WILLOW OF ASHES

NECROSEAM CHRONICLES BOOK I

NECROSEAM CHRONICLES

Available in eBook, Paperback, Hardcover,
and Audiobook (for select titles)

Prequel 1: Princess of Shadow and Dream
Prequel 2: Princess of Grim

Book I: Willow of Ashes
Book II: Orbs of Azure
Book III: Pearl of Emerald
Book IV: Phoenix of Scarlet
Book V: Blossom of Gold

OTHER WORKS BY ELLIE RAINE

Adult
Nightingale: A Paranormal Noir

Children's Illustration
Ballad of the Ice Fairy

WILLOW OF ASHES

NecroSeam Chronicles Book I

ELLIE RAINE

Willow of Ashes
NecroSeam Chronicles | Book One
Edition II

Copyright © 2018 by Ellie Raine

Cover Design by Ellie Raine
Interior Formatting by Tamara Cribley
Author Photograph by Melissa Giles Photography
Map © 2021 Chris Seckinger

Printed in the United States of America

ISBNs: 978-1-7320415-3-0 (Hardcover), 978-1-7320415-6-1 (Paperback), 978-1-7320415-9-2 (Ebook)

Library of Congress Control Number: 2018935664
First Printing, Edition II: 2018
First Printing, Edition I: 2016

Published by
ScyntheFy Press, LLC
www.ScyntheFy.com

For information about special discounts available for bulk purchases, sales promotions, fund-raising and educational needs, contact ScyntheFy Press at: www.ScyntheFy.com/contact For special bonus features and up-to-date news, visit the official NecroSeam web site: www.NecroSeam.com

For my darling husband, my loving family, and my incredible friends.
Thank you for your continued support and cheers.

AUTHOR'S NOTE

Dear Adventurer,

Sharpen your scythes and polish your armor, your journey through the world of Nirus begins here! What you hold in your hands is my life's blood—my heart and my passion that has grown as much as I have. I hope you enjoy reading this tale as much as I enjoyed writing it. So, pack your potions, gather your party, and don't forget your raven! And to help you along the way, check out the Nirussian travel guide in the back of this book.

Happy reading,
~Ellie Raine

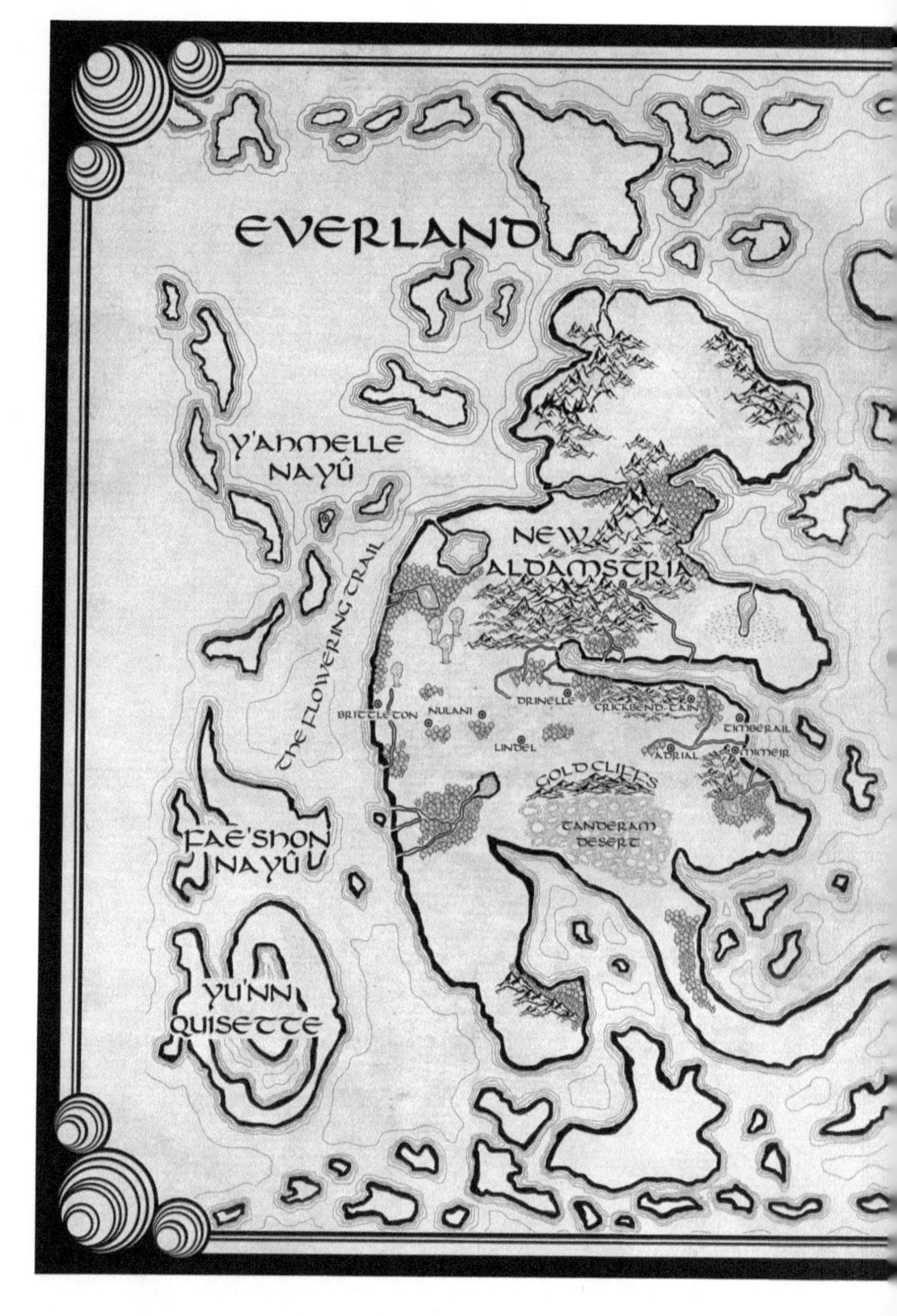

EVERLAND
Y'AHMELLE NAYÛ
NEW ALDAMSTRIA
THE FLOWERING TRAIL
BRITTLETON
NULANI
DRINELLE
CRICKBEND-TAIN
TIMBERAIL
LINDEL
ADRIAL
MIMEIR
COLD CLIFFS
TANDERAM DESERT
FAE'SHON NAYÛ
YU'NN QUISETTE

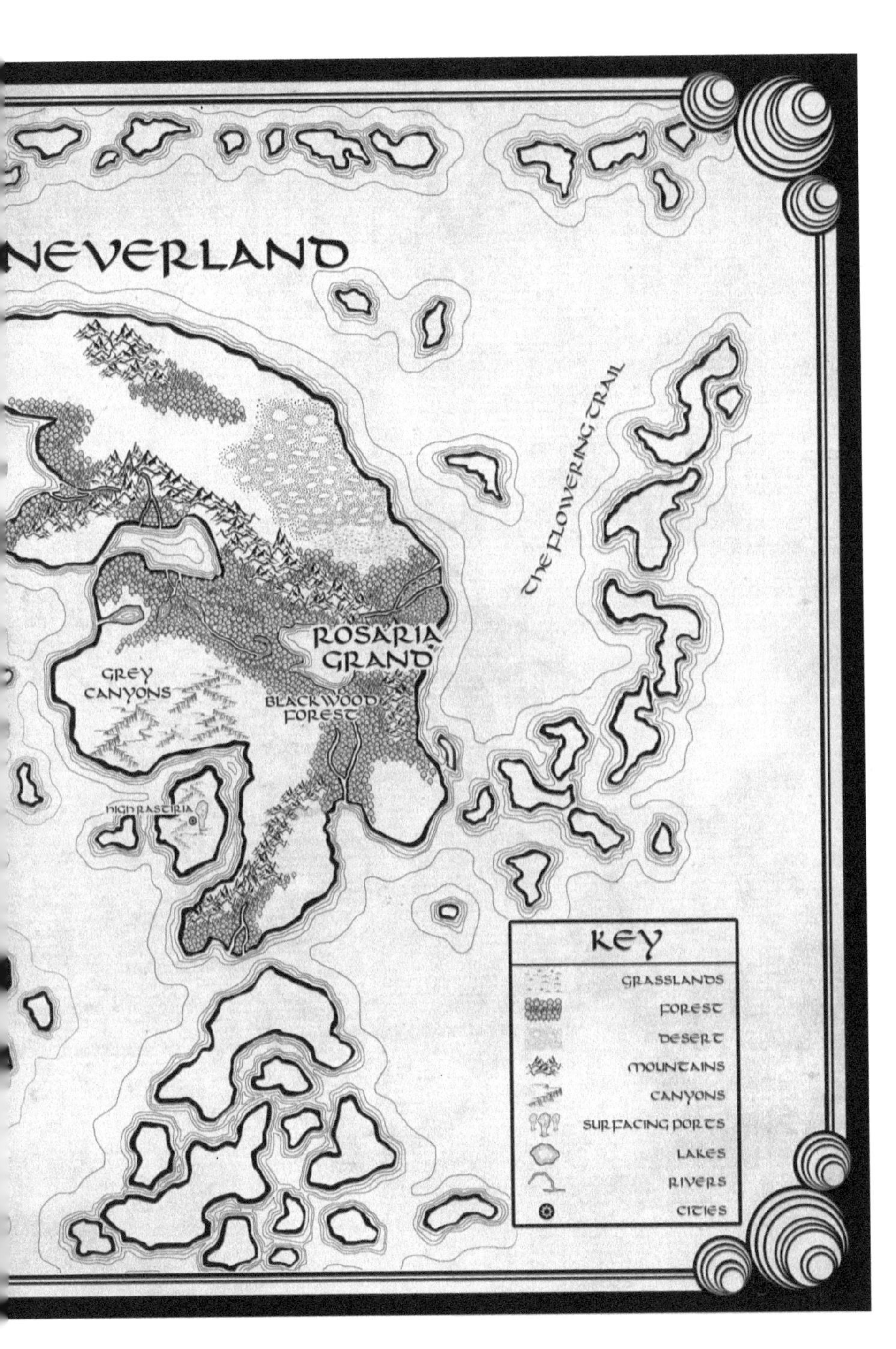

NEVERLAND
THE FLOWERING TRAIL
ROSARIA GRAND
GREY CANYONS
BLACKWOOD FOREST
HIGH RASTIRIA
KEY
GRASSLANDS
FOREST
DESERT
MOUNTAINS
CANYONS
SURFACING PORTS
LAKES
RIVERS
CITIES

TABLE OF CONTENTS

*"Iri, Father, forgive me. I've failed. My mistake
nearly ended us, and it may still yet.*

*"How long before the Shadowblood is born, to fix what I've done? The seal will
expire one day, it cannot keep our deaths contained… Please, send him soon.*

"I pray you choose better than I."

—The King of Dreams, 1596 A.B.

THE ASSASSIN IN THE STORM

XAVIER

"This must be a mistake?" a voice rippled in the darkness. "A farce… yes, that must be it. They mock us. I should hope they wouldn't choose one so young as our contender?"

I stirred out of my numbness, my temples pounding. Silver flares shimmered over my vision like trails of tumbling glitter as consciousness returned.

Where am I…? I was sure my sight had returned, yet I was surrounded by blackness, the world cloaked in shadow.

"No," that same voice hushed, wafting like smoke from the emptiness. "No, it is a mistake. The Gods wouldn't be so cruel. Surely, they'd meant to place such a burden on someone older? Someone more deserving of death…?"

A string of light split from above, and the canyons finally dripped into view. Water sprayed from the warring clouds like a vengeful waterfall, drenching my silken, ivory doublet and sticking my hair to my soaked cheeks. I was on my back, lying on rocks, the incessant water splashing my eyes.

What in Death is this water? Dazed, I watched the silver dots fade, and the canyons solidified. *Is there a leak in the ceiling?*

No, I wasn't in the caves anymore. I was on the surface… and the surface didn't have a ceiling, did it?

What had my textbooks called this? I pushed up to sit, groaning at the scrapes and cuts I fostered. *Ra… 'Rain'?*

I tried to stand, but my leg screamed with pain and I flopped onto the rocks again, panting. *Broken. Death, of all things, my BONES betray me. Alex would think it humorous, were he here.*

I paused, blinking away this 'rain'.

Alex! Where was my brother? And what in Bloods was I doing on the surface in the first place?

My head burst with an ache, and I rubbed it tenderly. My fingers came back red, the rain washing them clean. *I must have hit my head and fallen unconscious.* I concluded. *What had happened?*

I remembered attending a ball for Death's Festival. There had been dancing guests in the palace, a glorious banquet, lively music…

There had also been a fire. Yes, that's right! A fire had raged the ballroom. The littered bodies were branded into my memory, their skin melted away from their cheekbones. Though, that hadn't been the fire's doing. A man had poisoned them, slaughtered the guards, the guests, the staff… They were all dead.

We had escaped, I remembered. *We'd fled to the surface and ran through these canyons. The man had followed us and chased us to a cliff and…*

I lifted my gaze. A flash of light illuminated that very cliffside. I remembered toeing the edge, the rock crumbling under my boots.

We'd fallen down to this ledge. My head throbbed again, and I sucked in a wince. *Blast it, I'm sure Willow is not happy about—*

I stopped, horror splintering.

"Willow!" I screamed and scuttled over the rocks, my broken leg dragging behind me. The rain hissed and splattered in the wind, but her voice didn't ride the breeze. "*Willow—!*"

Icy fingers wrapped round my neck, crushing my windpipe.

"You'll have to forgive her," that same, gnarled voice from before rumbled. "Young Death is a tad… preoccupied."

A flash of light burst from the clouds, and a man's face brightened before my nose.

Memory raced back at that face. *Damn it all, the assassin!*

The man's broadened jaw was littered with black stubble, his yellow eyes so shocking, they were burned into my retinas.

His grip tightened on my throat, and he hoisted me over the ledge.

Beneath my dangling feet, ocean waves sloshed and churned like a feral animal, swirling and lapping in a nauseating rhythm.

A new light flashed—

I caught a glimpse of a girl, slumped on the rocks behind the yellow-eyed man. Her ashen hair stretched past her feet in a tangled mess over the rough stones, her azure eyes glazed as she laid unstirred, her face caked with dirt and blood. The once beautiful white dress was now ripped to tatters and stained crimson.

"Will… Willow…!" I wheezed under the man's grip. *Thank Bloods!* She must have fallen with me when the ledge gave way up top. *If anyone could pry this maniac off of me, it'd be she!* I clutched the man's slippery wrists, trying to free my breath. "Willow…! H-help…!"

She remained as still as the stones beneath her. Her lips were parted yet nothing sounded from her tongue. Her bright, azure eyes, however, were pried open.

"No…" I heard my soul shatter, a grueling, hollow sound. "No…! *NO!*" I kicked wildly, my claws grown and reaching for the man's face in hopes of scratching those savage eyes out of their damned sockets…! "What have you done to her?!" I screamed. "I'll kill you! The Seamstress can Cleanse me all She likes, *I'll kill you*—!"

A new pain made me gasp, my claws retracting.

The man's fingers slithered with blackened worms around my neck, the gooey strings pouring into my throat. They crawled up my skin and branched to my face, bulging over bones, licking past teeth and gums, slinking into my nasal cavity like oozing slugs. I screamed when the veins thrust their way to my eyes. Splotches blocked my vision, pressure balling behind the sockets.

—Sqrlch!

I shrieked in pain, a sluggish root jamming into my brain. The root squirmed and writhed like a viper rummaging for a meal.

Where… am I…? My mind blanked, like waking from a forgotten dream. *What was I… doing here?*

—Sqrlch!

Another serpent sank its fangs into my brain.

I… I can't breathe… My eyes bulged, seeing a strange man was strangling me. *Who was he? How had I gotten here…?*

Water splashed from the clouds like a terrible leak in the cavern's ceiling, my legs dangling over a cliffside, my vision spotted and patched.

What in Death is happening?

A squeal cut through the gale suddenly. I strained to look past the man, finding an ashen-haired girl lying on the rock. *Why does she look familiar?*

"Such a disappointment." The man crushed his thumbs over my voice box, his claws digging trenches. "And here I had looked forward to seeing the Shadowblood in all his glory."

He heaved and thrust me off the cliff, my stomach lurching sickly as I dropped. My screams faded as the sloshing waves below were sucked away, along with everything else as the world went black.

1

SOULBOUND

ALEXANDER

My placid reflection stared back at me from the polished, blackstone memorial they'd erected for my brother.

Xavier Madison Devouh, it read on the reflective surface, *Devoted son and brother. May the Seamstress guide his soul to a richer life full of peace and prosperity.*

I absently dragged my fingers over the carved letters.

My reflection showed an adolescent, pale face, my shadowy grey bangs tossed about my brow carelessly by the cavern winds. A satin doublet was fastened up to my neck with elegant, silver buttons, gold trim embroidered with intricate patterns along the hem and neckline. A burgundy cloak was clasped at my chest, the cowl collapsed over my shoulders.

My heterochromic eyes were reversed in the reflection. The one, sapphire eye was on the left of my face; the colorless, white eye on the right.

It isn't my face, is it? With the placement of the mismatched eyes, it was *he* who stood there. As though he hadn't vanished; as though the world hadn't shifted and died along with him.

"*... can't...*" his voice whispered in my thoughts, a high-pitched ring whining in my eardrums. "*Please...*"

I knuckled my throbbing skull, banishing the phantom voice. It had begun after he'd disappeared from that cliff on the surface. The voice began as a slight annoyance here and there, yet now it chewed at my thoughts incessantly.

I sucked in a long, shivering breath, then blew it out in a stream of cold fog. My wolf ears grew, draping solemnly to the sides of my neck as a sickness squeezed my chest.

"Alexander?" A soft voice hushed behind me.

I turned, one of my wolf ears swiveling when a woman stepped beside me.

She was a towering figure, wrapped in a fur cloak that hid her alabaster gown and thick coat. Delicate chains were clipped to her hair on both sides, glistening like silken strings that hung from her forehead in a 'V' shape, a diamond droplet glinting at the center. Her grey hair was braided and draped over one shoulder, precious gemstones frosting the strands.

She had wolf ears as well, though hers were naturally showing, unlike mine. My ears only grew in times of stress or sorrow, as most mammals were wont to do. In addition, she had a wavering tail curling round her skirts, which I didn't have with or without stress.

A tiny black bird, which I knew was named Ethil, gripped the woman's gloved finger, and she laid her other hand on my shoulder. "The memorial service ended hours ago," she murmured, her cloudy, blue eyes bloodshot. "Come… it's time we took our leave."

I turned back to my reflection in the blackstone memorial, stealing a final glance at my face.

A final glance at my brother.

"He is gone, Alex." My mother's boney fingers tightened on my shoulder. "Please."

"He wouldn't break his promise." I croaked. The face on the stone leaked with tears. "We promised to die together. Just as we'd come into this life, we were to *leave* it together. He wouldn't break it."

"*Break…*" his voice hushed in my thoughts. "*Promise… we… promised…*"

Mother's grip faltered, removing her hand. "Come… The ship departs soon. Your father is waiting."

Her footfalls clicked down the marble steps, crossing the yard toward the cemetery's exit. Wispy specters and ghosts floated between the tombstones, whispering prayers and murmuring the absurdity of how many new stones had been erected.

Many were lost in the fire last month. Many more were lost to the assassin. Even their ghosts had been destroyed from within their vessels—all the work of one, lone man.

I followed alongside Mother in silence, my soul stretching thinner as we walked away from my brother's blackstone slab.

When we rounded the palace's east wing, I looked to the terrace on the third floor. The latticed doors were shut, thick curtains drawn to hide the Death Princess's chambers within.

Willow had yet to leave her room since the incident. I'd heard she'd been found and rescued from the surface canyons, the assassin chased off. She'd returned to the caverns safely, yet the moment she'd come back, she shut herself in her chambers. She hadn't even come out for combat training all month. She *never* missed training, not in the last four years. Now, only a few servants saw her at all when they brought the heiress her meals.

She didn't come to the memorial today. I couldn't say I blamed her.

Mother and I crossed to the palace courtyard and climbed into the awaiting hover-coach, the silver buggy floating over the grey-stoned pathway as its exposed gears clattered, and the stabilizing hydraulics hissed with steam. The two horses harnessed to the front were whipped into motion, the coach lurching forward and gliding smoothly out of the palace grounds.

The cityscape ahead was lined with sharp spires and gothic buildings, wedged between rocky pillars that stretched from the cavern floor all the way to the ceiling, which was hidden in misty formations that trailed with gleaming, floating lights. The lights wafted in and out of the overcast, the ethereal orbs drifting calmly as they illuminated the caverns with a pale, grey filter.

We arrived at the harbor, merchants and sailors bustling along the vibrating boardwalks. I climbed out of the coach behind Mother, stepping aside as a scaled man with webbed ears stalked past me carrying two heavy crates of fish, then followed Mother to the pier.

Grim's seas were a vast series of wide rivers within the caverns, the lapping water split into branching straits by pillars and rock formations littered along the wide horizon. A thick fog clung to the hidden water's surface, the smoky, grey cloak twisting and licking like a living creature all its own.

I followed Mother along the pier and climbed up the ramp to board our awaiting ship.

The vessel bobbed in the rippling water, the cutting winds beating at the half-mast sails as the hired crew members pulled them down. A raven was perched on the crow's nest, its gaze sharp and inspecting as it cocked its head at me. It was my father's raven, Barrach, watching us to be sure we were all accounted for, and to alert us should any danger arise.

The crew cast us off, and we departed, Low Rastiria's harbor drifting farther and farther away.

"It will take nearly a month to arrive at the other Undercontinent," Mother said. "I suggest we all take this time to… to heal."

I grumbled. "Why are we returning to Low Everland so soon? I thought this was to be our permanent home."

She knelt to me. "It's only temporary, Alex. Your grandfather took over the role of the Death King's Eyes for these four years, and he's at his wits end. Your father is only returning to the post to interview new candidates. Once we're finished, and the role is filled, we'll return here."

"And return to the search?" My voice was tight with anger.

Mother paused. "They *are* still searching on the surface, Alex. They will keep searching, so we can give him a proper burial with a true funeral and—"

"He isn't dead!" I shouted. "He's still up there! He's alive! I... I hear him. It's growing clearer by the day, Mother, I can *hear* him...!" My vision blurred, eyes stinging.

Her own eyes misted and she pulled me in for an embrace, her fur cloak soft against my wet cheeks. "Oh, Alex..." She drew me at arm's length and cupped my face. "I do wish you were right."

She rose and strode into the cabin, delicately dabbing her eyes.

He's alive, damn it. I furiously rubbed my face dry. If they kept looking, they would find him and see.

"*...so much water...*" His voice hissed in my thoughts again, ringing in a shrill whine. "*I... can't breathe...*"

I hit my knuckles against the post, causing the raven at the crow's nest to croak at me angrily.

"Where are you?!" I hollered at the cavern's misted ceiling. The Floating Lights gently twirled and swam within the formations. "Why can I hear you...?"

I sank to my knees and curled against the post, shivering.

The nearby crew members had turned at my outburst, whispering that I'd gone mad.

Perhaps I am mad, I considered, hitting my head against the post like a miserable, hollow shell. *Was it him? Or was it merely my memory of him...?*

Heavy footfalls clunked toward me, and I craned my gaze up.

My father's vassal, Nathaniel, loomed over me, his burly arms set at his sides, his bear-ears perked in my direction from under his raggedy, black hair.

"Ye all right, lad?" Nathaniel asked, cocking a thick eyebrow. He wore a narrow hat with a long plume wavering at one side, and his coat was a stiff, indigo captain's uniform. Nathaniel scratched his scruffy beard and muttered. "Yer scarin' me crew, shoutin' at clouds like that..."

I hung my head. "I'm sorry, Nathaniel... I'll—"

A ghost suddenly phased through the post over my head, the pale specter's feathered hair curling at his cheeks. "Oh, leave the young sir alone,

Nathaniel!" the ghost, who was my mother's vassal, Aiden, chided the bear-shifter. "He's lost his twin, is this not punishment enough?"

Nathaniel's ears curled. "Aw, I Bloody know what the lad's goin' through! I was only sayin' nothing's gonna come out 'o—"

"Why don't we see what comes out of *you* when I shove an arrow through your throat and…!"

They kept to their blathering, and I sighed and crawled under them, walking to the ship's ledge.

I folded my arms over the rail, hearing the water lapping under the churning mists, the fog hiding the waves.

"Xavier?" I whispered, staring at the swirling, grey veil. "If I can hear you, can you hear me? Can you tell me where you are?"

"*It's… dark,*" his voice hushed in my thoughts. "*So dark…*"

"How can we find you? What can you see?"

"*Nothing.*" The voice dimmed. "*There is… nothing…*"

"We'll find you," I said, my teeth sharpening, claws growing long and scraping the wooden rail. "I don't care what they say, *I* will find you and bring you home."

"*Home…*" The voice was so soft I almost couldn't hear it. "*Home…*"

My hands balled, and I struck the rail… Then a shadow caught my eye from the mists below.

Within the light grey veil, dark splotches formed. A splintered mast of a ship peeked through the fog, its sails shredded and torn, beating in the cavern winds.

I twisted back to the arguing captain and ghost. "Nathaniel!" I called, getting the captain's attention. "Nathaniel, there's a wreckage here!"

Nathaniel and Aiden stopped their bickering, then came to meet me at the rail. Nathaniel produced a copper spyglass from his coat pocket and held it to his eye.

"The lad be right," he rumbled, sounding troubled. "Aye, I reckon that be the vessel what went missin' these last few days…"

He collapsed the spyglass with a *clack, clack, clack* and shoved it to my chest. "Lad, keep an eye on the mists down there. I'll tell the boys to fetch the dinghies."

I swallowed. "W-wait. How many days has the ship been missing?"

Nathaniel adjusted his plumed hat in a growl. "Three."

The warmth flushed from my cheeks. "Then… then wouldn't they be Changed—?"

"We'll take a look 'n see, lad," he said, tromping off to shout at his men.

I unfolded the spyglass, the lens quivering in my fingers. All I could see was fog. Fog and tall stalagmites, the rocky pillars sprouting from the water and stretching to the ceiling...

I focused on the wreckage's broken mast, seeing its tattered sails in greater detail through the lens. There were no bloodstains on that piece of the vessel. Perhaps the crew survived—

Skririririririri!

I ducked at the hideous shriek that split the fog, its high-pitched echo bouncing off the cavern's pillars, then dying into silence.

The raven at the crow's nest began to croak and caw ceaselessly, sounding the alarm.

The crew scrambled over the deck, Nathaniel shouting orders to take up arms.

Death! I sank to my knees and lifted the spyglass again, sweeping the lens over the fog. Shadows shifted behind the veil. They were creeping toward us, their hisses and bleats trumpeting louder as they neared.

I kept the lens focused on them, licking my lips and calling back, "Nathaniel, they're over here—!"

Skririririiii!

A dripping, skeletal creature leapt from the water and hooked its claws into my shoulder, *yanking* me overboard and dragging me into the water with a cold *splash!*

My pained curses bubbled in the dark waters, my shoulder burning as the creature still had me hooked, and it dragged me farther into the water's depths toward the shrouded floor—

My head hit a stalagmite. The creature's claws ripped out, and the cold water vanished from my skin as blackness swallowed me.

XAVIER

A freezing chill crashed over my skin.

I gasped, but sucked in water. I was drowning, my shoulder burning from puncture wounds.

Panicked, I found the brightness of the surface above, and swam upward. The water peeled away from my face and I wheezed in a reviving breath, coughing and spitting up the water.

Where am I?

I shivered in the freezing water, my burgundy cloak heavy around my shoulders. I unfastened it in case it threatened to drag me back into the water.

There was nothing but grey here. Churning mist draped the water everywhere I turned, I couldn't even see above it.

My wolf ears were already grown, fright shaking my soul as I trembled in the water. "H… hello?!" I cried, coughing. "Is anyone there?!"

My wolf ears picked up shouting within the mist. The voices were nearby.

"Help!" I called, swimming toward the voices, my shoulder hot with pain. "P-please…! I need help!"

A splash came behind me.

I whirled, but saw nothing. "H… hello—*Aaah!*"

Claws dug into my back, hooking me, and I screamed as I was dragged backward—

An arrow shot at the beast, the crystal tip plunging into its skull with an ear-splitting *crack!* The blow was so powerful, a spiral of wind rushed after it and cleared the mist in a wide circle around me.

The creature screamed in pain and released me, squirming into the water out of sight. Now that the mists had cleared, I saw a winged man flying above, a second arrow nocked along his bowstring.

"Young sir!" the bird-shifter called. He put away his bow and arrow and soared down to me, grasping my outstretched hand to pull me out of the water. "the Archer be praised, you're alive! Don't worry, your mother has exterminated the rest of them, all that's left was the one who'd dragged you under."

I blinked at the winged man, baffled. "My… mother?"

He flew us onto a ship's deck, and I fell over my knees and hacked the water from my lungs, quivering at the pain in my shoulder and back.

A wide circle had formed around me, and I heard a woman barking orders.

"Make way!" she commanded. "Make way, that is my son…! Alexander! Alexander, are you hurt?!"

The woman came hustling toward me, clad in a fur cloak and her braided hair tussled and frazzled around the twinkling gemstones pinned in the strands. She crouched and held a tender, gloved hand to my shoulder wound. "Bloods be good, you'll need medical attention… I'm glad I resurrected Aiden in time to find you." She turned to the winged man who'd flown me here. "Aiden, tell the ship nurse to treat Alexander immediately—"

"No," I said, panting over the floorboards. "I… I'm not Alex…"

But why do I know that name? The thought stabbed my brain, and I clutched my throbbing head. *I knew someone with that name… yes, I knew them well… but how?*

I shook my head. I had other priorities to see to. "Was another found?" I asked the woman. Death, but she looked familiar. I coughed. "Other than me? A girl, with white hair. She… she was with me—had you found her as well? Please, there is a man after us, I don't… I don't know what's happened to…"

My temples swelled, and I grunted, head shaking desperately.

The woman's breath died on her tongue. She squeezed my good shoulder and lifted my chin to face her, staring at my eyes. "Seamstress Cleanse me," she whispered, tears welling. "Xavier…?"

"Yes…" I said slowly, the name familiar. "Yes, that's right. That's my name… but I must find my friend." Her name returned in a blink. "I must find Willow."

"Oh, Nira be blessed…!" She took my hand eagerly and dragged me toward the cabin. "Lucas! Lucas, come look, we've found…!"

"Where am I…?" A voice trilled in my thoughts, a whining ring hitting my eardrums.

I screeched to a stop, the woman's grip pulled from my fingers.

"Who… who'd said that?" I asked, a chill prickling the hairs on my neck.

"Xavier?" the voice called, shaking. *"Xavier, can you hear me?"*

I knew that voice… it was… "Alex?" I whispered, remembering the name of my brother.

"Yes!" He laughed, though still sounded shaken. *"Where are you? It's so dark here… There's n-nothing. But I can see the ship. I can see Mother. Where are you?"*

"I… don't know," I admitted, gazing at the woman who now stared at me in shock. "Mother…" I said. "Yes, that's right. That's who you are—"

Her face suddenly shrank away, the world sucked into a funnel as I was thrown backward.

The world I'd seen had been condensed into a single, circular window, which hung suspended in an empty, black void I now floated in. All traces of pain had vanished, along with the chilled water soaking my garments and hair.

I stared at my hands, at my feet. I radiated with a soft light.

In the window, the woman leapt back. "Death's Head!" she shouted, her voice crystal clear and echoing all around this void. "Alexander…?"

The window streaked left and right, blinking. *"What in Death…?"* Alex's voice hissed. Hands appeared in the window, palms turning in examination. *"What was that place? Xavier…? Can you hear me?"*

I reached a hand at the window. It was like touching water, the images rippling under my fingers. I pushed on it, pulling myself through—

The void was sucked away behind me, and I collapsed into the outside world, cold and bleeding as the pain burned at my shoulder and back.

Screams echoed from my head.

"Alex?" I panted, searching the deck for him, but couldn't find him. My breaths grew ragged, the screams worsening. "Alex! Stop it, stop screaming…!"

I clutched my wolf ears, but it did nothing to blot out his frightened cries. I pushed on my skull desperately, staring at Mother. "Wh… what's happening…?"

Mother's grey face had drained white, whispering, "Great Mother below."

2

A NEW JOURNEY

XAVIER

I yawned in my seat, rubbing the sleep from my eyes as I put down my silverware, this morning's meal comfortably housed in my belly.

Our manor's expansive dining hall was decorated with silver chandeliers and ebony furniture, the walls dressed with eloquent paper where oil paintings of achromatic flowers hung. A grandfather clock soothingly knocked and tocked against the far corner, and the delicate, stringed music sang from a phonograph.

"How awful!" A pale ghost said from across the polished table, conversing with a second soul beside her. "They found no survivors?"

"None but two children." The second ghost straightened over her seat. Neither soul physically touched the furniture, but incorporeal beings were wont to float over cushions as though they were, well, corporeal. "I hear they were hidden in a cellar. It was a massacre, up on the surface. The valley was overrun with the Necrofera, even the Reapers who came to help were killed."

The first ghost wilted in sympathy. "Nira below, the poor dears! I've never heard of so many demons at once. Do you think the demons down here could do the same?"

"I certainly hope not, Nira forbid, but I do think…"

They chatted on, and I spied a butler entering the hall, balancing a tray of steaming tea.

"Ah, Thateus," I greeted. "Is that cinnamon and honey I smell?"

The butler chuckled. "Indeed it is, Young sirs. I had a feeling Lord Alexander wouldn't stray from his previous record of waking after you."

Thateus was our family's Head Vassal. Today his black-and-grey hair was slicked back with gel, his curling ram horns looking particularly polished and waxed.

"A correct feeling it was, Thateus," I commended. "And today is a special morning indeed. I've at last broken my old record for being 'the first awake in the most consecutive days'."

"Ah, then perhaps a celebration is due?" Thateus hummed as he poured me a cup of tea, its scented steam wafting from the silver rim. "I'll inform the other vassals to prepare a grand feast. And, of course, your available ancestors are welcome to partake?"

The two ghosts across the table soundlessly clapped their hands in excitement.

"Oh, how lovely, a new celebration!" The first, Ancestor Bathesda, sang in delight.

The second ghost, Bathesda's sister, Jilluh, murmured. "It's been ages since the ghosts gathered for anything, it's much overdue."

Bathesda's lips twisted at her spectral sister. "Ages? It's been three weeks!"

"Which is a long time for a ghost nearing three-hundred!" Jilluh huffed. "You and I are about ready to Descend to Nira any day now, Bathy. We have to enjoy the rest of our afterlives as much as we can, especially with our darling descendants, isn't that right, Xavier?"

I chuckled, taking my cup of tea. "I couldn't agree more, Ancestor."

Bathesda pushed contemplative fingers to her translucent lips. "Speaking of, Jilluh, what have you decided should be done to your vessel once you Descend?"

"Oh, I'm having my bones ground into meal and put in the crypts, of course. I hardly wish to clutter the family yard. When my soul is reborn, I'd rather leave room for my next vessel and…"

They chittered on happily as Thateus bowed to me. "Very well, Young sirs. I'll inform the staff and see what the cooks can offer. Have a good morning." He picked up the empty plate and took his leave.

I smiled, listening to the ghosts' conversations and raised the tea to my lips.

But I halted once the smooth liquid glinted in the pale light and reflected my face. A mismatched pair of blue-and-clear eyes stared up at me from the tea, belonging to a pale face framed in shadowy, grey hair.

"Well, if it isn't Alexander," I said. I watched the reflection of my lips move in the tea, which held his fainter reflection as well. "Nice of you to join us. Keeping the morning Dreamcatcher hard at work again, are we?"

I thought they could use the excitement. He grunted from my thoughts. In the tea, I watched him rub his eyes, his voice heavy with exhaustion. *My apologies. I woke early in the night. It took me some time to fall back asleep.*

"I see." I hummed quietly and sipped from the cup, erasing both of our reflections in the liquid. "You should know I've broken my previous record today, thanks to you. The ghosts are joining us to celebrate."

He snorted, declining a response.

"Oh!" One of the chatting ghosts chuckled across the table. "Is Alexander awake? Why, it's nearly half-past eight! That's quite late, even for him."

"Terribly late," the second specter agreed with a light gesture. "Is something amiss again?"

I raised pacifying hands in a laugh. "Not to worry, Ancestors. He only had a disturbed rest."

"—Young sirs?" a new voice called.

I twisted back, seeing a new ghost had phased through the wall. It was our mother's vassal, Aiden. Aiden's translucent wings fluttered silently as he approached.

"Aiden." I slung an arm over my seat. "Good morning."

"Good morning as well, young sirs." The spirit bowed, his wings dipping behind him. "Your Mistress has requested a meeting, once you're finished eating. She's waiting in her chambers."

"Very well. Thank you, Aiden. We'll be right up."

He bowed again and floated through the wall in a quiet ripple—then popped his head back out. "Oh, and do save some of that feast I heard about for me?" He added in a toothy grin. "I'll ask my *Da'torr* to resurrect me so I can enjoy it myself!"

"All right, all right," I said, rising and folding my napkin over the table. "I suppose Nathaniel will wish to do the same?"

"Tell him after the feast has already arrived," Aiden scoffed. "I would much like to see his pale face wilt as I eat whilst happily alive." He smiled wide and disappeared behind the wall.

I bowed to my ancestors, faring them well, and strode out of the dining hall, crossing to the corridor of this ancient castle, and climbed the curling stairway.

"What do you suppose Mistress wants, so early in the morning?" I hummed idly to Alexander. "It's not even Bright Light hours."

"Perhaps she's found a solution for us?" he offered from my thoughts.

I scowled, my tone souring. "I… think it's too late for a solution. How long has it been now? Five years?"

"Six, after next month."

I groaned.

At fourteen, I'd barely grown three whiskers before I was flung off that cliff—and awoke with my soul trapped in my brother. Six years of searching for the reason, searching for *anything* that hinted at an answer for why this had happened to us, yet we still had nothing. In no text had there been any mention of two souls sharing the same body; of two NecroSeams sewn to the same heart.

It seemed Alexander and I may be trapped this way for the rest of his life. And I, the parasite, would have to settle for inexistence, locked away in this city—in this damned manor—with naught but my family's ghosts to know I was still here.

If I could remember how it happened…

Pain splintered my temples, making me stagger. I gripped the railing when the manor wobbled, the memory met with blackness and pain…

I clasped a hand to my head, breathing slowly. *Damn it… Why can't I remember?* Collecting myself, I tugged on my lapel and continued up the stairs.

Thanks to that yellow-eyed lunatic, most of my past had been wiped clean. Though, now that I was almost twenty, I'd regained a fair amount of memories. But when it came to how I ended up like this, and *her*…

There was nothing.

I climbed to the third floor and headed for Mother and Father's chambers. Once reaching the elegantly carved doors, I knocked. A muffled 'enter' was called from within, and when I opened the doors, I found Mother waiting.

"Xavier," she said after glancing my way briefly before gliding her eyes back over the stack of papers that littered her desk. She held up a finger, signaling me to wait as one of her wolf ears folded down in concentration. She pushed up her reading glasses, peering through the lenses with strict scrutiny.

She wore her finer silks today. Her shadow-grey hair weaved over one shoulder with specks of ruby gems, wolf ears perking while her tail brushed the skirts of her black dress.

I closed the doors and stood at attention, wrapping my arms behind me.

The ever-nostalgic sounds of shuffling papers and the *tick- tick-tick* of her desk clock filled the lavish room, and I noted the bed looked recently fluffed. The servants must have made their rounds recently. They also seemed to have set the fire in the hearth along the wall, the scent of charred pinewood perfuming the chamber as embers snapped behind the iron bars.

After scanning the room and finding it empty of other bodies, I cleared my throat. "Will Father be joining us today?"

Mother hummed absently, eyes still focused on the papers. "He's arranging a few things for our trip to the surface. Guards must be placed accordingly, tickets and schedules must be made, a stand-in must watch over the manor..."

I nodded, offering a grunt. Then decided to ask, "Will a stand-in be necessary? Alexander and I will be here."

Her eyes flicked at me for a mere second, but it was enough to shut me up. A soldier didn't argue with his general.

She didn't have to answer, regardless. I already knew what that look meant. Alex and I weren't considered a viable stand-in, not in Father's eyes. Even if we were his heirs.

Mother set down her papers and folded her glasses with a tired sigh. "At ease, boys."

I allowed my posture to slack and my arms to fall at my sides. "You wished to speak with us, Mistress?"

"I did," she said, taking a sip of tea that had lost its steam. "I have some news for you both. You're already aware that your father and I have been asked to oversee this 'massacre' on the surface. I fear it's too dangerous to bring you both, namely because I'm unsure of what we're dealing with. The reports don't offer much detail."

"So," I began, failing to stifle my annoyance while sliding my hands in my trousers' pockets. "We're to stay here while you're gone, the usual protocol, hide our situation from whatever stand-in comes, and wait around until we hear back about Bianca's news. Is that about right?"

One corner of her lips lifted a fracture. "I never said you were staying here, Xavier."

I paused. "But you said..."

"Oh, you're not coming with us, either. If I don't know what to expect, I'm not comfortable bringing my apprentices. Especially when one, need I remind, isn't supposed to exist at the moment. High Everland's capital is one of the world's most Reaper-populated cities above the caves. It's far too much of a risk to bring you both, far too much."

She turned to her desk and rifled through the stack of papers, pulling out a few carefully selected pages. "You, my beloved students, are embarking on your own journey. Although, I suggest you fetch Jaq to accompany you. The Gods only know what trouble he'd cause with the stand-in, if left alone here."

"But… Mistress." My brow knitted. "Where are we going?"

Her lips relented and displayed a rare, genuine smile. "To your missing vessel, Xavier."

I raced out the manor and rushed through the front gardens, my breath fogging in the freezing gust, burgundy hood falling to my shoulders.

Grey clouds loomed overhead in their usual overcast, numerous balls of glowing light swirling within the ceiling-mist like floating glitter.

One of those pale, blue lights was falling from the ceiling now. It was a gentle descent, like a glowing bubble floating gracefully to the cavern's floor.

A laugh escaped me and I sprinted faster. As the ball of light neared the ground, I snatched it out of the air. The ball was cold against my palm and a frozen fog hazed around it. *A sign from the Seamstress*, I thought eagerly. *She must be sending me good fortune.* Smiling, I gripped the cold, glowing ball and dashed out of the gardens.

In the distance, I began to see many ghosts floating around my family's graveyard. One specter waved to me.

"Alexander!" he greeted cheerfully. "Or… perhaps Xavier?"

"It's Xavier, Great Grandfather!" I tossed the ball of light to him when I hurried by. "Here—for you, if you like! Newly fallen!

Thala ul wuw shefta!"

The light left a trail of chilled fog as it sparkled beautifully away from me, and the ghost caught the ball in his translucent hands, fumbling to keep it from dropping onto the pale grass at his misting feet.

The Fallen Lights were common in Grim, but they were certainly unique in their own way. They were one of the few objects ghosts could physically touch. Researchers weren't sure as to why this was, but many ghosts were happy to receive them as gifts regardless, especially from their descendants.

I rushed through the gates of our estate, catching sight of a horse-drawn, hovering coach. Its exposed gears and hissing stabilizers hummed softly as the Levi-stones embedded in its underside lifted the buggy off the ground to float gently behind the horses. *Perfect timing! I'm fortunate indeed.*

I sprinted after it and leapt onto the stepping platform. The floating buggy leaned at my added weight, its stabilizers hissing angrily, but I threw open the door and slid inside.

Several female servants turned to me in a start but chuckled when I latched the door behind me and took a seat. "Good morning, ladies," I greeted in a cheerful pant, hoping to mask my exhaustion with a smile.

"Good morning, young sirs," the servants giggled in unison, all giving polite nods.

The woman closest to me, a fox-shifter named Garra, spoke separately. "You seem awfully eager to run errands with us in town, young sirs. You very nearly tipped the coach!"

"Sorry for the start," I said. "I'm afraid we can't join you today, we're off to see Jaq. We've received news regarding our, er, dilemma."

A scale-skinned servant across from me, Laura, gasped. "Then you'll be back to your old selves again soon?"

"With some luck." My grin stretched until the muscles were sore. I hadn't been this exhilarated in years.

A large raven suddenly croaked from the window, and I saw the black bird had alighted onto the door's lamp fixture to follow me.

I winked at it. "Not long now, Mal," I said. "Your master will be rid of this parasite before your mangy tail feathers can molt next summer."

The bird's response was to turn up his diamond tail and give me a scoffing caw. Through the window, I watched us pass by all the large, masterfully decorated cemeteries with blackstone buildings and spiked, iron structures wedged in between. It was still within the hours of Growing Light, the floating balls twinkling overhead were a bright blue hue; almost their usual, pure white gleam as they swirled in graceful wisps within the billowing clouds of the caves' ceiling and weaved around the rocky pillars that climbed from the cavern floor all the way to the hidden ceiling.

If it was still this early, would Jaq even be awake? He had a terrible reputation for sleeping in if we didn't have training.

Damn it, Jaq, why did you have to be on break this week?

After the coach came to a stop, I hopped out and dashed toward Jaq's home. It took nearly ten minutes to arrive at the small cobbler shop on foot.

My pace slowed when I was outside the door, and I waved at the crow that was perched on the dangling sign above it.

"Good morning, Bridge," I panted in greeting to the crow.

She watched me curiously, her head cocking. The raven following me, Mal, soared down to greet her next, and I jerked the shop's door open. A bell jingled when I entered, and the customers' eyes snapped to me in horror.

Everyone suddenly jumped against the wall, knocking over boxes of shoes as they all dropped to the floor in a very, very low bow.

"G-g-good morning, High Howllord!" they squeaked, too afraid to pick their heads up from the floor.

As they shivered over the ground, all the mammals' furred ears sprouted from their heads. Those who had tails kept them firmly tucked, and the winged couple in the back made sure to glue their feathers to the floor in a dramatic bow.

Always the same with these shifters, I thought bitterly, sighing. Alexander and I could hardly walk anywhere outside the manor without people's spines shattering at the sight of us, petrified of our very existence. We had our father to thank for that—or rather, the role he played as the Death King's acting ambassador.

The only ones who *didn't* fear us were our fellow Reapers, none of whom occupied this cobbler's shop, at the moment.

Save for one man. At the center of the shop, the only shifter left standing was a scaled young man with sandy blond hair and rectangular, black-rimmed spectacles. He hefted several boxes of shoes that, I assumed, he was preparing to display near the front window.

The grey-skinned viper noticed the bowing customers first, glancing around with a knitted brow. Then he spotted me.

"Mates?" Jaq began, then quickly amended. "Uh—I mean… High Howllord." Jaq glanced at the lingering customers, who were now scurrying out the door.

He held his tongue, bowing to keep up the pretense until they were all gone. Once alone, he *thwacked* me sharp upside the head.

"The Death is wrong with you?" he demanded. "Comin' down here in that getup, it's like you're tryin' to scare off our customers."

"We have a new assignment," I puffed, still out of breath from the run over. "It's urgent."

He groaned. "Ah, Death no! Ya ain't cuttin' my break short. Mistress said I got a whole week off, ten days straight, full leave without exception—"

"You'll want to make this an exception."

"There'd better be a Gods damned invasion in the manor."

I grinned. "We heard back from Bianca."

He backpedaled, our old friend's name perking his scaled ears. "Oh. W-well, what'd she say? Good news?"

"In a way." A smirk tugged my lips. "While you've been twiddling your thumbs with shoelaces all week, she's found the soul that may know where I am."

His face finally sank with gravity. "You serious?"

"Deathly serious."

He gave a thrilled laugh, patting my shoulder with solid thumps. "Great! That's great! Then you'll be back to normal in no time, right? Let's hurry up 'n go talk to the guy."

"It's a woman, actually. And we can't. Well… not yet."

His expression soured. "Why not?"

"Her soul is apparently missing. The other ghosts say she went back to the surface without a Reaper to escort her."

"Well, ain't that just a Bloody inconvenience… what do we do, then?"

"That's what I'm trying to tell you, Jaq. We have our final assignment as apprentices." My grin was downright devilish now. "We're heading to the surface to be those escorting Reapers."

3

THE CAT AND THE RAVEN

OCTAVIUS

Pounding rattled the washroom stall door.

"Tavius," my older brother, Neal, called from the other side. "When you're done mopping in there, Mika wants you to wash the tables. 'Specially tables three and four, some kid puked out his guts."

"Gods damn it." I stopped my mopping and walked out of the stall, my cat ears growing in annoyance. "How bad?"

He tried and failed to hold back his chuckle. "It's a real masterpiece."

I massaged my eyes. "You deal with it. I'm busy in here. A drunkard pissed all over the floor again."

Neal snorted, unfastening his pants and took a piss in one of the urinals. "Tourists… Anyway, looks like you got it handled. Just bring everything out to the main floor."

I sighed, wheeling the mop and pail out of the stall. "I guess it's not like you ever do your own chores anyway."

"Bloods, will you chill?" He flushed and went to wash his hands at the sinks, inspecting himself in the mirror. He combed his fingers through his black hair, making an effort to keep it from sticking up, and patted his bronze cheeks with water. "The rest of us can't feel germs. You were practically made for this kind of work."

"I didn't ask to be the official janitor." I made my way to the main dining area and forced my ears to recede. "Bloody freeloader…"

I bent to pick up stray oyster shells from the floor, tossing the slime-coated husks in the nearest trashcan—

A swarm of prickles radiated over my fingers in response.

It was always an uncomfortable feeling, the prickling. Germs and bacteria may have been everywhere, but at least people could ignore them if they wanted to. For me, it gave off a kind of frequency. Like a buzzing in my head or vibration bouncing off my soul and echoing back, like some annoying radar.

I glanced back at Neal as he followed me to the café's main room. "I thought it was your turn to do tables tonight?" I asked.

"Would, but I've got a date," he said. "We'll have to cancel throwing-practice, too. If I pull this off right, I'll be back by morning."

"You're always back by morning… Who is it this time?"

"Don't really remember her name. Some customer from the lunch shift." He gave an annoying, toothy grin. "She had a friend with her, you know. Both tourists, so they won't know about your little… well, germ thing. I was going to try for both, but if you want, I can ask if—"

"I have tables to wash." *Damn it.* I was probably going to regret that later. But he was just so damn smug… I wasn't going to give him a reason to pull the 'I helped you out, you owe me' trick. I already did most of his workload, I didn't think I could handle anything else.

My cat ears came back, too irritated to keep them normal. "Just get out of here before they change their minds," I said and wheeled the mop around, heading for tables three and four.

Neal breathed a long, sympathetic sigh, following me. "Well, I tried. Can't say I wasn't looking after my little brother… Don't worry, Tavius." He ruffled the hair between my cat ears and took out a cigarette, lighting up. "We'll make you a man one of these days. Just need to find a girl that'll have you."

I already did, you cocky little… I let it go in a breath. Neal wouldn't know about my one-night stand. I never told anyone. It happened a long time ago, and I only just met the girl that night, so she probably wouldn't even remember me. Most likely, she was back in her big, exciting city, moving on with her life and perusing some dream career of hers… Unlike me.

Grudgingly, I started my work on the tables. And Holy Bloods was it bad. Red-orange vomit was splattered and dripping off the tables in gritty chunks, perfuming the place with that swelling, sour stink. I didn't even need to be near the stuff to feel the prickling from my 'germ radar'. It festered over my skin like invisible grains of sand.

Holding my breath, I took the mop and started swabbing the half-digested food, sloshing the sudsy water over the stained wood. It was near closing time, so there was only one group of customers left. The old vision-screen on the wall was flickering again, the news reporters fizzling.

I glanced at my little sister, Connaline, in the back, seeing she was bringing the last customers their desserts. The chubby sixteen-year-old had her hands full with plates, her orange cat ears perked while asking if the customers needed anything else.

Connie was the only one of us who didn't have black hair. She got her color from Mom. The rest of us had Dad's Grim-shaded hair, so we were usually mistaken as Grimlings when foreigners came by—which happened a lot, since we lived on a beach where travelers usually came to take a load off.

At the bar, my older sister, Mikani, was counting today's profits. She was scowling. Her fiancé, Ringëd, watched her with concerned eyes, leaning back against the other side of the counter with his tan arms crossed.

I guessed today didn't go so well for us. It'd been like this most days, lately. The only good thing about today was that it was Dualday night; one of the nights I usually visited Mom. The reminder was enough to have my cat ears recede.

The vision-screen flickered again, the reporter's voice fuzzing out of focus from the speakers. I left my rag on the table and went to the wall where the vision-gem was mounted. I rose to the balls of my feet and tapped the turquoise gem with a finger.

The screen of projected light sharpened into focus, and I stepped back to make sure it stayed that way.

"…Necrofera slaughter in the valley is still under Reaper investigation," the reporter announced.

A picture of a ruined village came on the screen. The scrolling text said it was Entrial Valley, near our kingdom's capital. Aged blood stains coated almost every inch of the place and countless mangled bodies were piled over the ground. All of their chests had been ripped open, their splintered ribs jutting out.

On the screen, a team of white-cloaked Reapers hauled away the bodies, probably to check if any of their NecroSeams were still tied. That didn't look likely. Those demons were the stuff of nightmares—only they were very real, and very dangerous. I thanked the Gardener I'd never seen one in person before. If I was lucky, it would stay that way.

"The Death King's Eyes has agreed to come oversee the situation," the reporter continued, *"which means we will be broadcasting a nation-wide alert: HIGH HOWLLORD LUCAS DEVOUH IS SURFACING. Be aware of the*

danger and do NOT cross his path. Stay away from the Eyes, if you value your life. He will not tolerate anyone foolish enough to distract him from his duties, so please remove yourself from his attention and be respectful, if you wish not to be beheaded.

"In other news, a break-in took place at a major armory in Lindel yesterday. Sellers claim a handful of Reaper scythes were the only items missing. The suspects were seen fleeing the crime scene: four hawk shifters who..."

A snapshot of four masked bird shifters appeared beside the reporter, three men and one woman. Their names hovered beside them in bright text, along with their sentences. They were set to be hung for breaking the Fourth Law of Death—whatever that was.

The nether-kingdom's regulations always had the harshest punishments, no matter which nation you lived in. *Death happens everywhere, to everyone,* as they say, *Grim just manages it, in their dark little hole in the ground.*

My mouth twisted at the screen, and I crossed my arms, looking at the four wanted bird shifters.

"The Carter Siblings, eh?" Ringëd said next to me suddenly. My sister's fiancé had come to watch the report.

Ringëd's cropped hair was creamy blond with brown tips, his long nose flat and stern, square chin speckled in light stubble. He was tan, but his skin wasn't as dark as an Everlander's bronze-complexion. His ancestry was from the other continent, Neverland, where they had lush forests to hide from the sun... which only made Ringëd even weirder, since he was born on an island from the Ocean realm's province to the west. That was probably the only reason he wasn't as pale as a Grimling.

"We've had some trouble with those four ourselves, a few weeks back," Ringëd grunted, looking at the Carter Siblings' pictures on the screen. He had that usual, analytical look of his, like he was still on duty, even though it was afterhours.

"Leave it to a Seeker to investigate off-the-clock," I muttered. "Guess your department never caught them?"

"No, we didn't. They must have skipped town too quick, looks like. Guess this explains where they disappeared to."

Clack! Clack!

Knocking came from the window next to us. A raven with white cheeks was pecking his beak against the glass. The bird cocked its head at me, cawing and fluttered its wings, head bobbing.

I grinned. "Looks like it's time to visit Mom."

The last customer finally paid their bill and left, so we closed for the night. I slung off my apron and hung it on the hook in the kitchen, then left the café with Ringëd.

When we stepped out, the raven fluttered onto my head as usual. I felt its talons lay gently over my hair, which cushioned their sharp points.

I was never sure how the raven knew to be careful when sitting there. To be honest, I wasn't sure of anything Shade did. He was still a feral bird, scavenged his food, came and went as he pleased, did everything your average bird did… he just followed me around sometimes. Okay, *most* times. He was weirdly obedient.

Ringëd and I walked along the boardwalk in silence for a while, and I watched the ocean hush in the spring breeze. It was a half-moon tonight. A good night to talk to Mom. I knew her soul couldn't hear me all the way in Grim, but it made me feel better to say what I was thinking out loud. I guessed I was practicing for when we actually *would* see her ghost—provided we had enough money to travel underground, one of these days.

"By the way, Tavius," Ringëd began, taking out a smoke and lighting it. He puffed for a second before letting out a smooth, dark cloud. "I've been meaning to talk to you about that raven of yours."

I grabbed Shade from my head protectively. "He stays outside like Mika wants," I said. "He hasn't brought in any more rat livers."

"R-at!" Shade cawed lowly. "Rat?"

"No rat, Shade." I scratched at his neck. The little guy liked to mimic some words every now and then. He didn't know too much, but it was still pretty cool.

"It's not that," said Ringëd. "It's what the bird means. Don't you want to know why it keeps following you?"

"Well, I stopped thinking about it." I moved my scratching fingers underneath Shade's beak, smiling when his throat gave a pleased coo. "You get used to him after a while. But, you know… I keep wondering what I'm going to do if he just flies off somewhere and doesn't come back. I don't know what I'd do. To be honest, I think it'd crush me, or… I don't know."

"Yeah, I've heard the bond is something special with them. Guess you have to be one to understand."

"Be one of what?"

He rubbed his neck. "Well, uh…" He sighed. "All right, look. I've seen other people who were followed by black birds. Back on my island, on the Marincian province."

"So, it's a Marincian thing?"

"It's more of a Grim thing, actually."

I gave him a scrunched look. "You think Shade mistook me for a Grimling?"

"No." He paused, then revised, "Well, maybe. I don't know. But that's not the point. Octavius, have you put some thought into what you want to do for a living?"

We stepped off the boardwalk and headed for the streets toward the cemetery. I grimaced at the reminder that I wasn't going anywhere with my life. At my current rate, I'd keel over in the middle of scrubbing toilets.

"What's the point?" I asked. "We've all been busy keeping the café running, so it's not like any of us have time to find an apprenticeship… I'm too old to take one up anyway. They're looking for sixteen-year-olds fresh out of school, or even younger. No one's going to take on a twenty-two-year-old busboy."

"See, that's what I wanted to talk about. You're already an apprentice. I would have told you about Shade when you first got him, but with Mikani being so stressed about you all keeping your house, it would have been too soon back then. But it's been a couple years already, so… I think it's about time you knew."

I was only more confused. "Knew what, though?"

We stopped outside the cemetery gate, and he hesitated. "Actually… you know what? Ask me tomorrow. I think your sister needs to hear it, too. She won't be happy, but she'll just have to deal with it. It's your life, anyway."

"Do I have to make some kind of choice?"

"Not really. Sort of…" He scratched his cheek. "Have you really never heard of this? It's basic curriculum back on my island. I didn't think about it much since it rarely happened, but I still knew. One of my ex-girlfriends was even chosen, actually."

"Chosen for what?"

He shook his head, taking another hit from his smoke. "I'll tell you tomorrow… don't stay in there too long, all right? Curfew starts in an hour." He stabbed a warning finger at my face. "And I'm serious. I may have pulled some strings the last time, but this time will be different. Your sister will actually have to pay bail, and you're all short for money as it is."

"Right…" I sighed.

With that, he left, heading down the road and turning a corner. I glanced down at Shade in my arms. "So, you actually mean something, huh? Do you even know what?"

The raven croaked in response, and I chuckled. "I'll take that as a 'no'."

I lifted Shade up, letting him fly out of my arms and perch on the fence. His diamond tail fanned out as he ruffled his black feathers, impatient.

The cemetery was pretty misty tonight, and the gate was locked as usual, so I had to find another way in. I walked along the length of the fence, counting iron bars until finding the three rods that were loose. Pulling them up, I ducked inside the cemetery, sliding the bars back in place so no one would see I'd snuck in.

I climbed the tallest hill and took my usual seat under the dead tree in front of Mom's grave, staring at the stone in silence while reading the engraved name on the stone: *Sirra-Lynn Abigail Treble.*

"Hey, Mom." I brushed my fingers over the chiseled letters. "Sorry I didn't bring flowers this time. We're running short on money..."

Time passed quickly as I talked. I knew she couldn't hear me, but I needed to feel like I could still talk to her, like she was still here with us in Everland, not down in those caves with the other ghosts.

I'd asked Ringëd once what Grim looked like. He'd visited there a few times as a kid, before he came here from his island. He said the caves were actually beautiful, brighter than what people up here expected. He said they had clouds in there, some kind of weird mist formations that covered the stalactites on the ceiling, but it never rained.

I tried to imagine what it would be like to live underground. It just seemed weird, to never see the sun, the moon, the stars, the rain...

How did the Grimlings stand it? Going their entire lives never seeing any of those things was just so... so...

I laid on my back, staring at the sky. Maybe I only thought it'd be terrible because I didn't live there? Maybe, to a Grimling, they'd think it'd be worse to live up here?

I grinned, deciding I'd save that question for when I visited Mom in person.

4

AN UNEXPECTED ALLY

XAVIER

"Anythin' yet?" asked Jaq in a quiet hush.

"No," I sighed dully. "Don't you think it's been long enough?"

"Shh! I just heard somethin'…"

Jaq pressed an ear against the cobbled road, holding his breath. I had my cheek over the rocks beside him, listening for signs of life underneath us.

My fingers tapped over the colorful stones as I bit down my fluttering anxiety. Keeping still was proving a challenge, but we'd already made an agreement with Jaq to test this theory. Despite my hurry, this was our first time on the surface… well, first time for them. I'd been above Grim's caves once before, but that wasn't a time I liked to remember. Not that I remembered much of it to begin with.

Alexander didn't share my patience. *"Tell him it's over."* His voice echoed from my thoughts. *"Must you indulge him at such an imperative time?"*

I turned to Jaq, about to follow through with my brother's request, when our friend held up a scaled finger. "Oh no, I know that look." Jaq pushed his glasses farther up his impeccably straight nose. "Whatever you're tellin' him, ya can shut it in there, Alex. Now I know I heard somethin' this time…"

We waited longer, listening, and when my own patience ebbed, I exhaled. "Jaq, we can't hear anything. It's a myth children fabricated."

"Maybe everyone's sleepin' down there!" He shuffled to his feet. "We should've tested it in Bright Light hours. It doesn't count at Dim Light."

I pushed myself up to stand beside him and chuckled, pulling my white, draping hood over my head. "Don't try and slither your way out of this one,

Jaq. We've won this wager. Everlanders can't hear us underground in Grim. Which means we're squad leader on the next hunt."

"Aw, come on!" Jaq threw up his hands, making the long chain that was wrapped around his left wrist jingle. "Ya can't both be squad leader! You were leader at the last hunt, Xavier."

I shrugged. "Then Alex will lead."

"That still ain't fair. You'll be leadin' half the time, like ya always end up doin'."

"We have to share control. We'd go mad in there, otherwise."

Jaq clicked his tongue and muttered, "Ain't Bloody fair…"

Croaking blurted from the raven and crow above us. The black birds were perched on the spiked fence of the cemetery, and they both looked down at us impatiently. Our feathered companions were just as eager as we were, it seemed.

Jaq groaned beside me, scratching his neck. His pale, scale-coated skin had become cracked and dry in this heat. Our friend grimaced while peeling off a thin layer of snakeskin from his neck.

"Why's the surface so hot?" He flicked the flaky skin away. "It ain't natural, I'm tellin' ya. Reptiles would probably die up here if they stayed out too long."

I raised an eyebrow. "Then how did your mother survive? Wasn't she a Landish viper?"

Jaq stretched his arms and gave a yawn, displaying his two long fangs before scratching at his neck once more. "Don't mean she liked it up here."

"Yes, that's all well and good," I heard my brother clip. *"Shall we get on with it, then? We haven't got all night, and I sure as Bloods don't want to be sitting in here until morning."*

"Right." I cleared my throat, focusing on the task at hand. Alex was right, this was our final mission as apprentices. We had to view this assignment as professionals.

The cemetery was misted in a thin fog, the gravestones casting long shadows from the light of a strange, half-filled object floating in the black ceiling—er, '*sky*'—over our heads.

"What *is* that thing?" Jaq asked, pointing to the glowing lemon wedge up there. "Why ain't none of the lights floatin' around?"

I hummed and rummaged through my pockets to produce the informational pamphlet we acquired at the Surfacing Port. The attendants were passing them out at the station.

"I believe the surface dwellers call it a 'moon'," I said, flipping through the pamphlet to find the proper section. I held it under a lamppost and showed it to Jaq. "It says here, it's some sort of planet, only smaller, and orbits Nirus. And those lights around it are apparently called 'stars'."

Jaq's nose scrunched at the pamphlet, comparing the printed photograph with the real thing. "Weird. So, it just sits up there? Does it ever fall, like our lights?"

I muttered, "I'd think if it did, it would blind whoever caught it."

He scratched his flaking chin. "Would that be extra *good* luck, or the worst luck 'a your life?

"Death if I know," I said, snatching the pamphlet back and stuffing it back in my trousers' pocket. "We can debate it when our mission is finished. Come, we've a ghost to find."

I rattled the locked gate, glaring at the chains keeping it closed. My wolf ears grew, and I gave an indignant snort, kicking the bars.

"Their office is closed at this hour," I mumbled, thinking. I glanced at our viper friend. "Jaq? Could we ask a favor?"

Already guessing my request, Jaq began unwinding the chain around his wrist. A metal ball dangled from the last link. "Give me a sec." Jaq pressed a thumb against the engraved rune on the ball, and the carving became lit with a golden sheen.

Soon, the sphere gleamed and began melting in his hand like thick, silver liquid. The metal rippled and waved in sleek folds, spreading itself thin until it molded into a short-handled, hooked blade. The liquid gave a hushed clash as it solidified in that shape, and took on its original, metal texture once again.

Jaq's crooked scythe was as smooth as glass, its flawless surface reflecting the light of the half-moon while emitting a bluish, glowing quality of its own.

Our friend tugged the attached chain, now ready to throw. He swirled the weapon, then tossed it up. The crooked blade latched to the top of the fence with a *clang* and Jaq pulled himself up. He scaled the tall fence and threw the chain back down to us, then hopped off and waved from the other side of the bars.

I climbed after him, grabbing his weapon off the fence, and jumped into the yard.

"All right," I said, handing him back his chain-scythe. "Keep your eyes open for any wandering ghosts. Her gravesite should be somewhere around here, and if she's anything like the ghosts we know, she'll be staring at it like a gnat to lamplight."

"And if she's not here?" asked Jaq, reverting his scythe into a ball that hung on the last link and wrapped the chain around his wrist.

"Then we'll…" I paused, my wolf ears perking. There came a soft mumbling from atop the hill, picked up by my amplified hearing.

"… hope everything's going all right for you, down in Grim," said what sounded like a boy's voice. A miserable sigh followed. "I bet the afterlife's easier than up here…"

Jaq didn't seem to hear anything and looked ready to question me, but I raised a quieting hand and crept up the hill. Jaq followed skeptically.

Once reaching the top, a black haired, bronze-skinned boy appeared within the mist. He sat before a grave with his knees tucked to his chest, murmuring gently as a boney tree loomed over him and the grave, cloaking them in a thin shadow.

Jaq and I hid behind two stone slabs, my wolf ears receding as we listened to the stranger talk.

"Mikani's worried, you know," he said. From his hair, I thought him a fellow Grimling, but that skin… it was so much darker than a cave-dweller's. Was he a local here on the surface? "She doesn't want to say anything, but Neal and I can tell. I think we might lose the café soon, if something doesn't change."

I peered over the edge of my shielding tombstone, searching for any ghosts he may be speaking with. *Is it the soul we were sent here to find?* My eyes strained in the half-moon's light, but when no souls came into view, I clicked my tongue. "False alarm. There's no soul here."

"I don't get it," Jaq mumbled, scratching his brow. "Is he just talkin' to the grave?"

Alexander hummed from my thoughts. *"I've heard those without soul-sight are wont to doing that. Perhaps it's a coping mechanism?"*

"Perhaps," I agreed curiously. What an odd thing to do. Don't they know the ghosts can't hear them? How bizarre.

"And Connaline's doing fine, I guess," continued the civilian, his tone more hopeful. "She'll be done with school this year, after next spring. Maybe we'll get enough money by then to come down and see you?"

Cawing burst overhead, interrupting him. A raven with white cheeks soared down to greet him, and it nestled over his hair. He grinned up at the bird. "And I guess I can introduce you to Shade." He reached a hand up to scratch the bird's neck. "He's pretty cool. Follows me around a lot."

"Well, Nira take me," I murmured, staring at the new raven. "It would seem we have another Brother up here."

The boy's raven twitched its head in our direction, and we ducked behind the graves. I thought we'd been caught, the raven turned away and began to fluff its wings. Screeches burst from its beak and the boy grabbed it to try and calm the Bloody thing.

"Shade?" He struggled with the bird's flailing wings. "Land, Shade, what's gotten into you?"

"R-un," the raven choked. "R-un…!"

Other screeches cried when *our* birds flew over. Alexander's raven fluttered onto my gravestone, and the crow went to scream at Jaq. They both sounded panicked.

"Death," I cursed over the noise.

Jaq caught the frantic crow in his arms and tried to hush the bird. I held the raven still cawing at me, trying to calm it down, but it only screeched louder.

"To ar-ms!" Mal croaked. "Dang-er! Dang-er…!"

He kept to his squawking, and I muttered through clenched teeth. "I heard, I heard! Damned bird…" I flicked my eyes upward, hissing, "Alex, will you shut him up?" The raven was *his*, and thus never listened to a damn word I ever said.

Alexander's voice rang in my thoughts. *"My turn."*

I felt something pull me back, a light, intangible tug that vibrated my soul. Alexander wanted to switch. Grudgingly, I closed my eyes and inhaled, then let the force pull me backward as the touch of warm air vanished from my skin. The panicking raven disappeared from my arms, breathing became meaningless and every sense of touch and smell and taste became… nothing.

"Thank you, Mal." My brother's voice echoed soothingly around me. "You've done well. Be calm, now."

I opened my eyes again. I was now inside the usual, isolating void. My prison. I stared out the large window in the surrounding abyss and watched as Alexander hushed the raven in his arms. Now that Mal was silenced, Alexander peered over the edge of the gravestone.

"What in Bloods got into you?" the black-haired boy asked the crying bird in his arms. "Void, calm down! You're going to get me arrested again—"

Skriiiiiiiii…!

A high-pitched shriek cracked through the mist, the cry leaving a hollow echo in the night. Alex tensed behind the grave. That hadn't been a noise any natural beast would make. It was gurgled, yet as sharp as the dullest knife to ever plunge through your eye sockets.

Rigidly, the boy rose. Irregular footsteps pattered behind the tree, and he flinched. A moment of quietness swelled before he crept toward the tree, keeping his white-cheeked raven against his chest.

"For Death's sake," Alexander muttered, moving out of our hiding place to head for the civilian. "Bloody idiot! If it's that horde we heard about from the valley—"

Another grating screech cried out.

The boy jolted and staggered away, the raven fluttering out of his arms and cawing from the tree instead. Black cat ears grew from the boy's head in fright.

Then, from the thinning fog emerged a sluggish shadow. The thing dripped rather than walked, its skin surging with tar-like syrup that quivered and pulsed over its limbs.

It stared at the boy with glowing white eyes, never blinking as it kept a cautious pace and sniffed the air. The form looked humanoid, but its slumped posture and crooked steps ruined that illusion. This wasn't a shifter. Not anymore. Its hollow eyes were wrenched open, glowing in the black liquid that slurped over its body.

It took another step forward, sloppy and disjointed. It raised its horned head and bleated a hideous, ripping scream, and more beasts came from the fog. Now, they all watched the cat shifter, who was frozen where he stood.

Alex broke into a full-on sprint, Jaq following as the raven and crow soared overhead and croaked furiously. Alex and Jaq gave three sharp whistles, ordering the birds to veer away to a safer location.

We were yards away when the boy noticed us coming, and he turned to make a run for our group—but his legs tripped over the gravestone he'd come to visit, and he tumbled to the dirt in a winded groan.

The beasts shrieked after him.

He tried to scuttle away, but a set of claws tore into his shoulder, making him stumble and cry out. He kicked the thing back, gripping the bloody gashes on his arm, but a second beast came and—

CRACK!

Jaq flung his chained scythe forward, and the blade fissured into the demon's head before it could take a chunk out of the boy's jugular.

"Damned freaks!" the viper spat, his fangs dripping with venom. "Ya ain't eatin' any souls tonight!"

With his chain-scythe stuck in the demon's skull, Jaq yanked it away from the boy. The beast whipped its head violently, and the scythe sliced out.

Black blood oozed from its head. The demon roared, hunching over, its joints popping out of place as it backed away.

Its head began to mend. The black tar strung together like sticky jelly until the creature's wound was newly healed. Then it ripped a vicious growl and leapt for Jaq.

Jaq whipped his chain round his shoulders, the blade whistling as it revolved full circle and tore the beast's head clean off. The skull rolled away from its flailing body, snapping from the ground. The ooze from its stubbed neck stretched like a tangle of writhing tendrils that slithered across the dirt, trying to reattach to its body.

Alexander ran to the headless demon, plunging one of his blades into the beast's chest.

"My, my," Alex grunted as he *ripped* the scythe over its heart. "Aren't we overdue for our reaping?"

A *snap* sounded under his blade, and the headless creature wilted. The disembodied head gave a muted scream from the ground, and the slithering, black tar soon fell still, evaporating in a hiss.

Once the tar cleared, the skeleton underneath clattered to the ground in a pile of bones and decayed flesh. The skull rolled before the trembling boy's feet, and he plugged his nose in disgust, lunging behind a grave to retch. The slosh of vomit gushed alongside his gags.

My brother's scythe still dripped with black blood, but the ooze soon hissed away, leaving the blade clean and glowing. Alex counted the remaining demons: there were seven left, all staring at him with glowing savage eyes as Alex slid his feet in a more prepared stance.

"Jaq, take the ones on the left," he said, cracking his neck. "We'll harvest the rest of these souls ourselves."

5

A REAPER'S DUTY

XAVIER

I t was a frenzy.

The creatures scrambled forward, shoving amongst themselves to be the first to feed, mandibles dripping with sludge. Every splatter slithered back to them, always moving like feral snakes over their disfigured forms.

The Necrofera couldn't die by normal methods. They were already dead to begin with, husks of the shifters they once were, blackened skeletons and mindless corpses drenched in their rotten souls.

Souls that we, as Reapers, were sworn to set free.

A creature leapt for Alex in a hungry scream. He ducked and arched his scythe upward, cutting through its chest and severing its NecroSeam with a sharp *snap!*

With the Seam reaped, the creature's soul was released from its vessel. The sludge evaporated like muck draining off skin, and its corpse fumbled behind us.

A second beast clawed for Alex's feet. He jumped and ripped into the creature's back, pulling the stuck beast toward him before flipping it on its back and tore the blade over its heart.

Snap! The demon's NecroSeam was cut, and with an agonized scream, it shriveled and died, the black tar evaporating.

Alex jerked his gaze to Jaq. Our friend was busy fighting two demons, his chain-scythe whipping round his shoulders in a wide perimeter.

Alex and I knew to leave Jaq be. His choice of weapon was advantageous for distances, but we couldn't jump into his fights without being tangled in his chain ourselves. That had been a hard lesson during the early years of our training.

Two beasts scurried for Jaq from opposing sides, and he crossed his feet and spun, his chain swirling around his neck in a smooth whistle as his scythe sliced through one demon's chest.

Snap!

More black ooze tainted the mist.

Jaq spun on his heels and crouched, swinging his blade upward to snag the second beast's chest. He *ripped* it free with a hard, grunting jerk then trotted toward us, the beast's corpse thumping to the dirt behind him—

A yell split our ears. The black-haired local ducked under a gravestone and scuttled away from the demons now preying on him, panicking as he hollered for help. *Blast it, they must have thought him the easier kill.*

Alex darted for him, and Jaq followed, the viper hurtling his blade at the closest beast preying on the boy. His blade sank into the creature's side, and he yanked it backward.

Alex slid between it and the boy, dirt puffing behind him as his feet scuffed to a halt. The boy's cat ears were folded to the nape of his neck in quivering terror.

The demon Jaq had caught shook itself loose and scurried back, healing its wound.

Jaq and Alex touched backs, the remaining three creatures circling.

"Boy," my brother barked to the cat behind us, not breaking his gaze from the beasts. "Is that your messenger?" Alex pointed a scythe at the white-cheeked raven still screeching overhead.

The boy sounded puzzled, his voice trembling. "Shade? I... I guess he's mine."

"Why haven't you told it to leave?"

"*Told* it?" he asked skeptically. "I can't get rid of it half the time! How the Land am I supposed to—"

"Three whistles."

The boy stopped. "What?"

"Give three whistles. Do it now, they all understand the Commands instinctually."

"Well, Bloods, if you know all that, then *you* do it!"

"We can't do it for you if it's not our messenger!" Alex hollered, annoyed. "Now will you shut your Bloody mouth and *do it already?*"

He winced, but soon did as asked. After delivering three short whistles, his screeching raven soared away to safety. The boy stared after it with wide, puzzled eyes.

"If he doesn't know basic messenger Commands," I muttered from the psyche, *"I'm betting he hasn't advanced past the wooden scythes in training."*

My window tilted as Alex cocked his head. "I'd say that's likely."

I hummed, considering. *"Give him one of ours."*

Alex's gaze flicked upward. "If his master hasn't granted him one, he isn't ready."

"At least offer him some protection."

"And if he's as good as Jaq and takes one of our kills?" He laughed. "I don't think so. We have claim. He probably doesn't even use close-range blades, he wouldn't know how to handle them."

The boy stammered behind us, "u-um… who're you talking to?"

"Just offer," I insisted. *"Even if he IS on par with Jaq, we'd still be disrespecting our Brother by denying him kill on a harvest."*

"And I should care why?" sighed Alex.

"It's the principle of the matter."

"Oh, well then, far be it from me to stain something as sacred as the principle." He snorted. "Sentimental ass…"

The boy gave an audible swallow. "What the Land are you… C-can you just hurry up and kill the things already?"

Jaq spat venom at the dirt. "No worries, newbie, there's only three of 'em left. We've hunted more than that hundreds 'a times, no problem."

"Oh, Bloods, I'm gonna die…" The boy hugged his knees and gulped down terrified gasps, burring his face in his shaking hands. "Are all Reapers this suicidal?"

My vision narrowed from the psyche, watching the boy through my window. *"Death's Head…"* I mumbled curiously. *"I don't think he knows."*

"So it would seem," Alex said, hefting his shoulders. "That would explain his ignorance, at the least."

The boy scratched his head vigorously, shouting, "*Who* are you talking to?!"

The demons were closing in. They seemed fully healed and ready to strike.

My brother flicked his eyes up briefly. "I've already killed three, and Jaq's had his two. Your turn, if you still want a go at them."

The boy's voice cracked behind us. "I can't kill those things!"

"Not you. You're obviously newly chosen." Alex jerked his head upward, which was a gesture meant for me. "Well then? Hurry and take your turn."

I pushed myself toward the window in the black void surrounding me.

Once my head passed through the window, I was brought out to the 'conscious' world. Alexander's scythes weighed down my hands; the warm air touched my skin again and, relieved to *feel*, I gripped the metal hilts with tight fingers.

A demon scrambled for me. I ducked and sliced its neck with one scythe while my other blade shot into its chest. I tore through its heart with a *snap* and shoved the corpse aside.

The second beast came next, and I blocked its claws with one scythe and plunged the other into its heart. *Snap!* Another Seam reaped. The demon's skeleton clattered to the dirt.

I pivoted to the final creature, frozen where it stood.

The demon glanced at its now dead companions, then swept its glowing eyes at me. I sighed and stepped toward it, my pace lax. This seemed to startle the thing. It gave a bleating squeal that dripped black saliva and scurried away from me.

I put away one scythe and tossed a hand behind me to signal Jaq, and I heard the viper give a heave. His chain-scythe flew into view and the blade hooked deep into the beast's back.

The demon screamed a shattering howl, like glass against stone, and fought to crawl away like a beetle pinned in place, its legs wiggling uselessly.

I swiveled one of my scythes idly, strolling over as the frantic creature writhed against Jaq's chain, the thing leaving claw marks in the dirt.

I took a deep breath, knelt, and *jammed* the long end of my scythe into its spine with a squishing plunge. The thing gave a final shriek as the blade pierced out the other side of its chest, and I twisted the scythe over its heart.

Snap!

It was done. The last rotten soul was released from its expired vessel. I gave a calming sigh and raised the blade to my chest.

"Nira Cleanse these souls of their rotten state." I bowed my head at the corpses surrounding us. "The Void is but a temporary house for your lost spirits, and with the guidance of the Mother Goddess, may the Great Unknown await you. Mercy befall your fate. Peace and safe passage to your rejuvenation. *Mu necros nechshali yettek...*"

I finished the prayer and glanced at Jaq, who'd saluted with a fist to his chest as well.

With the danger gone, I reverted my scythe back to its smaller, spherical form, and replaced the ball back on its magnetic holder around my neck, joining the one I'd put away earlier.

I felt Alex wanting to take my place again. He asked to do the honors of removing the corpses. *As if I had much choice.* The cleanup would have to be conducted by Alexander regardless. I wouldn't be any help with that, and neither would Jaq.

I allowed Alex to switch with me. As he took control, the touch of warm air vanished. I found myself back in the empty void with only the large window of my brother's vision to stare at.

Alexander raised a hand to the ruined corpses and skeletons. A birthmark of three black diamonds was displayed under his knuckles, and as my brother exhaled a long sigh, the mark began to gleam. The diamonds changed white and shrank, swirling over his skin, and soon enough, it morphed into a Death mark, looking like two scythes leaned back to back, gleaming white from below his knuckles.

His fingers leaked with black and violet lights, stretching and cradling the scattered pieces of corpses. Like a morbid conductor beholden to his orchestra, my brother weaved his shining hands in the night, the small glints of violet rippling after each solemn stroke and punctuated slash.

One by one, the bones clattered back together, the rotten, decayed puzzles piecing themselves in their proper spaces as though performing a ballet for the Seamstress.

But Alex's concentration was thrown when the civilian gave a startled gasp behind us.

"N-Necrovoker...!" he stammered, not so much out of fear, but rather of confusion and awe. "You're a Necrovoker?"

Alex glanced away from his eight boney puppets to give a humble nod. We saw the boy's cat ears had receded, calmer now that the beasts were dead, but he seemed disgusted by my brother's new company... and yet couldn't look away.

Alex hummed. "I take it you don't see many corpse-raisers up here?"

The boy shook his head.

Alex rolled his neck, and I heard a zipper of small cricks. "Well, I suppose it should come as no surprise. Death is Grim's element, not Everland's..."

Mal, Alexander's raven, fluttered down from the sky to perch over my brother's shoulder. Jaq's crow, Bridge, came to perch over the viper's arm as well, and the white-cheeked raven landed on the new boy's lanky hair.

While Alex had his new 'friends' line up before us, Jaq wrapped his chain around his wrist. "Ya got some guts, ya know," Jaq muttered to the shaken local. "Could've gotten yourself killed, goin' after 'em like that without a scythe."

"Yes, we can all agree that was a terribly stupid thing to do," Alex said, tapping a finger to his chin in thought. "Now, more importantly, what do we do with a Reaper who isn't aware he's one himself? I can't say I've ever come across such a case, but here we are."

The boy looked skeptical. "I... what? I'm not a—"

"Yes, you are," Alex contradicted. "Rather, you're a fellow apprentice." Alex unzipped his jacket to show the boy our badge that was pinned to the inside pocket. The badge held a silver raven in flight, and within an ebony rectangle read the words 'Reaper Apprentice'.

Jaq had a similar badge pinned to his belt. Alex gestured to the boy's raven. "That messenger chose you recently, I take it?"

The boy lifted the raven off his head and instead held it in his arms. "Uh, I mean, I wouldn't say *chose*... Shade just started following me a couple years back."

"A couple years?" We all echoed, though my response wasn't heard, except by Alexander.

Jaq rubbed his eyes under his glasses. "Bloods, kid, you're farther behind in your trainin' than I thought!"

He ducked his head sheepishly. "Look, I'm really not a Reaper."

"Not yet, true." Alex's gaze flicked to the boy's scratched shoulder, which was crusted with blood. "Regardless... it looks like you need a Healer. Shall we take you to a Clinic?"

The boy gripped his shoulder, looking at the cuts. His expression turned sick, but he swallowed and shook his head. "I'll get my little sister to heal it at home... She has remedy Hallows, and it's not that serious."

"Then let us take you there," Alex offered. "In case you run into any more... trouble?" He nodded to the clattering bones still standing at Alexander's command.

The boy shuddered. "S-sure, yeah... uhm, thanks..."

Jaq scrutinized the corpses with a sniff. "So, what do we do with them? If we file a report, Mistress will know we ran into trouble on our first day. She might summon us back if she thinks it's too dangerous."

Alex grimaced. "We'll leave them here. Drop an anonymous tip at a Raider's station explaining it. They can retrieve the vessels on their own time."

"Sounds good to me," Jaq approved.

Alex had the corpses lay themselves neatly behind the tree, and after he dismissed his Hallows, the violet streams of light around the corpses faded. His white Death mark changed into the black diamonds again on his right hand.

He turned to Jaq, who was staring at a grave under the twisted, dehydrated tree.

"Hold up," our scaled friend's eyes narrowed at the gravestone. "Isn't *this* who we're lookin' for?"

Alex crouched before the grave and read aloud, "Sirra-Lynn Abigail Treble." He laughed and patted the viper's back. "This is it! Good work, Jaq."

The local boy seemed nervous to ask. "Why were you looking for that grave?"

"This soul is missing from Grim," Alex explained.

The boy's bronze face blanched. "She's on the surface?"

"Our Mistress sent us here to find her." Alex twisted to search the cemetery for signs of a wandering specter. "Though… It doesn't look like her soul is present. Brilliant… I suppose we'll have to look at her old home next, or perhaps query her next-of-kin."

"Well, *I* got nothing," the boy muttered. "And she's not at home, either."

Alex narrowed an eye at him. "Er… I don't think we were properly introduced. Who are you?"

"Oh, uhm, Octavius Treble." He waved at the grave unceremoniously. "Sirra-Lynn was my mom."

Alex scratched his chin with interest, I could hear the rough scrape of his nails against his recently shaven skin. "Her son, eh? Convenient… If she's not at home, do you know where her ghost may have gone?"

The boy, Octavius, shrugged. "Not really. Oh, but maybe Rochelle's seen her in Nulani? They were good friends, she used to visit there a lot before she… well…"

Alexander cleared his throat, staying on topic. "And where is Nulani?"

"It's the next town over, just eastward. It takes hours to get there though, since you have to cross over the wastelands first."

Alex clasped a hand over Octavius's shoulder. "You can explain on the way. I think we'd best leave tonight and arrive by morning. I suggest you hurry and pack."

Octavius blinked. "You want me to come?"

Alex cocked an eyebrow and pulled out his informational pamphlet from his pocket, flapping it in a gesture. "Sir, we are *tourists*. I don't know the first damned thing about this surface of yours, and I personally would prefer to avoid any delays caused by our utter ignorance of this terrain. Your mother's afterlife is at stake—and I will *not* fail my final assignment because *I got lost*. We need a guide. And who better to guide us than the son of the very woman we're tracking?"

Octavius blushed and rubbed his neck. "Oh… yeah, that makes sense, I guess…"

"Besides." Alex rolled up the pamphlet and stuffed it back in his pocket, exhaling. "We don't know this 'Rochelle' woman or what she looks like. You sound familiar with her, so this task would go far more smoothly if we had someone to point us to her."

"Oh, right," he laughed nervously.

"Though," Alex continued, "you really ought to see to your injuries first. Never leave a fellow soldier unaided, as Mistress often stresses."

He glanced at the gashes on his shoulder. "It's really not that bad. It'll probably leave scars, but right now it just needs some disinfectant."

"Excellent idea—you can pick that up while you pack." Alex pushed him forward. "We'll have to tell your father, also, it's standard procedure to inform the spouse of such things."

"U-um, if you can find him, sure, go ahead and tell him… But he hasn't been home for years."

Alex stopped and turned to him, puzzled. "What do you mean?"

"He… he sort of… left, after Mom died." His voice fell morose. "My older sister just takes care of everyone now, so…"

Alex gave an awkward cough. "Oh… I see… *Khm kmm*, we'll just, er, explain it to your sister, then… Your mother could be in very serious danger. If any demons find her, like these ones here, she won't have a way to defend herself. Not without an escorting Reaper."

Octavius scratched his head. "Well, I don't want her to be eaten…"

"All the more reason to come."

He pursed his lips, and a hint of excitement flashed when he glanced past the cemetery gates.

"All right," he announced, "I'll come. It beats scrubbing tables, anyway. I just need to convince Mikani—"

Alex gave a hard *thump* on his back, making Octavius lurch forward and his raven flutter in his arms. "We'll sort it out," Alex said. "This search will be far smoother if we have Mrs. Trebles's son with us."

Octavius hugged his raven tighter and stared at his feet while making his way down the hill in front of us. When he glanced back, I caught his thrilled, disbelieving look, as if he'd been searching for some excuse to leave for years.

"Well, that was a stroke of fortune if I ever saw one." Alex muttered to me. My window bowed upward when he grinned. "It won't be long now,

Xavier. Once we find this ghost, we should find *you*. Then, with luck… we can keep our oath."

I smiled at the reminder. *"Born together."*

"Die together," he finished, voice hardened. "We'll fix that, soon enough."

6

CLATTERY CATS

XAVIER

Octavius led us to his home along the docks of Brittleton Beach. It was a quaint, two-story eatery called the Clattery Café, its yellow-painted sign crooked and chipped at the edges, flat roof covered in palm-tree fronds whose fingers ruffled in the sea breeze, sand grains puffing onto the docks. There was a single, flickering lamp at the door, the window curtains drawn and glowing dimly with after-hour lights.

Octavius pushed open the thick, oaken door and allowed Jaq and my brother entry.

The inner décor of the wide dining hall was, to put it bluntly, endearingly *tacky*. The walls were littered with fishing nets and rowing oars, a plastic, feral swordfish mounted between family photographs, and the splintered walls behind them were frayed with shavings falling all the way from trim to ceiling in two corners. The chairs were upturned and placed atop the tables, and Alex grunted a complaint that the bar counter stank of ale and disinfectant cleaner.

"Mika?" Octavius called, his voice carrying through the empty dining hall as he closed and locked the door behind us. "Mika, we need to talk. Something's come up."

Heavy footfalls thumped from a stairway in the back corner, and a black-haired, bronze-skinned woman marched down in a scowl.

"Where in the five Bloody realms have you been?" the woman, Mika, demanded, black cat ears growing from her head and curling back angrily, her feet like boulders against the stairs. "I called Ringëd to see if you were with him, and he said he left you at the cemetery *two hours* ago! Land, Tavius, what have I told you about staying after curfew—"

She froze when she reached the last step, spotting Jaq and my brother standing behind Octavius.

Her shoulders tensed. "Who're they?"

Alex raised a respectful fist to his chest and gave a shallow bow. "Alexander Dev... er, *Edric*, miss. And this is my associate, Jaqelle Mallory."

Jaq gave a fang-filled grin and thumped a fist to his own chest. "Call me Jaq, Ma'am."

She crossed the floor to scrutinize us skeptically, her nose crinkling as though smelling something foul. "Gardener sow me, you're paler than my grandma's spoiled chicken..." she muttered, inspecting my brother's grey hair, then looked at Jaq's sandy blond locks. "And what's with you? You got an Everlander's hair, but your scales are as grey as his."

"Half-blooded," explained Jaq proudly. "Da's a Grimish viper, my mother's a Landish snake."

"Uh-huh," She grunted, pulling out a packet of cigarettes and crushed one between her lips. She flicked her fingers—

A *puff* of orange flame ignited over her fingertips suddenly, and a smooth teardrop of fire wavered under the cigarette, burning the end that flared red as she sucked in a long breath, then exhaled smoke from her nostrils.

I blinked from the psyche, watching as she dismissed the fire with a wave of her hand. *"A Pyrovoker,"* I hummed, causing my brother's gaze to flick upward.

Alex murmured ponderously. "A fire-thrower here on the surface... I suppose given your Grimish hair, it shouldn't be too surprising. Are you immigrants, then?"

She puffed on her cigarette. "Everlandish, born and raised. Now who exactly are you? And what's with the birds?" She pointed her chin at the raven and crow on their shoulders, the birds cocking their heads to stare at her with one eye. She glanced at Octavius's white-cheeked raven as well, crossing her arms. "What, did Tavius find a crow club or something? If he offered you food, *he's* cooking it, because I..."

She paused when she turned to her brother, taking notice of the bleeding gashes on his shoulder. Her cigarette dropped to the floor, and her hastened slippers snuffed it out as she grabbed Octavius's arm. "Land, Tavius! What happened?! Gods, those are deep...!" She twisted toward the stairs, shouting. "Connie! Connie, wake up and get down here! Hurry!"

Octavius rubbed his neck in a mumble. "It's not that bad, Mika. Bloods, I'm just glad I'm still alive, if these guys hadn't been there, I'd be Fera food."

"Fera food?! Gardener, tell me you're joking!"

Jaq pushed his thumbs through his belt. "Fraid not, ma'am. Your brother here was almost a demon-salad."

Alexander set fists at his sides. "He was attacked by a small horde, nothing as devastating as the reports of your valleys, but nonetheless, he was fortunate we were there."

Hurried footfalls clambered down the steps, and a young teenager scampered down to us, followed by a different young man.

"What happened?" The thick girl panted, the run down having exhausted her, flabby arms holding onto the bar counter for support. Unlike Octavius and his two siblings, this girl's bronze skin befitted her silky, orange hair and honey-yellow eyes. *Was she a sister of his as well?*

The gentleman behind her looked like a taller replica of Octavius, no doubt an older brother, with the same black hair and green eyes as his brother and Pyrovoking sister, his nose even having the same sturdy bend.

The man found Octavius, and his gaze widened with worry. "Damn, Tavius! What'd you get yourself into this time?"

Octavius muttered. "*I* didn't do anything. And what are you doing back already, Neal? I thought you went out with those tourist girls."

Neal crossed the floor alongside the rotund girl. "They had too much to drink at their inn's tavern, so I made sure the inn keeper brought them to their room safe enough."

Octavius grunted. "Wow. Sorry, dude."

He shrugged. "They're here all week. They know where to find me if they want to try again… so what happened to your shoulder? And who're these guys?" He looked at Jaq and my brother, and laughed at their fluttering messengers. "Heh, hey! Look at that, Tavius. They got their own birds, just like you. Good for you, finding some friends. It's about damn time."

Their younger, chubby sister rushed to Octavius and grabbed his shoulder to look over the cuts. "Land," she breathed in concern, her hands shaking. "I'll go get some disinfectant! Stay right there, Tavius!"

She disappeared into the back kitchen, then reappeared a moment later with a rag and a pail of sudsy water. She dunked the rag in the pail and vigorously washed Octavius's wounds, pushing so hard, he winced.

"Bloods, these are deep," she said, uncertainty puckering her features, her orange cat ears folding to her neck. "I hope I can heal them enough."

Octavius grinned thinly. "I'd appreciate it, Connie."

The girl, Connie, sucked in a breath and clasped a hand on the cuts. From her wrist, a golden Land mark gleamed, looking like a sword made of sharp flower petals standing upright. Lights leaked from under her palm, seeping over Octavius's wound and sinking into the cuts. They began to mend, the skin scabbing over until they were naught but trailing scars across his shoulder.

Connie stepped back in a wheeze, bending over her knees as though that small feat had drained her terribly. "H… how was that?" she asked.

Octavius rolled his shoulder back, stretching it and wincing only slightly now. "Much better," he said, smiling at his younger sister. "Thanks, Connie. You're getting better at that."

She beamed in delight, her round face brightening.

The older sister grumbled. "All right, well… thanks for bringing him back. I'm guessing you guys are Reapers, since you helped him with the Necrofera?"

"Indeed we are, miss," Alexander said humbly. "Or rather, we are apprentices, carrying out our final assignment. Admittedly, we came to your home for reasons other than seeing your brother here safely."

She cocked an eyebrow. "Does it have something to do with those birds you guys are walking around with?"

"Yeah, that's about right," Jaq grinned wide and folded his arms behind his head, jingling the chain wrapped around his wrist. "Guess you don't know either, huh?"

"Know what?" She questioned.

Alex cleared his throat. "Miss Mika—"

"Mikani," she corrected sharply, irked.

Alex restarted. "Miss *Mikani*… Your brother has been chosen by a messenger raven. When a shifter is bonded with a messenger, it means they are henceforth apprentice Reapers."

There was a long silence from all of them.

Then Neal let out an incredulous laugh. "Tavius? A Death Knight? Bloods, I can only imagine *him* fighting demons, running around in circles screaming like a feral kitten!"

Connie jabbed him in the ribs in a scolding pout. "*I* can see it. That's so cool, Tavius!"

The only sibling who hadn't responded was the elder sister. Miss Mikani stared at Octavius blankly at first, then slowly pulled another cigarette from her packet and lit it between her lips with another fire summoned from her fingers, a soft, white gleam shining from her back shoulder. I presumed that was where her Death mark was hidden.

"So," Miss Mikani began, her brow creased in deep thought. "Tavius is a... a Reaper?"

"An apprentice," Alex said, nodding once. "Yes."

"And you know this because he's got a bird?"

"A messenger, yes."

Neal threw his hands in the air, protesting. "Hold up, hold up! How does a bird make you a Reaper?"

"They don't *make* us Reapers," Alex explained. "They come to those who are meant to become one."

Connie held a plump finger to her lips. "I've never heard of that."

"Me neither," Neal snorted. "Sounds like a load of crap to me, birds randomly going to find people."

"It's not quite as random as you seem to assume," muttered Alex, waving to Mal from his shoulder. The raven cocked its head and gave a low croak. "Messengers are a Reaper's companion," he explained. "Said to be kissed by the Seamstress, Nira, any feral black bird can be born as a messenger, though not all black birds are. The messengers are smarter than the average feral, have a longer lifespan and have certain senses that we shifters don't yet fully understand.

"One of those senses, for instance, is the call to find something—someone. They don't know at first for whom they're searching, but they know when that person has been found, due to a strange, but very strong initial bond shared with that shifter. Not much is fully understood about the bond, but what we do know is that with every shifter a messenger comes to, those shifters have particular traits that—"

"Whoa, okay." They all interrupted, Octavius included, their faces bunched in severe confusion. Octavius lifted a requesting finger. "Short answer?"

Jaq pushed up his glasses and explained more simply, "If a messenger chooses *you* to follow, you're meant to be a Reaper."

"I still don't get it," Neal complained. "How can a bird make someone a Reaper?"

"Again, they don't *make* us Reapers," Alex chewed, his annoyance budding. "They choose us if we're meant to become one. And once a Reaper has been chosen, like Octavius, they are apprentices from then on and must begin their training with a master Reaper. This brings us to our next business..."

Alex clapped a hand on Octavius's shoulder as he announced, "We would like to deliver him to Everland's capital city, to find a master Reaper who will train him."

They stared at us in shock. Miss Mikani stammered. "Wh… what? Tonight?"

"Yes," Alex said, "There is more, I'm afraid. It cannot be mere chance that we found your brother in that cemetery tonight. I suspect the Shepherd had a hand in our fate… You see." Alex stood taller and cupped his hands tentatively. "We were there on a mission to find your mother's missing ghost."

"Missing?" The young Connie squeaked, her orange cat ears perked straight up. "She's not in Grim?"

"It would seem not. In fact, the spectral residents sharing her after-home reported she had undertaken a vassalship with a Necrovoker some years ago. They claim she'd visited every month or so, but this past year, she disappeared entirely. The last they saw of her, she was surfacing with her Necrovoker to attend to business of sorts. Yet, she is nowhere to be found… and without an escorting Reaper, we fear she may be in grave danger, especially with that horde in your valleys."

Octavius chimed in helpfully. "We're going to Nulani to see Rochelle. I figured if anyone's seen her around, it'd be her."

Miss Mikani took a deep hit of her cigarette, looking as though she wished to melt into a seat, but hadn't the mind to pull one of the upturned chairs down from the tables.

"So." She breathed out a smooth stream of smoke that licked over her head like a ribbon of grey water. "Your 'assignment' is to be her escort?"

"It is," Alex confirmed. "And we wish to bring Octavius with us, since he not only should be finding a master Reaper in the capital, but is also able to recognize your mother and any affiliates of hers. Not to mention," Alex murmured in an embarrassed cough. "We're not exactly familiar with your surface and its customs… admittedly, we're new to these highlands as of tonight. A guide would help us find your mother faster."

"Yeah… yeah, that makes sense…" She deliberated over another hit from her cigarette, Neal and Connie waiting in silence around her. Then, she squeezed her eyes shut. "Well… Tavius, what do you want to do?"

Octavius froze. "What?"

"You want to go and help them find Mom?" She gestured with her cigarette, smoke curling. "And… I guess find a… a *master Reaper* or whatever?"

Octavius's fists balled, and he swallowed visibly. "Yeah," he said at last. "Yeah, I do."

She sighed, a hollow ring to her tone. "Well… go and pack, then."

"It's all right?" He asked, uncertain. "It was my turn to pay the electric bill and—"

"We'll take care of that," she said, though reluctantly. "There's still three of us here. Besides, you're not a kid anymore. You can do what you want, you're overage, you make your own decisions. Just…" She clicked her tongue and muttered. "Just bring Mom back here to say hi before you put her back down in the caves, yeah?"

Octavius's face split with a thrilled, toothy grin. "Yeah…! Yeah, you bet! Thanks, Mika!"

He bolted past her and his siblings and darted up the stairs, perhaps to pack.

Alex hummed. "Well. That was simple. Thank you, Miss Mi—"

Miss Mikani snagged his jacket by the collar and yanked him close to her snarled nose, her green glare more jagged than crystal shards.

"Listen here, Reaper," she warned, her teeth sharpening in her gums and cat ears curled tight to her head. "If anything happens to my brother—*anything*—I will find you and burn you to a mangled heap of bones and ash." The hand that gripped his jacket erupted in a small flame, singing the cloth and heating the metal zipper until it blushed red. She growled low, "You hear me?"

"Y-yes!" Alex managed, shaking his surprise. "Well heard!"

"Good." She shoved him back, and he stumbled into Jaq, who righted him. She dismissed her fire Hallows in a puff of smoke and set a fist at her hip, adding, "And you'd better take care of my Mom, too."

Alex patted his now ruined jacket in a rueful mutter. "And I suppose you'll demand I find your father next, then?"

She snorted and spun on her heels, heading for the kitchen. "If you find *him*, feel free to shove him off a mountain and feed him to the Fera. Now if you don't mind, I need a *long* smoke."

She vanished into the kitchen, the door swinging closed behind her, leaving Alexander and Jaq standing rigidly with the remaining two siblings.

Octavius came trotting down the steps then, hauling a large duffle bag over a shoulder. His raven flew to an upturned chair leg, fluttering excitedly.

"Ready!" Octavius announced in a pleasant pant.

Alex cleared his throat, as though shaking Miss Mikani's warning from mind. "Splendid. Let's be off, then. We'll want to catch the earliest train."

Octavius nodded in a splitting smile, hugged his older brother and younger sister, and left with Alexander and Jaq.

Our new Brother stole a final glance at his home as we strode along the boardwalk, messengers soaring overhead, and he broke into a thrilled laugh.

7

PROPER PROTOCOL

LILLI

"I'm telling you…!" The rust haired steward pushed me forward, scarcely biting back his irritation. "The ground will *not* crumble under your feet! Just step off, miss! You're holding up the other passengers!"

I wished to believe him, but Nira damn me, I simply couldn't bring myself to let go of the metal doorframe. My claws left trails of scratch marks in the steel, my fox ears grown and folded down the nape of my neck. I stared at the abysmal metal steps leading to the ground, which I could swear shrank farther and farther away the more I looked.

I swallowed. "You're sure…? I won't be too heavy and fall back down to Grim?"

"Please, Howless, you aren't the size of a blasted mountain! We're at least four leagues above the lower crust, and another mile from Grim's ground level. You won't fall, now just… get… off!"

He shoved me out and I nearly lost balance when hopping onto the first metal step. A sudden gust of foul smelling wind rushed upward from the geyser's hollow pit under the bridge, rendering me rigid as my long, grey hair was ruffled, blocking my view. I quickly brushed the strands away, the bell tied to my bundled hair jingling.

Damn it, girl, you can do this! You've faced worse horrors than a Bloody staircase.

Breathing in the sulfur-scented air, I very carefully slunk down the steps.

My gaze fell to the gap between the Surfacing Pod and the station's platform, the empty chasm daunting under my feet. I clung to the safety rail, petrified of falling through and plunging far, far below into the geyser's pool back in Grim. Even if I survived the fall, the scalding water would surely char me to death. Fire itself couldn't burn my skin, but I knew boiling water would indeed cause damage. I had the scars on my back from years of training to prove as much.

The geyser's stream had already settled, having lifted our pod to the surface successfully. It would be perhaps another half hour before the next stream was scheduled to begin, to bring other Grimlings to the surface, or back home to the caves.

Once reaching the final step, I held my breath, shutting my lids tight before hopping onto solid ground in a cringe. My feet hit stone, and I peeked open an eye.

Thank the Gods…! I was fine. The ground wasn't cracked around my feet nor even disturbed.

I blew out a relieved sigh, thankful the surface ground seemed just as secure as Grim's floor. *This isn't so terrible.* I straightened and tugged my hood over my head as my fox ears receded. *It almost feels like being on the actual ground. I may be able to do this after all.*

The other passengers filed out of the pod after me, and I glanced round, searching for my companion. There were many blond and brown-haired shifters here, more than I'd ever seen in my life. Only a few black, white and grey haired Grimlings, like myself, could be accounted for. And that was only noting the difference in hair. Bloods, Everlanders were all so… *colorful.* I counted at least four different degrees of skin tone in the station. A few shifters had pinkish hues while others held darker brown complexions. But the vast majority had a deep, velvety bronze shade.

I suppose I'll have to grow accustomed to being the minority. I couldn't help but wonder if this was a product of this famous 'sun' I'd heard so much about. Why else would the Grimlings be exempt of such color?

"Jewel?" I called, my voice reverberating in the station's echo chamber. I winced at the volume. It drew an unwanted amount of attention. Instead, I gave a quiet whistle.

A twitter sounded above, and a small, canary-sized crow fluttered down, alighting on my shoulder. I smiled. "Well, we're here, Jewel. We're actually on the surface."

She twittered happily.

Jewel was a songcrow, a rare breed native to Grim. She didn't croak like other black birds, she whistled in lovely chimes. I'd had Jewel since I was a child. Yes, she was remarkably smaller than most messengers, but I loved her all the same. Her small size fit my small height, as I often told others. We matched.

"Young Howless?" called a uniformed woman across the station. She waved for me to join her and the rest of the tourists she was leading. "Please come with us! We'll have you all escorted to your desired inns once an officer has been assigned to your party. Remember, for your safety, a curfew is in place here in Everland, and punishment for breaking curfew is more severe and costly than in Grim. You cannot roam about the surface cities without an escort, or you may find yourself in a prison cell until the penalty fee is paid." She clapped her hands cheerfully. "To save you all that inconvenience, we advise you to stay with your escorts until you've properly settled."

Bloods, imprisonment? For taking a nightly stroll? One would think the news of a demon massacre would be enough to make anyone hesitate to wander the streets at night.

The attendant woman separated us into groups of ten. My company consisted of all noble citizens, dressed in splendid fabrics and glittering jewelry. I tugged my warm, velvet hood over my face, hoping not to be recognized by the other Grim barons.

The privileged nobility were assigned two Rockraiders, gold-plated knights of the Land realm who had swords strapped to their belts that were hidden in intricately-designed scabbards. I found it odd that their weapons were fully formed and not enchanted into smaller forms during peacetime, as the Reapers did for their scythes. Perhaps in Everland, keeping their weapons displayed was a symbolic gesture?

The lower-class parties were assigned spear-wielding Footrunners, common police officers. We had Footrunners in Grim as well, though their leather armor was a midnight black, instead of the woody brown I was now seeing on these fine officers. The designs were slightly different as well, the metal buckles a dull brass instead of iron, and the ailettes were flat at their shoulders instead of spiked with curling, claw-like ends.

Our noble troupe congregated through the Surfacing Port to the connecting train station, led by the Rockraiders. I skipped after them as we all paid for our tickets and filed inside the first-class compartment.

"Wait, little Howless!" the rust haired steward from the Surfacing Pod hollered, and I paused outside the train's doorway. He trotted to me and panted. "I almost forgot, Howless. I need to stamp your passport."

"My passport?" With an innocent finger pressed to my chin, I played the role of a ditzy schoolgirl and pretended I wasn't a stowaway. "Why, you've already stamped it."

His brow puckered. "I did?"

"Don't tell me you've already forgotten?" I frowned as if hurt by his mistake. "It was only a few moments ago. Do you find me so disinteresting that I don't even hold a spot in your memory?"

He flushed. "Er, well…"

"How very rude!" I fanned an ostentatious hand over my chest, voice rising to attract attention from the other passengers, embarrassing the poor man. "Don't tell me you've mistaken me for another Grimlette? Do we all look the same to you?"

He reddened further. "I-I didn't mean…! Er, no, of course not, my lady. Trust me, it's hard to mistake you, especially, since you're so—er—*youthful*, with such elderly hair—"

"Elderly?!" My eye twitched with actual offense, fox ears sprouting. "I'll have you know that grey is a most becoming hair color for youths in my nation! The elderly are hardly the majority of that percentage!"

He shrank back. "Y-yes, my lady! Of course—I, I meant no disrespect!"

"Well, you've given it! You all but called me an old hag. Do I look old to you, sir?"

"N-not at all! I-I've just never seen such lovely hair on such a—er—young lady in all my—"

"So now I look like a bumbling pup who can't walk on her own two legs? Gods man, is no insult beneath you? Nira knows I should file a complaint to the manager of this establishment—"

"No! Er, I-I'm deeply sorry, your ladyship. I'll, uhm, just… Here, I-let me help you in…!"

He presented his hand in a frazzled smile, allowing me to take it. I was sure to give an exaggerated huff while stepping onto the train. "Thank you, sir. But you'll be lucky if I choose this port to return home. Best think twice before mouthing off to a valued passenger, hadn't we?"

"Yes, my lady…" He wilted. "A thousand pardons… Please, enjoy the rest of your visit…"

I winced as he skulked away, his leaden steps dragging in shame. *Perhaps my act had been too harsh. I need to learn to balance this façade, to be stern not cruel.*

The doors closed, and the hover-train soon hummed to life. Steam plumed from the pipe at the front of the vehicle as we started through the tunnels of the canyons, heading south toward the coastal city of Timberail.

I took a seat beside a window, staring at my reflection against the blackness of the tunnel. My glittering amulet glinted from around my neck, its many jewels and diamonds sparkling in the train's lamplight. Once we exited the dark tunnel, I gasped at the black void these surface dwellers called a 'sky'. There was a large object shining down from it, like a glowing lemon wedge. Sprinkled all around the sky were tiny, stationary lights as well.

"Look, Jewel," I murmured to my little crow, who was perched on the seat's back next to me. "Their lights don't move like ours in Grim. Do you think they fall more frequently?"

"They don't fall at all," a Howless informed behind me. "They're called 'stars'. They're nothing like our lights in Grim." She leaned forward and pointed out the window to show me. "And that bigger light there, that's called the 'moon', if you remember from your foreign-culture lessons, assuming you've undergone proper schooling."

The baroness had jet black hair with tiny bits of sapphire pinned beautifully between her braids. She wore a silver wedding-vine and droplet over her forehead, and her painted red lips rolled into a pleasant smile. "This is your first time on the surface, isn't it, Howless?"

I blushed. "Am I that obvious?"

"Painfully. But don't fret. I know it can be intimidating at first, but in time you'll find there's not much difference between our kingdoms... yet at the same time, you'll find many differences."

"Which will I find more of?"

"The latter, admittedly," she chuckled and placed her hands on her lap. "But life does go on here much the same as the caves. Of course, in your case, you might find a severe lack of ghosts floating about. Not that I can see any myself, but I have a feeling you can."

"How could you tell?" I asked, genuinely surprised.

She gestured to the white birthmark below my right collarbone. "You have a Death mark there. That mark means you're either a Necrovoker or a Pyrovoker. Since both elements come from the same realm, you only have one mark. I simply took a guess, knowing I had half a chance of being correct."

You actually had no chance of being incorrect, I thought. But she wouldn't have known about my second element. It's rare to find anyone with two types of Hallows.

"And." The woman flicked her eyes at the crow sitting on the chair beside me. "You have a messenger. Which makes you a Reaper, or at least an apprentice. You'd be required to wear those soul-seeing masks unless you could already see the ghosts naturally."

I gave her a forced smile, uncomfortable to be under such imposing inspection. "How perceptive of you, Howless."

She seemed to take my cordial tone as an invitation to further scrutinize my face. "You seem somewhat young to be traveling on your own, though… Are you even twenty yet?"

"I have another year or so."

"I thought as much. What brings you here to the surface? Is it Reaping business? Have you come to collect a soul?"

"I'm not here for a reaping. I have other duties that require my attention."

I could see she wanted me to expound. *Well, why not?* I was finally on the surface, my quest had officially begun.

"I'm looking for someone," I said. "He's been lost for a long time, and I think he may be here in High Everland somewhere."

"Who would you be looking for?"

"A Grim boy… well, I suppose he's more of a *man* now, after so long, just shy of twenty. He has different colored eyes. You haven't seen him, have you?"

She thought a moment, her face contorting with dread. "Different colored…? Good Gods, girl, you don't mean…" She stopped, then chuckled. "No, of course not. Forgive me, Howless, I thought for a moment you were speaking of the High Howllord's son, Alexander Devouh."

I laughed with her. "No, no, certainly not. I already know where he is."

"Who doesn't?" She waved an amused hand. "Sorry for the scare. I suppose every Grimling jumps at the description. Old habits, you know."

"Er… Yes?" I wasn't sure which old habits she meant, but thought it best to play it off.

She was still chuckling to herself. "Ridiculous. To think you'd actually be looking for the young Howllord. Can you imagine?"

I kept my smile in place, despite my confusion. "Yes, absurd… But I *am* looking for his brother, Howllord Xavier Devouh."

Her laughter choked.

The entire compartment fell silent, all heads snapping to me in disbelief and animal ears sprouting from their heads.

"You what?" a blond lord demanded, voice shaking. "Why in Land's name would you be looking for *him*? Or any of them?"

The other nobility agreed after him, Howllords and Roarlords alike.

I raised a skeptical eyebrow. "I have a task to complete. I must find Howllord Xavier before returning home."

The Howless, who'd only moments ago had been welcoming, now regarded me like a dangerous beast that belonged in the zoo.

"Well!" she hissed, moving to the far wall to keep her distance. "If you have a death wish, you can enjoy yourself alone in that task, girl…! My gravest regards to your soul!"

The train came to a slow stop as we entered Timberail's main station. When the doors slid open, everyone rushed out with the escorting Rockraiders, who hustled after the retreating crowd in their clattering armor.

Stiffly, I rose and shuffled out with my crow. The crowd made a wide perimeter around me, scurrying about their business in the echoing station.

"Uhm," I began, starting toward one of the cringing Raiders nearby, "am I not owed an escort to—"

Jewel suddenly perked over my shoulder and burst into a flurry of violent twitters, buzzing overhead.

Then screams rippled through the station.

The Raider in front of me shoved through the crowd with his comrades, drawing their swords, the station's speakers blaring with frantic alarms.

My fox ears grew with a sudden rush of adrenaline—

A hideous screech peeled through the station.

Creatures suddenly slithered through the mass, their squirming skin wriggling as their joints cracked and popped out of place.

Demons! I dug my heels into the tiled floor and braced as the mass of fleeing shifters shoved past me. *But we're nowhere near the valleys!*

I struggled against the retreating traffic, pulling out the ornate hair-stick that was speared through my pulled-up strands.

"Move!" I demanded, wading toward the beasts at a hazardously slow rate. "I must get through—!"

A disgusting creature hooked its fangs into a too-slow steward.

"No!" I shoved against the current too late, watching as the demon ripped the man to shreds in a mess of blood and torn muscles, his soul ripped out and vanishing down the beast's throat.

As I ran toward it, I pressed the rippled engraving carved into my hairstick. The ornament grew with a golden glitter, stretching in my hand, and a crescent, silver blade extended from the top to mold into my staved scythe.

I gave a furious scream and hooked my scythe into the demon. With a spray of black blood, a *snap* sounded, and once the beast dropped, the syrupy tar evaporated, and the creature's rotten soul was set free.

I panted in a sickened rage, gazing upon the pulpy corpse I'd been too late to save. Then I sucked in a breath and searched my surroundings, my fox ears curling determinedly.

Five more beasts ravaged the crowd, some feasting on fresh corpses, others hissing at Raiders who swung their swords like useless flyswatters. Their weapons couldn't harm these creatures. *But my scythe can.*

Grip tightening over my staff, I rushed for the closest demon that was terrorizing a Raider. I rolled the staff round my neck and ripped the blade across the thing's chest.

Snap!

My swing sent its corpse hurtling away.

I rushed from one beast to the next, scythe singing with the assuring purchase of metal severing bones and squirming sludge, tearing through each chest before they had time to recover.

A winged Fera screeched above, spiraling teeth-first for my head. I hopped back and wheeled my scythe upward. The weapon whistled as it caught the flying beast's neck. I heaved the beast down and gave a final, whipping twirl in the opposite direction. The crooked blade met the beast's heart.

Snap!

I gave a few finishing spins to slow my scythe's natural rhythm, ending with the staff tucked under my arm and the curved blade arched overhead. The trailing circles of black blood soon evaporated and, scanning the terrain to make sure no demons remained, I broke my combative stance.

The scent of aged flesh thickened from the clutter of slumped corpses at my feet.

Jewel fluttered to my shoulder, chirping lowly in concern. "Where..." I panted, adrenaline still pounding in my chest. "Did these things come from...? We're nowhere near the valleys..."

Several Raiders circled me, their stunned faces red with exertion as they stared beguiled at me.

I puffed, sweeping my scythe forward in a gesture. "Are there any more?"

They all shook their heads.

"Thank Death." I lowered my scythe in a long exhale then held a reverent fist to my chest as I cleared my throat and recited the traditional Grimish prayer, *Tidings for the Rotten.*

"Nira Cleanse these souls of their rotten state," I began, bowing my head respectfully, "and may the Goddess guide your lost spirits through the Great Unknown. Mercy befall your fate, tormented ones… May you find peace and safe passage as you seek rejuvenation. *Mu necros neschali yettek…*"

I lifted my head and looked toward the Raiders still surrounding me. "Now," I said, causing the men to jolt. "Someone call for the Healers. Some of the fallen may still be alive."

One man broke away to do as told, but the others stayed behind, as if awaiting orders. *Bloods, these men look petrified. Clearly, they haven't a clue how demon attacks are dealt with.*

"Someone else," I added, "call the Reapers at the capital and summon them down here to retrieve any corpses who still have their souls… if any *hadn't* been eaten. We need them here within three days to reap the souls, else these corpses will turn into more demons."

One Raider scratched his nose. "U-uh… Why can't *you* reap them now?"

My posture slacked and I gave him an exasperated look. "Do you see how many corpses there are? There must be several dozen! One Reaper can hardly look after a handful of souls while bringing them to Grim, do you honestly expect me to escort *this* many without risking a second attack of Fera feasting on the rest of them? No."

I paced between the Raiders, gesturing absently as I recalled what my tutors had explained about Reaper policy in this land. "From what I've studied, High Everland's protocol is different from Grim's… Your Reapers aren't allowed to station in your cities, except for your capital. Which means a special law is set for this particular scenario. These corpses must be guarded in the morgue until the capital's Reapers arrive to free their souls. Though, in the event that no Reapers come within three days, the morgue's pathologist is exclusively allowed to use an emergency scythe and reap the souls instead, to prevent them from rotting."

The men stared at me blankly, unfathomably lost.

I sighed, rubbing my temple. "Oh, will someone just call the morgue?"

One man ran off to do as instructed, and I nodded to the cluster Raiders still present. "You all, spread out and keep the station secured. We must be absolutely certain no demons remain to ambush us while our guard is down." I snagged the shoulder of the last man before he followed his comrades. "You, find a ledger and follow me. I need a record of how many souls were eaten, and how many are still tied to their vessels."

He swallowed visibly and did as told, hustling into the station's office to procure a ledger and quill.

I had my scythe revert to its smaller, hair-stick form and speared it through my tangled strands, giving a silent prayer for the deceased shifters as I waited for him to return.

Then I stiffened when a movement caught my eye.

A figure hooded in a snow-white cloak lingered by the station's exit. Folded behind his back were black, feathered wings.

Another Reaper? I thought, my brow knitting.

His feathers were a Grimish black hue, so he must have been a visiting Grimling, such as myself. *Had he helped during the chaos?*

The Reaper was staring at me, standing under the shadow of a pillar, as if hiding from the Raiders who were scattered throughout the station. The top half of his face was veiled by his draping hood, and he declined to approach. Then he turned on his heels, unfolded his wings and took flight, disappearing out the exit.

Confused, I stared after him, glancing at my messenger crow who was perched on my shoulder. *Perhaps he thought I had a handle on the situation and didn't need his help?*

The Raider returned with a ledger and quill, and I strode toward the corpses with him following at my heels.

"Oh," I said, turning to the Raider. "After we're through here, I don't suppose you'll escort me to an inn? I think I've frightened off the Raider I'd been assigned."

"*Me* escort *you?*" the man questioned shrilly. He laughed. "Howless, after tonight, I wouldn't be the one doing the escorting. *I* want protection home! I-I'll even pay!"

I frowned, cocking my head at Jewel, who chirped from my shoulder. "Hm. I suppose that's sensible."

8

SOUL-SIGHT

XAVIER

"Is this him…?" a woman's voice whispered. "The Shadow…?"

I barely heard her over the screaming storm. The yellow-eyed man's boney fingers squeezed my throat as he extended me over the cliff, rain spattering in the gale. Willow lay on the rocks at his feet, silent as a corpse. If she hadn't spoken just now, who had…?

"It is half of him," a man murmured. "The one that was lost."

"Then we've found him?" the woman asked. "We may begin?"

The voices came from above. I craned my gaze, blinking the rain from my lashes. Three silhouettes peered over the cliff, looking down at me. One was a lion-eared woman, hiding behind a blond man, his amber eyes glinting when a flash erupted from the storm.

"No," said the man, hushed. "Something is not right."

"Yes, something is wrong," a fox-eared woman beside them agreed. "Perhaps we must consult Dream. More observation may be needed… Dream will decide if it is time."

Who were they—?

My killer crushed my windpipe, and black veins spewed from his hands. His fingers loosened from my neck, and the world drifted into darkness.

I jolted in my seat, scrambling to grab the cliff.

My fingers touched nothing.

Another Bloody dream, I realized with relief. And annoyance. *That memory is coming more frequently. I wonder, is it because I'm close to finding my body?*

But who were those… *other* people, from the dream? Their faces were slipping from memory, but I could have sworn there were others on the cliff this time. That had never happened before. Perhaps it was a creation of my subconscious?

I turned my gaze to the compartment's window and saw the sky outside was still dark with twinkling, stationary lights. What were those called again? 'Stars'?

The scenery outside zipped by smoothly, our private compartment rocking softly in a quiet hum. The ride was so gentle, even our company's black birds were asleep on the luggage shelves above us, their heads tucked in their wings, undisturbed. The loudest noise came from Jaq's snoring beside me, his face scrunched against the wall as he drooled over the polished wood.

"You okay, Alex?" Octavius asked from the seat across from me. It seemed he'd been awake for some time.

He was leaned back in the leather seat with his legs crossed, and he held a circular discus I recognized as a communicator. From the large gem in the center of the device, around many buttons and turning gears, a beam of light projected in the air to make a flattened screen of translucent light. The communicator's display gave Octavius's face a bluish glow.

I almost questioned why he'd called me 'Alex' when I remembered and shut my mouth. *He doesn't know of me.* Instead, I gave a tired sigh and rubbed my eyes. "I'm fine."

"You were talking in your sleep," he said. "And you had a random spike of adrenaline. Was it a nightmare?"

I gave him a skeptical look. "Something like that… how did you know my adren—"

"A guess," he answered quickly. Perhaps too quickly. He gave a small cough. "I, um, saw you were thrashing around a lot, so…" He dropped his gaze to his com-screen and changed subject. "s-so, um… about this Reaper thing, and messengers choosing you and whatever… What I can't figure out is why *I* was chosen?"

I hummed. "To be frank, no one's entirely sure if there's one specific reason. But among those the messengers follow, all tend to have at least one trait in common."

"What trait?"

My head cocked. "We strive to protect others, more or less. Whether souls are deceased or still living, we're the first to come to their aid when needed. Your raven sensed this trait about you; it's a great honor to be chosen. It's not something to waste, as you've done by waiting so long to find a master."

"O-oh… sorry…" He rubbed his neck, flushing.

I chuckled. "Don't be. It isn't your fault you didn't know. Perhaps it's only common knowledge in…" A glare caught my eye from the window. My gaze shifted to the scenery outside. "Nira!" I flew out of my seat, horrified as I pressed my face to the glass. "What's happened to the Sky realm?!"

Octavius followed my gaze but couldn't seem to find anything strange. "What?"

"The 'sky'!" I shouted, waving frantically at the window. "It-it *changed*! It was just black, but now it's… it's red! Is it burning or… Death, something must have happened to the Sky realm! One of the islands must have exploded—just there! That red ball!"

He snorted a laugh.

"I see nothing funny about this!" I hurried to shake Jaq awake. "Jaq! Jaq, wake up you damned idiot, we have to get out of here!"

Jaq fumbled awake, hurrying to his feet. He saw the bleeding sky outside, cursing while we argued about what to do. We could jump off the train and find shelter. But would that be safe? What if the explosion expanded out to us? Maybe the caves of Grim would be better protection—

Octavius laughed harder. He clutched his stomach, as if to keep his insides from bursting. It took him some time to recover before he could wheeze. "Holy Land, calm down! Bloody tourists. Is this not in that pamphlet of yours?"

I snapped my fingers. "Ah, yes! The pamphlet!" I hurried to retrieve it, flipping through pages with shaking hands. "That's right, this could be some terrifying, common occurrence in this realm! Which means they must have a standard safety procedure for us to follow… Where is it…"

"You've never been on the surface before, have you?" he asked with a smirk.

I hesitated. "Well… no." Technically, I *had* been on the surface once before, years ago, but that was during a storm. This was different. There were no clouds in sight, here.

Octavius's chuckles exacerbated at our panicked faces. "That's normal, all right? We're not going to die or anything. It's called 'sun rise'."

We stared at him. Jaq stabbed a finger at the glowing, red ball of fire. "That's the 'sun'?"

"But why is it red?" I demanded. "Our textbooks have only shown a yellow sun. And your sky is supposed to be blue."

He shrugged. "It changes throughout the day. Trust me, it's normal. The Sky realm is fine, nothing is burning."

Jaq and I, shifted our gazes back to the window, still wary.

"Wait a minute…" Octavius muttered. He stared at me with slitted lids. "Alex, weren't your eyes the other way yesterday?"

My worry over the sky dissolved. "Sorry?"

"Your eyes." He squinted harder. "I thought the blue one was…" He shook his head. "Never mind… Weird, I guess I forgot."

Jaq and I exchanged a glance. Then I asked Octavius, "you, er, don't happen to be a Necrovoker, do you?"

"No," he said. "Why?"

I blew out a breath. "Thank Bloods… I mean—er, just curious. I thought for a moment you could see souls."

Octavius rubbed his fingers nervously. "I, um… I can, actually."

I jumped. "What?"

"I have soul-sight." He looked uneasy. "But I'm not a Necrovoker."

"That's not possible," I protested. "You're not wearing an enchanted mask."

He looked at Jaq pointedly. "Neither is he."

Jaq slipped off his glasses to showcase them. "Don't need to. My glasses have the right Evocation sealed in them."

"No one can naturally see ghosts unless they evoke death Hallows," I finished.

Octavius glanced away. "Well, I can see them."

I lifted my right hand, palm turned toward my face. "Do you see anything here?"

He peered at the hand with confusion. "Uh. A hand? What about it?"

"The mark. Can you see it?"

"You mean *that* mark?" Octavius pointed to the back of my left hand instead. "The tattoo of Nirus's Crest? That's on your other hand. What, did you forget which one you had it inked on?"

Jaq and I shared perplexed glances.

Even when *I* was in control, those who weren't dead or a Necrovoker could only see Alexander's mark, on his right hand. That went for our mirrored eyes, also. He shouldn't see me at all.

"It's not a tattoo," I corrected, suspicious now. "It's my Evocator's birthmark."

Octavius leaned closer to better see my left hand, his eyes wide with interest. "Woah, really? But all the kingdoms have their own mark. That doesn't belong to one."

"I know," I murmured, grimacing. "Believe you me, my parents were just as confused. They upturned every book they could find on abnormal Evocators throughout history and still came up empty."

"I thought you were a Necrovoker? Shouldn't you have a Death mark?"

"I do." My tone was still suspicious, though I tried to mask it with a hum. "Half the time, anyway. It only appears when I evoke my Hallows. And technically speaking, I'm half a Necrovoker."

"What does that mean?"

I paused, remembering I was pretending to be my brother. "Necrovokers have two halves of the death element. There's the Hallows of deceased vessels, and the Hallows of souls. I can only control vessels, but I have no power over souls."

That was the reverse of the truth. I was the twin with the soul half, Alexander controlled the vessels. In other words: he resurrected the corpse, and I tied the soul inside.

Octavius only looked more befuddled. "Wait. If you can control dead vessels, why didn't you just take control of the Necrofera when they were attacking us? Wouldn't that have been easier?"

"If it were possible, I suppose it would have been," I said. "Necrovokers can't affect the Fera that way. Since they're a merging of their rotten souls and vessels, the Hallows doesn't work. Not effectively, anyway. It's sloppy at best, and controlling a rotten soul is like trying to grab soap with oily hands."

"Er, okay… but I've never heard of a halved Evocator anyway. Does that happen a lot where you're from?"

"Well… no. From what we've researched over the years, I don't think it's ever happened *anywhere*. There's no documentation of Hallows splitting."

He laughed. "And you looked at me like I was the weird one?"

I scratched behind an ear, seeing the irony. I decided a subject change was in order. "You're certain you aren't a Necrovoker?"

"Super certain." He crossed his arms. "I think I would have known something like that by now. That Hallows isn't anywhere in our family history. We have fire and healing and… uh…" He glanced away. "Well, Neal is Hallowless. And-and so am I."

"Do any of your siblings have soul-sight?"

"Just me."

"And you're not dead, are you?"

He gave a flat stare. "Do I look dead to you?"

"You'd be surprised how difficult it is to tell. You could be a Necrovoker's vassal."

"A what?" He asked, bemused.

"A vassal." I knuckled my brow as I explained. "See, you could be a dead soul tied to your old corpse that has been resurrected and brought back to life for a time. It's something we can do. We see a lot of different ghosts and vassals in Grim. All of my family's servants are vassals, for instance, since we can't hire any living shifters who aren't scared Deathless of us."

He cocked an eyebrow. "You have servants?"

My teeth clicked shut.

It was his turn to be suspicious now. "Wait a minute. Are you a nobleman?"

"Don't be ridiculous." I tried to act offended. "If I were a noble, would I be wearing trousers with holes in the knees?"

"You wouldn't be calling them trousers, for one thing," he muttered.

"Well I… I have a unique choice of vocabulary."

"Which sounds even more aristocratic with the Grimish accent." He chuckled. "And not to mention the servants—"

"That's not important! *Kmm-hmm*! Now…! You're *sure* you're not a vassal?"

"Bloods, I'm alive, all right? So I can see souls, it's not a big deal."

I sat down, deflating as I snorted and glanced out the window. "I beg to differ…"

Against the red sky, a cityscape appeared in the distance, like silhouettes of flat-tipped fingers reaching over the horizon hungrily.

"Ah, brilliant!" I clapped my hands. "We're nearly there. You're sure this Rochelle woman will know where your mother is?"

Seeming glad to be on a different topic, he nodded. "If anyone would know, it'd be Rochelle. Mom would always visit her when she was alive. If she came up here and didn't come home, I'd bet she went to Rochelle."

"Splendid." I rose and zipped up my jacket, the tag snagging at the semi-melted tooth—which had been our parting gift from Octavius's short tempered, fire-spewing sister. I glowered, sighing. "Hopefully, this will only take a day or two and we can get in, get out and be on our way before anyone notices we're up here."

He frowned at me. "Why don't you want anyone knowing you're up here?"

"It, er…" I cleared my throat and threw open the compartment door in a nervous laugh. "*Ahem*, e-excuse me, I need the lavatory!"

I hurried out, leaving him and his incessant questions behind.

9

A SEER'S FERRET

RINGËD

Istepped into the Clattery Café with leaden steps, stretching my neck and making audible *cricks* as my Seeker brothers filed inside after me, filling the place up.

The feral ferret on my shoulder gave growling snickers.

"<Salvation!>" Kurn said. His language was in the form of heavy breaths and low guttural sounds, but I understood him all the same. I was supposed to be a ferret-shifter anyway.

Well, *supposed* to be.

"<I was starting to think we'd never escape that sea of paperwork,>" the ferret whined from my shoulder, rolling on his back theatrically. "<We've spent hours in that sweatshop of an office. *Hours!* You'd best count your Mel, Ringëd. I hate to say this, you know I hate it, but if you starve me like that again, I'm afraid I'll have to fire you. You're perhaps the worst butler I've ever employed.>"

"Guess I should update my résumé, then," I hummed. "You don't pull punches, do you?"

The ferret bowed his head with a solemn sigh. "<It had to be said, Ringëd. But look on the bright side. You may not be the *best* butler, but you're certainly one of my favorites.>"

I grinned, scratching behind one of his ears. "Thanks, bud. Right back at'cha."

Kurn was a delusional little pet. He was under the impression that he was the exiled emperor of a planet called *Hcah-Ah-Ah-Hcah,* and that he was sent to this world after the rebellion took siege of his palace, yadda, yadda, yadda… something like that.

I just found him being sold by a random peddler in my home island, Y'ahmelle Nayû. The little guy made me laugh, so I bought him. He's been pretty useful for investigative work, too. I get him to crawl around in vents to overhear conversations and find things in tight places my hand can't squeeze into. Best ten Gôshel I ever spent.

Mika's little sister, Connaline, perked up behind the hostess counter when I walked in, the teen's orange cat ears flicking up.

"Ringëd!" Connaline's plump arms waved at me and the rest of the boys. "Hi, fellas!"

The department called back cheerily.

I leaned against her hostess counter. "How's it going, sweetheart?"

Connie scooped up Kurn when he scuttled down my arm to demand food from her.

She sighed. "It's complicated, I guess. Hey little guy." She giggled while petting the ferret, not understanding Kurn's demanding pants when he called her a deaf wench.

"Complicated how?" I asked.

She shrugged. "Well, uh… have you talked to Mika yet?"

"I'm about to. Is something up?"

"She's, uh… well, you know. She's Mika."

I winced. She must have been extra pissed today. *That'll make this conversation harder.*

I promised Octavius yesterday that I'd tell him about that raven of his. The kid had no Bloody idea, none of them did. I intended to change that today.

"You guys are kind of late, aren't you?" Connie asked while swooping between tables to pass out menus. She'd left Kurn on the counter. "You totally missed the lunch rush."

I grimaced and picked up the ferret. "Yeah, well… finding the Carter Siblings and fighting for priority rights with extradition is really putting us all under pressure."

Her cat ears swiveled with interest. "Sounds complicated. So, the Carter Siblings are in Lindel now, right? You think they're still there?"

"Let's hope so." I zipped up my brass-orange vest—part of my Footrunner uniform—and adjusted my officer's badge pinned to the breast-pocket.

We had cloth uniforms instead of the leather or metal armor Runners usually wore. We weren't part of the spear-holding troops. We were a different branch, the Seeker department. We found things and people, figured out how crimes happened and where to track down the suspects. Not as glamorous as what the bronze-heads did, but the Artist can paint me a fool, I wouldn't trade it for anything.

Connie started taking everyone's orders, and I decided to get a drink. I'd need one for *this* conversation. Maybe two.

I went to the bar and sat between two other Runners. Kurn crawled down from my shoulder and pattered onto the counter, heading for the black-haired bartender who was having a smoke.

"<You there!>" Kurn snickered at Connie's brother, Neal. "<As I've tried *exhaustingly* to tell your dimwitted sister, I demand service. All these bi-pedal mongrels have been attended to, but where is *my* attention?>"

"He-e-ey, it's the little emperor!" Neal grinned and flicked the ash off his smoke. "You want something to eat, little man?"

"<Indeed I do, good sir!>" Kurn ran up his arm and pawed at Neal's cheek. "<I'm glad to see someone here has a bit of courtesy! You have my thanks, dark-headed one.>"

Neal didn't actually understand Kurn, but he picked up on body language pretty well. The kid would make a good Seeker, always noticing the little details. He was too old to pick up an apprenticeship, being twenty-three, but… *Oscha*, maybe I could pull some strings on the force and squeeze him into the training program. Once I told Octavius of his apprenticeship, Neal would probably feel left out, especially since he was the older brother. Maybe the offer would lift his spirits a bit.

Neal went to the pastry shelves off to the left and picked up a mini-muffin, setting it on the counter for the feral ferret. "You're in luck, Kurn. We got your favorite today."

Kurn scuttled off his shoulder to sniff at the muffin. "<Apricot? Splendid! I'll file a request to the unruly female in charge and get you a raise, my good man.>"

Kurn nibbled happily at the muffin, and Neal slid a glass of scotch my way down the bar before I even had to ask for it.

"Little late there, Ringëd," said Neal as he poured two mugs of ale for a new pair of customers.

I nodded appreciatively for the drink and took a swig. "Just doing some paperwork on the Carter Siblings. They skipped town for Lindel, looks like, but they were caught stealing down here before then, so we're trying to push our way into Lindel's Seeker branch to get them extradited. Takes a lot of politicking, it's a Bloody nightmare."

Neal folded his arms on the counter in front of me. "Nightmare's not over yet. Mika's pissed."

"So I hear. But your sister's always pissed."

He plucked the cigarette from his lips and chuckled, smoke curling with each breath. "Not like this. You haven't answered any of her calls today, have you?"

I rubbed my scruffy chin, swirling the scotch. The smell burned my nostrils as I took another swig. "Lost my com this morning," I explained. "Dropped it on the street and a horse smashed the living Void out of it. Why? Something happen?"

"Dude." Neal folded his arms over the counter, leaning forward. "Octavius left."

I choked on the drink, slamming down the glass. "*Khff-khff!*—wha— *khff*—what? When?"

"Last night." He tossed his head back, flipping his black bangs. "Apparently, he got himself into some trouble when he was visiting Mom's grave. Necrofera showed up."

"Artist sink me!" I cursed, cupping my mouth. "Is he all right?"

"Yeah, craziest thing happened. Some Reapers came in and killed them all. Octavius is lucky as Land to be alive; he came back with just a few scratches on him."

He traced his fingers over his shoulder to give a visual. "But that's not even the best part," he went on. "These Reapers had some ravens with them, just like Octavius, and they said—"

"He's a Reaper, too," I finished for him, hunching over the bar. "So, he found out, huh?"

"You knew?"

I finished the scotch, and Neal poured me another glass. "Yeah, I knew. I was actually going to tell him about it today."

"Guess these guys beat you to it. They went to Nulani to find Rochelle, to see if she'd seen Mom's ghost... But, uh, I was wondering. If he's supposed to be a Reaper..." His green eyes shined eagerly. "Can you tell if I'm gonna be one?"

I pinched the bridge of my nose. *As expected.*

"First off," I said, "I think your sister could use a break from losing her siblings this week. Second: No, Neal, you're not going to be a Reaper. A black bird has to follow you first, that's what the messengers mean."

"But what if I get one later? What about then?"

"Cornelius." I propped my elbows on the counter. "Why would you want to be a Reaper? You think fighting demons that can rip you open is buckets of fun?"

He shrugged. "It'd beat being locked up in this place forever. It's not fair that Tavius gets to leave just 'cus of some bird."

I sighed and set down my drink. "We'll talk about this some other time. Is your sister in the back?"

He nodded, and I pushed off the counter. "Right. Time to do some damage control."

I walked to the back of the café and pushed open the kitchen door—something flashed in my head at the touch, the Dream mark on my left shoulder gleaming from under my uniform. It was a past vision:

Mika shoved open the kitchen door, storming past the ovens and stovetops in a furious mutter. She threw open the back door outside.

The vision faded.

"Getting a smoke, then," I grunted and followed the path she'd taken outside.

Prophetic Hallows was really useful if you were a Seeker. It made investigating a lot easier. Well, it would have been better if I could See the Present or Future. But all I usually saw was the Past. Still, it was nice to have.

I opened the back door, finding Mika leaning against the wall, smoking. I went to stand beside her and she offered me a cigarette.

I took the offered smoke as she flicked her fingers and made a small flame ignite out of nowhere, her Death mark lighting on her back shoulder. She hit me up with the fire, then went back to puffing on her own smoke.

"Wondered when you'd get here," she muttered. "Did Neal tell you what happened?"

"Yeah." I let out a cloud, watching the streams flow rhythmically between us. "You know, I was going to tell Octavius about it today. I was going to have you there for it, though. I didn't think he'd just leave right when he found out."

"Well he did." Her tone was harsh. "Those Reapers had a good argument, though. Apparently, our mom's soul went missing from Grim. Her ghost's here on the surface somewhere, so Octavius went to help them look for her."

"Uh." I flicked her a sideways look. "Wow?"

She exhaled a new stream. "Yeah. *Wow.*"

"You're taking it well. Thought you'd be setting the kitchen on fire, to be honest. Wouldn't be the first time, like after your dad left."

"We need this place. We'd be bankrupt without it. It's hard enough to convince the tax collectors that the bastard still runs the place, and Neal's signature-forging skills aren't up to par yet to fool the banks into transferring ownership."

"You could just quit," I said. "I could get us our own place, we could actually get married one of these days and have a couple kids."

"I already have 'a couple kids' to look after," she grumbled. "But, well... I guess I got one less now, huh?"

I pushed my back against the wall. "Couldn't keep him here forever, Mika. He'd have to leave eventually, with that messenger. Even if those Reapers didn't come in yesterday, there might have been some other group coming in here to tell him later."

Her tongue clicked. "Maybe the later group wouldn't have been as weird. These guys were something strange, Ringëd. One of them sounded like some Grimish lord dressed in normal clothes, trying to blend in or something. Had weird eyes, too."

"Weird how?"

She bounced a hand in the air, trying to think back. "I don't know, just... just weird. They were two different colors. I think he might have been blind in one eye."

I stopped cold, almost swallowing my smoke.

"Wait." I raised a halting hand at her, shutting my eyes. "Wait, wait, wait. This guy... He didn't have grey hair, did he?"

Her brow scrunched. "Obviously. He's a Grimling, most of them have grey hair, even if they're young."

"Did you get a look at his hands? Did one of them have some weird mark on them—like three diamonds?"

"I don't know, I didn't look."

I whipped a hand to my belt and hurriedly unfastened the velvet pouch dangling at my side. I loosened the strings tying it closed and plucked out the fist-sized, crystal ball, shoving the orb at her face.

"Did he look like this?!" I all but shouted, evoking my prophetic Hallows, azure lights sparkling from my fingertips and pouring into the crystal ball.

From the lights swirled a man's face, the vision gleaming with its own light in the orb, to show Mika what *I* had Seen with my Third Eye for twenty Gods damned years.

The face was a chalky, pale grey hue, mismatched blue-and-clear eyes staring out from the orb's clear surface, shadowy grey hair framing his cleanly shaven jaw in feathery curls.

Mika blinked at the face. "That's him!" She said, pointing. "That's exactly him!"

"*M'ëd Gingette!*" I cursed in my native, Marincian language. "And you just let him leave?!"

She stared at me. "W-well, yeah. Mom's soul was missing, they had to do their job."

"*Oscha*, Mika, do you even… Gods damn it!" I threw down the smoke and snuffed it out with a foot, shoving open the door. "I have to go."

She started after me when I stormed inside. "What?" she asked. "Where?"

"To find that Grimling!" I shoved open the front door, ignoring my shouting coworkers when they tried to get my attention.

Mika panicked and ran behind me out to the boardwalk, snagging my wrist. "Wait! You can't leave, I-I just lost Octavius, and…!"

I slowed, hesitating. *Gods damn it*, I cursed to myself. *I'm doing exactly what I told Neal NOT to do.*

I sighed, taking her hands. "Mika. Do you remember those visions I told you about? The ones I've been Seeing since I was a kid?"

Her face tightened. "The one with those Grimling boys?"

I pointed down the boardwalk. "That Reaper you met was *him*. The same Gods damned Grimling I've been Seeing visions of for twenty years. *Twenty years*, Mika—of unwanted visions, of questions, of never getting any answers—and now you tell me your brother just walked out with *that same guy*?" I squeezed her fingers. "Please. This may be my only chance to figure out why these visions keep happening. When I have my answers, I swear, I'll come straight back." I grinned, kissing her fingers. "And maybe we can finally have that wedding?"

Mikani snorted a laugh, even though her eyes were misting. "Bloods, you're relentless. Ringëd, I'm just not ready—"

"For *Oscha's* sake, Mika, we've been engaged for years," I groaned. "When will you be ready? Bloods, you don't even wear the vines I gave you."

She blushed. "It… It just doesn't feel right, since…"

I sighed. "I know, I know… it was bad timing on my part, huh?"

She shrugged, sniffing. "You didn't know my mom was going to die that night."

"But I get it. I just… I really think she'd want you to wear them." An idea hit me, and I grinned wide. "I got it! When I find Octavius, I'll help him find your mom's ghost. And when I do, I'll drag her back here and have *her* tell you to Bloody marry me already."

She grumbled, blushing. "Ringëd…"

I kissed her cheek and skipped backward in a laugh, hollering, "Find yourself a nice dress while I'm gone, honey! Don't stand me up at the altar, all right?"

She stamped a foot, scowling after me. But I saw her flush and snort a laugh.

10

NULANI

XAVIER

"Surface Travel Advisory," Alexander read aloud from his informational pamphlet, squinting painfully from the glaring ball of light beaming overhead. "When out in the sunlight, it is suggested for a Grimling to acquire various protective-wear to avoid potential damage."

He scowled, shoving the pamphlet to his nose. "Without any previous exposure to the surface sun, cave-dwellers are greatly at risk of afflictions such as sun-burning and retinal damage, with a chance of… temporary *blindness*?"

Alex crushed the pamphlet in a fist and groaned, rubbing his stinging eyes. "Is *that* what's happening to me?!"

Jaq also pushed his thumbs over his eyes beside us. "Why wasn't that at the *front*?!"

Octavius, unaffected by the sun, shrugged. "It's not that bad. Your eyes need to adjust."

"Adjust?" Alex cried, wiping pained tears as he tugged his hood further over his face for shade. "My eyeballs are on fire! How do you adjust to *fire*?"

"Just stay in the shade," Octavius suggested. "Give it a while. I see Grimlings travel up here all the time at my café, they get used to it."

Alex heaved another groan, dabbing at the water clinging to his lids. "Bloods, we need to hurry and find this woman before I *do* go blind."

Octavius leaned against the sandstone wall of the alley and hummed. "We'll keep looking. But I think your eyes need a rest."

Alex grumbled and glared at the bustling crowd passing us in the streets of Central Nulani.

I floated in the black abyss of my brother's psyche, watching through the disc-like window. Though I didn't feel the pain he was suffering, I saw bright patches blot his vision. I did not envy him.

Alex stuffed the pamphlet in his pocket. "Are you sure she's in this town?" he asked Octavius. "If we came here just so I could go blind, I will *not* be in a cheery mood… thus far, none of the Healing Clinics have her on record. You said she was a doctor, didn't you?"

Octavius swept his gaze over the sea of faces that passed by the alley, long shadows dancing over him. "She is, yeah. And she's lived here for as long as I can remember. I don't think she moved. And besides, it's only been a day, maybe we've been looking in the wrong districts?"

Alex shrugged ruefully, and Jaq peeled off a layer of dried snakeskin from his neck, grimacing.

We were within the heart of the Southern Nulani marketplace. There were merchant booths scattered across the bazaar in cramped aisles, shifters of bronze and brown skins buzzing through the narrow paths of this intricate maze.

The buildings were squared and flat-roofed, with cloth awnings that crowned the doorways in splendid crimson and purple fabrics. There were few metal structures, but this was the historic district, so I supposed the city wished to preserve the old-styled buildings.

The overall *wideness* of this country was staggering. *There's no ceiling up there*, I marveled in silence, noting the absence of rocky pillars that would otherwise bring a familiar, cramped feeling to our Grimish cities. The lack of spiked roofs and sharp spires capping the buildings made the space that much more open, winged shifters seeming to have little trouble maneuvering their self-managed traffic.

Music strummed from a street performer's lute, the man garbed in a sleeveless vest and thin sirwal. Clapping castanets and dancing in the crowd was a woman accompanying him. She wore a sheer, lavender skirt that fluttered as she twirled, the color bright against her brass-toned skin. This realm was vastly different from the caves, so bright and colorful, vibrant and lively…

Of course, a land was expected to be *lively* when it lacked a populace of dead ghosts.

"So, um," Octavius began. "What's this Reaper training stuff going to be like? What am I going to learn?"

"Everything you need to know to be a Reaper," answered Alex in a sniff, his stinging lids seeming to have calmed slightly.

Octavius rolled a rock under his sandal. "Does any of that include *not* fighting rotten demons?"

"Yes, actually. You'll learn the messengers' whistling Commands, the proper etiquette for reaping a soul and escorting them to Grim… and then, of course, there's the creed."

His head lifted. "What creed?"

"The Reaper's Creed. Our code of honor, what we live by. All the realm's knights have one, the Reapers are no exception."

His gaze brightened, like a youth reading of fabled heroes and epic adventures, eager to hear how the story unfolds. "W-what is it? Can I learn it now?"

"Er…" The low scrape of claws against skin echoed as Alex scratched an ear. "It's a bit long. You won't memorize it right away. It may be best if we write it down for you to study."

Octavius mumbled. "Okay… Oh, um, hey—I've been meaning to ask, but… Is that white eye blind?" He pointed. "Your left one?"

My window shook as Alex rolled his eyes. This was a common question for us. "No," Alex said, "the pigment is merely gone."

"How'd it get like that? Was there some kind of accident?"

Alex hummed. "Nothing of the sort. We were born this way."

Octavius backpedaled, frowning drastically as he took a breath. "*We?*"

Alex paused. Then cleared his throat. "I… have a brother."

"Oh." Octavius laughed, as if he should have guessed. "And his eyes are like yours?"

"In a way—"

Jaq pushed down Alex's shoulders, intercepting in a grin. "They sure are, 'cept they're reversed. Like lookin' in a mirror."

Octavius gaped. "Woah, cool! How'd that happen?"

"Void if we know," Jaq said as Alex shoved him off. "Prob'ly comes with bein' identical. They got the same kinda Evocator's mark, too, but they're on different—"

Alex elbowed him in the ribs, growling. "Shut it…"

Jaq snorted. "I ain't tellin' the important parts."

"It's more than…" Alex glared at Octavius, who stared at us. My brother grabbed Jaq's arm and pulled the viper away. "Excuse us."

Once out of earshot, Alex turned on Jaq. "It's more than we want him to know. You can't blurt out every detail whenever it suits you."

"It ain't every detail!" Jaq protested. "It wasn't nothin' worth knowin'—"

"Then I suppose you wouldn't mind if we told him about *you*?" He stabbed a threatening finger at the viper's chest. "What about this 'illiterate peasant' charade you insist on playing? Perhaps we'll let it slip that this isn't your real persona."

He bristled, glasses slipping down his nose. "That… That is my personal business," he huffed, suddenly well-articulated and haughty. He flung an arm over Alex's shoulder and pulled him in, hushing under his breath. "Mind you, you're not Sir Honesty about such things either. You outright told him you weren't a baron. At least I didn't lie."

"*Failing to mention it* is just as dishonest," Alex accused, pulling Jaq's shoulder down to bring his scaled ear closer, muttering through clenched teeth. "And you damn well know we have to keep our title from him. If he knew who we were, he'd be running home screaming for his life before we ever found his mother."

Jaq grunted. "Fair."

"Let us handle the talking. Until we say otherwise, no mentioning of Xavier unless it's straight from *our* mouth. Understood?"

Jaq gave an indignant snort, shoving off him and straightening as he slipped back into his peasant-persona. "Fine. And no mentionin' my business either, ya hear?"

They hit knuckles to bind their agreement, and Alex sniffed. "Deal."

They returned to Octavius, who stared beguiled at them.

"Apologies," Alex began. "Boundaries had to be set, you understand."

Octavius shrugged. "Uh, sure. But, um, if you have a brother, why isn't he up here with you? He's not a Reaper?"

Alex sighed, shutting his eyes. "Damn you, Jaq…" He addressed Octavius with a sharp inhale. "It's… rather complicated."

"How?"

Alex rubbed under his nose. "Well… he's dead."

For once, Octavius was silent.

"Oh," he offered after a time, unsure how to respond. "Um, sorry…"

Alex cleared his throat and stepped out of the alley's protective shade. "We should keep moving—*arghh…!*"

Alex groaned in agony, clutching his eyes. Then from the psyche, an invisible force pulled me toward the window.

Death! I panicked, straining against his pull and scrambling to stay inside, where I was free of pain. "*No, no, no…!*" I shouted into the void surrounding me. "*Don't you dare!*"

He growled and yanked my soul through the window.

Hot air touched my face, sweat covered my garments and the blistering sunlight shot pain in my eyes like hot, metal rods spearing through grapes.

"Ahhh!" I doubled over and held a hand over my watering retinas. Someone may as well have splashed my pupils with fire. "Gods damn it, you bastard…!"

"You all right?" Octavius asked over me, failing to hide his amused smirk.

I seethed, tugging my hood to block the light, though it was of little help. "I'll be fine… Bloody sun…"

With a hand covering my burnt eyes, I stormed into the bazaar.

As we were squeezed in the midst of the bazaar, slowly wading through the traffic, Jaq let out a miserable groan.

"Death, I'm starvin'!" His stomach rumbled beside us, and he clutched his belly. The viper's mouth watered as he boorishly inhaled the peppered steam wafting from the multitude of vendors and eateries in the bazaar's cramped aisles. "Can we stop already, mates? We've been walkin' for hours! Can't we make food the priority? Just for a bit?"

I nearly lost my footing when a woman shouldered me in her hurry. "We've wasted enough time thanks to this damned sun. Can't you wait until we've searched the next clinic?"

His stomach moaned again, and his face cinched up. "I can't wait another damn minute! I'm smellin' chicken, 'n beef, 'n rat—"

A squat, married couple gasped in disgust as they walked by him, shying away from Jaq as rounded mouse ears grew from their heads in fright.

Jaq flushed and called abashedly. "*Feral* rat! Uh, I didn't mean…!"

The couple stormed off in a huff.

Octavius snickered next to him. "Smooth."

Jaq glowered and peeled off his eyeglasses, wiping them with his shirt. "Wouldn't've said it so loud if the damn steam didn't fog up my lenses… It's not like I *saw* 'em there…"

The viper's stomach gave a third, angry groan, and his bones seems to drip gloomily.

I sighed, relenting. "Oh, all right, go find yourself a meal. It's painful just hearing you moan about it."

"Yes!" Excited now, Jaq extended a scaled hand to me, as if asking for something.

I snapped my fingers. "Right. Money."

I grabbed the Storagebox that was strapped to my belt. The translucent blue block was solid, but within its see-though walls was our luggage, shrunken and condensed in the box's weightless field. I pushed my hand against one surface of the block, and my fingers sank inside as quiet ripples spread across it. Then I pinched the tiny money-pouch lingering at the bottom and pulled it out of the block. Once the pouch touched the outside air, the bag grew to regular size and weight in the palm of my hand. I untied the string around the pouch and plucked out ten brown, spiked beads of Mel. Our pamphlet told us this color was the lowest denomination of Landish currency.

I poured the beads into Jaq's outstretched hand. "This should be enough. Let us know if you need more. Mistress has stressed that she and Master are funding our travel expenses in full."

Jaq nodded in thanks and licked his lips, tongue slitting hungrily between his fangs as I watched him trot to one of the steaming booths, leaving Octavius and me to wait.

"So," Octavius pursed his lips, looking at the scythe-spheres around my neck. "Just wondering, when am I going to get a weapon for the Necrofera? If I'm supposed to fight demons, I don't want a repeat of last night."

"That's reasonable," I encouraged, setting fists at my sides in a cheerful smile. "What style would you prefer, in a scythe?"

His brow scrunched. "Style?"

"Close range, long distance, something in-between?"

"Oh, um… I guess…" He blushed. "I don't know. I've never held a sword, let alone a scythe."

I chuckled. "It's all right, not many come into this apprenticeship with prior combat experience. That's why we train."

"Does it have to be a scythe though?" He asked.

"Can a sword cut stalks of wheat?" I questioned. "Yes. Does that make it the most efficient weapon for the job? No."

His stare blanked at me.

I tapped my chest. "A Reaper's task is to cut a spectral thread in a shifter's heart: the NecroSeam. Think of it like… like *sewing*. You wouldn't use a knife to cut your thread. You would either use scissors or a ripping tool. Scythes are that ripping tool—they're curved to provide the most efficient and optimal method of cutting the NecroSeam as quickly as possible. Regardless, it's not as if swords can kill demons in the first place."

"Why not?"

I plucked off one of my scythe-spheres and made my blade materialize, a soft, blue glow emanating from its surface. "You see how our blades give off this light?"

He nodded, staring at his reflection in the curved, glassy surface with awe.

"This light is from Spiritcrystal," I explained. "It's dimmer than a pure-crystal blade, but only because it's alloyed with a physical metal." I turned the blade idly, displaying its radiant glow from various angles. "Spiritcrystal is the only mineral a soul cannot pass through. They're also alloyed with olium, for better protection."

"Why can't this crystal stuff cut the vessel by itself?"

"Well, it can touch a soul," I explained, "but not physical skin—living or dead. It'll phase through without harm or damage. Blacksmiths must wear gloves to handle the crystal at all, and they usually alloy the scythes with olium for its light weight and durability."

Octavius nodded thoughtfully. "Okay, cool. Do you think they sell them here?"

I considered. "They may, if you find an armory. You need your messenger with you as proof that you're a Reaper. It's against the Third Law of Death for anyone except Reapers to possess scythes, so the sellers must see proof of knighthood or apprenticeship."

Octavius shifted his gaze to the bazaar. "Got it… Then, I'll see if there's one around here. Come on, Shade!" He trotted into the crowd with his raven, and I chuckled—

Someone stumbled into me.

"Oh, terribly sorry!" The young man responsible waved in apology. But he perked when meeting my eyes.

He was well dressed, his skin showing the faint texture of tanned scales. His chocolate eyes peered at me from under half-moon spectacles and he wore a nobleman's suit, short sleeved and finely pressed as silver designs were expertly stitched into the trim. Draped over his shoulders was a deep maroon cloak, fastened by several rows of dangling chains that were hooked to silver buttons. His hood was folded over his back, revealing his gentle face in the hot sunlight.

The scaled man, a Roarlord as I guessed, adjusted his glasses, his golden suit shimmering in the bright sunlight.

"What a unique pair of eyes," the Roarlord murmured, fascinated as his stare lingered on my face. "Is your left side blind?"

"Er… no." My nerves twisted when he leaned closer. "My vision is fine."

The Roarlord cocked his head. "Grey hair… and an accent also, which makes you a Grimling. What brings you to the surface?"

"Sightseeing."

He frowned, but soon gave an amiable laugh. "A secret, is it? Yes, you look like someone on a mission, so grave and focused… Could you be looking for someone?"

I sidestepped around him. "I have somewhere to be. Please excuse me."

Heedless, he followed at my side. "Where are you headed, then? I thought perhaps we could share stories over a pint?"

"That's kind of you, but I have a… friend to find."

I hung a left with a brisk twist. Still, he pursued.

"A friend?" he echoed. "No, that doesn't sound right. I think the one you're searching for is… closer. A relation? A brother… a twin?"

I halted.

His chuckles turned shrewd. "Another hit, is it? I wonder, does he have the same odd eyes? Only reversed?"

My stare soured, wolf ears sprouting. "You know who I am, don't you?"

"I wouldn't say that." He looked up to ponder. "Or, perhaps I would? That's an interesting question, I'm afraid there isn't a simple answer… where are you going?"

I shoved into the crowd, and he followed again. "I've upset you." He sighed dismally. "Please, forgive me. It was just an assumption, with your twin."

"Leave, if you know what's good for you. You people usually run by now, regardless—"

Cawing burst overhead as Mal flew down to me, screaming. I tried to catch him, but he jerked away.

I felt that familiar tug on my soul: Alex wanted to switch. I allowed the vibration to pull my soul inside the psyche as Alex took control. Now that *he* was out, Mal finally perched on his shoulder without protest.

The raven ducked his head and hissed at a passerby, ruffling his feathers at a hooded girl who came to stand beside the nosy Roarlord.

Her face was shrouded in shadow from the hood she tugged over her silken, grey hair. She couldn't be older than us, but her hair was a metallic, iron shade, the exposed strands shining in the sunlight. *Grimish hair.* And yet her skin was a warm, brassy hue, like Octavius.

The raven screeched at the girl, and pointed cat ears sprouted under her grey hair in annoyance.

"Mal!" Alex tried to calm him. "Be still! It's only another shifter, control yourself."

"Wr-ong!" croaked Mal. "Wr-ong!"

"A black bird?" The Roarlord sounded surprised. "You're a Reaper?"

"Apprentice," Alexander corrected. Mal continued to screech at the girl. He gave the man an odd look. "You… truly don't know who I am?"

He smiled. "I'm afraid I don't."

"Perhaps that's best." Mal's croaking heightened, and Alex squirmed to quiet him. "Apologies, he's not usually so incessant. I think your companion frightened him."

The Roarlord looked at the cat-eared girl. "Cilia? Have you been tormenting this Reaper's black bird?"

"Hardly," she huffed. "I was only walking. Honestly, you should know me better, Macarius."

The Roarlord, Macarius, gave a laugh. "I suppose your messenger has a fear of cats, then."

Alex scrutinized the girl, trying to better see her hidden face. "You look familiar, miss… have we met?"

The girl tugged her hood. "I don't believe we have."

Macarius hummed. "Perhaps your messenger was frightened of her earlier today?"

"Not likely…" Alexander considered. "Though, I'm surprised you know of the messengers. The shifters here seem to be lacking in Reapers. They don't know much about us."

"They're also lacking Arborvokers, I noticed," Macarius muttered. "The plant-growers stay in this new continent you call Never… land…" He trailed off, gaze flicking to Alexander's hand. "Is that an Evocator's mark?"

Alexander glanced at the black diamonds resting over his knuckles. "Oh, er, yes."

"May I?" He held out a requesting hand.

Alex hesitated, but presented his hand, allowing Macarius to grasp it with curious fingers. "Interesting… So, you have the Crest of Nirus?"

"We—I'm not sure what it means." Alexander sounded uncertain at the Roarlord's sudden interest. "I'm only a Necrovoker."

"And I suppose your… twin… possesses a similar mark? On his other hand, yes?"

Alex retracted his fingers. "Were these also assumptions?"

Macarius cupped his hands politely, his smile placating. "Precisely."

"Macarius," the Grim girl, Cilia, interrupted. "We haven't time for a chat, if you recall?"

"Ah, yes." Macarius bowed to us. "I'm afraid we have more pressing matters. Thank you for the… intriguing conversation."

They turned to leave.

"Ah!" Macarius pivoted back. "What is your name, young Reaper?"

My brother took a moment to answer, his voice careful. "Alexander."

The Roarlord's smile twisted. "I have a feeling we'll meet again, soon, Alexander… Good day."

He and Cilia strode into the crowd, and Mal finally calmed, huffing tiredly from all his yelling.

"*Well,*" I said from the psyche, perplexed. "*That was odd.*"

Alex stared after where they'd left, his gaze narrowing. "Indeed…" He pivoted and pushed through the crowd, keeping Mal shielded from the passersby. "Come, let's find the others… I don't like Mal's mood. He's pulling at our Bond painfully tight, and I have a strange feeling we won't want to be here much longer."

TO ARMS

OCTAVIUS

"A scythe?" the blacksmith questioned behind his iron mask, turning to look at me through the dark-glass slit.

"U-um…" I shook in place, my feet stuck to the hardwood at that freaky mask. "Y-y… yeah… If you h-have any, I guess…"

I'd found this small armory in one of the corner buildings on the north end of the bazaar. The door was propped open, so I'd just walked in. The smith wore a work-apron covered in soot and grime, sweat beading the back of his brown neck and dripping under his shirt.

Sitting in the back as she rubbed an oiled cloth over a broadsword was a teenaged girl, maybe fourteen or fifteen, with oil-stained, dark skin and sharp eyes that narrowed suspiciously at me, a long braid hanging down her back. She was probably the smith's daughter, since they had the same shade of light-brown rabbit ears, except *his* were draped down the sides of his neck and wet with sweat.

In front of me, the smith stared from behind that creepy slit in the iron mask, a deep grumble vibrating this throat that made my head sink into my shoulders. *Bloods, I wish I could see his face.* Or, on second thought, maybe his face was a thousand times scarier than that expressionless mask.

The metal mask looked at Shade next, who was nestled on my head and biting an itch on his tailfeathers.

"Ah!" the guy grunted cheerfully, his voice muffled under the iron plate. "An apprentice. For a minute there, I thought you were trying to pull a fast one on me. Can't be too careful these days, those damned Carter Siblings are running amuck out there, stealing from armories like mine."

He put down his hammer and turned away from the forge, the fire licking smoothly as embers popped, the heat wavering over my face and making me sweat.

The smith leaned back on his creaky stool and lifted his mask. Surprisingly, even though his body was as thick as a mountain, his face wasn't as scary as I was imagining. His wide-set nose and rubbery cheeks were dusted with black streaks, but he had kind, round eyes that smiled along with his bearded lips.

"So then, apprentice Reaper," he said, patting his dirty gloves over his apron, which was lined with weird tools and various, small hammers. "What are you doing down here? You all are supposed to be stationed up in the capital."

"I-I'm visiting family," I lied. "My Master's still up there, but he thought I should, uh, get my own scythe down here if I could."

"Well…" He scratched his head, smearing soot over his hair. "I guess we have a few models in stock. They were supposed to be delivered to the capital station, but the orders were canceled last minute. I was planning to save them for future orders, but if you got the Mel, take your pick."

I wiped a drop of sweat from my cheek. "U-um… thanks."

"What style you looking for?"

"I, uh… I don't know."

His probably-daughter flicked me a sideways look from the back, and the smith cocked an eyebrow. "What have you been training with?"

"I-I, uh… I'm sort of new and…" Bloods, my hands were shaking. This guy was *huge*! All it would take was one punch to the face and my skull would be crushed by those tree-trunk arms. "My-my master wanted me to have some protection. Because of the valleys."

He frowned, his face bunching up and looking all serious. *Crap, he isn't buying it! Why did I bother coming here?*

He blew out a breath. "All right. Fair enough." He swept one of those enormous arms to a wall covered in glowing weapons, where the girl sat in the corner. "Come have a look at what we've got. See if anything catches your eye."

I wheezed out a relieved sigh. "Th-thanks!"

He nodded and pulled his mask over his face again, hammering at an axe with sharp *clanks* piercing the forge.

I crossed the floor, passing all the swords and bows and spears, poking at a benched whetstone, and stopped at the wall of scythes.

They were so *cool*! Some of them had long staves, others had short handles, there was one with a chain, like Jaq's, twin blades and sickles with wider hooks, some with a brighter glow and some with dimmer lights…

My eyes ran over each one from top to bottom, left to right. Then repeated. *Land, which one?*

Next to me, the teenaged girl flicked a judging look my way, dragging the oiled rag over the blade in her lap. "Trouble choosing?" she hummed, smirking like she'd thought of a joke about me.

I laughed nervously. "Y-yeah, I guess… So, um, I guess that's your dad or something?"

"Uncle," she said, standing to put the sword on an empty mount over the wall. She took off her gloves and wiped her hands on her dirty overalls, then crossed her arms. "My parents aren't exactly… *around* anymore."

I rubbed my neck. "Oh."

It got awkwardly silent, and as a distraction, I picked up a staved scythe that was propped against a wall, pretending to examine it, as if I knew whether or not one of these things was any good.

"Whoa," I said, surprised, "it's super light."

"Yeah," the young teen said, "Reaper scythes are usually alloyed with Olium. Super light, but super durable. I just finished learning how to make these myself."

"You're his apprentice?" I asked.

She slid her hands in her overall pockets. "Sure am. Been training at the forge since I was a kid, when Uncle Henry took me in."

"Cool." I lifted the staved scythe experimentally, waving it around really slow to see what it felt like. It kind of had a pendulum feel to it, but there were counter weights at the bottom of the staff to keep it balanced. "You know, this doesn't seem so hard—"

C-clang! THUNK-KLUNK-KLUNK!

The long blade swiveled when my grip loosened too much, and it smacked two sickles off their mounts in super loud clatters, making me cringe, Shade fluttering from my head.

From the front of the shop, the blacksmith's masked face snapped toward me.

I carefully leaned the scythe back on the wall. "S-sorry…"

The smith shook his head. "Be careful back there, you hear? Those aren't toys, they'll cut you open just as well as any sword in here."

I nodded vigorously, flushing. "R-right!"

The teen girl giggled and called over, "I'll watch him, Uncle."

"Keep that Reaper out of trouble, Vendy," he grunted, returning to his work.

The girl, Vendy, grinned at me—then her hands glittered with a golden light, and a Land mark shined from her neck.

The two sickles that'd dropped on the floor quivered, that golden light blooming around the blades now, and they lifted in the air between me and Vendy as she raised her hands to them.

"Try these," she suggested, "they might be easier. Looked like a staffed scythe wasn't your thing anyway."

"Thanks…" I gawked in awe at the floating sickles, carefully gripping their hilts. "S-so, you're a Terravoker?"

The lights faded from her hands, and she gave a crooked-toothed smile. "You bet. I take after Uncle Henry. Smithing is easier when you're a rock-molder."

"Cool." I tested swinging the sickles, then frowned. "Wait, wouldn't I have to get super close to kill a Fera with these?" I shivered, remembering the demons from yesterday. I also remembered how the puke tasted from being so scared. "Uh-um, maybe something with more distance?"

"Well," Vendy hummed and took the sickles back, using her golden Hallows to have them float back to their mounts, then scanned the wall alongside me. "Maybe a chain—?"

Chraawww! Shade burst suddenly, flailing from my head out of nowhere. *Chraa-aaa-aww!*

He went berserk, tugging my hair painfully.

"Ow, *ow!*" I pulled him off, holding him to my chest. "Shade, what the…"

Screams ripped from outside the shop. Through the open doorway, I saw people running in the streets and shrieking.

The blacksmith set down his hammer and rose, grabbing the nearest sword on his worktable. "What in Land is going on out there?"

Vendy followed his example and thrust a glowing hand to the wall of swords beside her, the blade she'd been oiling before rising off its mount and flying to her hand as she ran to her uncle's side.

I looked at Shade, the bird still screeching wildly. He wriggled out of my arms and screeched from a spearhead instead. That puke started coming up again.

"Oh, Land." I whipped my head around the armory, panic thundering. *Think, think, think, think, think—*

"Those!" I shouted, fumbling to a pile of steel throwing knives at the front counter. I scooped them together and rolled them in a nearby apron so they wouldn't cut my arms up, then ran outside.

"Hey!" the blacksmith hollered after me under the doorframe. "You have to pay for those!"

"I'm borrowing them!" I called, rushing into the crowd. "I'll bring them back afterward…!"

XAVIER

Civilians scrambled out of the bazaar, toppling booths and shoving aside any shifters in their way.

"What's happening?!" Alex yelled into the mass, his gaze sweeping the crowd in hopes of catching someone's—anyone's—ear. "H-hey! What's happened?! What is…!"

Mal was screeching overhead, flailing frantically.

"Is he…" I began in disbelief. *"Is he giving warning hollers? For Fera?"*

"It damn well feels like it!" Alex shouted, stumbling to keep his balance as shifters skirted by him without heed. "Our Bond is pulling so hard, it feels like he's trying to rip out my soul!"

"But demons are nocturnal!" I sputtered at my window. *"Why would they be out during the day—?"*

A pedestrian's throat burst in a spray of black ooze inches from Alexander's face. A long, thin claw was piercing out of the man's neck from behind, and slowly, his body collapsed at our feet.

A shadowed creature stood before us now. It clicked and bent its twisted spine, lifting its blackened skull and ripping a gargled shriek that spattered writhing tendrils from its sharpened teeth, scuttling toward us.

Alex plucked the two scythe-spheres from his neck chain, his weapons materializing in time for him to tear the blades into the beast's chest, *snapping* its NecroSeam.

We were veiled in the following black mist when the corpse hit the ground.

"Where's Jaq?" I hollered from the psyche, searching the fleeing crowd for the viper from my agitating window. If I could just have a fuller view…!

Alex whirled, yelling, "Jaq?!"

If our friend gave a reply, we couldn't hear it over the noise. Jaq was lost in the sea of terrified shifters, who were dropping like flies as the streets began to flood with bodies. Alexander heaved against the current, his wolf ears grown.

"Find higher ground!" I shouted.

"Working on it!" He hopped onto an abandoned wooden booth for refuge.

From this vantage, we had a better scope of the scene—not that it told us anything we didn't already know. The demons were everywhere. Even in the skies, there was a swarm of winged Fera flocking in a dark cloud and casting a looming shadow over the once sparkling bazaar.

"What is this...?" Alex whispered, his grown claws digging into the wood. "There must be hundreds...!"

"This has to be the pack from the valleys!" My voice shook, realizing something. *"Death! I think I know why that Grim girl was hiding her face from us!"*

"The girl?" Alex questioned, sounding confused why I'd brought it up at a time like this. "Why?"

"Her pupils must have been white!"

"Bloody Death... That must be why Mal was acting strange around her." He leapt down and broke into a sprint. "Jaq, you picked the worst time to get lost!"

With every corner turned, more bodies were added to the death toll, their chests cracked open with ribs jutting out of soaked chunks, demons feasting on their bounty. Alex could only fend off so many. This amount was too much for us.

—Mid-sprint, Alex's head snapped to a rabbit-eared girl with a long braid, swinging a broadsword with heaving grunts at the gelatinous beasts.

She thrust and sliced at them, but each blow was for naught. They mended with their sticky sludge each time, unharmed.

"Damn it!" The girl growled, and her hands suddenly glittered with gold light. "Should have grabbed the scythes instead...!"

The cobblestones glittered with the same golden light as her hands, and the ground *cracked* under her feet.

A vicious breath heaved from her throat, rabbit ears curling back, and the golden lights spewing from her fingers *ripped* the stones from the ground and formed into a sword in her hands.

A Terravoker!

Young though she was, the girl weaved through the cluster of demons with such speed and precision, she may as well have danced between them. She sliced and beat at the creatures, ripping the stones from under them to trap the Fera in stone cells, but each time, as before, they only glopped back together, untouched—

A beast drove its claws into her chest. She screamed as it *cracked!* Her ribs open, piercing her exposed heart, blood spattering over its shadowy nails.

Her cries died into silence.

Snap!

The creature sliced the Seam in her heart, and her screams returned, the girl's newly pale figure rising from her body.

"It's her ghost!" I shouted at Alexander from the psyche.

"Take over!" Alexander called back, and hurriedly stumbled into the physical world.

Ignoring the relieving rush of tangibility, I bounded for the screaming soul and plunged my scythe into the demon's chest, ripping its rotted Seam and littering the cobblestones with its corpse. I snapped my gaze up at the girl's confused, floating spirit.

"Come with us!" I hollered, putting away one of my scythes and clutched the girl's ghostly arm—which rippled coolly under my fingers as if touching liquid air—and pulled her away with me.

This was why I'd switched with Alex. He couldn't touch a soul. I was the only one of us with that ability.

"W-what's going on?" the ghost girl squeaked as I veered right, dragging her along. "Wait... wait, it's *you*—!"

"Watch it!" a familiar voice called ahead. I turned the corner and saw Jaq.

"Jaq!" I hurried to him, relief flooding as I pulled the ghost girl with me. "Thank the Seamstress and all her melancholy!"

Like us, Jaq had apparently been killing as many Fera as he could, and his chain-scythe was now hooked onto a winged demon flapping above him.

"Mates!" he called after seeing me, his boots dragging over the ground as his captured beast tugged the chain with angry screeches. "What in Death is goin—*huah!*"

He was lifted in the air, his legs flailing about while he tried to jerk the weapon out, but the Fera swung him forward—throwing him straight into me.

Jaq and I collided with wrecking-ball impact, throwing both of us to the ground as his blade finally sliced free of the demon and clattered to the cobblestone. I shoved Jaq off and shuffled to my feet, trying to find the ghost girl I'd lost hold of. *Ah, there!* By the apple stand.

I started for her, but the winged Fera that had escaped Jaq's leash swooped down and dug its claws into the ghost's shoulders.

I screamed when its teeth found purchase. *"No—!"*

A whistle of air shot past my ear, a knife thrown between Jaq and me.

The knife plunged into the winged demon attacking the girl's ghost. Spidering, black veins suddenly crawled away from the knife's blade and spread over the beast. The thing screamed and writhed, and when the veins finally hissed away from the new corpse, the newly cleaned knife remained stuck between its ribs.

Jaq and I slowly pivoted back, bewildered.

Scattered across the ground were a dozen corpses, all with throwing knives protruding from their bodies.

And right in the middle of the mess was Octavius.

He was perched on a merchant's table with his hand cocked at his ear, pinching the tip of another knife, ready to throw. Spewing from his hand and crawling over the knife were black, jagged veins that slithered and crept around the blade like a web of poison.

Octavius's left ankle was shining with the white light of a Death mark; a mark that the straps of his sandals had hidden.

Octavius jerked up when he saw us, the black energy of Hallows disappearing from his hand as he dropped the knife in a start. He seemed frightened, but whether from the demons or guilt of being caught doing… whatever this was, I couldn't tell.

There came a long, tensed silence, which was eerie in the chaos around us. My gaze was fixed on the white glow of Octavius's ankle; on his hidden Death mark.

"Octavius?" I began uncertainly. Then a vibration tugged at my soul, so quick I barely realized Alex wanted to switch before I was forced back into the psyche.

I stumbled in the void, regaining focus as I saw Alexander glare at the cat shifter, his voice furious. "I thought you said you were Hallowless?"

Octavius blinked. "Y, your eyes just switched—!" He jerked back when a winged beast dove down in front of him.

He stumbled to the ground and hurriedly grabbed two more knives from the bundle he had tucked to his side in a rolled-up apron, flinging them at the demon. The knives had been coated in black veins when he launched them, and once the blades cracked into its skull, the veins spread onto the Fera.

The creature dropped, shaking its head and struggling to heal the veins spidering over its head. Octavius hopped on the stand again and took another knife by the blade.

Drawing out a long breath, the same black veins sprouted from his fingers and coated the knife. He threw it at the demon with incredible speed and struck its chest. The veins rooted into the beast's heart at contact and the Fera curled into itself, screaming.

When the last of the liquid evaporated, its corpse collapsed to the ground. It lay motionless, the knives still protruding from its skull and chest.

My brother's gaze shifted back to Octavius, eyes wide and skeptical. "Octavius?" He pointed at the corpse with a scythe. "How did that just die?"

The cat's face reddened. "It… it only works if I hit their chests."

"If you hit their… what are you—?"

"Hey!" Jaq clipped behind us. "I'm not sure if you noticed, but we're still busy here!"

"Aye!" a new man called beside Jaq—a rabbit-eared behemoth that slashed at the creatures with such force, he threw them back several yards at a time. He tossed his head at Octavius and shouted, "I'm glad as Bloods you brought reinforcements, Reaper!"

"M-me, too!" Octavius called back, hopping off the booth to run toward us.

Alex and Octavius touched backs and joined Jaq and the burly swordsman. Alex stole a glance at the ghost girl we kept a protective circle around, and I saw through his vision that she had the same rabbit ears and sturdy nose as the new man.

"Uncle!" She hollered right behind him, though his ears didn't so much as twitch, her spectral voice unheard by his soul-deaf ears. "Uncle, be careful…!"

We were caught in the center of the horde, and Octavius gripped his last two knives with trembling hands.

The demons seemed to be waiting for something. A command? Whatever it was, we had no desire to speed up their decision to kill us.

Alexander risked a glance at Octavius. "What sort of knives are those?"

"I-I don't know the brand," he said, "just some throwing—"

"I meant how are you killing those things with them?"

He swallowed. "Y-you said I just had to cut their NecroSeams and they'd die."

"Those knives can't touch their NecroSeams. They aren't made with Spiritcrystal."

"Yeah, I-I know. I just sort of… added something."

"Added? Added what?"

His head ducked. "I don't know, just, uh… some poison or something?"

"What the Death does that—?"

"Well, this is unexpected," a new voice suddenly sounded above. "Looks like we caught some little Reapers, didn't we?"

12

DEMON COMMANDER

XAVIER

Our heads snapped up to the man who'd spoken. He was sitting on the edge of a rooftop, one leg dangling over the side and kicking against the brick. Placed before his eyes were strange, red-shaded spectacles, the lenses shaped like small circles with thin, wired-frames. The stranger had a large nose and long face, skin a velvety brown, and he had twitching horse ears sprouting from the sides of his head. His coarse brown hair was swayed to one side and the skin on his hands was textured like hooves.

He gave a thoughtful grin while looking down at us from the roof. "Lucky me. Cilia wanted some Reapers, too. We just didn't expect any to be outside the capital."

Alexander hesitated, checking to make sure the horde of Fera surrounding them *wasn't* advancing before calling up to the man. "Who are you?"

"The name's Lucrine." He gave a two-fingered salute. The gesture was oddly amiable.

He pushed himself over the edge and came hurtling down from the roof, startling all of us as he landed feet first onto the cobbled road and fractured the ground around him with a powerful *crack!*

He was uninjured, acting as though he *hadn't* dropped thirty feet from the ground like a two-ton boulder, and walked toward us with his hands sliding into his pockets in a casual stroll. The surrounding demons made a path for the man, much like royal guardsmen making way for their captain.

Lucrine's red glasses slipped down his nose, and before he pushed them back over his eyes, I caught a glimpse of his white pupils: two glowing lights within his brown irises.

"I'm in charge of this little pack," Lucrine told us. "Not a bad bunch, eh? Some of them need more training, but hey, they're coming along fine enough."

"Another Sentient." Alex lifted his scythes. "What is your Hallows?"

Lucrine laughed and put his hands over his sides. His friendly demeanor was annoyingly off-putting. "Oh, I might be a Sentient, but I'm not an Evocator. I used to be one of them, actually." He threw a thumb over his shoulder, referring to the disgusting beasts awaiting his command. "But a hundred or so years of eating souls helps ya gain some... awareness."

"Then a Class 2," Alex growled. "Is the Grim girl one of you also? Or is she a Class 1?"

"I'll have to go with the latter, if that's what ya call us," Lucrine answered. "She's got fire, in case you were wondering. Quick word of caution, while we're at it: Not someone you want to mess with. You'll want to keep that in mind after you've Changed, not that you'll remember much by then."

Alex's fingers tightened around his scythes. "We won't become one of you."

Lucrine cocked an eyebrow, turned back to his horde of Necrofera, then looked back at us. He started laughing. "Kid. You're outnumbered. If ya actually think you're going to live through this, ya got some imagination." He snapped his fingers, getting the attention of the demons behind him. "Fellas? Have at it. Keep their souls tied for me, too, will ya?"

The beasts charged, and we braced for impact. Octavius panicked and threw his last two blades at the closest demon. One of them missed and the other barely snagged its collarbone. Just like before, the beast died. Jaq and Alex prepared their counterstrikes... but the beasts came to a sudden halt, at the command of Lucrine.

The demons turned to their superior, seeming confused. Lucrine was staring off into the distance as if listening to something we couldn't hear.

"Are ya Bloody serious?" he questioned to no one. "I just found some Reapers here, that's what you..." He paused, as if to listen, then gave a click of his tongue. "Ah, fine... Come on, fellas. Time to leave."

Lucrine started away from us with the demons following. "Ya got lucky, Reapers, I'll tell ya that," he called with a dismissive wave. "Have fun with life, while ya still got it. We'll be back to finish our little game here."

We all watched in disbelief as the parade of beasts trotted away. Perplexed, we peered after them, dozens upon dozens of demons funneling out of the bazaar… and disappearing.

What were we supposed to do in this situation? Chase after them? We'd be killed, no doubt about it… in all our years of training, Mistress never once mentioned what action to take when a damned army of Fera were… fleeing? Regrouping? It was so bizarre, Alex's feet were plastered to the ground, not a clue how to react.

Soon enough, all fell silent. There were no more screams splitting from the townspeople, and the beasts' screeches faded into nothing.

It was like they'd just… vanished.

Jaq's shoulders dropped. "What the Death just happened?"

"Why would they leave?" Alex's brow furrowed.

Octavius collapsed to his knees and puffed the remaining panic from his lungs. "Who cares! Bloods, I thought that was it right there, I really did…!"

The burly swordsman patted Octavius's back, coughing a guffaw. "You did good, Reaper! Didn't expect you to be a knife-thrower, and a damned good one at that. How about I make you some throwing-scythes, eh? No charge."

Alex put away his scythes and looked at Jaq. "That other Sentient must have told Lucrine to stop. That Cilia girl. She sounded like the lead commander."

"Definitely." Jaq wound his chain around his wrist. "I ain't never seen a pack that big run away."

"We've never seen a pack that big at all. And *you*." Alex turned on Octavius, who was still wheezing over the ground beside the swordsman.

Alex knelt and offered a hand to the cat. Octavius grabbed it and Alex pulled him to his feet.

"Firstly," Alex began, "Brilliant aim. We didn't know you were already trained with throwing knives."

Octavius leaned over his knees and panted. "Y-yeah… My brother Neal and… and I use the cutting boards at home. Never thought I'd be using that to keep myself alive."

"Right. Secondly." Alex rubbed his temple. "What did you mean you added *poison* to the knives?"

Octavius straightened with a deep breath, stretching his back. "I don't actually know if it was poison. I mean, it could have been, for all I know, it came out on instinct. Whatever it was, it was apparently enough to make their Seams deteriorate."

Alex stared at him. "Deteriorate?"

"Well, it wasn't working like I would have wanted it to, if I knew I could do that." Octavius rolled his head back. "Ideally, their souls would have been destroyed altogether, right? But I guess my Hallows isn't strong enough for that… So, I just worked with what I had. I wasn't about to question it when it was the only thing keeping me alive."

"Necrovokers can only *control* death, Octavius. We don't have anything that can *cause* it, let alone destroy souls."

"I know. I'm not a Necrovoker."

"Then what are…" Alex went rigid, and Octavius wheeled an egging hand in the air, as if telling us to keep trying. "No," Alex muttered. "But that's impossible?"

Octavius deflated, seeming miserably accustomed to our reaction. "Void, don't I wish."

Jaq seemed lost beside us, scratching his scaled nose. "What is it?"

"He…" Alex dumbly pointed at Octavius. "He's an Infeciovoker. Aren't you?"

Octavius gave a glum tilt of his head, took an apprehensive breath and spread his arms, gesturing to himself. "The guy with infection Hallows, at your service…"

Jaq's eyes bulged. "No way…! No Bloody way—a real one?"

"I thought they were extinct!" Alex laughed. "Holy Bloods! Mistress will not believe this…!"

Octavius rubbed an uncomfortable shoulder as they circled him with intrigue. "Can you guys stop?" he pleaded. "This is kind of why I didn't say anything before."

"But your kind died out centuries ago!" Alex cried. "Your Hallows is the lost element from the Death realm—only the royal family of Grim has it! And even they don't have that element alone."

Octavius massaged his eyes, looking annoyed and severely uneasy. "Yeah, I know. That's all I ever hear after someone finds out."

"Bloods, I thought we'd never see another one." Alex rubbed his chin. "Why didn't you tell us, though? Something like this—"

Octavius jerked an accusing finger at him. "And your eyes are still different! I freaking saw it, they just switched randomly!"

"That's why you can see souls, also, isn't it? Because you infect both the soul and the vessel?"

"*Why* did your eyes randomly change?" He pressed, annoyed that he was ignored. "That kind of thing doesn't happen—!"

"Never mind my blasted eyes, man, you may as well be a fossil with feet. That hardly compares. Why didn't you tell us sooner?"

Octavius's cat ears began to recede now that the danger was gone, but he still looked frustrated. "Because when I tell people, they either don't believe me and want me to prove it—which makes them freak out after I 'demonstrate'—or they avoid me like I'm going to give them the plague. Most of the time, it's the second one." He sighed and muttered. "I didn't think you'd take me with you to find my mom. I wanted to help find her, so I wasn't going to risk it."

Jaq punched the cat's shoulder. "Ya don't give us enough credit, Tavius. I mean, as impossible as it is that you have an extinct element, we're still gonna take ya with us."

"Nira knows we'd be fools not to." Alex crossed his arms. "You know more about your mother than us, and perhaps if she sees you out here, she'll be more likely to show herself. No, having your help is certainly…"

Alex trailed off, his gaze drifting past Octavius.

That swordsman had wandered into the crowd of bodies. He stood over one girl's corpse, kneeling as he scooped her in his arms, his cheeks stained with tears. "Vendy…?" He choked, holding the girl close and weeping over her body.

It was the body of the ghost girl we had protected. She loomed over the man now, the pale specter reaching for his back, though he couldn't feel her touch.

Alex set his jaw and strode to them. "I'm sorry," Alex said to the swordsman. "We couldn't save her vessel… but we were able to save her soul."

The man lifted his gaze to Alex, blinking through tears. "Her… her soul…? She wasn't eaten…?"

"She wasn't," Alex assured softly, gesturing to the ghost he couldn't see. "She's with you now, above you. I think… she may be the only soul we saved today."

He searched for the girl's ghost with soul-blind eyes, holding her ruined body tighter as a sob squeezed out his throat. "Vendy…? Vendy, can you hear me…?"

Alex relayed her reply so he could hear her words. "She can."

"Vendy, I'm sorry…!" His voice cinched painfully, breaths quivering. "I'm sorry…! I promised to take care of you, and I…!" He shut his drenched eyes, then looked at Alex. "You… you'll take her to Grim, won't you? See her safe…?"

Alex exchanged a sorrowed glance with Jaq, then nodded to the man. "Yes. It is our duty. However, we still have another soul to find. We can offer your loved one protection while we search for our quarry and descend with both of them, if this is suitable?"

He heaved a breath, but nodded, lifting the girl's body as he rose to his feet. "Come. I've a debt to pay, with that one." He threw his head at Octavius. "If you're going to help guard my niece's soul, you'd better be armed with the right weapon, Reaper."

We followed the man through the ruined bazaar, and Alex solemnly pulled out our com. With the level of devastation that happened here, we had no choice but to follow standard protocol and summon the Healers and capital Reapers. No souls were spared save for the girl floating beside Alex, but the other Reapers would certainly wish to conduct an investigation and track down the horde that vanished. Not to mention post guards in case the creatures returned—

"Are you hurt, Ana?" a gruff voice suddenly asked a few yards away, catching our attention.

A blond man was fishing a woman from a broken pile of wood. His hideous face was riddled with scars, his skin puckered and lined so much, it was a challenge to find a single patch of bare skin. He had bulging muscles and was clad in thick, brass armor, two swords strapped to his back in a cross shape. A gold coin glinted from around his neck, shining in Alexander's eye and making him wince.

Others survived?

The man's armor was different from the Rockraiders, who now searched the bazaar. It was dulled and dented from abuse, and he wore no helm, allowing his short, sweat-drenched hair to fall free at his ears, a lion-tail twitching behind his legs.

He picked up a Landish woman from the wreckage, lifting her with his thick arms as easily as a sack of daisies. When she was gently set on her feet again, she brushed her dampened, orange cloak free of splinters and sighed, whispering. "I am unharmed, Kurrick… thank you." Her lion-ears folded downward, her tail swishing. "Though, I fear this trip has proven to be more dangerous than we suspected, and so soon into our observations."

"Indeed," the warrior man, Kurrick, growled. Then his gaze snapped straight to us.

Alex tensed under that amber gaze, as though speared by a lance and pinned in place. Though, I had this peculiar feeling… There was something strange about the warrior's face. Something familiar, as though I'd seen him in a dream…

Alexander's gaze shifted to the stones beneath the warrior. The road had been lifted into many spikes along the path, as if the cobblestones had been torn out and stretched into spears by some unknown force, protecting the space the woman had occupied moments ago. My gaze shot to the warrior's ugly, scar-burdened face again. *Another Terravoker?*

The man's arm was bleeding, punctures visible from a bite wound. The woman with him took notice and quickly clasped her hands around the marks, a golden light sparkling under her palm. The wound was sealed in a matter of seconds, and the man thanked her, leading her out of the bazaar as she tugged her hood over her face to cloak her features in shadow.

And a Healer is with him?

She glanced back and caught Alexander's gaze. From under her hood, I could barely spy her crimson eyes and curly brown hair, the strands wispy like flower petals. She had a young face, early twenties at best. A glimmer of jewelry shined from one of her lion-ears just before she turned forward and ducked away with the warrior.

Odd… I frowned in the psyche as a nagging nostalgia tugged at my thoughts. *Where have I seen those two before?*

Alex's gaze lingered after them for a moment longer, then he snorted and resumed following the others to the burly swordsman's home.

13

A NECROVOKER'S BLOODPACT

XAVIER

We waited in the cramped kitchen of the Blacksmith's livingspace above his shop. The sharp sounds of a hammer clanged against metal beneath the dusty floorboards under our feet.

Jaq sat at the rickety table beside me, Octavius seated in his own chair across from us and murmuring to the girl, Vendy's, ghost. Her body lay on the tattered couch in the next room, cleaned and wrapped in a soft blanket, as though she were merely sleeping.

We'd been here for hours, night having fallen long ago. The Blacksmith had taken some time to speak with his niece's ghost when we'd first arrived, able to see and hear her after I enchanted a pair of spectacles to give him soul-sight, and then he went to work downstairs, preparing Octavius's 'gift'.

Now, at last, the hammering ceased beneath the floorboards, and the blacksmith's heavy footfalls climbed the stairs in the corner, the man hefting a silver case in his arms. It was opened to display its contents, silvery, hooked throwing-scythes stacked neatly in several compartments, with a single long, thin sickle curved around them like a glowing-blue frame.

He strode to Octavius and presented him the case.

"I've never made throwing-scythes before," the smith said gruffly, "but I've made plenty of knives and scythes separately, so it was a quick forge. Especially with Terravoking. I used the scythes I'd already forged to make this batch, so the alloying had already been made. You'll need to strap these holsters to your belt to keep them close to you. The blades are small enough that they don't need to have a safe-form. Except the sickle."

The smith plucked the sickle from the case and touched his thumb against the sealing-rune. The thin blade glowed and melted into a ball, resembling our own scythe-spheres. He placed the ball back in the case and cleared his throat. "You'll still want this blade in case you run out of throwing ammo. I suggest you have your teammates help you figure out how to swing it right."

Octavius took the case and marveled at his new weapons. "Th-thanks, sir…"

The Blacksmith pulled off his soot-ridden gloves. "Call me Henry. Now, I've got something for *all* of you. Wait here."

He trotted back down the stairs, then clattering metal sounded as he returned to the kitchen, hefting five sets of armor on his shoulders, setting the lot on the kitchen table.

"With a horde like that on the loose, I'll be damned if I send soldiers off without plate." He swept a thick arm over the load. "These are forged with Olium and iron, so they'll be heavier than your weapons. But an added thickness will keep those things' claws from ripping through."

Alex stared at the heap of armor, his mouth agape. We'd worn armor during training, but nothing *this* splendid. The silvery shoulder-guards were slightly spiked and engraved with knotted designs, the breastplate polished to a mirror-like finish, chainmail latticed under each matching piece.

Jaq laughed in a thrill and lifted one of the sets, turning it over in wide-eyed admiration. "Bloods, look at these things! You made these just now?"

The smith, Henry, laughed. "Land, no! It takes weeks to make armor sets. Those had been from a previous order for a squad in the capital. But the order was canceled, along with several scythe commissions. The squad they were for had been killed in the valleys. Probably by the same horde that came here."

"Mournful Seamstress…" Alex rubbed brooding fingers over an embossing on the breastplate. It was a fanciful design of the Death King's emblem; of the Death mark.

Henry grunted and lowered into a chair, still wearing the pair of soul-sight spectacles I'd enchanted for him, turning to his niece's ghost who lingered beside him. "Well, Vendy," he said to her. "Have you given some thought about the other… option?"

Alex's brow furrowed at the smith. "What other option?"

The ghost girl explained, "It was something me and Uncle Henry talked about while he was down there forging." She took a hesitant breath, then blew it out with an air of resolve. "And after thinking it over, I decided… I want to make a Bloodpact with you."

Alex nearly fell out of his chair, and I jerked to attention from the psyche, sputtering along with him, *"What?"*

"Uncle Henry told me about Necrovokers making Bloodpacts with ghosts," Vendy said. "He told me about them having vassals to help them with tasks and missions and things like that… oh, and combat, too. Uncle's trained me with the sword since I was a kid, and my Terravoking is decent, too—"

"Do you understand what forming a Bloodpact means?" Alex demanded, dumbfounded. "Once a Pact is made, it cannot be undone until—"

"The Master Necrovoker dies," Vendy finished. "I know. And I'm okay with that… if you do something for *me*."

Alex sat back, still beguiled, but a new understanding dawned on both of us. "Ah. there is something you wish to do before we return to Grim?"

The ghost nodded. "I… made a promise to my parents. Before they were executed."

Octavius went rigid beside her. "Executed? That's what you meant when you said your parents weren't around anymore?"

"When Vendy was small," Henry said, "my brother and his wife were hanged for speaking out against Everland's king." His hands balled, anger bubbling as he growled. "Everland's *fake* king…"

Octavius's expression was noticeably tight now. "Oh, Land," he said meekly. "You're with the rebellion?"

Jaq shot him a questioning glance. "What rebellion?"

"Well, um…" Octavius pulled on his knuckles nervously, peeking over his shoulder as if worried someone were listening at the windows. He licked his lips and whispered. "Some people think King Galden isn't the rightful heir to Everland's throne, since… um…"

Henry folded his burly arms and rasped, "Since he isn't the Relicblood of Land."

Octavius's cat ears grew, and he ducked his head, hissing under his breath. "Not so loud…! Bloods, do you want to get *us* hanged?"

Alex waved his hands hurriedly. "Hang on, hang on! Are you telling me simply *stating a fact* is grounds for a hanging?"

Henry's scowl was Deathly serious. "Yes. That's what got my brother hanged, along with hundreds of others over the centuries we've been straining to keep this rebellion alive."

Vendy's ghost set determined fists at her sides. "And I'll make a Bloodpact with you and provide aid where needed if *you* let me stay up here until we give Galden the boot and have the *rightful* heir replace him."

Alex's stare flattened at her. "Do you expect to be released when we die of old age? Waiting an eternity for a dead prophet-king to crawl out of his unmarked grave? The true Relicblood of Land died five centuries ago. Only four Relic Bloodlines are still alive, in case you haven't noticed. You think Land's incarnation will just pop back into existence now, after his rebirth is long overdue—nearly twice over?" He laughed and leaned back in his creaking seat, crossing his legs. "I'd pay to see what Death thought of *that* idea."

Vendy motioned to slam her spectral hands over the table, but the action was as silent as a breath, her hands phasing through the wood without contact. The anger in her voice, however, rang clear as shattered glass. "The real heir is coming back *this century!*" she insisted. "We have a ton of Seers in the rebellion, and all of them had the exact same vision. And, for whatever reason…" She motioned to push her ghostly fist against the table and leaned toward us. "*You* are in every one of those visions."

Alex blinked. "Er… I'm what now?"

"You're foretold to bring back the Relicblood of Land," Vendy said. "Both you, *and* your brother."

Alex cursed and pushed forward, sinking his elbows into the table with a grimace. "If you know my brother… then I take it you know who I am?"

"From the minute I saw your eyes," she said, unflinching. "We *all* knew you'd surface here eventually. All of our oracles Saw it coming. They said we had to wait until you surfaced on your own, and this would mark the day our Relicblood was going to return soon."

Jaq threw a lazy arm over his chair's back, peeling off a shedding layer of snakeskin from his nose. "Well, if that ain't the biggest load of Bonedragon turd I ever heard."

"Agreed," Alex muttered. "I've heard many fabricated stories about my family, but I think that's the most unique thus far."

"It isn't a…" She stamped a soundless foot. "Gardener sow me! It doesn't matter if you believe us or not. Will you make a Bloodpact with me or not? My offer still stands to help you out, even if you don't think you can keep your end of the bargain."

"And will you end up regretting this decision if we *can't?*" Alex asked. "I'll be honest, I've never made a Bloodpact with a soul before. It's been called into question whether I'm even able to make one at all. I can only manipulate corpses. Physical pieces—bones, muscle, skin—I can't touch a soul."

Vendy's translucent glare speared right back at us. "But your brother can."

I tensed in the psyche. Why did it feel like she was staring directly at *me?*

"I know he's in there," she said, "He switched with you while we were running from the Fera. *He* could touch me. *He* can form the Pact, for both of you. You're twins, right? Same blood. Should work fine."

Alex ground his teeth, and a wave of dread washed through me from the psyche. *Death!* We'd been too busy with the horde to worry about our exposure...

Octavius suddenly shot up a hand. "Um," he began. "Can someone explain what's going on?"

Alex ignored him. Instead, he slowly pushed to his feet and leaned over the table to match Vendy's glare. "If we agree to a Bloodpact," he said venomously. "Will you agree to speak of this to *no one?*"

She gave a crooked-toothed grin. "Won't you be able to command it, anyway? I hear a direct order is impossible for vassals to disobey."

"Deal." Alex grabbed one of Octavius's new throwing scythes and *sliced* his palm, drawing a line of blood. "Shall we give this a try, Xavier?"

I pushed myself through the psyche's window—and was thrust into the physical world, taking my brother's place, my palm stinging from the cut he'd made. I reached my bleeding hand toward Vendy's ghost.

She grinned and clasped it eagerly.

My blood exploded through her translucent arm, branching off like a tangled cluster of pulsing veins, that small amount stretching thin, yet pooling through her soul like red ink in water.

"I, Xavier Madison Devouh," I began, reciting the Bloodpact's sacred Oath as we'd been taught—though never tested—when we were boys. "And my brother, Alexander Edric Devouh, do hereby swear to protect and foster this deceased soul, Vendy..." I looked at her in question.

She huffed with a swing of her head. "Vendrea Milly Cauldwell."

"Vendrea Milly Cauldwell," I repeated, "for the remainder of our breathing lives, to the best of our ability, or may our souls be punished in the Void where Nira's wrath will be set upon us."

Vendy's smile turned smug. "And I swear just the same, blah, blah, blah, and... done!"

I sighed. "How very formal of you... I do hope you won't regret this?"

"Nah." Her ghost smiled. "I've made up my mind. I'll do what I can to help you out, so long as you help *me* out."

I chuckled. "Well. It isn't the most traditional vow, but it's a vow nonetheless."

The last of my branching blood poured into her soul's chest and swirled into itself, disappearing in a hush.

A rolling chill prickled through me as the Pact took effect, the hairs on my neck shocked straight up. The wash of static settled to a simmering buzz in my soul, filling a reserve that hadn't been there before. I shivered, the buzz thumping along with my pulse.

"Well, then," I murmured, tugging my coat and nodding to the ghost. Bloods, why did I feel so *invigorated?* I found myself smiling like a giddy child at the ghost, my blood pumping on a dazed high from this new Pact that bound us together. "Welcome to our vassalship. Congratulations, good to have you aboard." I glanced at her lifeless body, still wrapped along the couch in the other room. I hummed. "Perhaps we ought to find your vessel a proper Storagecoffin before we leave. For now, I suppose Alex should resurrect you."

Octavius blinked from his seat, staring at me; at my eyes.

"But…" Octavius sputtered, the man tragically, tragically confused. He lifted a limp finger at me. "You *are* Alex…" He didn't sound as certain of that statement as he probably intended.

I sighed. *Another loose end to see to.* Well, he'd seen and heard enough, and nearly died alongside us. Perhaps he was owed some form of… closure.

I scooped up a set of armor from the table and slung it over my shoulder. "Save your questions, Octavius," I said wearily, yielding to a yawn. "We'll explain on the way to the next city. Now come. We best hadn't dally in this town, lest we want that horde to come back and finish the job."

The blacksmith grunted his agreement and grabbed a Storagebox from the counter, shoving in the rest of the armor sets and muttering about gathering other weapons for the trip, in preparation. *Marvelous,* I thought with a withered sigh. *Apparently, he expects to join us as well.*

Jaq lifted from his seat to follow me as I strode toward Vendy's corpse.

She lay wrapped like a bouquet of flowers along the tattered cushions, the gore of her opened chest cavity hidden. Her dark face had started to pale within the hours of her death, lips turning blue.

"Alex?" I called.

As summoned, my brother took control, and I fell back into the black void of the psyche. I watched through his vision as he evoked his violet-glowing Hallows, and jumpstarted Vendy's heart.

A gasping breath was sucked in through the empty vessel's lips, and the color flooded back to her skin, her lungs rising and falling steadily with breath.

"Your turn," Alex announced.

I took his place in the physical world once more, and wove Vendy's soul a temporary NecroSeam, the violet lights stringing from my fingertips like smoke and wrapping into a shining thread within her ghostly chest. Gripping that thread, I pulled the ghost into the vessel, the spirit sinking inside and disappearing. With determined, threading strokes, I tied the soul to its awaiting vessel.

Vendy's eyes snapped open, and she shot upright, squirming to free herself of her blanketed prison.

"Hello again, Vendy," I said, smiling. "Welcome back to life."

She wiggled her fingers, giggling. "Cool! Thanks, Masters."

I offered her a hand. "You don't have to call us Master. "*Da'torr*" is more traditional."

Her nose scrunched. "What's that mean?"

"It's short for *Shelic Da'torr*, or "Life Giver" in Grimish. It's far more accurate than Master, which tends to give the impression that we *own* the dead, when in actuality, it's a mutual contract."

"Huh. Okay, sure. Whatever helps remind me that I'm dead."

Henry came in then, carrying a sword hidden within a scabbard, and handed it to Vendy. "Now that that been settled," he said, "Here is your new blade, Vendy. Now that you're a vassal of a Reaper, you better be equipped like one."

Vendy took the sword and unsheathed it. The double-edged blade gleamed with a blue light, and Vendy blinked.

"Is this Spiritcrystal?" she asked.

"Sure is," said Henry. "I used the last of what I had down there to make you that."

Octavius gawked at the glowing sword, aghast. "W-wait!" he interrupted. "I thought only Reapers were allowed to have Spiritcrystal weapons?"

I hummed. "There are exceptions, one that extends to a Reaper's vassals. If they're expected to fight demons alongside their Necrovokers, they're allowed to wield the same weapons. Or rather, weapons of their choice, made with the same material."

"Huh…" Octavius rubbed his neck. "I guess that makes sense."

Harsh knocking pounded at the door from downstairs.

From the kitchen, Henry went still. The knocking continued.

"Henry?" A woman's voice called, concerned. "Henry, are you there? Are you or Vendy hurt?"

Henry relaxed, calling down. "We're here! Don't knock down my door, woman, I'll make you pay for the repairs!" He pointed at me sternly. "Don't say a thing about what happened to Vendy. As far as she knows, Vendy is still alive."

He disappeared down the stairs, and I heard the door squeal open beneath us.

The woman sighed in relief down below. "Oh, Bloods be good, Henry, when I heard what happened here, I ran right over with the rest of the clinic! Are you and Vendy all right? You're both safe?"

"We're fine, we're fine," Henry assured. "Horrible timing those demons had, heh… you see, we're going on holiday. We were just about to leave, actually, so you've caught us at an awkward time, Rochelle—"

"Rochelle?" Octavius, Jaq and I piped at once, all of us craning down the stairwell.

The woman at the door was a reptilian shifter with dark scales coating her smooth skin, her hair a bright shade of blond, nearly the same color as the doctor's coat hanging from her shoulders.

Octavius laughed in delight and trotted down to greet the woman. "Ms. Maya! It *is* you—do you remember me? It's Octavius, Sirra-Lynn's son!"

The woman blinked at him in shock. "S… Sirra's son? Shel Almighty, little Tavius? You're… *not* little!"

He grinned and rubbed his nose. "Guess it's been a while since you visited, huh?"

Jaq and I skeptically climbed down to join them, though neither of us had found our voices yet. Instead, we let Octavius wave toward us in a gesture. "Hey, um, Ms. Maya, these are my friends. They're up here looking for Mom's ghost. They said she's gone missing and we thought you might have an idea where she could be."

The woman stumbled to keep up, scratching her head and stammering. "I-I suppose… er… Oh, I'm sorry, Tavius. I haven't heard from her since the funeral. I wish I could offer more… oh! Have you gone to see Maveric? Her old Healing Master? She would be more likely to see him than me."

"Oh." Octavius's disappointment was plain in his posture. "Well, where does *he* live?"

"He lives a few cities over, in Lindel," she explained. "Farther inland."

Octavius twisted to me, his cheer returning. "Perfect. That's on the way to the capital."

14

GREEDY FERRET

RINGËD

I kicked the splintered wreckage of a broken crate in Nulani's bazaar, the streetlamps dimly showing me the crappy state of the place.

I bent to touch my fingers to a dried spot of blood on the cobblestones, my Third Eye opening as I evoked my prophetic Hallows. Through someone else's eyes, a scene played like a film.

Screams ripped through the bazaar, shifters scurrying out of the aisles and toppling booths, Necrofera ripping off arms and cracking open ribs in a splatter of blood.

The narrator of this scene heaved raw breaths, his heart thundering and panic hurling his legs forward to find an escape—

Pain shocked his brain, a claw pushed through the side of his head as he collapsed...

The vision ended, and my own perspective blinked back to the dark street in the present time.

"Artist sink me," I cursed, rising. "A Fera attack? Way out here?"

"<What!>" the breathy snickers of Kurn piped, the feral ferret's head popping out of the messenger bag at my waist. He was chewing on a dried apricot he'd apparently stolen from the box in there. His round ears swiveled as he got a lay of the land, the mask-patterned fur hugging his eyes now sweeping over the ruined bazaar. "<What danger have you brought me to this time, butler! Demons, here? You assured me they were in the valleys to the east!>"

"They were," I said, getting out a smoke and lighting it. "They moved a long way to get here. But why, damn it? It doesn't make sense."

Kurn's breaths were questioning. "<So then? Where is the strange-eyed one? Whatever transpired here seems to have passed hours ago.>"

I took a hit from my smoke. "I don't know. But I can start with Rochelle, find where she lives." I dug into my satchel and lowered a handkerchief to his nose. "This used to be hers, see if you can get a scent off it, Kurn."

Kurn sniffed at the cotton fibers, then his ears swiveled right and he swung his head that way. "<Ah, yes! I remember that scent. The woman who smelled like buttercream and apples, some years back. That is a scent I won't soon forget."

He tossed the dried apricot he was nibbling on and scurried out of the bag, touching to the stones and hobbled rightward. "<Come along, Ringëd! Perhaps if we're quick enough, she'll make those scrumptious raisin cookies she used to make!>"

Suspicious, I rummaged through the bag and snatched the box of apricots I was saving for snacks. I shook it, and a small *tpt, tpt, tpt* rattled. *One left.* It had been a full box.

"You fat little bandit!" I stomped after him, and he scurried faster, seeing he was in for some real trouble now. "You're damned lucky I don't have claws! I'd scratch you up so bad, those snacks would pour outta you like a split waterskin—"

"Hey!" a guy shouted at me from down-a-ways. He fumbled over the bazaar's wreckage to get to me, hefting his spear and pointing the tip at me to stop me from going forward. "You're in a restricted area, and it's past curfew—!"

"Yeah, yeah, pipe down will ya?" I zipped open my vest to show him the badge pinned to the inside fabric, the brass shield reading *Officer Ringëd Fleetfürt, B.B. Seeker Department.* "I'm exempt from curfew, just like you, pal."

"Oh." He lifted his spear and leaned on it instead. "Sorry. Guess I'm kinda jumpy, after what happened this morning."

"No kidding." I pulled the cigarette free from my lips and waved it in a smoky circle. "So, uh, about the Reapers that were here for it. You don't happen to know where they went, do you?"

His eyes splintered open, his grip on the spear starting to shake. "Th-th-them…? Why do you want to know that?"

"I got my reasons," I said. "Do you know where they are or not? I'm in the middle of an investigation, I don't have time to dick around here."

The spear-toting Runner rubbed his neck nervously, hound ears growing from his head. "You didn't see the news?"

I raised an eyebrow. "No. Why?"

"They got his face on camera during the attack," he said, shivering so bad I was worried he'd have a seizure. "One of the Grimlings. He… he's…" He lowered his tone to a frightened whisper, leaning closer to my furless, human ear. "He's the son of Lucas Devouh…"

I frowned. "Uh. *Who?*"

He jumped back like I'd bit him. "You don't know who Lucas Devouh is?!"

"I was raised on a Marincian island," I said. "I don't know half the damn nobles in Everland, let alone Grim."

"Shel, mate, all you have to know is to stay away from them!" he squeaked, shuffling back. "They're bad news, all of them! They'll chop off your head as soon as look at you! Trust me, mate, you don't want to go looking for his son!"

"Uh… right," I muttered, chewing my cigarette. "Then, uh… do you know where they went so I can… *avoid* them?"

He shook his head, cheeks flapping. "No idea and I don't care to know. Seriously mate, stay away if you want to keep your head."

I pursed my lips and nodded once. "Ah, yep. Will do. Have a good night." I spun on my heels and hurried after Kurn, who was waiting for me in the streets. I stuffed my hands in my pockets. *Pschal frettre renn, feather-headed idiot.*

The kid wasn't going to cut off my head, and neither was his old man. Bloods, the only one who'd come close to it would be their mother, but even she had standards. That kid may as well be like a nephew to me, in a weird way. I mean, I'd been seeing visions of those two for twenty damn years, it was hard not to know just about everything about them.

Well, except their family names, apparently. Weird, how that one thing never came up in the visions. But even weirder was how that Runner reacted to them. I knew the Grimlings down there had that reaction around them, but I didn't think it extended up here to High Everland. *Weird.*

I tossed my smoke and crushed it under my boot, following the feral ferret who scuttled down an alley to find Rochelle.

With some luck, maybe *she* would know where to find that kid.

15

RUDE AWAKENING

LILLI

Thunk!

The steel pole beside my seat quivered when I rapped my forehead against its cool surface.

Thunk! Thunk! Thunk!

My stomach groaned, dragging down my shoulders and pushing a pained grimace out my throat.

I was going to starve if I didn't eat soon. But I couldn't afford the train's services any more. When was this blasted ride going to end? It'd been hours since we left the last station!

Thunk!

I surely looked like a madwoman, hitting my head on a pole in the middle of the compartment, but I needed a distraction from my hollow stomach.

The train echoed through the tunnels of the station, and I clutched the glittering amulet dangling from my neck, sighing. I turned to the window across from me and saw my solemn face staring back. Powdered strands of grey hair curled out my cloak's hood, my onyx eyes bloodshot as the small black bird was perched on my shoulder, resting.

What was worse, that marked the second town, yet still no luck.

After Timberail, I'd traveled to the city of Mimeir and was now headed to Adrial toward the west. Xavier had to be here in Everland somewhere. The Neverland continent had already been searched by many others, so he couldn't have been there. I would turn this continent inside-out, if I had to.

I glanced around the rest of the compartment. I was running so low on money that I couldn't afford a first-class ticket, let alone food. I was the only noble in here. It felt odd to travel in a lower-class compartment. With my fine clothing and jewelry, I felt incredibly out of place. Perhaps I should have invested in something less conspicuous?

Looking at Jewel on my shoulder, I raised a finger to the small black bird and stroked her feathers to help comfort myself—then I stiffened when my sleeve dropped down to show my wrist.

The back of my hand was shedding and, horrified, I quickly pulled the sleeve back over it so I didn't have to look. I'd gone without my cloak for half an hour yesterday and discovered something the Landish shifters called a 'sunburn'.

Bloody sun! Who knew it was such a menace? It was much too glaring and just looking up at the sky would have my eyes watering. And now I find out that it burns your skin if exposed too long? Horrible! Just horrible.

"Is that her?" A whispering woman caught my attention. She sat a few seats down from me in the same row, murmuring to a man beside her. I assumed they were married, since wedding-vines dangled from the woman's hair. It connected at her forehead with two white jewels, and a third diamond droplet hung from their connecting links.

"It has to be," the man agreed. To match the woman's wedding-vines, this man wore a gold ring around his left, fourth finger and had a small diamond earring pierced to his left ear—which meant he was, indeed, this woman's husband. I only flicked my eyes at them briefly before glancing the other way, hoping they didn't catch me staring back.

"We don't have cloaks like that up here," the husband said. "Such a long hood, and a dreary dress... And look at her hair. It's grey."

"Is there a problem with my hair color?" I snapped, my fox ears sprouting. "It's rude to whisper things about someone sitting right in front of you."

"Oh!—er, sorry, Howless!" The husband bowed his head, his face red. "We meant no disrespect, we were just surprised...! Landish shifters don't have grey hair unless they're old."

He cringed when I shot him a deadly glare, annoyance flooding. Why was *everyone* calling me old?

"But-but you look really young!" the woman amended hastily, bowing also. "And we heard about the Fera attack earlier this afternoon in Mimeir. They said a young Grim girl killed them all by herself. It was on the news."

"And you assumed this was me?" *Death. If I was talked about already, word may spread to Grim that I was here. I couldn't have that.*

The man hesitated. "Well, you are a Grimlette, aren't you?"

"Clearly," I muttered.

"And you have a Death mark there." He gestured to the white Death mark below my right collarbone. "So, if anyone could have killed them, I'd put my Mel on you."

I felt as though he'd given me a bit too much credit. "If anyone has the right weapon, they'll have just as good a chance," I said.

"Against twenty of them?"

I remembered the attack: the Fera had appeared as I was coming out of the library. I thought it was unusual to see such a large pack, especially during daylight. Demons were usually nocturnal. I will admit, they gave me more trouble than my first tussle, but it was nothing I couldn't handle. "There were twenty-two," I corrected.

The woman's eyes widened. "I didn't know Reapers could be so young."

"I'm actually an apprentice." *I suppose there was no point in denying it.*

"Apprentice?" She echoed. "Shouldn't you have a master, then?"

"I do. He's back in Grim. I'm simply away for a short time."

"All by yourself?"

"I am fully capable of taking care of myself, thank you."

She gave a light laugh, trying to diffuse the tension. "I don't doubt that, I'm just impressed. What's your name?"

I considered if there was harm in telling them. Either way, it was best to offer as little information as possible. "It's… er, Lilli."

"What a lovely name." The man leaned forward, smiling. "So, what brings you to Everland, Howless Lilli?"

"I'm searching for a Grim man. He's a wolf shifter with heterochromia, two different eye colors. Have you seen him, by chance?"

The man scratched his neck. "That sounds vaguely familiar. How old is he?"

"I suppose he'll be twenty on the first of Spiridel."

"Oh, I see what's going on." The woman grinned. "A lost love, is he?"

I blushed.

She chuckled. "Don't be embarrassed. It's common for girls your age to hunt for men."

"That's right," the man agreed in a laugh. "You look almost of age to wed, aren't you? Nearing twenty, I'm guessing, like your missing someone?"

"I-I'll be nineteen in another month… but that's not why—"

"Ah, still have another year until womanhood, then." The wife nodded in understanding. "Well, best luck in finding your man. Make sure he gives you your vines like a proper gentleman should." There was a wink in her eye with that last comment.

"Er, yes…" I mumbled. "Thank you…"

"Ah! Wait." The husband glanced up in thought. "I remember now. You said this Grimling of yours had different eye colors?"

My head perked up. "Yes! One is blue and the other doesn't have any color. Have you seen him?"

"He's a Reaper also, isn't he?" His expression soured and he gave a low hum. "Sounds like that man we saw on the news about the Nulani massacre."

"He's in Nulani?" I barely had the breath to speak. "In High Everland?"

"Yes, but that report said he was, er…" His head ducked and he spoke in a quieter voice so the other passengers couldn't hear him. "He's Lucas Devouh's son."

I suppressed a groan, swiftly tiring of this realm's shared paranoia toward the Devouhs. "And?"

The couple gawked at me. His wife was the first to speak, her lion ears growing in fright. "You're intentionally looking for the Devouh's son?"

"Yes. I've been tasked with finding him as soon as possible. It's been six years since he disappeared, but I swore to find him and return him home."

"Six years?" The man's own lion ears sprouted. "Why in Shel's name would you…" His mouth closed. "Oh. Wait. You mean you're looking for their *other* son?"

"Oh." The woman glanced at him in surprise. "You mean the brother?"

My arms folded expectantly. "Yes. I'm looking for High Howllord Xavier."

The man scratched his head. "I see… I don't know what you've heard, but that son died a long time ago. It was all over the news when the family came back to Low Everland."

"He's alive," I assured. "You said yourself he was in Nulani."

"That was the brother. The one who came back with the family."

This had my brow knitting. "Alexander wouldn't be on the surface. It had to be Xavier."

"The report said it was the other one," the woman disagreed. "But I guess… they could have been wrong?"

"Yes." Annoyance bubbled again. "They were wrong. If Alexander had surfaced here, I would have known about it long before I left."

The man pursed his lips. "You're not still going to look for him, are you?"

"Why wouldn't I?"

He peered around the compartment, making sure no one was listening. "You're from Low *Neverland*, aren't you?"

His tone made me squirm. How had he known that?

He didn't wait for my response and kept his voice low. "Listen to me. The Devouhs are dangerous. Trust me when I say you don't want to cross paths with any of them. You'll likely lose your head over it."

I stared at him, dumbfounded. "You must be joking?"

"You're not taught about them in Neverland, are you?" the woman asked. "I guess it makes sense, if you don't live right above them on this continent… but we don't want you to throw yourself into the wolves' cave, Howless. Nothing good can come from running into the Devouhs. It's best to stay clear."

"Er," I began, their wary gazes discomforting. "Thank you for your concern, but I think I'm familiar enough with the Devouhs to know my neck is safe from being severed."

The man's eyes turned grave. "If you're sure, then… we'll pray for you. Just please take care. Remember what we told you."

I cleared my throat and gave a slow nod, turning away to glance at Jewel in puzzlement. *What is wrong with this realm? Everyone's scared Deathless of my quarry.*

An announcement fizzled from the speakers of the train, the conductor informing us the ride was to take two more hours before arrival. *Wonderful.* Two more hours of starving…

I could think of nothing better to do than rest to keep my mind off of food. It had been some time since I slept anyway. Between searching up and down the streets of High Mimeir for Xavier and the Necrofera attack, I was exhausted. And hungry. How was I already running so low on money? I suppose I'd left Grim on such short notice, I could only bring what I had with me at the time… If I wanted to get to Nulani—where Xavier was supposedly spotted—I had to save what little beads I had left. This trip was turning out to be harder than anticipated.

I closed my eyes with a quiet sigh and after a few moments, the sounds around me faded away while sleep dragged me into submission.

I sat along the ground, my back leaned against a black-barked tree. The air was cold against my skin and I could barely see my breath fog in the darkness. The only source of light came from a lantern on the grass beside me. I stared ahead, a thicket of willow trees rustling in the misted night.

I picked up the lantern and rose, tip-toeing into the forest I recognized as the Weeping Woods, in Grim.

A figure strode past. I only caught a glimpse of the shadow- grey hair disappearing through a row of dreary branches.

Xavier?

In a daze, I followed, catching another glimpse of him turning elsewhere. I trailed behind through the veiling trees, their leaves weaving in the gentle wind as they sent a roar of whispers throughout the forest. I hurried to catch him, but with every turn I made, he would make another.

Ash began to fall.

The light flakes swirled in the mist, and the melodic twinkling of wind chimes clued me in to what we approached. The Relic was close, the Requiem's tune echoing in the distance. I caught a flurry of ash in my extended hand, examining it with questioning eyes.

How could this be?

Xavier's ever illusive figure made another turn before vanishing behind the final row of branches, leading into the hidden cavern where the Relic awaited.

But he shouldn't know of this place. The Relics were sacred. Forgotten... Forbidden to speak of.

How had he known where to find it?

—SCREEEeeeeeCRASH!

My eyes flew open at the sound of shattering glass.

Jewel hollered before me and I jumped to my feet, still not fully awake while stumbling blearily over the floor. The passengers screamed, ducking under their seats to avoid the flying glass shards.

From the jagged, open windows came the darkened figures of Necrofera, which swarmed into the train's compartment.

Oh, for Death's sake!

I let out an aggravated growl and pulled the black ornament from my hair, gripping my scythe after it stretched into my hands with a golden shimmer. *Is there no end to this madness?*

My head snapped to a Fera crawling on the ceiling. It dropped to the floor and I hopped away, thrashing my scythe across its chest to cut its NecroSeam.

Many wary gasps followed the trail of my blade, the passengers huddled at the other end of the compartment and shying away from the weapon.

I pulled back, worried of hitting someone by accident—then a row of sharp teeth sank into my boot and pierced my leg, making me yelp. I cut down the beast responsible, but stepped back with my hurt leg and tumbled to the floor, boot seeping fresh blood, the punctures pulsing hotly.

I shook to my feet, favoring one leg, and limped down the aisle while trying to tear through as many demons as I could. Avoiding the metal poles and cramped, cushioned seats was a challenge, and with each rotten Fera killed, it seemed three more would take its place.

How many are there? My blade hooked a metal pole and I swung round to avoid a predator.

"Death!" I slashed at the beast, but tripped over a corpse, my scythe clattering to the ground and sliding away. The thing jumped for me.

Kshat—Kshat! Spliksh!

The Fera was shot with something from within the crowd of passengers, and as the glass pellets shattered onto the demon, a cracking bolt of lightning spread across its tar-like skin. I ducked when the demon flew past my head and thudded onto the far wall, its muscles stunned by the static volts.

Kshat—Kshat!

More shots fired at the remaining Fera, each paralyzed with bolts of lightning as I staggered to my feet.

The shots had come from two armored Footrunners who'd come onboard from a different compartment. They wielded golden Shotri, combat devices with gears and whirring springs, used to blast pellets of elemental magic at high velocities from a thin, cylindrical barrel. These two Runners must have been on security duty here, thank Bloods.

"Grab your scythe, miss Reaper!" one of the Runners urged, shattering another electric orb onto a recovering demon.

I limped to my scythe and took hold of it once more as I killed the stiffened demons with a few, final strikes.

After the last Fera's sloshing skin evaporated, the Runners lowered their Shotri. My shaking legs collapsed, lungs wheezing while the train came to a stop. We'd arrived at the station in High Adrial and the doors slid open. *Nira be blessed!* I thought in a pant. *It's finally over.*

But why did it all stop so suddenly? Was that really all of them, or had the rest fled?

"Medic!" a Runner called at the screen of light coming from his communicator. "We need a Medic! Adrial Station, Eastern District—there's been a Necrofera attack!"

"Bring a Healer, too," the other added, crouching beside me. He removed his helm and slid his breast plate over his head, taking off his brown tunic next and tearing it.

He told me to remove my boot, where I'd been bitten. I did as ordered, and he took the torn strip of his tunic to tie around my soaking wound, knotting it tight to slow the bleeding.

"That'll do before the Medics get here," he said. "Are you all right?"

"I'll be fine," I sighed. "Thank you. Truly. I might have met my end, had you not been onboard."

"It's part of our job." The Runner gave a relieved grin and rocked back on his heels. He had a rubbery, pig-like face, with a particular softness touching his smile. It was a kind face. He wiped sweat off his wrinkled forehead. "We might not be knights or anything, but we try to help however we can."

"And what help you've been." I clasped his hand in thanks. "Had you been a Grimish Runner, you would have been honored well."

The compartment emptied soon after the doors opened, and perhaps twenty minutes passed when three women dressed in brown tunics came hurrying into the station and crouched over me. *The Medics.*

Shocked at my wound, they set their boxes of medical supplies on the floor and untied the strip of cloth the Runner had tied for me earlier. My leg was sticky with blood and the Medics were quick to treat the bite wound.

Once everything was cleaned, a Healer dressed in an ivory coat hurriedly crouched next to me and held his hand over my leg.

A golden Land mark glowed from his wrist as a thin layer of my skin regenerated over the punctures, making me wince while feeling the tissue stretch painfully. The sting eased as the holes were sealed from the man's remedy Hallows, and after he was finished, he leaned back and let out a sigh.

"That should do it, miss Reaper." He gave a gentle smile. "Just take it easy on that leg, I can only do this much. It will take some time to heal completely, and it may still be a bit tender when you apply pressure. Just drink this for a day or two, and you should be fine."

He handed me a glass bottle with strange, bluish liquid inside. *Ah, a healing tonic.* I've drunk these before. I grimaced while taking the bottle, remembering the awful taste, but appreciated the prescription all the same. I pushed the bottle into my Storagesphere, which was tied by a silver chain around my waist, and watched it shrink and descend down to the bottom with the rest of my luggage. I rose, using my scythe as a crutch and replaced the wet boot back over my foot.

"Thank you." My breath was still heavy, and I reached into my Storagesphere again to pull out my pouch of Mel beads. "How much do I owe you for your help?"

His smile widened and he chuckled, placing a hand over mine to stop me from plucking out the beads. "I should be asking you that. You were the only patient I needed to see here. Everyone else is in your debt. From what I've been hearing on the news, these Fera have been going on a killing spree in the other towns as well."

Seeing that he wasn't going to take my Mel—for which I was thankful, since I was running short—I replaced the money pouch back in my Storagesphere and had my scythe shrink to its smaller, hair-stick form, slipping the ornament into my tangled hair.

I shuffled out of the train alongside the Healer. "Do these attacks happen often in Everland?" I asked.

The Healer shook his head. "We hardly get any reports on them at all. And it's usually just a few, it's never been this many."

"So, they waited for me to visit before coming out of hiding…"

"Hey!" a loud, demanding voice reverberated from the other side of the platform. A group of armored Rockraiders were trotting toward us. "Was it another attack?" the Raiders hollered.

I sighed and glanced at the Healer beside me, muttering, "And here comes another round of ordering *grown men* how to deal with basic Fera protocol. What joy."

After several hours of leading the charge in processing the attack and having the Fera corpses carted off to the morgue, I finally left the station, rubbing at a migraine, Jewel chirping wearily from my shoulder.

"Honestly, these Everlanders are as clueless as feral crabs caught between metal tongs," I muttered to Jewel. "Shouldn't they know their own Bloody laws? How such things are handled? They're the ones who banned our Reapers from their cities, you'd think they'd have a handle on how to deal with Fera *without* us. Yet they're relying on a foreigner to remind them of their own policies—!"

A feather fluttered down, long and black, glinting with a greenish sheen from the streetlamp above me. I caught the feather and lifted my gaze to the sky, confused.

This feather is too long to be Jewel's—

I stiffened. Perched on a roof nearby was a hooded figure, watching me. His dark wings were folded down as he stared at me from under his hood. Jewel began to twitter up at him, her chirps shrill.

I examined the long, black feather curiously, my gaze shifting from it to the winged man. *Ah, it must be his*, I concluded. *Isn't he the Reaper I'd seen in Timberail? And I could swear I saw those wings in Adrial earlier today. Has he been helping me kill the Fera all this time?*

"You're that same Reaper from before, aren't you?" I called, hesitant at his constant stare.

He said nothing, and my lips pursed. "What is your name?"

He turned away before looking back at me, his face shadowed deeply in his draping Reaper's cowl. "Janson."

"Are you following me, Sir Janson?"

"If that's what you want to think," he rumbled. "Whatever excuse I can use to legally leave the capital is a good one."

My head tilted, and I was growing annoyed at Jewel's constant chirping. "Why have you left, then? Is it because of the attacks? You want to help the people in the other towns without the Raiders knowing?"

"If I'm found, I'll be imprisoned. But I'll stay out as long as the Fera are behaving like this."

"Do you mean you wish to travel together?"

His head shook. "You've attracted too much attention already, Howless. And it's actually legal for you to be in other cities. You're not Landish."

"You don't look Landish yourself, Sir Janson." I pinched the feather's spine and raised it up for him to see, twirling it. "Your feathers are black."

He gave an agreeing tilt of his head. "I'm a transfer from Grim. I've been a Landish citizen for a few years now. I still have to abide by the laws here."

"If you don't wish to travel together, then what do you plan to do? Follow me in the shadows until I return home?"

He glanced away in thought. "Maybe. That's something to consider, at least. I'll keep an eye on you if the Fera show up again. I'll come to help if you need it."

I drew in a breath to reply, but his wings flexed and he took to the sky, flying behind the buildings of Adrial's cityscape.

Jewel had finally stopped her twittering and I gave a sigh, not sure I was comfortable knowing a knighted Reaper would be watching me during my stay here. I opened my hand to look at the feather again… but it was gone. My hand was empty.

16

CHANGING EYES

XAVIER

Alexander slid the train's private compartment door closed with a loud *ca-clack* behind him.

Our newly grown party seemed to have settled in well enough. Henry sat at the far corner and checked his dufflebag full of Storageboxes—which he'd stuffed with nearly the entirety of his shop's wares, all shrunken into multiple cubes, thinking he might have a chance at selling them along our travels—while the newly resurrected Vendy sat beside him. She was surprisingly composed, despite her recent death. She did seem a bit distant, her eyes glazing in a brooding thought at times, but she wasn't completely stoic. Her hands ran over her long braid as if in a trance, and her foot tapped every now and then.

Jaq sat to the left, his back leaned against the wall by the door with one leg propped on the seat and the other swinging lazily over the edge.

Octavius sat beside him, his hands in his pockets and feet crossed, staring out the window at the setting sun. He looked stiff and uncomfortable, his face set in a desperate scowl, as if trying to find the answers of the universe by the sheer will of his mental focus.

My brother sank into the seat across from Octavius and folded his arms. He too glanced out the window to watch the dimming sky.

The three black birds were perched on luggage shelves, their heads tucked under their wings to rest during the ride, feathers glowing with the orange light outside.

We were now on our way to Lindel. Rochelle had said a man named Maveric Liste lived in that town and may be of more help, for finding

Sirra-Lynn. He had been her old master Healer, during her apprenticing days. Rochelle gave us a photograph to recognize him by once we arrived in Lindel and, hopefully, he would have answers.

But for now, as the hover-train hummed toward Lindel, we had a different matter to address. One that, it sounded like, Alex was already on top of.

"Octavius." Alexander dropped his eyes to the carpeted floor and cupped his hands. "What are your plans after we find your mother?"

Octavius glanced away from the window to look at us. "What do you mean?"

"When we find your mother, what do you plan to do? Are you going to find a master Reaper at the capital here in Everland, or do you plan to escort her with us back to Grim and find a master there?"

"I haven't thought about it. Why?"

"If you recall, we promised you answers to some obvious questions you had of us." Alex stretched forward. "What happened in Nulani… well, we could have died. *You* could have died, all because we insisted you come with us on this hunt. We can't guarantee something like that won't happen again. With a horde that large, who knows where they went. That said, this trip may put you in danger again. If you want to return home now, we understand—"

"Are you insane?" he blurted. "If my mom's soul is up here with those things running around, I want to find her as soon as possible. I'm not going back home just because it's dangerous."

Alex combed a hand through his hair. "Very well… In that case, we think it's only fair that you know why you're being put in danger. The full reason. But we can't tell you outright unless you agree to travel back to Grim with us and train under our own master and mistress, after all this is over."

His green eyes were skeptical. "Why would I have to do that for you to tell me?"

"Because if we tell you, we need assurance you won't tell others. Vendy is obligated to do as we ask, even if she chooses to object, and Henry seems to be well versed in the art of keeping secrets, considering his affiliation with this land's rebellion… but you, Octavius, are an outlier. If you train with us, you'll be obligated to keep our secret."

He removed a hand from his pocket to rub his neck. "Uhm, oh… okay. I needed a master Reaper anyway, right? What am I supposed to know? Something about why your eyes change?"

Alex took a moment of silence, probably to think of how to begin. "Are you familiar with the six Laws of Death, Octavius?"

"Sort of." He had a thoughtful look. "Something about only Reapers being allowed to have scythes and obviously the one that says not to kill other shifters."

"Forbidding murder is the First Law, yes. The Second Law states that a deceased soul must never be left to rot, and their NecroSeam must be reaped once their vessel has died. The Third law forbids the release of a shifter's soul before their vessel's time has ended, and the Fourth law states that only Reapers, their vassals and their apprentices can use weapons made with pure or alloyed Spiritcrystal."

Jaq adjusted his glasses beside us and added, "Then the Fifth Law says if a shifter's Seam is cut early, the vessel has to be put to rest, since they're pretty much already dead without their soul and the Seam can't be reattached once it's cut. The Sixth Law just says not to harm or hold any black birds captive, 'cus that would prevent future Reapers from bein' chosen."

"Okay." Octavius seemed determined to grasp all this. "What does that have to do with anything, though?"

My brother fidgeted an uncomfortable shoulder. "We may be in violation of two of those Laws. The Second and Third. At least, we might be. We're still not entirely certain."

Octavius gave a skeptical laugh. "I think you'd know if you let someone's Seam go un-reaped or not."

"We actually *have* allowed that to happen." Alex licked his lips and glanced at Jaq, who only shrugged. Alex's head dropped before giving a sigh. "You remember the brother I told you about? And what happened to him?"

Octavius scratched his nose. "You said he died… you mean you didn't reap his Seam?"

"Correct."

"So…" Horror pulled Octavius's features. "He's a Necrofera?"

"No, no." Alex shrugged with his hands. "Nothing like that. He's right here."

Octavius frowned. "Uh… where?"

I sighed from the psyche. *This looks to be my cue.*

I entered through the open window of the psyche, and once I took my brother's place, relishing the sensation of *feeling* the train's gentle vibration, I straightened in my seat.

Octavius blinked. "H-hey! Your eyes just!"

"We know," I interrupted, raising a pacifying hand. "I apologize for the late introduction. A certain discretion comes with the territory, you understand."

He stared at me.

"I'm Xavier," I offered. "Pleasure to formally meet you. Though, you and I have spoken on several occasions already, so I suppose it sounds rather redundant at this point."

"Uh." He lifted a weak finger. "You don't actually have a brother, do you?"

"I *am* the brother. We're both sharing his vessel."

"But I…" Octavius didn't seem sure what to ask first. He ended up giving us a withered look and settled with: "*How?*"

Alexander took my place. "We'll explain. Some years ago, my brother was thrown over a cliff here on the surface lands and was lost in the sea. After Xavier went missing, his soul awoke… well, attached to me."

I switched out to add, "Now both of our NecroSeams are tied to his heart. And since I was proclaimed dead, if the Death King knew I was here, he would sentence my Seam to be forcefully reaped, as the Second Law of Death commands."

"And if they did that," my brother continued after switching. "They would cut my Seam also, and our parents would possibly be executed as punishment for keeping a deceased soul's NecroSeam tied. So, to avoid any of that, we need to find Xavier's body. We think it might be alive… with your mother."

Octavius's nose scrunched. "Uh… w-wait, wait! If you're serious, why would your body be with my mom?"

"*His* body." Alex circled a finger. "I'm Alex. Pay attention to the blue eye, mine is on the right."

Octavius massaged his temples. "Ugh, fine, whatever… what does my mom have to do with any of this?"

"We believe she is affiliated with an underground organization known as *Land's Tailors*. It's a hidden group within the Healing community that's located somewhere in the Land realm, if it exists at all. Rumor has it, this group illegally houses vessels whose souls had been released before their deaths, and is kept secret since, as mentioned previously, it is against the Fifth Law of Death to keep them alive.

"Your mother evoked the elemental Hallows of remedy, according to her file. We have a friend with the same Hallows, who's studying under a very renowned Healer in High Everland's capital. Bianca… Our friend… well, her master swore he'd seen Sirra-Lynn recently when he took a trip to a Marincian island near this continent's coast. He knew she'd died years ago, so obviously, he was shocked to see her alive and well."

Octavius was even more confused now. "My mom's alive?"

"No," said Alex, and I nearly winced at his insensitive tone. "We've confirmed she was dead, we interviewed other ghosts who knew her while she was in Grim. But they say she left the caves years ago, undertaking a vassalship with a Necrovoker, as Vendy had done with us."

"I thought you said she wasn't being escorted by a Reaper?"

"Not every Necrovoker is a Reaper. We don't know who this other corpseraiser is, but that's all we've heard on the situation. Bianca's master overheard your mother speaking with someone about a 'missing Devouh boy' who was found years ago and was being cared for. They thought his soul was long destroyed, killed in his dreams. He'd supposedly been there for six years, which is the same timeframe that my brother went missing."

Octavius tapped a knuckle over his lips ponderously. "Devouh… That's right, you said that was your name earlier. But why does that sound familiar—?"

"—N-never mind that!" I hurriedly switched with Alex and blurted, then cleared my throat, dialing back my tone. "Needless to say, we had men search for your mother on that island, but we couldn't find her. Though we *did* learn where your mother's gravesite was located. So, we came up here ourselves, hoping to find her and question her about my body."

"Land…" Octavius scratched his head. "You know how weird this whole thing sounds, right?"

"Oh, we're well aware of the absurdity." My grin was stale. "But again, it's important that you not tell anyone else."

"As if anyone would believe me. But, um…" He folded his arms. "How do you know he—uh, *you're* still alive? What if your vessel actually is dead?"

I raised a hand to my chest. "We think there's a good chance I'm still alive. After all, my Seam was never cut and I'm not rotten, so… we think the fact I haven't changed into a Necrofera is a good sign."

"Does that even count as a sign, though? I've never heard of something like this happening."

"Neither have we," I lamented. "But I'm willing to give myself the benefit of the doubt and assume I can still have a life."

He groaned and rubbed his eyes. "Land, this is too weird… How long has this been going on exactly?"

"Six years," I grunted.

"Shel Almighty, if I had to live in my asshole brother for more than a minute, I'd lose my damn mind."

I nodded solemnly, humming. "You get used to it. Death, do you get used to it…"

17

PROGRESS REPORT

XAVIER

Hours into the train ride, our communicator bleated to life from Alexander's pocket, springs and coils whirling in quiet whistles. Alex plucked it out to answer, and a screen of translucent light projected, displaying a very familiar woman's scowling face.

Mistress.

Her shadowed hair was neatly pinned up and draping over her shoulder, storm-blue eyes absent of cheer. Her grey wolf ears were perked in our direction, remaining silent as if expecting us to speak first.

Accustomed to the cold gaze, Alexander didn't falter while offering her a respectful nod. "Mistress. We meant to call you."

"Spare me," she grunted. *"You've never ventured to call when you've caused trouble before, you're not about to start now. I will be brief: I've seen the reports."*

I watched from the psyche's window as Alex raised up a fist and coughed. "Of course you did… well, we're all alive, if that is what you wondered."

"It was." Her tone was resentful. *"Forgive this old woman for giving a damn about the wellbeing of her danger-pining students. Where are you now?"*

"Heading to Lindel," answered Alex.

She cocked a pencil-thin eyebrow. *"Is that where Sirra-Lynn was found?"*

"It's where we should find our next lead, at the least."

She gave an exasperated huff. *"Well, as long as you're leaving Nulani, that's all the better. We believe a Class 1 Sentient was behind that attack earlier, the same Pyrovoker from the valleys. If you find her, do not engage. Repeat: do not engage. You're not ready to face such a threat unsupervised."*

"With all due respect, Mistress," muttered Alex. "We already have. It's a wonder we're still standing now, but the fact is, they ran off. There's no telling where they went, or why they left us alive."

"All the more reason to find security elsewhere, which I'm glad you're seeing to. I will not have my students caught up in a mess like that again. If this continues, we may ask that you postpone your search until this problem is dealt with."

"Understood… though I should hope relocating to Lindel will solve the issue. And even after this, Mistress, we've an obligation to fulfill to someone." Alex hesitated, glancing at Henry and our resurrected vassal, Vendy, across the compartment. "We picked up a few additions since we surfaced. Xavier and I have formed a Bloodpact with the only surviving ghost from Nulani's attack."

Mistress grew still on the screen. *"You were able to form a Pact? With both of you?"*

"We were," Alex agreed. "We didn't have much choice but to try, regardless. The ghost noticed our changing eyes while we were protecting her. Xavier had to be out during that time, since I couldn't touch her. She wished to form a Pact with us in exchange for her silence."

"Bloods be praised, your first vassal…" she sounded in awe. *"Well, I suppose if she insisted, you certainly made the right choice. What is her name? I'll have to tell your father, he'll be so proud."*

Alex cleared his throat and turned the com screen toward Vendy. "Well, er, her name is Vendy. She is a Terravoker and Blacksmith's apprentice."

Vendy wasn't exactly the image of poise, reclined in her seat with a boot propped up, her overalls wrinkled and her loose braid sloppily tossed over a shoulder. The teen idly used her Terravoking to fiddle with three floating Mel beads above her gloved palm, her brown rabbit ears turning to the screen. She waved to Mistress with that crooked-toothed grin of hers.

"Well, Ms. Vendy," Mistress greeted pleasantly, her expression drunken with glee. *"Welcome to the family, dear! We'll have to introduce you to the other vassals, we can celebrate upon your return to Grim—"*

"Not just yet, Mistress," Alex interrupted, turning the screen to face Mistress again. "Vendy's request for forming the Pact was to allow her more time on the surface, to see through a… family vow. We're not sure if she's able to fulfill this vow, but we've agreed to give her a chance to try, to the best of her ability. Once she is satisfied either way, she will consign herself to follow wherever we choose to go."

"Ah," Mistress said, thoughtful. *"Then I suppose if you've made such a promise for the Pact, you must see it through... But I stand by my earlier order. If this demon situation continues, both your search and Vendy's vow must be postponed. You can both resume once it is dealt with... but this is only if the horde worsens. Nulani was drastically farther than the valleys where they first appeared, there is no telling if they'll reappear or where. Currently, I suggest you come to the capital for reinforcements after you've questioned this Maveric fellow."*

"Yes, Mistress," Alex saluted with a fist to his chest. Then he had an afterthought. "Ah, and there is something else. We acquired a new Brother when we surfaced to Brittleton." Alex turned the communicator to Octavius now, who stiffened. "This is Octavius, one of Sirra-Lynn's sons. He is accompanying us to find his mother."

Our mistress gave a confused look from the screen when Octavius waved a nervous hand at her.

"Ah, the other Reaper from the reports." She inspected him. *"Who is your master, if I may ask? I don't recall seeing anyone use throwing-scythes before, but you seem to be commendably trained."*

Alex turned the screen back us. "He has yet to find a master. He's, er, self-trained, you could say."

Her gaze turned suspicious. *"Then where did he find those scythes to kill off the demons? The view on the screens was a bit blurred, but the Fera were certainly dying. Were they stolen, or did you have a hand in it, Alexander?"*

"Not stolen," Alex emphasized. "It's difficult to explain. But Mistress... since he doesn't have a master, we were hoping you could take up Octavius as another apprentice. There's been a bit of a complication. He, er... knows of Xavier."

Her eyes split with seething fury. *"You told a Bloody stranger of...! Nira, do you have any idea what you've done—?"*

I pushed through the psyche's window and switched with Alex, taking his place in the physical world to address Mistress. "He's taken an oath of silence. Hiding was difficult, given that he could see me. He has soul-sight... But he's agreed to train under our supervision, so we can keep an eye on him."

"As if I take any students that fall at my doorstep?" she growled, wolf ears curling in offense. *"All potential apprentices must first pass my entrance examinations. Or did you forget that you both almost failed that very test?"*

My eye twitched, and I heard Alex growl from my thoughts. "That's not important."

"Oh yes, it is. Do you have any idea the shame it would have brought me if my own sons failed my student examinations? And believe you me, I would have tossed you off to a different teacher, don't think you had any special treatment just because you both fought for elbow room in my belly before you clawed your way out of my—"

"Mother!"

"I'm only making a point," she snorted. *"Death, Jaq did better than you on that test. Even if you'd both failed, I still would have taken up Jaq in a heartbeat."*

Jaq laughed beside us, but grunted into silence when I jabbed him hard in the ribs.

Mother continued. *"My point is, I'll not make an exception for a stray cat simply because you couldn't keep your wagging tongue still for a single week. Exam first. Decision after."*

I took a long breath. "Mistress. Your exam is to take the potential students on a Fera harvest and see how they fare. Well, you saw the reports. You even said you saw him fight. So let's pretend our little skirmish back there was the test. Now you tell me: Did he pass?"

She glowered at me, oh Death did she glower. There were times when staring at my mother could be akin to having a line of cross-eyed bowmen aim for a crabapple on your head. Many men have cowered under that look. Many have nearly pissed themselves in front of the whole court, in fact. It wasn't a glare one easily matched, at least not with much confidence. Even through the screen, it was terrifying.

But it was still through a screen. And she wasn't anywhere near us now, so it wasn't as though she could string my feet to a tree this time.

Better yet, I knew I had her. I saw the relenting glint in her storm-blue eyes, and she grudgingly shut her lids. *"Now I have to explain this to your father… Fine. He passed. I'll file the apprenticing papers tomorrow… and I'll hold him to his word on staying silent. Mark my words, if he so much as utters a single syllable—"*

"He won't."

"I won't!" Octavius echoed meekly.

"Very well… I'll send his badge as soon as there's time. We're still trying to sort out this massacre situation in the valleys…"

Her eyes flicked away in an afterthought. *"I never expected to find another Necrovoker up on the surface, though. We're a rare breed in the other realms."*

"Oh, he's not a Necrovoker, Mistress." I grinned. The train began to slow, and we glanced out the window to see we were approaching Lindel's station at last. "I'll explain another time. It looks as though we've arrived in Lindel."

"Ah, one of your grandfather's inns is there, I'll make a call to inform the manager—"

"No!" I bit back my tone, noticing Octavius was staring at me. "Er, I mean, that's fine, Mistress. We'll find a different inn."

"Absolutely not. I want to be sure you make it there in one piece, and our connections up there only extend to that specific chain."

"Mistress," I assured. "We'll be fine on our own."

"Xavier, if you or Alex so much as arrive at the Howler's Inn a MILLISECOND later than nine o'clock, I will strip you of your badges and you'll find some other profession to take up."

My teeth clicked shut.

She began muttering under her breath. *"Defying orders from a superior officer... bah! If you hope to be a knight, you'd best start acting like one... Now. Howler's Inn. Nine o'clock. Status updates aside, I'll not have my apprentices take shelter in some commoner's shack. It'd be absurd to see gentlemen of your standing staying anywhere else."*

Octavius shot me a suspicious glance. "So, I was right. You guys *are* nobles?"

"Of course they are," Mistress huffed before I could deny it. *"What in Nirus would make you think otherwise?"*

Octavius almost laughed. "The clothes threw me off."

"Oh, for Death's sake! What have I told you boys about those peasantry rags?"

"Mother," I chewed. "That's hardly relevant."

"Your attire is always relevant when you have a reputation to uphold."

"Could we focus our attention on something more important? Like, say, us almost being killed today?"

"And I'm happy to see you're all right. But you're representing the Devouh Household while in the public's eyes."

Octavius tapped a thoughtful finger to his chin. "Devouh, Devouh... I swear I've heard that name before..."

I flushed, growling, "Mother, could you keep it down—"

"You can't expect the court to take you seriously if you dress like a peasant," she prattled on. *"Your father is already furious—"*

"Oh, what else is new?" I scoffed. "If he cares so much, tell him to do something groundbreaking and call us himself for once."

She bristled on the screen. *"Your father is a busy man, even more so than me. As much as he'd like to call, he has important matters to settle about this massacre in the valley. And besides, you saw him just last month at his social."*

"Yes, for five whole minutes," I muttered.

"Xavier—"

"So sorry, Mother, but we seem to have arrived. We'd best be off."

Clink!

I promptly ended the call as the train screeched to a stop. We'd reached Lindel's station. I glanced at Octavius and Jaq, who were pointedly silent, as were Vendy and Henry, and I nodded for them to follow as we stalked out of the compartment.

Stepping onto the smoky platform, the messengers flew out with us. Octavius lugged behind, weighed down by the duffle bag strapped to his shoulder.

I supposed he didn't have the money to afford a Storagebox. They were so much easier to carry around, shrinking your luggage in size and weight, thanks to the gel-like gems found in Everland's mines. They came pre-made to shrink whatever was shoved into it, but manufacturers cut the gems in designer fashions with various models these days. Henry had several in that bag of his, carrying his vast array of wares that had been in his shop in Nulani. I had to wonder how many weapons he traded for so many boxes.

"So, uhm," Octavius began as his white-cheeked raven nestled onto his head. "That was your mistress Reaper?"

I tugged my hood up, feeling Alex's own raven settle onto my shoulder. Mal was never comfortable around me, but he could tolerate it most times. "Yes," I answered.

"And she's also your mom?"

I muttered. "What ever gave you that idea?"

"If you don't like it so much, why didn't you pick someone else to train under?"

"If you had the opportunity to have the most renowned Reaper in all of Grim to have as your master, would you have turned your nose up and chosen someone lesser?"

His step faltered. "She's that good?"

"Damn near the best. You should see the line of hopefuls for her entrance tests."

"How many have passed before?"

"Including the four of us?" I flexed out my hand, then curled my thumb to wave the remaining four fingers.

The color flushed from his cheeks. "That's it?"

"That's it," Jaq agreed, the viper smirking so wide, his fangs were showing. "And that's only the entrance exam. If you're scared now, wait 'till you get to the final. Goin' up against a Sentient is way more dangerous than the demons we've been fightin'. And by the looks of it, we're being followed by two."

He shivered. "Oh… what exactly is a Sentient, anyway?"

My eyes squinted at him, seeing he was serious. Did we not explain this? "That horse-shifter from Nulani earlier?" I said. "He was what we call a Class 2 Sentient."

"So, it's some kind of person?"

"It's a kind of Necrofera. There are three classes of demons. When a shifter's soul rots and merges with the corpse, they change into a Class 3 Fera, which is the typical demon we've been seeing: dumb, blackened, hungry and have no control over instinct.

"But if one survives long enough to eat, say, ten-thousand souls, then they become sentient and regain their humanoid form again. They're still demons that hunt for souls, but they're more powerful. They're no longer ruled by instinct alone. Now, they can blend with the living shifters and strategize. That's the Class 2 type. Less common. I'm surprised we found one, demons don't usually live long enough to become a Sentient."

"Okay…" Octavius rubbed his neck, absorbing the new knowledge. "What about this Pyrovoker your mistress was talking about? The one responsible for the valley massacre?"

"She is a Class 1 Sentient."

"What's the difference?"

"When an Evocator's soul rots," I said, "they immediately look the same as when they were alive and keep their Hallows. They don't start as a common, lesser Fera. They're initially superior. The only physical change you can tell with any Sentient, though, is that all of them have white pupils."

Jaq added beside us, "and some time durin' the change, they lose their memories of bein' alive and sorta wake up from nothin'."

"Oh…" Octavius gave a short breath and hurried ahead. "Let's, um, get inside somewhere. I'm getting creeped out talking about demons who don't look like demons…"

I smeared a hand over my face and grumbled. "Right. I suppose Mistress will know if we don't go to the right inn… Knowing her, she'll call them to check. I think I'll let you handle it, Alex."

Alex groaned from my thoughts. *Why must I do it?*

"Because it's you everyone knows about. They all think I'm dead."

"That's beside the…"

"Ah, ah, ah." I held up an expectant finger. "Let's not forget that I took the fall last month at Father's social. Howless Laraine had a tremor and couldn't keep hold of her champagne, so I had to walk all the way across the parlor wearing her drink on my trousers before retrieving a new pair. You owe me this time."

He clicked his tongue and I felt him about to switch.

"Fine…"

I let him take control and fell back into the void, watching him continue down the street with the others through the window of his vision.

"Let's get this over with, then," he mumbled miserably.

18

STALKER IN THE SHADOWS

MACARIUS

"Keep back, Cilia," I warned the young grey-haired girl beside me, sweeping an arm in front of her before she could take another step. "We don't want their birds to sense you."

We waited behind a corner building, watching the Reapers and their party stroll into the large city of Lindel. They didn't seem to notice they'd been followed on the train, and it wouldn't be in my favor to make ourselves known now.

Cilia gave a sigh, perhaps out of boredom, as she withdrew her hood. The disgusting scar running across the base of her neck was puckered and smooth, along with the matching marks looping her wrists.

She leaned against the brick structure. "The Bloody birds can't sense my Weight from this distance," she said. "Not as long as I keep it suppressed."

"I wasn't aware you could suppress it." I eyed her narrowly. "Your kind always seem to have new rules, the more you speak of them. Are there facts you're leaving hidden, I wonder?"

She muttered, "Not purposefully. They come to me as we go along. It's merely that there's so much of our culture to teach you, how do you expect me to remember everything in a moment's notice?"

"Culture," I chuckled, "*Our culture*, she says… walking corpses with principles, though most of their population is mindless, vicious beasts? Such a strange world you live in now, my dear."

She declined to acknowledge that, instead asking, "Why did you have me stop Lucrine? He hadn't had much chance to gather more soldiers. I wasn't even able to have any fun myself."

I stared at my hands, rubbing my scaled thumbs over the pads of my fingertips. I'd been so close… I'd had him right in my grasp. *I even touched the Crest with my own fingers…!* I could have ended it there. I could have finished him that moment, easily. I could have brought the world that much closer to salvation.

But that would have only solved half the problem, I reminded myself. *This has to be dealt with carefully. All at once, where I could watch everything unfold myself.*

"Well," I began, my hands clenching. "We couldn't let the boy die, could we?"

"Yes," she said, "We could have." Her arms folded. "He was a Necrovoker. He would have made a fair Sentient, at least."

"If we'd Changed him, he would have lost his memories."

Her stare flattened, white pupils glowing within those green orbs of hers. "Is there something you don't want him to forget?"

"His brother," I hushed, the sound of it pushing a chuckle from me. *Brother… twin, even. I should have guessed such a parallel.*

"Need I ask why?" Cilia drawled dully.

"If you'd been paying attention, you wouldn't." I tried not to sound short, though I could feel my scales growing more prominent over my skin. "That is the same boy from the Death palace six years ago. Or, his brother, I suppose… His twin. It's just as he described… What are the odds?"

She cocked an eyebrow at me. "Just as *who* described?"

The shadow-haired boy turned a corner with his companions. I pursued in silence, Cilia striding at my side.

"Macarius?" She began, her look impatient when I ignored her question.

"I was told the boy had been killed," I murmured. "I wasn't told he had a twin."

"Why does it matter?" she puffed, hands on hips. "Can I not run up there now and kill all of them? I can even do it quietly, no one will stir from their beds. I didn't have any exercise in Nulani, at least allow me a short jog?"

Such a child. She always had been, though. She was twenty when she died, and now seemed to be stuck in that immature temperament. Not that I was much older. We were the same age, numerically, but I'd physically grown six years ahead, after I'd escaped my timeless prison. Still, it was odd that I should find her again, after so long. That was poetic irony for you, I supposed.

"Because he also has the Crest on his hand," I explained, "you will stay your claws. He and his brother, it would seem, are two halves of the one person I needed dead years ago."

"If you wanted Lucrine to kill him, why didn't you let him do so in Nulani? Why have we followed them here?"

I stopped at the corner the boys had turned a few moments ago, and I barely caught a glimpse of them turning down a different street. "He claims to be searching for his brother."

"I thought you said his brother was already dead?"

"I was told he was." I felt my fangs grow longer, following after the Reapers. "But even if that boy had been proclaimed dead, why would his twin come looking for him after so many years? It seems strange, Cilia. It's too much of a coincidence."

"What do you mean?"

My voice fell quiet, thoughtful. "When I was given word that the boy with the Crest was killed, I didn't expect to run into his Bloody twin. And I find him just as we begin the first stage? One doesn't decide to search for their dead twin after six years, Cilia. He must have reason to believe his brother is alive."

"And?"

"And if he *is* alive, I have two serious problems."

"So, kill this twin and you'll have one less problem."

"Then how will I find the second, if he is alive?" I felt my tongue slit, angry that she still didn't understand. But could I blame her for being a twit? It didn't seem fair. Intelligence was something you were born with—or without. Still, the glands in my mouth began to build with venom, I could taste the poison leaking from my fangs.

"This isn't something to be taken lightly," I said. "I want you and Lucrine to follow the boy. Find where they're staying. But do so at a distance, those black birds will give you away, and they'll move elsewhere before showing us what we need."

She gave a sigh and rested a delicate hand over her hip. "Very well… If you insist on wasting time… Lucrine is on his way here with the others. I'll tell them to wait in the wastelands."

I adjusted the spectacles over my eyes, regarding her with a bit more appreciation. She may not have been very bright, but at least she was obliging. More than she ever was before. And that, in its own right, was more satisfying than anything I could have imagined.

"If the boy does find his brother," I said, "you can have your fun, Cilia."

19

A STREET APART

LILLI

"What do you think, Jewel?" I stared at the silver lettering of the Howler's Inn hanging from the entrance of the fifty-story building before me.

It was a mixture of modern architecture and historic design, silvery metal embedded with smooth stone that was carved with intricate pillars and gilded trim that hugged the windows. The structure's many brilliant lights gave its trailing terraces a vibrant, whitish glow, as if filled with thousands of Fallen Lights from Grim's caves.

But this realm wouldn't have the Fallen Lights, would it? It was far too hot. *Perhaps they could do with some of our Lights,* I thought, my heart sinking at the reminder of home. *At least they would dampen some of this ghastly heat.*

"What if he's in there?" I glanced at the small crow perched on my shoulder. "He could be staying there right now and I could be just outside."

Jewel gave a low hum and I shook my head. "No… he wouldn't be there, would he? He wouldn't remember his family if he lost his memories… Bloods, he may have even forgotten his own name. I doubt he remembers me, either."

I tried to imagine what he would look like: older, taller, different yet still the same, with that usual comforting smile and those kind, mismatched eyes… He could have spent these last six years alone on the surface, or was perhaps taken in by a strange family, given a different identity, waiting for the answers to his past… answers that I could bring him.

I grabbed the Storagesphere chained to my waist and peered into its clear surface. The little grey pouch inside was empty beside the shrunken, spare clothes—which were all worn and dirty, since I didn't have the money to have them washed. The spiked beads of Mel had been drained from the train ride here to Lindel, so for the first time in my life, I was destitute.

I gazed up at the clock tower across the street from the Howler's Inn. Its glowering face stared down at me from atop the enormous temple and the night sky loomed behind it like a timeless void.

The temple may once have been a magnificent structure, but now its flat, stone walls were chipped in some places and various vines were rotted and dry, their color a dull brown instead of green. There was a large symbol etched on the wooden doors, resembling flower petals of diamonds which took the form of a sword standing upright; the hilt was the usual tri-leaf of diamonds, the Crest of Nirus, only upside-down.

It was a Land mark, this realm's patriotic emblem and the symbol a shifter was born with if they were blessed with Hallows from this country. It also doubled as the crest of Shel, the God of life and power.

But surrounding Shel's sigil were four others. The emblems of Ushar, Rin, Iri and Nira created a joined, square frame around it.

A Harmonist temple, I noted, admiring the stained-glass windows looming at the front of the building. They each depicted different scenes of the Gods.

One displayed the child God of Dreams, Iri. The Shepherd was an azure haired, fox-eared boy wielding a crook that was tied with a bell. In the stain-glass, He stood atop a mountain's cliff, sweeping His crook toward the sky, three shining Orbs of Azure gleaming in the air before Him.

Playing in the storms surrounding the Shepherd was His elder brother, the God of Sky, Ushar. The Archer's scarlet dragon wings were spread wide as He played in the storm, His bow aimed at a mighty Phoenix of Scarlet that flew alongside Him.

In the other window showed the beautiful God of Ocean, Rin. The Artist commanded the seas with a graceful dance in the waters, His scaled dragon tail and flowing emerald hair wavering in the stain-glass shapes. With His trident in one hand and a paintbrush in the other, He stood before a colossal, icy clam that held an enormous Pearl of Emerald.

In the same window, far beneath the Artist's waters and standing within hollowed caverns twinkling with Floating Lights, was His mother: the Death Goddess, Nira. The Seamstress was depicted with wolf ears and long, ashen hair as She guided the souls of a sunken ship to the caves with Her shining scythe in one hand and a sewing needle, which trailed a shimmering thread, in the other, leading the souls to a towering Willow of Ashes that flaked with brilliant white powder.

On the final window above the doors, in the largest, flower-shaped frame, was the golden, lion-eared Father God of life: Shel. The Gardener was clad in golden armor matching his hair and bright eyes, a sword in one fist and a humble gardening spade in the other, a seed sprouting into a Blossom of Gold on the tool.

This temple must be for a SHELISH faction of Harmonism, I amended, noting how much larger the Gardener's window stood compared to the others.

We Harmonists had a joined belief in all the Gods of Nirus, but each followed different philosophies. Whichever God you wished to emulate in life would determine the faction you joined. I was accustomed to a *Nirian* Harmonist temple, where the Death Goddess was featured more than the rest. It was odd to see Shel in Her place. And the brilliant gold, purple and orange colors of the glass had me mesmerized. It was beautiful… but also a bit of an eyesore, admittedly.

Lovely as it was, the new images and bright colors were unsettlingly foreign. The conflicting hues were giving me a headache, and I rubbed my eyes.

Oh, what am I to do now? I thought with a sigh. Without any money, I couldn't travel to the next town and I'd have no hope of finding Xavier, if he was still in Nulani. I didn't have any money for food, either… or a place to sleep.

Sighing again, I walked up the steps of the temple. After pushing open the doors and peeking inside, I was relieved to find it abandoned, and closed the doors. I sat along one of the dust coated benches, on a side where the walls weren't chipped and opening into the ceiling's wooden framework, where birds had nested.

Jewel settled into a ball on my shoulder as I tried to find a comfortable position to sleep, without success, and let out a grimace.

I didn't like this realm very much.

Most of the people I'd come across have either been rude or scared Deathless of the man I was searching for, it was too hot, and the whole nation had a serious Necrofera infestation. The train ride in Adrial was the worst yet, I thought it would never end. If Sir Janson hadn't been on the train's roof—at least, I assumed that's where he'd been—to kill off the rest of the Fera, I may not have made it out alive.

Why were there so many here? There's usually only five or six at a time, fifteen at most. A Sentient must be leading them all together. That was the only answer that made any damned sense.

But that would mean the Sentient was following me since Timberail. Would it really do that? No one knew I was here, so why would a demon?

I rolled on my side. This trip may have been a bad idea. I've never had to sleep on a stiff, wooden bench before, and I've never been this hungry. I missed home...

Tears stung and I wiped them dry. I grabbed the amulet around my neck and clicked the glittering cover open, winding back the dial and let the twinkling music play.

My eyes closed, imagining myself back home where my father would sing this to me as a child. My lips formed the words, whispering the old language with the music. It helped me calm, and I tried to fall asleep on the uncomfortable bench.

I pray Father can forgive me for leaving... and Matthiel.

Matthiel. I'd nearly forgotten about my recent betrothal. He'd proposed the very night I left home. I'd originally agreed, but after learning Xavier was alive... well, my life had been put on hold when I was given this mission.

Find Xavier, I was ordered, *and reunite him with his brother.*

But why? None of it made sense... How was I to know if my 'quest' was even viable? I could be trekking along a wild-wolf chase for all I knew.

I squeezed my eyes shut. Death, I wanted to go home. It was safe and familiar there. I was moving on with my life, about to start a new family with Matthiel, take on my duties and responsibilities, finally step forward to the future...

But I knew there was nothing for me at home. Not anymore. That ideal future wouldn't be waiting for me on my return.

Only my execution would welcome me back.

And so I'd better have Xavier with me before then.

20

THE DEVOUHS

XAVIER

Alexander paused outside the Howler's Inn, Mal cocking his head from my brother's shoulder.

"Hmm?" Alex intoned, his head twisting to the raven. "What's wrong, Mal?"

Mal bobbed his head curiously, lifting a hesitant talon and croaked, "O-dd. O-dd…" The raven stared at the Harmonist temple across the street.

Beside us, Vendy took a defensive stance. "More demons?"

"Bloody Void," Henry cursed, rummaging into his bag to find a weapon. "I swear if I have to go through another attack, I'm going to—"

"No," Alex murmured, his brow knitting. "Mal feels something… familiar. Something to do with the temple?"

Mal croaked and twitched his head. Then he seemed to lose interest and bit at an itch on his wing.

Octavius scratched his cheek, hefting his awkward duffle bag. "Guess it wasn't that important?"

"Perhaps not…" Alex didn't sound satisfied, sweeping his gaze to the temple with narrow lids.

GONG!

His eyes jerked to the looming clock tower above, its glass face glowing alongside the almost-round moon.

GONG!

His eyes widened in panic when he read the clock's hands: *Nine 'O clock.*

"Death, we're late!" Alex rushed up the steps of the Howler's Inn. "Mistress better not have called them already…!"

He threw open the glass doors, keeping his shoulders hunched and grown wolf ears folded down the nape of his neck. Jaq and Octavius hustled to keep pace with Alexander's brisk steps.

From the psyche, I watched our company cross the marble floor of the luxury inn's lobby, voices of lounging shifters bouncing off the arched, golden ceiling. The guests of the Howler's Inn were high-class citizens and traveling nobility, their demeanor as refined as their silken garments. The women's jewelry and wedding-vines glittered in the chandeliers' lights from the golden ceiling, shining along the glimmering walls which, not surprisingly, shared the same golden sheen as everything else in this Bloody realm.

I didn't like the gold, personally. It was much too glaring, not as subtle as the silver décor in which I was accustomed to in Grim. But, as Grandfather Edric would argue, knowing your customers was the key to a successful business. Since his inns had many foreign locations in the other realms, I supposed it made sense to adopt the more popular themes from the local cultures… Tacky and gaudy though it may be.

We were by far the most underdressed customers in the Howler's Inn. And the barons noticed. Oh, they glanced away to pretend we didn't exist, but Nira knew they noticed, stealing disgusted glances at us and murmuring under their breaths as we passed.

Alexander pulled on his hood, dropping his gaze—and mine, by consequence—to the floor.

Music played from a stringed quartet in the corner, and when Alexander rounded the trickling stone fountain in the center of the lobby, we hurried to the gilded, caged doors of the lift. We breathed a small sigh of relief once reaching it—

"Excuse me!" An orange-haired man in a tanned uniform came from the crowd, pointing an accusing finger at us. "Do you have a reservation?"

Alex squirmed. "Er… yes." He promptly jabbed the lift's call button, his foot tapping as he watched the glass box that was far over our heads descend on its tracks toward us.

The steward wasn't convinced. "I'm sorry, but you'll have to leave if you don't have a reservation. You're disturbing the guests with your feral birds."

"We have a reservation." Alexander crossed his arms, his eyes stuck to the gently falling lift as it reached the gilded cages on the floors above us.

"We'll be staying in the master suite, which I presume is on the top floor, as it usually is. I'll call for a key once we reach our quarters."

"Now see here!" the steward grabbed Alexander's hood and yanked it down, turning him by the arm strictly. "This is no place for hooligans! Please leave before I have the guards escort you… y-you…"

The man froze, staring at Alexander's mismatched eyes. The color fled from his cheeks. "Y… Young Howllord Devouh…?"

The chatter in the lobby vanished.

The music screeched to a stop, and the noble crowd of Roarlords and Roaresses turned their attention straight to us. Wine glasses shattered in the painful silence.

Alex's finger became a woodpecker against the call button.

"Y-Y-Young Howllord Devouh…!" the steward squeaked, his back cracking in an apologetic bow. "I—I mean *High* Howllord! I-I… I'm terribly sorry! I didn't realize—I-I didn't see your eyes! P-p-please forgive my rudeness…!"

To our side, Jaq failed to stifle a snicker.

Alexander looked about the crowd of stunned faces, their dark skin growing pale and animal ears sprouting.

Alex swung his head left. That section of the crowd jumped in terrified gasps and scattered to hide behind one another, more wine glasses shattering. He turned his head right, and that section followed the first's example, scrambling several yards back as if a simple glare would cause them to drop dead where they stood.

"Your… your m… m-m-mother called just a moment ago about your arrival…!" The steward's breath was jagged, rabbit ears grown and draped down his neck. "But I… I wasn't expecting you to look like a…" He stopped himself and slid a nervous hand over his orange hair. "I-I'll go retrieve your key…!" His voice cracked with 'key' and he stumbled into the crowd, running into half a dozen Roarlords along the way—all of whom didn't mind, as they themselves were too busy escaping.

In a matter of fringed seconds, the lobby had emptied, leaving behind only the clutter of broken glass and seeping wine on the floor.

Alex hid his face with a hand, groaning. Vendy let out a clucking laugh, and Henry snorted beside her.

"Um," began Octavius sheepishly. The cat inched away from us. "Okay. *Now* I remember where I heard that name…"

Ding!

The damned lift finally arrived.

Once the gilded cage door clattered open, and the glass door behind it followed suit, Alexander spared no time to shuffle into the carpeted box. The liftman inside jumped at the sight of us, and hurriedly stumbled out.

Cranking gears and springs clinked to life from the inner workings of the lift, and a single vial, snapping with trapped lightning, sparked from the panel that displayed the floor numbers.

Jaq followed us inside with an entertained smirk, Vendy hopped on before Henry's heavy weight shook the box… yet Octavius lingered outside.

"Well?" Alex barked at the cat, declining to peel his eyes off the maroon carpet of the lift. "Are you going to stand there like a drooling idiot or get in?"

Gulping deep, hesitant breaths, Octavius stepped in, his legs trembling. His cat ears had grown and Octavius shuffled carefully around us, pressing himself against the farthest wall.

The steward returned and gave us the key to our room—well, the man attempted to. When Alexander reached for the key, the steward cringed and jerked his hand back before my brother could grab it. Jaq took the key from him instead.

"Th-th-th-there you are, Howllord…!" the steward built up the courage to say, shying away. "We've had the servants prepare your room fittingly! P-please call if you need anything!" His tone suggested he never wanted us to call.

"Yes," Alexander grunted dully, then shoved a lever forward, locking it in place with a loud *clank* and cranked it in a circle, closing the gilded cage door outside, then closed the inner doors of the box. We were familiar enough with how these contraptions worked that we didn't need assistance to maneuver it. Grandfather Edric had been more than eager to teach us in Grim when we were boys, so the concept was nothing new.

Alex punched the desired floor's button, and the lift sparked to life, the Shockvial in the wall giving the machine power to move upward. We watched the floor numbers brighten with small *dings* as we ascended.

"So…" Octavius kept his back stuck to the wall. He seemed to be stopping himself from cringing, pinned like a feral crab awaiting the hour when his legs would be ripped off and drained of their stuffing. "You're a High Howllord."

"Yes." Alex drummed impatient fingers on the lever, watching the floors rise.

Octavius swallowed audibly. "Wh-which makes your f… father…?"

"The Death King's Eyes," Alex growled, but squeezed his eyes shut, calming. "Yes. Any more questions?"

"Um," began Octavius, "j… just one…"

"We're not going to hang you."

He wheezed out the breath he'd been holding. "Shel Almighty, thank you…!"

Ding!

We reached the top floor.

Alex went through the rounds of shoving the lever in place and cranking it, opening the glass doors and the cage, then stepped into a wide, sienna-carpeted hallway. Two cleaning maids pushed a hovering cart of fragrant sprays and fresh rags, the women flinching as Alexander made his way past them.

"Y-Young Howllord!" they gasped, looking at his mismatched eyes. "Good-good evening!"

Alexander jerked his head away, a single grunt his reply.

"We've c-cleaned the quarters for you and your-your friends!" One stuttered. "All three bedchambers and the lounge! And the banisters of the balconies! All spotless!"

He muttered. "Yes. Good. I think."

"Will you… will you need room service, Young Howl… H-H-*High* Howllord?"

"No. We'll be retiring for tonight."

"Of-of course, High Howllord!" They gave petrified bows, their gazes following him as he scurried down the hall, his hands stuffed in his coat pockets.

When we reached the last set of doors, Alexander snatched the key from Jaq and rammed it into the keyhole, cranking open the lock with a sawing *crrrrr-clack* and pushed on the doors, storming into the expansive, finely-furnished quarters.

The messengers flew inside ahead of him, alighting outside a large, open window. Jaq's crow, Bridge, *thunked* her head on the crystal chandelier on her way out, rattling the dangling jewels.

Despite its newly quivering light, the chandelier gleamed steady starlight over the lounge-hall of these chambers, illuminating the brilliant shine of gold trim and suede, rustic couches with gilded frames. The floors were dressed with burgundy carpet that trailed with dark swirls, only stopping in the corner when it met a curling stairwell leading up to an open, railed hallway, where I assumed the bedchambers awaited, if the floorplan for this master suite was the same as those in Grim.

Alexander shrugged out of his jacket and threw it to the floor, disregarding the intricately carved coat hanger by the doors.

"So much for anonymity," he muttered. "Can't we be greeted with a simple, 'hello, how are you?'"

Even after the others shuffled in and Jaq shut the door, Octavius was still frozen in place.

"So… so earlier, on the com," Octavius said, "that was High Howless Devouh? She's going to train me?"

"Yes." Alexander sighed, knuckling his temple. He drifted to the wet-bar in the back and rummaged through the cabinets, grabbing several bottles of liquor and inspecting the labels. Henry joined us and grabbed himself a drink, offering one to Jaq as well.

"And," my brother added blithely, finding a vessel of peppermint-licorice scotch and poured himself a glass, throwing it down his throat and pouring himself another, "if you can catch our father for more than an hour, he'll be training you as well. He's our Master, if mostly in writing."

Octavius's face cracked in horror. "W-what?!"

"Don't even think of having second thoughts," Alex warned. Mal flew to his shoulder, and the raven pushed its beak against my brother's bristly jaw. He took another, lighter glug of his drink. "You gave us your word that you'd train with us, and you've already passed Mistress's entrance exam. That exam was also to place you with our master."

"You didn't tell me he was Lucas Bloody Devouh!" Octavius cried, Shade giving an agreeing *b-ad*! From his head. "What if I mess something up and he cuts off my head?!"

"He won't cut off your head," Alex grumbled, rubbing his eyes. "He's not the tyrant Howllord Endlser was before him. Stop believing the idiots who tell you otherwise."

Octavius slumped against the wall, trying to keep his breath steady. "I'm dreaming. That's it. It's a nightmare. This whole week has just been a nightmare."

Alex found the ice bucket on the wet-bar and plucked two cubes with the metal tongs, plunking them in his glass and rattling them. "You do realize that apprenticing under a High Howllord means you'll have diplomatic authority over everyone on this continent, and will *prevent* you from being executed by anyone?"

Octavius's head lifted, one cat ear perked. "R… Really?"

Jaq laughed and climbed the stairs toward the bedchambers. "Yep. Might as well get used to it, Tavius. Ya can almost get away with anythin', even if you're not related to him. Those are the perks that come with apprenticin' under the High Howllord. Everyone's gotta respect ya."

Octavius rubbed his shoulder. "I never thought about it like that..."

Alexander patted Mal's head from his shoulder in a dreary sigh. "Can't we have one week without people screaming at the sight of us? That's all we ask. One Bloody week."

Octavius's cat ears receded, and he inched his way to the bar beside us. "S... sorry. It's just—I can't believe your dad's the High Howllord of the entire Undercontinent."

Alex gave a half-nod and mumbled. "And our mother is the First Fangs of Low Everland, which makes her the commanding general of the Reapers under *and* over this continent, to be technical. Political and military power within one house... makes for perhaps the strictest parents in history."

"Bloods, you're practically royalty! I mean, your parents are the ones who meet *our* king when the Death King has anything to say, right?"

Mal hopped off Alexander's shoulder to join Bridge outside the open window, Shade flying after him from Octavius's head.

"Yes," Alex said, "our father is good friends with King Serdin. He was once his Second Hand, before this. It should come as no surprise that His Majesty Death chose him as his ambassador."

"Land..."

Alex hesitated. "You're not planning to bolt out the window, are you?"

"N-no." Octavius's gaze flicked to the window, as though now considering it. Then he shook his head. "But... but I don't get it. You're not... *bloodthirsty*, like everyone says... but what about your dad? He's not going to kill me for being around you guys, is he?"

"For the love of... *Why* does everyone think our father is anything like the previous Eyes?"

"Uh," Octavius lifted a finger. "Because he keeps sentencing people to death?"

I switched with Alex sternly, the air vents fanning coldly against my cheeks as the drink warmed my belly. "As if your king up here doesn't do the very same?" I countered. "And those are only criminals who are given the death penalty, which, mind you, had been sentenced by a different council of law. Our father simply approves those decisions and makes sure their souls are treated well afterwards, provided they aren't psychopathic murderers who'd go on a killing spree if resurrected again."

Octavius muttered. "Yeah, sounds like a real saint..."

I sighed. "Look. Our father isn't—*gugh!*" I took a sip of Alexander's peppermint-licorice drink and spit it out. I grimaced at the bottle and rummaged through the cabinets to find something more suitable, pouring myself a separate bottle of cinnamon whiskey instead. "Bloody disgusting, licorice…"

I took a rueful swig of my *better* drink to drown out the horrible taste, exhaling as I went on with my thought. "Our father isn't perfect. Void, he's certainly not much of a father most times, but he isn't what you think. He does have reasons for approving those penalties, just as your king has his reasons for the very same thing. Our father doesn't cut off heads left and right for personal gain, as Lord Endsler had done before him. Why do you think my father took over?"

Octavius leaned against the back of the suede couch. "But what about the people who used to be your dad's servants? I heard he killed the whole staff and enslaved their ghosts."

Alexander demanded to switch, and I obliged to give him reign. "First," he began, "You're thinking of, yet again, the *previous* Eyes of the Death King. Second, our father has only sentenced *one* staff member to death, after she poisoned my soup and nearly killed me. And mind you, this was not the first attempt a staff member had made on my life. She had been the 48th servant to try that year, and the only one who'd nearly been successful. While those before her had simply been imprisoned, my father had decided to put an end to the attempts after I was sent to the hospital. He made her an example and had her hanged for her crimes, and he stopped hiring *living* servants. He decided the only staff members he could trust were the ghosts who had sworn a vassalship to him."

"Third," I said after I switched and crossed the hall, sitting along the windowsill, the opened frame looming behind me and drawing in the outside scents, the clock tower glowing bright. "Those same ghosts had *been* the vassals of the previous Eyes. And you were right, they had been enslaved into service with Lord Endsler… but it was my father who freed them. Not that anyone is brave enough to ask any of them, of course, so even their gratitude is spat upon by the presumptuous rumors and terrified gossip…"

Mal fluttered onto my knee from outside. A string of meat hung from the raven's beak and he swallowed the last of his scavenged meal.

"Watch your heads, watch your insides," I sang morosely, my voice quieting, *"Else they ride with the Death King's Eyes. Cold and brutish, kills the foolish, comes Lord Lucas, the Terribly Ruthless."*

Silence swelled, and I loosened a slow, hollow breath. "Alex and I have spent our lives hearing that nursery rhyme wherever we went. Children sang it to our faces, their parents taught them in the safety of their homes…"

Octavius had fallen silent.

I circled a hand. "Of course, it's an updated rendition of the rhyme. Its subject was originally meant for Lord Endlser: the Bloody Ender, as they called him. Endlser was a Necrovoker, but I tell you now, not all Necrovokers respect the dead. Endlser would kill for his own gain, enslave their ghosts, break apart families…" The warm air suddenly dampened and chilled, and I rubbed my arms in a shiver. "They all came to our father, when he beheaded Lord Endlser. They thanked him, offered their service—begged for it. They had nowhere else to go, after the demon was gone. The damage he'd caused was done… For all our father's faults, he is not another Bloody Ender. Yet the trauma still bleeds like a fresh wound that will never be cleaned, forever tainting the name of the Death King's Eyes…"

We'd lapsed into a sorrowed silence for a time. Henry and Vendy, seeming to have already known about our family history and thought nothing of it, chatted by the wet-bar, the Blacksmith swiping Vendy's glass from her sternly and muttering that she wasn't old enough to drink such things, dead or not.

Only when Mal began preening his feathers over my knee did Octavius clear his throat and point to the raven. "So, er… is-is Mal both of your messengers, since there's two of you in there?"

An obvious distraction. But, well, I supposed I could use one as well.

"He's Alexander's." I glared at the raven, who cawed at me, illustrating his dissatisfaction by turning away. The damned bird had never fancied me. "In truth, I don't have a messenger. I… went missing before it could find me."

"Oh." Octavius looked sorry for bringing it up.

I sighed. "It's all right. If he's still looking for me, perhaps he'll come when I find my body." My smile was stale. "But first… well, I suppose we'll have to find your mother before I start hoping for anything more."

Octavius seemed to cheer at the mention of his mother. He stared down at Shade by his feet. "Yeah… You know, I'm starting to wonder if Mom went to find my dad. If she heard he left, maybe she went to bring him back?"

I hummed, recalling that he'd mentioned his father before. "Perhaps," I considered. "The theory isn't so farfetched, I shouldn't think. You don't know where your father is?"

"He just left one night, after mom died." He pulled out a wallet from his pocket, retrieving a photograph. He stared at it solemnly. "We haven't heard from him since. He could be anywhere by now."

I rose to peer at the picture myself, asking, "Why did he leave?"

"That's what I want to know," he said, a faint grimace tugging his face. "We got back home from my mom's funeral, and we all just went to bed… I couldn't sleep, though. I heard someone walking around the café downstairs, so I went to look. I saw Dad all packed and heading out the door, and he only stopped after I asked where he was going. All he said was, 'You have to look after the others, now. You and Mika. Keep them safe'. And then he walked out, and never came back."

I scanned the photograph. There were five figures huddled over a sandy beach, the sun shining from a blue sky above. They were all in swimwear, smiling, save for one girl with black hair, who scowled at her two younger brothers who kicked sand in her eyes as they ran by.

I recognized each face. The scowling girl was his elder sister, Mika, the boys were Octavius and his brother, Neal, the little girl with orange hair, Connie… The mother was there also, holding the youngest in her arms with a radiant grin, her cat ears perked. She and Connie looked much alike, only the girl's eyes were yellow, and the mother's were pale green.

"Where is your father?" I asked, searching for the face I had yet to see.

"He was taking the picture." He said and pulled out another photograph. It was a smaller one, crumpled from abuse. He handed it to me. "This is him. Mom took this one, so he could be in it. It's one of the only pictures I have left of him—"

CRASH!

A vase shattered when I stumbled into its table, startling Vendy and Henry and causing Octavius to flinch. I dropped the photograph, recoiling as if it'd stung me. The paper fluttered down, swaying between us before it settled over the carpet, his father's face staring up at me.

The man smiled above Octavius, wrapping an endearing arm around him, his face broad and gruff with stubble, hair the same shade of black like his son's, skin the same bronze hue…

But his eyes, glistening in the sunlight, were a piercing, honey yellow.

"This…" I began, the hairs on my neck prickling. My lungs hollowed and iced, throat sticking as it dried in ragged breaths. "*This* is your father?"

"Yeah." Octavius lifted to his feet in surprise. "Wait. Do you know him?"

"I… n-no! No, it's not that." I laughed weakly, bending to pick up the vase's ceramic pieces, hoping it would distract me from screaming. "I was… *shocked*. At how… how alike you looked." I cleared my throat behind a quivering fist. "N-now, your father—he doesn't… he doesn't share your Hallows, does he? You're the only Infeciovoker in your family, yes?"

"No, I got it from him." Octavius cocked an eyebrow. "Are you all right? Your ears are growing."

"It's nothing! I was just… surprised! Er, since your mother was a Healer, also. Those Hallows are opposites, so I thought it was a, er… fitting match…"

He retrieved the photograph from the carpet, inspecting it with a furrowed brow. "Uh, yeah. I guess it was fitting… You sure you're all right? You look like you're going to puke."

"I'm fine." I forced a smile, but it twitched. "I'm… I'm tired. Yes. It's been a long day, nearly killed by a mob of demons. I-I suppose I need a night's rest."

He rubbed his neck, replacing the photographs in his wallet. "Oh. Right, sure."

I abandoned the vase pieces on a nearby table and barreled up the stairs. My grip was tight on the rail, insides twisting. I struggled to not seem rushed, yet adrenaline shrieked in my thoughts so gratingly I could barely hear Alexander swearing from the psyche.

When I reached the upper hall, Jaq's door opened.

"Mates?" Jaq held a communicator, the projected screen turned away from his face. "What broke?"

"Nothing." I shoved open the nearest bedchamber door, nausea heating.

"That didn't sound like nothing." Jaq held the com up in a gesture. "And Bianca's on com. She's still at the capital with her master Healer and wants to know when we're going to meet—"

"Later!"

I slammed the door and backed against the wood with a *thunk!* Panic tangled my gut, bile bubbling. The acid flooded up, and I hurried to the private washroom—

Vomited in the sink.

"Nira save us, he doesn't know." My arms shook against the marble counter, keeping myself stable. "He… he doesn't know a Gods damned thing."

"What do we do?" Alex asked from my thoughts. *"If he stays with us…"*

He didn't finish. He hadn't a need to.

"If Octavius stays with us," I said, "we may meet *him* again. And if that happens…" Sickness rose again, but I swallowed it. Those honey-yellow eyes were burned into my memory from the photograph; from my nightmares that have haunted me for six Gods damned years. "He'll kill you, Alex," I whispered. "As he'd killed me."

21

FOREIGN FESTIVITIES

LILLI

This trip was a terrible idea.

I wandered through the crowded streets of Lindel with a scowl, Jewel fluttering at my side. This awful, afternoon sun was still too bright and the small amount of shade my cloak offered wasn't enough for the harsh glare.

How am I to find Xavier now? I sluggishly walked along the blockade of shifters who'd made way for the parade, my heavy feet shuffling miserably. The bite wound on my leg had begun flaring painfully again. I'd taken my medicated tonic, but the swelling still ached like Death.

Barely a week has past, and I've already depleted what little money I'd had, I thought drearily, sighing. *Why is everything in this realm so expensive? Our travel fares in Grim are nothing like these prices...*

I stopped to give my swollen leg a rest, rubbing the wound under my boot tenderly, the parade marching past in the street.

There was some sort of festival today. Dancers were dressed in gold silks while musicians blurted their trumpets and bugles. Drummers clanked their rims and beat deep vibrations that shook the pit of my stomach; flag bearers strutted past me with gold, brown and purple ribbons that fluttered from their banners, and each section of the parade was separated by a line of Rockraiders who rode on the backs of Landragons.

I'd never seen the other realms' dragons. The reptilian creatures in front of me had leathery skin that was pimpled in rough pockmarks. They had scrunched snouts with small horns at their peaks, and thin, long ears that bowed to the middle of their backs. They were bipedal with no arms and were dressed in gilded armor, their saddles made of brown leather. They had skinny, wispy tails which mimicked their long ears, waving to and fro while the beasts honked and trotted onward.

From my cultural studies, I'd heard that Landragons secreted a strange ooze from their bumps at times, which had healing qualities when applied to wounds. Healing was one of the Land realm's Hallows. *So, it's true*, I thought with intrigue. *For every element of Hallows, there is a dragon of the same type.*

The only exception to this rule was the Dream realm's elements. But that kingdom was on a different physical plane entirely, and so had no dragons. Though, as the King of Dreams would argue, Aspirre's dragons were the ones we dreamed of in our sleep.

A troop of Footrunners followed behind the Raiders, all on horseback and wearing less beautiful, bronze armor while holding spears. Maidens weaved through the crowd carrying baskets of golden tulips, showering spectators with the petals and handing out woven lays to young girls.

One maiden came and pulled down my hood, placing a tulip behind my ear. She smiled warmly as she brushed back my grey hair, wished me a cheery King's Day, and pranced to the next woman to do the same.

My stomach echoed with a hollow growl, and I clutched my aching belly. Though the festival was exciting, my hunger was too overwhelming for me to enjoy it. I looked into my Storagesphere, seeing that my shrunken pouch of Mel was flat and empty. I'd used the remaining beads for the train ride here yesterday—and that meant I couldn't reach Nulani. I was stuck in Lindel now.

I hadn't seen nor heard from Sir Janson since the last time we met in High Adrial, either. Was he still watching me from somewhere? Perhaps *he* would have money...

When my stomach gave another groan in protest, I glanced at a merchant booth selling apples with longing eyes. The apples may not have been in season, but they still looked delicious from here.

Something tugged my skirt then.

I glanced down. A small, copper-haired girl had snagged my hem. She had curling sheep horns sprouting from her head and looked at me with wide, brown eyes above a button nose.

She tugged my skirt again, as if asking me to kneel.

I complied and lowered to her. "Yes?"

"Ain't you the Reaper missy from the screens?" she asked, rocking on her heels.

"Er, yes. I am." Had everyone seen those reports except me? *Perhaps I should pay more attention to the news.*

"Why ain't you with your friends?" Her head cocked curiously. "Did you get lost?"

"Friends? What do you mean?"

"The other Reapers from the screens." She lifted her tiny hands in a matter-of-fact gesture. "They were all in Nulani. But you ain't with them."

Could she mean Xavier? "I… didn't come with them." I could only assume Xavier was with a group, since she mentioned multiple Reapers. "But I'm trying to meet them. I simply haven't enough Mel to travel yet." *Or enough to eat*, I lamented in silence.

My stomach screamed again, angry. I had to stop myself from cringing. The beating drums from the parade only made my gut lurch more. "Er, do you know what this festival is about?" I asked, attempting to distract myself.

The girl pointed at a passing flag bearer, directing my attention to the gold and brown banner flapping in the breeze.

"Well yeah," she said, "everyone knows that. Today's King's Day. Mum says a long time ago, the first king of Everland was crowned."

The flag held a stenciled face of a bearded lion-shifter, wearing a crown that was crested with gold mountains.

"The first king…?" I asked. "Do you mean the first to be crowned *after* Land's Relic Bloodline was lost?"

"My mum says there was wars after the continents broke up," she explained. "Said it was bad times. Then the Arborvokers and Terravokers moved to their own lands. The rock people came here to Everland, and the plant people went to Neverland." Her chin jerked to the flag again. "Today's the day King Setthick was crowned as the new ruler, so Mum says we cele-brate our 'declaration of separation' from Neverland."

"I see…" What an odd thing to celebrate. Why was it seen as a blessing for a realm to be divided, after a thousand years of peace and unity? I sup-posed when the Land realm lost their Relic Bloodline, the nation underwent a harsh paradigm shift.

The girl tugged my skirt again, shyly this time. "Um, missy Reaper?"

"Yes?"

She pointed at Jewel, who was perched on my shoulder. "Why's that birdy following you?"

"Ah." I scooped Jewel up and presented her to the girl. "She's my companion. She's been with me since I was a little girl, just like you. Would you like to hold her?"

The girl's eyes sparkled, reaching out to take Jewel. My messenger hopped into her palms and chirped, ruffling her feathers and making the girl giggle. "She's so soft! Where can I get one?"

I chuckled and slipped the gold tulip from my ear, placing it behind hers. "There may already be one looking for you. It simply needs time to find where you are."

She rubbed Jewel against her cheek, reveling in my crow's plushness. The girl was called by her mother then, and she gave Jewel back before saying goodbye, curtseying politely, and rushed to find her parents in the crowd.

I rose in a sigh, clutching my stomach as it gave another moan. The apple vendor was still in sight, and I stared at the fruit hungrily. *If only I had enough Mel...*

"... still not certain of his whereabouts," a lion-eared woman said as she passed me. She was struggling to keep pace with the burly man pushing through the crowd.

The man had two swords strapped to his back in a cross-shape, his face coated in thick stubble. The woman tripped along behind him, frantic while her lion tail waved behind her. "We have nothing to report to Dream. How long are we to wait before speaking with the boy directly?"

My ears perked. *Dream? Does she mean King Dream, of Aspirre?*

I followed them, suspicious, watching the man shake his head. "We mustn't act too soon, Ana," he said. "Dream's instructions were to find both of them before explaining anything."

"Yes, but," The woman had a meek voice, almost a whisper. "Perhaps the other will show himself after we tell them?"

"We wait. I do not understand what's happened with those two, but I have a feeling it is something devious, with the way they are hiding. If we confront them now, we may never know. We will wait."

The woman took a small breath, conceding. "Yes, Kurrick..."

—A passing man hurtled into me, and I stumbled to the ground. My offender had been carrying a bag of produce and wine, and before I could even blink, he rushed off as if he hadn't noticed me at all. He'd been wearing a doctor's coat, his face stricken with horror before he disappeared into the crowd, round leopard ears folded down. *What on Nirus...?*

I pushed myself up to look for the pair of lions, but they'd vanished.

What had they been discussing? Why mention Dream? They didn't look like Dreamcatchers; the man especially had looked like a warrior. But I supposed looks could be deceiving.

My stomach moaned, crumbling. Hunger forced its way to my attention again, and I gazed at the fruit vendor from before. I was closer now, only a few yards away.

I watched a young, skinny boy slink beside the vendor, shoveling a sack-full of apples without the merchant's notice. He was a dark-skinned boy, with long, feathered hair and chestnut wings sprouting from his back, a red and black scarf wrapped around his throat, his near-skeletal torso bare.

Once he'd gathered enough apples, hurried as though stocking up on emergency supplies, he flew to the roofs, disappearing with his stolen goods.

Perhaps I can sneak one, also? My stomach groaned encouragingly. *Just one.* That wouldn't hurt anyone, would it?

I started for the booth, ducking behind various shifters and flower maidens to hide. Once reaching the booth, I crouched off to the side, staying out of sight from the merchant who was busy chatting with a customer.

Very cautiously, I reached for the first apple, and the minute I snatched it down, I devoured it in a matter of seconds.

Eugh! If I wasn't so hungry, I wouldn't have touched this mush. There was barely any juice, it was only a soft, bruised, *warm* block of grits.

Though, despite the disgusting taste, my stomach still howled. I plucked another apple from the booth, finishing that one and continued with another. With each one finished, my feeding became ravenous—like every bite was a reminder of how little I've had to eat, and if I didn't gulp it down quickly enough, it would disappear. I finished six in mere moments and almost took the last bite of the seventh—

Someone snagged my wrist.

"What we got here?" a man plated in gilded armor barked. He grabbed my other wrist and twisted my arms behind my back, yanking me to my feet. I yelped as he shoved me against the booth to face the merchant. "A little thief, are ya?"

"I-I wasn't…!" I craned back and caught a glimpse of the sword strapped to my captor's belt, noticing the badge pinned to his chainmail. *Damn it all! A Rockraider.*

"Have you got the Mel to pay for all those?" The Raider pointed at the discarded apple cores scattered around me.

"I… I was just going to…" My face warmed as a flock of eyes turned to me from the crowd. I felt like a fool, being forced to bend over the booth. I was glad as Death I'd thought to wear leggings under my short-skirted gown.

"Lasnic," the Raider called to the merchant, who noticed me now. His face was anything but pleased once he spotted the apple cores at my feet. "Got yourself a pretty little thief."

The merchant's arms crossed. "Are you the one that's been snatching my apples all month? Land's Blade, I've been losing a good chunk of beads because of you."

"Want me to bring 'er in?" the Raider asked.

Death, no…! I couldn't grab my scythe if my arms were held down, and I didn't wish to *physically* hurt him with fire, if I could help it… Not only that, but using any other element besides Necrovoking may give me away. Those reports have already shown me as having death Hallows, if they learn I'm also a Pyrovoker, then a dual-Evocator will attract suspicion.

The merchant snorted approvingly. "Lock her up for a long time, yeah. Keep her away from my booth, 'n everyone else. And looks like she's been swiping from the richer districts, too. Probably thought she wouldn't get caught as a foreigner."

The merchant grasped my chin, turning my head in examination. "Either that, or she's a runaway out of money. Maybe look up her family name. See if she's got parents who can pay me back—"

Panicked, I clasped the Raider's gauntlets behind me, my Death mark gleaming from my collarbone. *Seamstress prick me, I can't be found yet!*

Orange fire exploded from my hands.

The Raider hollered in pain, his armor heating, the scent of burning skin simmering under his plate. He screamed and released me, ripping off his gauntlets—but the skin had melted and clung to the metal, peeling off like dripping cheese.

I extinguished my fire, smoke licking around my shaking fingers. "I'm sorry!" I gasped, horrified at his disfigured arms. I grew sick. "I… I'm sorry…!" I bit back tears and dashed away—

Crack!

Something struck the back of my skull, so powerful that my vision went dark, and I collapsed. I could barely hear the fading voice of the Raider above me…

Then I was drowned in silence.

22

THE REAPER'S CREED

XAVIER

Clack!

I slammed down my mug and grunted at the bartender. "Another."

The bartender cocked an eyebrow at me, trying to see under my shielding fingers that hid my heterochromic eyes, and shrugged, filling my mug with foaming ale once more.

I knocked it back in a hard glug. Foam trickled down my chin but I didn't care, *clacking* the mug on the counter again in a vicious breath, swirling the rest of my drink in a brooding grumble.

"'I am a guide of fallen souls, for those Death's taken hold','" I heard Octavius read quietly in the hazy tavern, the surrounding chatter nearly drowning him out to my left.

I flicked my gaze at him, lids narrowed into thin, suspicious slits.

Octavius held the paper to his face with one hand and absently drummed his fingers on his mug with the other. "'Not a bringer of the end, all souls I will defend… Never will I turn away if there are Seams untied; beside my Brothers I will stand, living or otherwise'…"

He groaned, flattening onto the counter. "I have to memorize this whole thing?"

Between us, Jaq wiped his spectacles with his tunic before replacing them on his nose. "Just keep readin' it every day," the viper suggested. "It's not like ya gotta commit it to memory right away. It'll take time. Why rush it?"

Octavius stared into his mug and grumbled. "I don't know. I guess I just feel way behind with this stuff, since I'm getting into it so late. I want to catch up."

Jaq grunted, rubbing his scaled chin. "Fair enough. Here, maybe it'll help if ya think of it as separate parts. There's an opening call, and an answer that follows it. Right, mates?"

Jaq twisted to look at me, but I'd stopped paying attention. I hunched over the sticky counter, hood drawn up to cover my grey hair while my arms shielded my face, hoping no one in this tavern would recognize me. Henry was in the corner of the tavern playing a game of billiards, Vendy perched on the table's ledge and glancing back at me on occasion, as if to be sure she wasn't needed.

"Mates?" Jaq prodded me with a finger and looked at my almost-finished ale, which I still swirled idly. "How many of those have ya had?"

My voice was a dismal mutter. "Four." Or was it five? I hadn't been keeping count. So long as my thoughts were muddled and distracted, it was enough.

We're harboring the son of my killer. My gaze drifted to Octavius down the counter again. For a moment, I imagined the cat's green eyes bleeding yellow. *The reason I remember nothing, the reason I'm trapped in my brother... It's because of his father. And blast it, the poor fool hasn't a damned clue.*

How was I to tell him? Should I bother? He hadn't seen his father in years, knew nothing of his crimes, of his affiliation to us...

That photograph had brought it all back. That face, those eyes... the smile had been the only difference. The memory of the cliff had bled into my dreams last night, like a festering wound that had burst, those honey eyes bright and burning in the darkness of the thrashing storm, the quarreling sea lapping under my feet...

He doesn't know. I snorted a laugh. *He doesn't know any of it.* I broke into quivering laughter, pounding the bar counter as I heaved entertained chortles.

"What?" asked Jaq, puzzled. "What's so funny?"

"I'll be the death of us all," I mused, still snickering darkly. "It's only a matter of time now. The Shepherd's sands have begun to pour, and we are but the meager grains dripping along the timeline. Dripping, dripping, dripping..." My laughs became twisted and hollow, and I held a hand to my face, snickering. "Dripping, dripping, dripping..."

"Uh, yeah... all right, mate." Jaq plucked the mug from my lax fingers. "I think ya've had enough. We still gotta look for Maveric, I need ya walking straight, got me?"

I pushed my thumbs into my lids, groaning. "I'm fine."

"Fine, huh? What day is it?"

I propped up my chin with a fist, the tavern swaying slightly. "Mm… Triniday?"

"That was yesterday. It's Catday now. But close enough." He thumped my back. "Come on, we've already paid. Let's get outta here before someone sees your drunk ass."

"You have a… Monk class…?"

"I think he said a trunk latch," Alex pondered blearily from my thoughts. The drink was affecting him in the psyche, as well. *"No, a… buck rash?"*

"What is a buck rash?"

"I'm not sure… but I guess Jaq has it."

"He has a buck rash? Jaq, really, you should get that checked…"

Jaq's laughter doubled, and the nearby patrons and bartenders spurt into guffaws as Jaq guided me off the stool, leading us out to the streets.

Bleary, I cleared my throat, focusing my thoughts on contacting our vassal. "Vendy," I said aloud, leaning on Jaq as we moved down the street. A wash of static hit my brain as I spoke. "We're relocating outside… bring Henry and come meet us."

It took a moment for her reply to sound in my thoughts. *Uh… Da'torr? Why can I hear you in my head?*

"It's something like telepathy," I explained, slurring slightly as I rubbed my eyes. "A Necrovoker and their vassal can share a communication line, while separated."

A long moment of silence came.

I sighed. "We can't read your thoughts, Vendy. You have to speak aloud."

She snorted. *Well, that's no fun.*

"Just come out here and stay close. We ought to keep together."

Right. Coming.

The static in my brain fizzled into silence as the connection line ended.

I told Jaq to stop so we could give Vendy and Henry time to meet us, and I leaned against a wall, the world tumbling dizzily. There was a festival today. Shifters strode through the town in a merry bustle, dancers and flag bearers skipping through the masses with gold ribbons that fluttered in the wind.

My gaze flicked to Octavius behind us. He was reading from that paper again, scratching his nose as he scanned the Creed's lines intently.

"You're quite set on learning that today, uh?" I asked, stumbling only once when I went to read over the cat's shoulder, leaning on him for support.

"Uh, y… yeah." Octavius inched his head away from me, looking uneasy as he shifted under my weight.

Hmm. He was acting nervous. Not surprising, though. I'd avoided him at a ten feet radius all day. Surely, he'd noticed. I admit, it hadn't been my proudest of moments, but I… needed time. Time to think, time to calm myself. Octavius was the son of my killer. What did that mean for Octavius himself…?

Fool, I chided in silence. Guilt festered, and I glanced up at the messengers circling above us. *Octavius isn't his father.*

The thought sobered me some, and I gritted my teeth.

"The easiest way to remember the creed," I explained, clearing my throat, "is by rehearsing it with someone else."

Octavius's head lifted, seeming surprised that I was involving myself in his studies. "O-oh. Really?"

"Yes, it's much easier that way." I rocked my head toward Jaq. "For instance, if I say the line: 'I'll let not actions souls once took deter me from my duty', Jaq would respond with…"

"'I will forgive old histories and never show one cruelty'," Jaq answered on cue.

"Precisely," I chuckled, my mood cheering as I continued the creed. "'I am a destined guard who has been chosen from the masses'."

"'Who only kneels and places faith within the wolf of ashes'."

"'Protect, defend, preserve and foster every life and afterlife'."

"'With this creed I will swear to conquer rotted strife'."

"'I am a knight of Death',"

"'A Reaper of Grim',"

We both spoke the last lines in unison. "'Whether this life or the next, both in life and after death'."

Octavius had been reading along with us, then folded the paper when we finished. "I'm a little confused about the 'wolf of ashes' part, though. How does that work?"

"It means we serve the Death King as his honored knights," I said, walking into the crowd while there was an opening in the traffic. "The Relicblood of Death is always an ashen wolf, no matter what shift the outside parent is."

"I know that much. I meant…" He took a separate breath, perhaps to search for the proper words. "I've never even been to Grim before. My ruler's always been King Galden. I mean, how do I switch allegiances like that? Am I going to get hanged for treason or something?"

"Good Gods, no," I said, "an apprentice is marked as serving the Death King the moment their messenger finds them. So, in that respect, you've officially been allied with the Death King for the past couple years, you were simply unaware of it. But sentimentally speaking, I suppose your allegiance changes the moment you wish it to. If your king hanged anyone for such a thing, it would be *he* who'd be tried for treason, by the Death King no less."

He flicked his eyes up at our flying messengers in thought. "So, I don't have to follow King Galden's laws anymore?"

"Er… well, you're still an Everlandish *citizen*, so some of those laws still apply to you," I said. "If you'd chosen to apprentice here on the surface, then you'd be obligated to relocate to the capital, since we're not allowed to station in the other cities here. But since you've agreed to come to Grim and train with us, you don't have to obey that particular law. Until you change citizenship, you're in a pending status and have a 'transitioning immunity' to some laws. Reapers have that privilege with all kingdoms, since we're needed in all the realms, yet we only serve one king."

His brow scrunched helplessly. "Sounds complicated."

I waved dismissively. "Best not to concern yourself. Your situation is different, regardless. You're an apprentice of the Death King's Eyes, *and* the commanding general of Grim's military. You'll have a wide variety of privileges."

Trumpets suddenly blasted to life from behind a blockade of people in the next street. *A parade?* I watched the marching shifters idly, sobering. *What was this festival?* Judging from the sheer number of people, it must have been a particularly special day for these Everlanders. There were maidens passing out lays to young girls, men holding banners and tossing around streamers… and I, apparently, didn't stand out among the widely inebriated crowd.

I stretched taller, trying to gain a better view of the parade, but lost my footing and stumbled into someone.

The man I collided with dropped his sack of raw meat and bread, and I barely caught the bottle of red wine just before it hit the ground.

"My apologies," I said, rising to hand him the bottle.

"Oh, thank you!" The stranger gave a light, embarrassed laugh and took the bottle—then stiffened after meeting my eyes. "Y-Young Howllord!" He staggered back, nearly dropping the bottle again. "Forgive me, I-I-I didn't see you there!"

His hair was a rusted yellow with black, ringed spots. His leopard ears had grown in fright, angular face layered with a yellow beard that pointed down his chin and trailed up his jaw.

I peered at him closely, my swirling vision sharpening. "Hang on. Don't I know you?"

"I-I'm quite sure that you don't!" He attempted a smile, but it came out as a wince.

I rubbed my chin, absently noting that Alex needed a shave. "I'm sure I've seen your face before… wait." I reached into my Storagebox and pulled out the photograph of Sirra-Lynn and her former master. I glanced at it, then compared it to the man in front of me. "Maveric Liste?" I asked.

The man flinched, brown eyes terrified. "I-I… er, yes…?"

I gave Jaq and Octavius a bewildered—albeit thrilled—glance, thanking Nira for my good luck. "Dr. Liste! So, you are here. We wished to ask you about Miss Sirra-Lynn Treble."

"S… Sirra-Lynn?" Maveric squeaked. "I'm sorry, High Howllord, but I d-d-don't know anyone by that name!"

I held the photograph to his pointed nose. "She's right here with you. She was your apprentice once, wasn't she?"

His head ducked and he gave a nervous laugh. "Oh, er, Sirra- Lynn…! Yes, I—er, I remember now! Ha, ha! Ha…"

I clapped my hands and got right to business. "Doctor, I'm afraid we have troubling news. Sirra-Lynn's soul is missing from Grim. We think she may have surfaced here without an escorting Reaper, and we were hoping you may have some idea where she could be?"

He shuffled back. "I-I-I'm sorry, High Howllord, but I don't know any of that—!"

Alexander switched with me and snatched the man's wrist before he could run.

"Dr. Liste." Alex's growl echoed in the psyche I now occupied. "This is important. We're looking for *his* mother." He threw his head at Octavius. "And *I'm* looking for my brother."

The doctor swallowed hard, voice quivering. "Your… y-your brother?"

"I believe you know the one." Alexander pulled him closer to speak softer. "We've heard rumors about Land's Tailors, Dr. Liste. If it exists, I want to know if my brother is there alive."

"You weren't supposed to come looking for him…! H-he…!" Maveric glanced round the open market.

"What is it?" Alex hissed, his grip tightening on Maveric's shirt collar. "Is he there?"

"We can't talk here." Maveric inched back toward the crowd again. "Not right now. Tomorrow… in the clinic off Lumber Street, eastern district. C… come at noon."

He stumbled into the mass of shifters and peered over his shoulder while disappearing behind the corner buildings.

Alexander pushed himself inside the psyche while I took control again. I stared after Maveric, then spun to Jaq and Octavius. "I think…" I laughed. "I think he knew…! He must have known I was there. I have to be alive!"

They both laughed with me, sharing the glory of our victory—

"Don't…!" a small voice cried behind. "R-run already! Run while ya can…!"

I turned, perplexed. Within the crowd, a winged child wriggled on the ground, his feathered head shoved against the stones by a Footrunner's strict hand. "Thought you could take off with stolen goods just like that, boy?" The officer snorted. "I been looking for you, little brat. Couldn't run forever, eh?"

"We gotta leave…!" the boy squealed, his chestnut wings flailing desperately. "It ain't gonna be good, it ain't!"

He scarcely looked older than six. Around his scrawny neck was a red-and-black striped scarf, and his tan shorts were too big for his boney legs. He was barebacked, ribs pushing through his thin, brown skin from his chest, his spine sharply defined.

"We gotta leave!" The starved boy kicked and screamed. "We gotta leave or we're dead! We're all dead…!"

He began sobbing. Perhaps it was the remnants of the drink, but the sounds had my teeth sharpening.

I stepped in. "Release him."

The Runner kept his focus on the boy, pushing his face to the stones. "Keep walking, buddy. This isn't your problem."

The boy blinked through his tears, craning to look at me. "Uncle…!" His wriggling intensified. "Uncle! That's my uncle, lemme go…!"

"Nice try, kid," scoffed the officer. "Maybe next… time…" The Runner finally looked at me. He found my eyes and shot to his feet. "Bloody Shel…! H-High Howllord…!"

Damn those reporters. Well, anonymity was fun while it lasted. I may as well use the authority to my advantage now. "Do you have a problem with my… nephew, officer?"

The boy, now released, ran over and clung to my leg. The Runner shook in his bronze armor. "A-ah! S-so he was with you, High Howllord…! I-I-I see you're a busy man, so I'll just… I-I'll…!"

He shoved off without another wasted syllable, leaving me with the boy, who winced at the fresh scrape on his cheek. I bent to touch his face, evoking my Hallows, fingers glowing violet as my Death mark appeared below my knuckles.

With a slow breath, I recalled the feeling of numbness; of that cottony feeling that comes with an anesthetic. Keeping the memory fresh in mind, I pushed the feeling through my fingers and transferred it over the boy's cheek.

This was part of a Necrovoker's abilities. Part of my half, at least. The soul half. Sensory-illusions could be cast onto others, so long as I'd felt the sensations myself in the past. It did, however, require the receiver to be unaware that the feeling was fake. It wasn't a physical sensation—just an illusion I gave to a person's soul. Normally, one would argue that illusions were restricted to Decepiovokers, but those Evocations were purely visual, meant for the eyes. Tactile tricks were for the soul, which was my department.

When the sensory-illusion took effect, the boy sighed in relief, his wings bowing. "Thanks Uncle."

I cocked an eyebrow at the tiny bird. "I may have played along to get him off, and you're quite welcome, but you and I both know I'm not your uncle."

He frowned at me, squinting as though he had trouble seeing my face. "Hey, where's your beard, uncle? And why d'ya look like…" He paused, something dawning in his eyes. He slapped his hands over his mouth and shied back. "Oh! S-sorry! We're not there yet…" He hit his head and muttered. "Stupid, stupid…! Forgot what year it was again…!"

Octavius and Jaq came trotting up to us, both looking at the boy with concerned expressions.

Jaq crouched over his knees to match the boy's eye level. "Ya okay, kiddo?" asked Jaq, looking him over. "What was the Runner doin' all that for, little guy?"

The child went bug-eyed at Jaq, like the viper had just held up the biggest lollipop he'd ever seen in his life.

Jaq prodded the boy's head with a finger. "Kid? You okay? He didn't hit ya too hard in the head, did he?"

The boy snapped out of his daydream and shook his head. "N-no. Ya can't be here. It's too early. And they're commin', ya gotta leave—we all gotta leave."

He stumbled into the mass. Startled, I called after him. "Wait! Who's coming?"

"Ya gotta leave now while ya can!" he hollered back at me.

Suddenly, a small crow fluttered from the sky to perch on the boy's shoulder. It hid in the shaggy veil of his long, feathered hair.

A Reaper? So young?

The young Reaper twisted back but didn't slow his pace. "They're already here! Go and get outta here, Uncle Xavier! It's too early…!"

He disappeared, leaving me slack jawed beside Jaq and Octavius.

"Uh." Octavius inched his baffled gaze to me. "Did you tell him your name?"

"No," I said.

Jaq rubbed his shoulder. "He didn't see your eyes, did he?"

"Not unless he was a walking corpse," I muttered.

"Then what the Death was that about?"

My head shook, and I could only stare after where the child had left.

"Hey, Da'torr!" Vendy called behind, and I spun to find her and Henry trotting toward us. Vendy hopped up and down, trying to see over the crowd, frowning in disappointment. "Aw, did we miss the dancers? I love the dancers!"

I shook my thoughts of that strange child, remembering the more important encounter of the day, and grinned. "You missed more than dancers, Vendy. We found Maveric Liste." My grin cracked with devilish delight. "We'll have our answers tomorrow."

23

PRISON BREAK

LILLI

Long ago with times discord, there came the Children of Relics…
My eyes slit open, a man's voice echoing in song as I came to, head throbbing. A stringed instrument plinked softly as he sang, and in a daze, I sat up.

One for each realm, they came to be the rulers thought angelic

From Land to Death, beginning and end: Land, Sky, Ocean, Dream and Death

From Land to Death, beginning and end: Land, Sky, Ocean, Dream and Death

My long, grey hair was splayed across the grimy floor, frazzled and loose, my ribbon and bell missing. My hands were covered with strange gloves. Try as I may, they wouldn't come off, my wrists bound by metal shackles that were chained to the stones at my feet.

Something rubbed against my knees as well. It felt like a thin fabric was separating them from the floor.

My breath fled when I glanced down.

I was wearing loose trousers, the ragged hems reaching my ankles. I was also in a greasy, thin-sleeved tunic that was riddled with holes and strange stains. I recognized neither of these articles.

Where are my clothes? I wondered with a disgusted shiver, the next thought making my skin crawl. *And who in Bloods changed them?*

Panicking, I reached for my ear, breathing in relief to feel that the small earcuff, if nothing else, was still secured.

Bloods, I must be more careful. I didn't know where my amulet and scythe-ornament were, but if I'd lost the earcuff, it could have been far worse.

I twisted to examine my surroundings. In the dim light of this dungeon, I saw the walls were made of stone, the place stinking of feral rat droppings and mildew. The front wall was nothing more than iron bars caging me in. There was a single, orange lamp hanging outside where the hallway waited, along with a stairway. Jewel was nowhere in sight.

They threw me in prison. Glorious.

I glared at the gloves squeezing my hands. *Dampening gloves.* They were woven with rubbery fabric, coated in the secretions of an exotic plant found in the Sky realm. My tutors had called it Yinklît Gel. The sticky substance was known to nullify any elemental Evocation.

I noticed my boots had been replaced with shoes of the same material, so using the soles of my feet to release my Hallows was out of the question as well.

I swept my gaze to the stone wall on my right. The unseen man, likely a fellow inmate, still sang and plucked his stringed instrument.

Those with all three Blessings were the kings, and queen, the Gods did bring

With crowning marks to prove their right, they served to quell the thriving strife

Didn't I know this song? I vaguely remembered the tune from my history studies… Ah! Yes, that was it: *The Ode of Hope.* According to my tutors, it was written centuries past, when the Land King was first killed. It was sung in hopes of catching the ear of the lost heir.

Long ago with Bloodlines passed, the King of Land had been our cost.

Without a king, the Land is lost, cracked and broken, torn and crossed

I shuffled to the wall and pressed an ear against the stone. *Well,* I thought, *at least I'm not alone in this prison.* Would he be keen on escaping with me? I would certainly need help, with these dampening gloves.

His song wavered on.

And though our Bloodline may be lost, he will appear to us again

One day he will return we know, the rightful throne will be obtained

From Land to Death, First and Fifth: Land, Sky, Ocean, Dream and Death

From Land to Death, First and Fifth: Land, Sky, Ocean, Dream and…

He halted.

It was silent for a time, then he chuckled. "Awake are we? I'm sorry if my song is bothering you, little Grimlette. Would you like me to stop?"

I had to take a shocked moment before answering. "How… Er… Hang on. How did you know I was from Grim if you can't see me?"

"Aside from your accent? They brought you in after me," he explained. "You were asleep at the time. There's no mistaking that youthful grey hair, not on these surface lands."

Youthful! Nira, bless this man! Finally, someone had the sense to know the difference between an old woman and a young girl. "I see," I said, then paused. "But how did you know I was awake?"

His tone was pleasant, ignoring the question. "You wanted to ask me something, Grimlette? I can't imagine why you'd press yourself against the wall like that, otherwise."

"How—?"

"Another time. What is your question?"

I shook off my confusion, making a mental note to pester him about those things later. There was a more pressing matter that needed my attention. "I had a proposal for you, if you'd accept," I explained. "I thought, perhaps, you'd be interested in… well…"

"Escaping together?" he guessed, quite on point. "Well, that depends. Why were you thrown in here?"

I blushed. "I may have eaten some apples without paying."

He clucked a laugh. "Gardener's Spade! Your excuse is pettier than mine."

"May I ask?"

"I told a Raider the Day of Revival was approaching. The true king of Land will take his throne again sooner than he thinks, don't doubt it." His tone was proud. "He wasn't too pleased to hear it."

"He… imprisoned you over a belief?"

"It's not as uncommon as you might think, Grimlette." His voice grew rugged and dismal. "It's a crime of treason to claim King Galden isn't the rightful heir… Especially on a day that celebrates his ancestor's crowning. Oh, don't look so surprised, Grimlette. It's normal here. You may want to close your mouth, by the way, there are bugs flying about."

My mouth clamped shut, bristling. *Oh, that is IT!* I'd had enough of this game. "*How* can you see me?"

His glum chuckles bounced in the dim prison, and I jumped when one of the stones slid back from the wall with a grinding crunch, leaving a square hole that let me see into the next cell.

The opening was just big enough to show the goat-horned man's head, and he smiled at me. "These cells aren't very well-made."

His skin was a deep shade of brown, and his auburn hair was dreaded with red beads—with the exception of one green bead, which was isolated on a single strand dangling by his chin.

"Since your only crime is feeding yourself," he mused. "I see no harm in helping you. Let me see your shackles."

Thankful, I lifted my hands to the hole, and the man plucked out a small, thin rod from his hair, along with a short blade that'd been hidden.

"If one plans to openly express his disliking for the king," he hummed while sticking the rod and blade into my cuffs' lock, twiddling them around. "Then one must be prepared for imprisonment on a regular basis. Can't spread the word of our Relicblood's return if I'm executed, now can I?"

My shackles popped open, and I ripped the dampening gloves off my hands. My fingers were sticky from the nullifying, Yinklît Gel residue, and I wiped them on my trousers. "Thank you… er…"

"Linolius." He gave another smile. "Or Linus, if you like. I can remove the leg shackles as well?"

I glanced down at the cuffs, shaking my head. "That won't be necessary. I have a way to deal with them, now that my hands are free. And this hole is too high for you to reach, regardless—"

Another block of stone slid out of the wall, this time near the floor. "There are three other loose stones on this wall," he said, "but they're much too high to do any good. Not to mention, I can't reach them anyway."

"How do you know where all these openings are if you can't reach them?"

"You're a perceptive one," he muttered. "Come, slide those chains over here."

I knew he was purposefully ignoring my questions, and although agitated, I conceded. I could have used my Pyrovoking to heat the chains to a brittle temperature and free myself, but I supposed his approach was simpler, and would help conserve my stamina. If I ran into any Raiders during my escape, I would want to preserve my power to fend them off.

I wouldn't want to kill them, though, Gods no… I could barely stomach the sight of that Raider's cooked arms—a disfiguring scar that he would carry for the rest of his life… *because of me.*

I grew sick, calming in an exhale. *No.* I would avoid the likes of that if I could. I'd only need to slow them down if they pursued. They didn't deserve the death penalty for carrying out their task as guards. I was the stranger here, the law breaker. That wasn't their fault.

Linus undid my shackles, which clattered to the floor. I rose to the higher hole, ripping off the dampening shoes and grimaced as I wiped at the sticky gel that coated my bare feet.

"Thank you," I said, relieved.

"But of course… Howless." There was a mocking twinge with that last word. His fingers slid thoughtfully over my old shackles, his eyes glazing while touching them. He grinned. "A bit lost, aren't we? I believe your post is down below."

I didn't like that tone. Did he know, somehow? "What do you mean?"

"Never you mind, Howless." He chuckled, as if calling me that was a joke only he understood. "I believe our escape is overdue?"

I grumbled in annoyance, rubbing my raw wrists. "I suppose… Have you a plan, then?"

"Of course. But we have to wait, first."

"Wait for what?"

With a grinding scrape, he slid the stone back in place and quickly replaced the second.

Footfalls sounded from the top of the stairwell.

"All right, street scum," a voice called from above. "The gallows have a gift for you. On your feet."

I hurried to my cell bars, peering through.

A gold-plated Raider took a ring of keys from his belt. There was another knight with him, and five bronze-plated Footrunners accompanied them. The two Raiders had swords strapped to their belts, and four Runners held spears, the last having only a Shotri holstered at his waist.

I recognized one of the Raiders. He was the knight who'd captured me. He was a thick man, heavyset at his gut with legs the size of small tree trunks. He'd taken off his gauntlets to wrap his burned wrists in bandages and gauze.

I winced at the bloodied dressings. *Nira forgive me for such sins…* I prayed the Healers could help him well enough.

He unlocked Linus's cell door, and the bars squeaked open. The second, scaled Raider jerked Linus to his feet.

I was confused when they walked out, seeing the goat-shifter was still in shackles. His chains were longer than mine had been, and he didn't have dampening gloves. I supposed he didn't have any dangerous Hallows like me, but I expected him to have taken the shackles off by now. Had he run out of time?

More importantly, I thought, frowning when Linus began chuckling to himself, *why is he laughing at such a time?*

"Wipe that smile off before I rip it off," the reptilian Raider warned as he dragged Linus out of the cell. The man had a crooked, hooked nose that leaned to one side, lips chapped and tan scales flaking in some places. "And I don't know what you're laughing at. You think being strung up to dry is funny?"

"Certainly not," Linus disagreed in mock cheer. "You, however, will be a grand source of ridicule when the heir has you beheaded for treason."

He gave a nasally laugh. "Is that right? Kheh! Kheh, heh—" He fell into a coughing fit. Once it settled, he set a hand on his armored belly. "Guess I didn't learn my lesson when your friends told me the same thing before they hung yesterday, eh?"

Linus only smiled wider, the gesture vindictive.

"Well." The scaled Raider snorted, spitting a disgusting blob of black sludge. It smelled like chewing tobacco. "You'll get your turn in a few minutes. And you can thank one of your little friends for that. He cracked, told us all about your little hideout before we put him out. Should probably pick your friends better when you're a ghost—"

Linus *jammed* his elbow into the man's side. The knight grunted in a start, releasing Linus.

Death's ghost, he's free! I clutched my cell bars, thrilled as I watched the goat swiftly sidestepped around the Raider and twirled behind him with such dexterity, his feet may as well have grown wings. His feet shifted, ready to make a dash for it, and…

Linus pulled a sleight-of-hand and drew out the scaled knight's sword from its scabbard, the steel glinting in the firelight with a long scrape. My thudding heart dulled. His grin turned wild, and with shackled hands—

Linus slit the sharp metal over the knight's throat.

Blood sputtered from the Raider's neck as he collapsed to the ground, crimson dripping from Linus's blade. Linus's eyes were stale when he stared at the fatter, stunned Raider and the five Footrunners behind him.

"Wh… what…?" I stammered, horrified. "What are you doing…?"

Linus didn't break his gaze from the other men. "Providing an escape for you, my little Grimlette."

"W-wait! Not like this—!"

The thicker Raider drew out his sword, and four Runners prepared their spears, the fifth cocking his Shotri. The fifth let loose a stream of Shockspheres at Linus. The goat crouched under the spheres, which shattered against the wall behind him and aimlessly spewed bolts of lightning, and he rushed for the Runner.

I screamed when he drove his sword into the man's stomach—puncturing through the breastplate—and shoved the Runner to the ground, pulling out his soaked weapon.

The remaining Runners thrust their spears at him, and Linus twirled between the staves, slicing without pause.

I quickly evoked my flame Hallows, my hands heating with an orange fire as I directed the flames at the iron bars caging me in. The metal warmed, rising until the rods blushed red.

"Stop!" I increased heat so the bars would melt faster. I couldn't fling the fire, for fear of hitting the other men. Linus moved too swiftly for me to aim with confidence.

Red painted the walls, bones and lances fracturing at the force of Linus' blows. Now, only the rotund Raider remained.

"Demon…!" The Raider quivered, his grip tight over his sword's hilt. The smell of urine swelled as a wet spot dripped from the man's leg onto the floor. "Rebels aren't trained like…! L-like…!"

"How does that old creed go again?" Linus sighed, stepping over the soldier's fallen comrades. "Ah, yes. 'My courage is my honor, and my honor is my strength'. You seem to have forgotten that bit, haven't you, Brother?"

The Raider inched back. "H… how do you know that? That's only taught to Raiders—"

Linus darted for him. Their swords clanged, the blood on Linus's blade flicking onto the man's startled face. He swung for Linus's head, and the goat twirled behind him and stabbed backward, plunging his blade through his foe's back while the tip pierced out his chest.

My cell bars finally met their brittle temperature and I broke open a large hole for me to climb out. I rushed for them, hands blazing with licking flames.

Linus slid his sword out of the man's chest and kicked his corpse to the floor. Then he bent over the Raider's remains to retrieve the crimson-spattered keys that'd dropped during the slaughter, calmly unlocking his shackles.

"You'd best leave before others come down, little Grimlette," he advised with an invigorated inhale through his nose, as if this dank dungeon was an open field, and the horrors at his feet were nothing more than a patch of delightful daisies. "We wouldn't want anyone thinking this mess is yours, mm?"

I stood a safe distance back, teeth barred and grown fox ears curled back. The floor was a maze of red ooze now, stray drips trailing between the cracks and seeping to my feet.

"How could you…?" My voice shook. "I could have waited until they were gone to free myself. I… I could have…"

His face sagged with exhaustion, lids heavy with dark circles. "Two of them were planning to trade you off to a whore house for a fair sum," he said, massaging his neck. "Unnamed foreigners make the best illicit products here. Harder to track."

"I… I still would have escaped by my own means."

"Oh, I don't doubt that. This way was just simpler, I thought. Much faster. You see? You're already free to walk out, and with no hassle or shameful groping."

"It doesn't matter what they would have done!" I shouted, blinking enraged tears. "They didn't deserve this! I… I charge you for breaking the First Law of Death…!" My sharpened teeth ground so hard, my gums grew sore. "Those found guilty of needless murder receive the death penalty themselves!"

"If you had the mind to burn me alive, you would have done it already," he grunted, rubbing his lids tiredly. "Don't trouble yourself. You'd be breaking the very law you seek to enforce, anyway." He cast me a sidelong glance, then grinned at my new, loathing glare. "Oh, you can't hide it from me, Grimlette. You cannot end a life before its time so frivolously."

I kept my flaming hands up while he walked past me and entered his old cell.

"I'm not a Necrofera," he went on, "so you won't harm me so long as you aren't under attack." He retrieved his stringed instrument and threw his blood-stained sword to the ground. The clatter echoed against the stone walls surrounding us.

He hummed. "Now that the men are already dead, and I pose no threat to you, I'm afraid there's no legal incentive for you to harm me. Your only duty now would be to apprehend me. But I'll not go willingly, and you'd have to kill me to convince me otherwise. Though, you can't do that, can you?"

He gave a pleasant smile, the speckled blood on his face dripping between his lips. "No, you can't yet bring yourself to commit such sacrilege. I've felt it, little one. Yours is an honorable soul. You'll not strike down a man without arms—"

"Watch me!" I swept up his discarded sword and rushed for him. He hadn't time to blink before I leapt up and kicked him to the soiled floor, pinning him with my knee, bringing the blade's tip to his chest…

I froze.

My fingers gripped the sword's hilt with shaking fingers, arms poised to drive the steel into his heart. They wouldn't move.

I saw myself, seconds into the future, the blade sinking into the soft muscle and ending it. His eyes would dim. His face would pale. The blood would seep from the wound, his breath would fade to silence.

It would have been so simple… I'd done it hundreds of time with the Necrofera, this wouldn't have been any different. *Yet why couldn't I do it…?*

"As I'd said," exhaled Linus. "It's not in you. My time has not come. And you cannot interfere with my fate, not so dismissively. It's part of your heritage. Now tell me, will you go against your instinct, little fox-wolf?"

I stiffened, the blade still aimed at his heart. "How did you know I was half wolf?"

"Hybrids are quite rare, aren't they? To have both traits of parents with different shifts, it's such an oddity… Normally, only the dominant trait is given to the offspring."

"I said how did you know?" He was toying with me, and I was long beyond aggravated. "You seem to know more than you should—about everything. Where are you getting your information?"

"Observation," he said simply, smiling. "Your ears are thin and large, like a fox, yet your claws are not prim and delicate. They are thick and strong, much like your teeth. That, along with your quick temper, is typically known to wolf shifters."

"And everything else you seem to know about me? Like where my 'post' is? We'd barely spoken in our cells, yet you act as if you know who I am. How?"

He couldn't contain his chuckling. "Come now, Grimlette. You should know the answer."

He seized my pinning knee and twisted it upward, tossing me aside like a sack of feathers. He was strong, more than I'd anticipated. No wonder those men hadn't give him much of a fight.

I was shoved against the stone wall and fumbled to regain footing, gripping the sword firmly as Linus rose to his feet.

"I'd said before that I merely observe and deduce. I did not lie."

It finally hit me. "You're a Seer," I said. "That's how you know things you shouldn't?"

"Very good," he praised. "Prophetic Hallows does come in handy at times. Though I'll admit, I'm not as talented with past and future events. What I See is mostly the present; who someone truly is, and what they seek. You, for instance, are not just any stray Howless visiting the surface on holiday. You seek a man with heterochromia. Someone has sent you after him... Who is your employer, might I ask?"

"If you don't already know, then it's not your concern."

"Oh, but it is." He retrieved his stringed instrument from the floor and began plucking out of habit, leaning against the wall casually. "You see, I seek the same man. I wish to know who my competition is."

"Why are you looking for Xavier?"

He continued plucking as he gave me a curious look. "Not only Xavier, Howless. I also seek his brother. I have reason to believe those twins have an importance—one that we, as a nation, cannot afford to lose."

My hairs stood on end. I'd heard this before, from the King of Dreams. He was the one who'd sent me here. *Find Xavier,* he'd said, *and reunite him with his brother. With one missing, there will be nothing left for us.*

What had he meant...?

I blinked, suddenly noticing what the bard was playing on his instrument. The tune was all too familiar, melancholy and lamenting.

"That song," I whispered, shock twisting my glower. "How do you know that song?"

He closed his eyes, still plucking the strings. "It was playing in your subconscious, when you had me pinned. Curious though, it felt important to you. What is so special about this Requiem?"

"That prayer holds more meaning than a monster like you deserves to know. You disgrace its birthplace with your tainted fingers."

He gave a soft hum and started up the stairs, still playing. "Fascinating. Well, I'd best be off. Oh, and you're holding that sword all wrong, Howless. Your hands are too far apart, and your positioning is poor, stance too close, and weight too far back. Perhaps you are better suited for a scythe?"

I blushed and trotted to the bottom step, calling up. "Wait!" He paused at the top, finally ceasing his music. "Yes?"

"You… you called him your Brother." My throat was tight as I lowered the sword. My voice quieted. "That Rockraider. Was he truly your Brother-in-arms?"

He gave a long, solemn exhale. "Once, perhaps. They were all traitors to the true heir, after swearing their allegiance to a false ruler. My king will return, I heed you wait and see… And he will take the throne away from this imposter. When that happens, he'll know my loyalty remains with him. Best luck to you, fox-wolf. I believe we'll be in touch."

He disappeared upstairs, leaving me alone in the cellar. Nausea churned as the smell of fresh death permeated. It took me some time before I found the courage to drop the sword and climb after him.

When I reached the upper floor, which was thankfully empty, Linus had gone. I found my belongings in a box under a desk, which had apparently been confiscated after the Raiders imprisoned me. I thanked the Gods it was all here, clothes and all. Though, I hadn't time to change here. I quickly grabbed my amulet and other possessions, shoving them into my Storagesphere.

I tied up my hair with the ribbon and bell while I hurried out, sliding my scythe-ornament into the messy bundle.

Once outside, I jumped into the bustling crowd, the festival's music still blaring as it had been earlier. It was strange, how the once energizing notes now made my chest ache. The vibrations were only a daunting reminder of its new, hollow pain.

I found an alley and hid within it, pressing my back against the brick, sliding to the ground with a heavy heart.

A twitter sounded above, and I saw my little crow was fluttering down to me. I cupped the bird in my hands. "Jewel…! I'm sorry. I made you wait so long…"

I felt like retching, the stink of fresh blood clinging to my nostrils. I may have been accustomed to death, but only *after* it was done. And I'd never been proclaimed as the reason anyone had to die.

I folded my legs to my chest. "I-I need to stay focused, Jewel. I came here to find Xavier, not get involved with a… Jewel?"

The bird had buzzed out of my hands and perked her head, as if listening. Sensing. An eerie stillness overcame the alley as I stared at her, our Bond taut and tensed.

"Jewel?" I asked again, cautious. "Please, no. Don't you dare…"

I was cut off when Jewel began to chirp sharply, her cries rising to a violent scream. She fluttered out of the alley with warning songs.

"Oh, Gods damn it all!" I groaned.

I jumped up to follow the crow while slipping out the hair ornament to ready my scythe.

Nothing for it now. If there were demons here, they weren't going to kill themselves. *I couldn't save those men from a madman.* My teeth barred, scythe materializing. *But I can still help others from the…!*

I gasped and dug in my heels, skidding to a stop.

The warmth fled from my face.

There were *hundreds* of beasts…! Fifteen or twenty, I could handle—barely—but this many? I was still weak from hunger and my stomach ached terribly. The pain was almost crippling, the apples weren't enough. My leg was still sore from the previous wound in Adrial, and the running I'd just done had only aggravated it.

My eyes trailed the approaching swarm as the townspeople caught sight of the looming creatures. Screams sounded, followed by a stampede of terrified shifters rushing past me to escape. I stood frozen, eyes glazed at the Fera crawling from the buildings.

On a different day, in my own realm, I may have stood a chance against a *fifth* this many. But if I fought this amount, I couldn't kill them all. It would only be an invitation for a quicker death than I've been expecting. If I wanted to survive until my proper execution date, I had to run.

And so I did.

24

RALLY THE REAPERS

XAVIER

In the midst of the festival, our black birds began crying, their screeches panicked.

"To ar-ms!" Mal cawed. "Ar-ms!"

"B-ad!" croaked Shade alongside him. "B-ad! B-ad! B-ad!"

Under their ceaseless hollering, a haunting silence fell over the crowd. Then a quiet swell of noise rose from the distance. It was a soft chatter at first, but as we listened, the screams ripped clear and bloodied.

Sirens blared to life, so loud I had to block my grown wolf ears, the screams worsening. We had to brace ourselves from the people shoving past us.

Then we saw the cause.

"Nira help us," I whispered.

A swarm of Fera slithered into the streets, clambering over the buildings and crawling down the walls like a hive of squirming insects. Their bones cracked and popped as they marched, those in the back hurrying to keep pace with the frontline, as if they'd made some disorganized formation. It was a parade of death.

Though, oddly, they stayed within a single street, flooding through like a river confined in a canal. Just as quickly as they flowed in, they vanished behind the buildings one street down from us.

"Death!" Jaq hurried to unwind the chain around his wrist, preparing his scythe. "Again?!"

"Of course again!" I yelled over the blaring sirens, twisting to Henry. "Henry, armor!"

"On it!" Henry had already thrown open his dufflebag and yanked out our armor sets, tossing them to each of us. "Get on what you can, we don't have time for all the pieces!"

I threw on my chainmail, then tugged on my breastplate and already-attached shoulderguards, the weight sinking over my limbs as I slipped on the gauntlets next. Henry tossed us visor-less helms, and I slid mine on, nodding to Octavius—whom I saw had already strapped the holsters of his throwing-scythes on his belt and legs.

"Get somewhere high and cover us as much as you're able," I told Octavius.

"R-right!" He veered off and snagged a ladder bolted to the side of a building, climbing up.

I then plucked the two scythe-spheres from my neck-chain, arming myself. Vendy and Henry had donned their own brass armor and equipped themselves with longswords—and Vendy's Spiritcrystal blade.

I nodded to them. "Henry, with Jaq. Vendy, with me. If you're killed, Alex will have to resurrect you again, so stay close."

Vendy pounded her breastplate with a determined fist. "You got it!"

Teams assigned, we darted forward—

CROOOOOHHHHCH…!

The earsplitting sound of crunching boulders made us skid to a stop.

"What the Death was that?" Jaq asked.

A second roar erupted, and the ground shook. The pavement cracked under our feet.

CROOOOOOHHHHCH…! That sound came again, like rocks scraping and clattering down a mountain. An enormous shadow cast over us. Our eyes splintered upward.

A colossal beast was breaking its way between the buildings, five stories tall, scales made of rock, joints grinding like teeth gnawing on brick. And it wasn't alone. Three more of these walking mountains stormed into the marketplace, crashing into buildings.

Vendy staggered at my side, lowering her sword in shock. "Stonedragons?!"

"Now?!" Henry looked dumbfounded. "They're supposed to be in hibernation until winter!"

"Welp," Jaq said with a swallow. "They're awake now."

"We can't fight dragons!" I shouted, and almost heaved up bile when a cluster of people were crushed by the dragon's boulder-like feet, bones and organs sloshing back to the ground when its leg lifted. I glanced at Vendy uncertainly. "Can we?"

A roar sounded from one of the Stonedragons, and a dark shadow engulfed her and me. Panicking, we skidded to either side of the shadow.

SMASH!

The dragon's foot fractured the ground where we'd been standing.

"Where did these damned dragons come from?!" Jaq hollered from some distance away, he and Henry hacking away at the dragon's foot in vain.

"Void if I know!" I called over the noise, panting as the four of us sprinted away.

"They should be hibernating!" Vendy yelled, hustling at my side, our heavy armor clattering. "We don't have the right weapons for dragons!"

"Or experience!" I panted.

Jaq pointed forward with his curved blade. "What about them?"

A squad of gold plated Rockraiders barreled toward us, their swords drawn and visors lowered.

The Land Knights charged for the dragon. Their heavy blades clanged against the beast's rocky hide. Some managed to spear their swords between the scales, and the dragon let out an echoing screech as the bits were torn from its skin, leaving bloody lesions.

"Ah, right, good," I exhaled sharply. "They'll handle those things. Come, let's do our part and exterminate the Fera."

Jaq grimaced. "Ya mean *try* to?"

"Either way!" Vendy groaned and sped ahead. "Come on already!"

"Vendy!" I called, catching up to her. "Remember what I said about staying close!"

She idly cocked her sword over a shoulder as she ran, her rabbit ears folding from under her helm, and gave a snort. "Yeah, yeah. If I get ripped open, *Da'torr* Alex has to resurrect me again. Hey, but what happens to my soul if I *do* die again? Will I slip out like last time?"

"Not if I feed more Hallows into your temporary Seam," I said, realizing that was probably a good idea, and shoved my violet-glowing hand at her chest. I was wearing gauntlets, so the purple lights were hazy and jagged, but the Hallows seeped through the fabric well enough. I poured the smoky energy into Vendy's chest, the lights seeping under her breastplate from the neck, and I felt a wave of satisfying static as I reinforced her temporary NecroSeam with an added strength. "There," I said, puffing. "That will keep your soul secure, even if your vessel expires."

She grinned. "Great! You know, I could get used to this 'being dead' gig."

I gave a grimacing nod to the side. "I suppose you haven't much choice, have you?"

Jaq and Henry ran at the other side of the street, keeping pace with us, until the demons came within sight again.

Lucrine and Cilia are definitely leading a horde this large. My gaze whipped about, spying all the victims scattered on the road. They were dead, certainly, but their chests were left unmolested. No ribs were cracked open, nor even scratched, by the look of it. *Are they ignoring the souls? Instead of eating them?* In Nulani, all but Vendy had been devoured within seconds. Why change their behavior now?

The road ended at a corner street. The Fera were piling at the bend… then, they stopped.

What in Nirus?

Vendy sped ahead of me, veering to the side to jump atop a stack of wooden crates. Her long braid wavered behind her as she leapt over the demon's heads and disappeared within the eerily-still mass.

"Damn it, Vendy!" I followed her path and jumped atop the stack of crates, leaping over the horde and landing in a crouch within the eye of the mass. "Do I have to give you a direct command to stay the Death *beside us*—?"

I froze, staggering. Vendy and I weren't alone in the eye.

A Grimish girl was backed against a window, surrounded by the horde with Vendy and me. The Grimlette's eyes flicked to my face—and she stiffened.

I stayed crouched in the center with Vendy, confused, all of us staring at one another.

The Grimlette's long hair was a light shade of charcoal, the strands twirling in messy curls that wavered in the wind like silken ribbons. Her loose tunic and long trousers were tattered and splotched with grease, the dark brown color contrasting her Grim-pale skin.

Fastened in her grip was a staved scythe, and beside her flew a black bird the size of a canary, fluttering in a blur at her side.

Another Reaper? My brow knitted desperately, the Grimlette matching my dumbfounded look. *Here?*

My gaze darted to the crowding Fera, which hadn't moved. They hissed and snarled, but kept their distance, and Vendy circled me protectively, her Crystal sword raised at the ready by her ear. *Are they targeting this Reaper?*

I twisted to the Grimlette, my wolf ears curled. "Do you have backup here?" I asked.

"I… I suppose if you only count yourselves," she said, sounding both relieved and awe stricken. "Bloods be good, is it really…?"

"H-hey!" Jaq hollered from behind the cluster, his head bobbing up and down beside Henry. "Why'd they stop?"

My eyes swept the roofs to check the buildings, something catching my eye. My lids narrowed at a distant figure watching us from a balcony. It was the horse-shifter from Nulani.

"Lucrine…" I growled, gaze inching to the Grimlette behind me. "Hold your guard. There is a Sentient up there. I have a feeling he's here for you."

Her teeth sharpened. "I Bloody knew it…!"

"What does he want with you?"

"*That*, I don't know. This is the first time he's shown himself."

I craned to look at Lucrine again. The Sentient shook his head and walked through his balcony's doorway—

The Fera shrieked and charged.

Vendy skidded in front of me and evoked her rock Hallows, the ground before us stretching into deadly spikes and spearing the first line of beasts who came for us. She sprinted in a wide perimeter around the Grimlette and myself, forming a circle with those ground-spikes that were aimed away from us like a barrier.

Though, it only served to slow the creatures, unable to kill them or cause permanent damage. The beasts crawled over Vendy's barrier and skittered inside screeching.

"Vendy, try and trap them!" I called.

"On it!" She yelled, slicing into a Fera with her crystal sword, then fell back and used her Terravoking to stretch her spikes into domed cages around the beasts, ensnaring as many as she could.

A winged beast spiraled toward me, and I thrust my blade at its head. But something suddenly shot through its chest. The creature dropped with an agonized screech and shriveled in place as the black glop disappeared from the corpse.

A glowing, throwing-scythe was sticking out of its back, having been shot through its heart from the front. I looked up at the roofs, finding Octavius waving down to me. I gave him an appreciative nod, then remembered we had a new comrade to assist.

Where has the Grimlette gone?

I searched the chaos frantically, but the sludge-infested beasts were too thick to see even Jaq, and *he* was the tallest of us.

Then I heard the Grimlette grunt to my right. I spun on my heels in time to see her wheel her scythe round, slicing off a cluster of Fera heads in one swift draw. She reaped their Seams in a matter of twirling seconds, her arms crossing and dipping, shifting and bowing in a rhythmic dance.

My step faltered. There was something familiar about that style of reaping. It was delicate, yet powerful and precise as trails of black blood circled her.

"*When I hold a scythe,*" a young girl's voice echoed in my memory. "*I feel like I can do anything. My father swears when I first held one, I danced with it, as if I ought to have been born with it in my grasp…*"

My stare blanked at the Grimlette. *Do I… know her?*

She took a dazed moment to rest and leaned on her scythe. She was limping, clutching her leg—

Skririririii!

A glopping creature pounced for her. She jerked her staff up to block, but lost her footing, favoring one side. She collapsed under the demon, wheezing under its weight, arms quivering to keep her scythe, and the demon, above her.

She ripped a determined growl. "I'm so… Bloody tired of… you bastards…!"

Her grasp slipped, and her arms gave way.

"No!" My legs burst forward.

I thrust my blades into the demon's back, tearing down its spine and kicked it off her. "Are you all right?!" I shouted, perhaps louder than necessary. Patience had left me. I knew her. I *Bloody knew her.*

She gawked at me, as though my face had grown a bizarre, alien head.

I yanked her up by the arm. "Are you hurt?"

Sorrowed Death, she was shorter than even Vendy. She couldn't have been more than five feet tall, my neck had to crane drastically low to see her stunned face. Yet, she didn't seem as young as my teenaged vassal. While Vendy was tall for her age, this Grimlette was short for hers.

Exhaustion leaked from her breath, her tattered clothes and tangled hair amplifying her drained visage. What in Bloods had she been through? How long had she been fighting these things?

"Vendy," I said to my vassal. "Guard the Grimlette. She's exhausted and she'll be as good as dead if she loses focus in the middle of this—"

A beast drove its claws into my arm, digging deep into an open space in my armor. I gave a hard grunt at the pain, the cuts seeping with blood.

"*Da'torr!*" Vendy bolted for me—

I staggered backward and tripped over a littered corpse, stumbling to my back. I lost my scythes, the weapons clattering and skidding away as the demon shrieked for me.

Then Vendy's golden Hallows glittered over the ground in front of me, and she had the stones stretch into a long spike that skewered the beast through the chest. The demon was trapped in the spire, wriggling uselessly in the air.

Vendy sprinted over and helped me to my feet, panting as she had the ground stretch into another spiked wall around us and the Grimlette.

"That's far enough, fellas," a new voice barked from within the horde.

Lucrine appeared, his arms spread and waving the creatures away like a shepherd directing livestock. I hurried to pick up my scythes, touching backs with Vendy, the Grimlette gripping her staved scythe furiously and joining us in a tight triangular formation.

"Party's over," Lucrine announced to the grudgingly retreating horde. "Go back to your nest! All of ya! This ain't your fight, got that? Bloody mongrels." Lucrine twisted to us, his white pupils lackadaisical. "Sorry about them. Slight miscommunication on our part. We got it fixed right, though, so no worries."

"Stay back!" I shouted. "Draw any closer and we'll send you straight to the Void!"

Lucrine's large nose scrunched. Then he laughed. "Kid, you couldn't scratch an *itch* for me. Why don't ya wait a few years before messing with the big leagues, yeah?" He turned away and started after the horde he'd dismissed.

"You won't live long enough to see that day, demon," the girl spat behind me. She stepped forward, cocking her scythe. "If you're here to kill me, I suggest you finish me off now. Else be finished yourself!" She sprinted for Lucrine, vaulting over Vendy's spiked wall. "I will not be stalked by any more of your beasts…!"

Lucrine sighed and absently bent his neck, evading the Grimlette's swing. He grabbed her staff and kicked her stomach. The girl was sent flying back. She crashed against the brick buildings and collapsed to the ground, coughing.

Vendy and I dashed between them and took a guarded stance. "What do you want with her?" I demanded.

Lucrine paused. "Her? Bloods, you have no idea." Lucrine chuckled and shook his head. "Really, though, I have to go. Cilia's not going to be in a cheery mood if I don't leave already."

"Then she'll have to be disappointed." I bounded for him, knowing the Grimlette had been right: if we let him retreat now, these attacks would never end.

Lucrine hopped away from my first strike, and I swung again, barely missing his horse ear. He ducked behind me and *cracked* his elbow against my spine, grabbing me by the hair and shoved me to the ground. My cheek scrapped the warm street, and Lucrine gave a disgruntled sigh as he pushed my head down with a foot.

"Look kid," he said, "I like your guts, but I've been ordered to keep ya alive for now. We can play later, all right—?"

"Get off him!" Vendy snarled and leapt for the Sentient, plunging her sword into the demon's shoulder—

He shoved her off, plucking her sword out and *rammed* the blade through Vendy's throat.

Vendy sputtered, lips and throat dripping with blood, and she collapsed beside me.

"Dumb little insects," Lucrine spat above me, ripping Vendy's sword out of her neck and tossing it aside with a clatter. Then the pressure disappeared from my temple. "We'll catch ya later."

I pushed up, catching the last of him and his grotesque soldiers scattering away.

"Get… get back here!" I wheezed, my spine and head throbbing. I rolled to my stomach, looking at Vendy's blood-soaked corpse. "Bloody Death… Alex?"

Alex switched with me, and I watched from the psyche as he declined to lift off his stomach, panting, and touched a violet-glowing hand over Vendy's reddened breastplate. Her neck wound healed, and she soon gasped awake. "Land!" She jolted upright. "That Bloody *hurt.*"

"So much for… getting used to this 'dead gig', eh?" Alex puffed, pushing to his feet. He helped Vendy up next. "Now, where did that Grimlette go?"

SMASH!

A boulder-like dragon's foot crushed the building in front of us, shaking the ground. Alex fumbled back and cursed, watching the Stonedragon smash its way toward us. "Gods damn it!"

Coughing sounded behind us, and Alex found the Grimlette laying on a pile of stone rubble. He sprinted to her, hoisting her up and dragged her away from the colossus, its enormous feet erupting behind.

"The… the demon…" The Grimlette hacked up dust and debris, spit dripping from her chin as she limped behind us. "Where…?"

"He's gone." Alex shoved her down to avoid the dragon's swinging tail, then pulled her aside. "We have other matters to tend to at the moment!"

The three hurried around the dragon as it clambered after us, breaking the street in its wake. Vendy was forced to sprint on its other side, trying like Death not to be crushed under its steps.

"There must be a way to stop that thing," I said from the psyche.

"Well," Alex panted. "I'm open to ideas."

The Grimlette beside us gave a skeptical breath. "You expect me to think of something?"

"Not you," Alex muttered.

We spotted Jaq and Henry running toward us, hollering.

"Mates!" the viper called when we caught up with them. Octavius had hopped down from the roofs to join the two as well, and we all ran from the destructive dragon.

Jaq glanced at the new Grimlette. "Who're you?"

Alex answered for her. "A Sister Reaper. Run now, ask later."

Henry panted. "Where'd the demons go?"

"They're gone—don't ask why. Though, we're currently taking ideas on how to kill *that* thing if you're in a contributing mood."

Jaq pointed ahead with his scythe, drawing attention to the carcass of a *dead* Stonedragon on the adjacent street. "Can you resurrect that thing and make it fight the other one?"

The Grimlette sounded exasperated behind us. "That giant? I'm only one person! And I'm exhausted enough as it is!"

That made Alex snap back to her. I only now noticed the Death mark below her collarbone. *Another Necrovoker.*

"*You* may be too exhausted," Alex said. "But I'm not."

From my window, I watched him put away his scythes and he leapt onto the enormous carcass of the dragon, pressing his hands against its exposed underbelly. His birthmark of black diamonds brightened and changed into a white Death mark as he evoked his Hallows, grunting as the magic poured into the beast's skin.

The creature shuddered under him.

He slid down when it rose, its blood sloshing as Alex dragged his hands— and his new puppet—toward the living dragon chasing us.

The resurrected beast complied without protest, sluggishly clashing with the other dragon. Its horned head slammed against the enemy's side, and it crashed into a nearby building.

Alex winced on impact.

"Death." He watched the beasts engage in clumsy combat, more build-ings crumbling. "We don't want to cause more destruction... There has to be another way. My Hallows will only hold something that large for so long without a direct casting."

"Woa-hoh!" Vendy cried excitedly as she hopped to our side, watching the dueling dragons with giggling delight. "That was so cool, *Da'torr*! You resurrected that huge thing?"

Alex shrugged. "I may not have studied dragon anatomy, but its bones and organs were already in place. It wasn't as difficult as you may think. At least, not for me."

"*Show off,*" I snorted from the psyche.

The Grimlette stared at Alex in shock, blinking like a feral guppy. "How did you do that?"

Alex gave her an odd look. "I believe you saw how."

"But you can't... hang on. What happened to your eyes?"

Alex stiffened, realizing she could see the difference between our het-erochromia. He turned away to let me take control again, and when I was outside, I addressed her again. "Pardon? What about my eyes?"

Her features wrenched in disbelief, clearly registering that my eyes had returned to normal. Confused, she clutched her head. Perhaps she assumed she'd sustained an injury during battle and had simply imagined our 'chang-ing eyes'. *Good.* We could use that excuse later.

I brushed past her, watching the battling dragons intently. I noticed a small bare spot on the living dragon's belly, the scales already pried off. The Rockraiders must have tried to kill it and failed, many lances and swords still stuck in the beast's ribs. Our scythes wouldn't be long enough to reach the thing's heart, we'd need one of those lances.

"Vendy, with me," I told our vassal, hurrying to the beasts with the rabbit, my eyes fixed on one lance sticking out of the creature's foot. "How is your aim?"

Vendy's nose scrunched. "Aim?"

"There's a bare spot on the dragon's underbelly. If you can use your Terravoking to throw one of those lances at that spot, it may be enough to strike its heart."

Vendy squinted at the dragon to look. "What spot? You mean that *tiny speck?*"

"That's the one."

"*Da'torr*, I'm not a markswoman. Every time I've tried throwing any kind of lance, it just goes flat and smacks the target with the staff—"

"Then perhaps I can assist?" The Grimlette suddenly piped from my other side. *When in Void had she started following us?*

The resurrected dragon was abruptly knocked back by the living beast, and all of us scattered away from its fumbled step. We were finally close enough to the opposing dragon, and I leaped over a pile of rubble, then wrenched the lance out of the thing's foot.

I glanced at the Grimlette, cocking an eyebrow at her. "You think you can hit that spot?"

"I've trained with every staved weapon there is," she said, pulling back her long, grey strands and tightening her hair-ribbon to keep them in place.

"Better qualified than I," I agreed, then tossed her the staff. "Aim surely."

She twirled the lance under an arm, nodded, then slid under the beast and cocked the weapon back, preparing to strike.

But she was thrown down when our undead-dragon slammed to the ground, causing a powerful tremor. Alexander's Hallows had run out, and the beast was dead once more. The living dragon trumpeted in triumph, raising its front legs and throwing them down, ready to crunch the Grimlette beneath.

I dove for her, clumsily grabbing her arm, and skidded both of us away as the dragon's foot landed behind us.

"Might I—*khmm! Khmm!*—offer some advice?" I coughed up dust as we pushed upright. "Perhaps you ought to try *not* being crushed on this next try?"

"I'll consider it," she muttered, grabbing the lance again and running back under the dragon. Vendy and I followed her, ready to grab her in case the dragon tried to step on her again.

I saw that Octavius had found a lance of his own and drove it into the dragon's front foot. He clung to the staff for dear life, yelling each time he was lifted off the ground and brought back down, lifted up, and brought down.

Jaq had caught the creature by its tail with his chain scythe, but it was proving useless. The dragon was too heavy for him to slow. Henry wildly hacked at the thing's toes with his broadsword, the blade clanging noisily over the dragon's rocky hide.

The Grimlette dashed with a nimble flourish of dodging steps under the dragon, and as she vaulted herself upward with the staff's dull end, she thrust the lance into the dragon's bare spot, her aim deadly sure.

Though, as impressive as it had been, the lance still didn't sink in very deep. She pushed with all her might, fox ears curling, but the spear wouldn't budge any deeper.

"It's stuck…!" she grunted. "The skin's too thick!"

She yelped when the beast thrashed about, careening around the corner street. She let go of the lance and we fell behind, dodging its feet frantically—

The beast suddenly screamed to a stop.

The ground itself had cracked apart and burst upward, stretching into two, towering sharp spikes that glowed with a golden light, and *stabbed* into the dragon's right foot, keeping it trapped. Similar spikes burst into its other feet, and two barely missed Octavius's head.

"Vendy?" I panted, looking at our vassal in question and pointing at the enormous spikes. They had been far larger than I'd seen Vendy produce before. "Was that your doing?"

Vendy shook her head, equally confused. "Uh, no. Uncle? Was that you?"

"Not mine!" Henry called from the back of the dragon, the Blacksmith ducking under the beast's swishing tail.

Where had that come from? I searched the street for oddities. Then I caught a glimpse of a blond, lion tailed man staring at us from an alleyway. *That same Terravoker from Nulani? What is HE doing here?*

With the dragon's feet skewered by the spikes, it shrieked and writhed, the thick spires cracking and chipping.

"Vendy!" I yelled to the teen. "The lance is in place!"

Vendy nodded and evoked her golden Hallows, heaving her glowing hands upward in a vicious *thrust*. The metal spearhead of the lance gleamed with the same golden light, and it drove into the beast's heart at Vendy's command.

The beast wailed in pain, swaying limp, and crashed against a building while the Sister and I ran to safety. Jaq, Henry and Octavius sprinted to our side to watch the giant fall, giving a final grumble before its eyes glazed, and became still.

"Yes!" Vendy punched the air, hopping in excited circles. "We did it, we did it, we did it!"

"Holy Bloods," I panted in shock. "We… actually *did*."

"It looks like that was the last one, too," Jaq noted, glancing around. "I don't hear any more of them."

"That was too close." Octavius let out a relieved breath, patting his chest.

Henry grunted and sheathed his sword. "I don't think we'll be that lucky next time."

I grimaced. "Let's hope there isn't a next—*mmng…!*"

My pained groan tried to escape, but I sucked on my teeth to keep from screaming. The bleeding wound on my left arm swelled, the cuts burning, pressure building like someone trying to pry their boney fingers under the skin. The numbness of adrenaline had apparently faded, and the pain simmered there all at once. "Damned demons…"

The Grimlette gave a concerned frown, her fox ears still grown and folded. "You're hurt?" she asked. Dread contorted her face with small creases. The look was… familiar.

Nostalgia hit again, like a tiny leak spewing from a cracked dam. *How do I know her?*

Alex cleared his throat from my thoughts, and I blinked. "Hmm?—oh, er, sorry?"

"You have cuts on your arm," the Grimlette said, hesitant to reach a hand to the slits.

"I'll be fi…*nngh…!*" I'd rolled back the shoulder, but recoiled when the cuts swelled again. I clutched my arm. It wasn't debilitating, but Death did it sting.

The Grimlette snagged my left hand. "Clearly you aren't fine. Death, they're deep… You'll need a Healer. Though, I have a tonic that may help as well."

I felt the blood pour down my arm and drip over the back of my gauntlet—which she removed curiously. She lifted my newly bare fingers closer to her face, brushing her thumbs over my skin to wipe away the blood covering my Evocator's mark of black diamonds.

Her eyes went wide, and a smile stretched her lips. "Nira, it *is* you…"

A scuffle of feet echoed through the street. A troupe of armored Raiders came to examine the wreckage, looking at the corpses and yelling commands for the Runners to search for survivors.

The Grimlette flinched at the sight of the Raiders. She cursed, shoving past me and fleeing.

"W-wait…!" I called after her, but she'd already wheeled round a corner and disappeared.

"What the Death was that about?" Jaq questioned.

Octavius scratched his head. "Weird. Who was she, anyway?"

"I'm not sure…" I admitted, dismayed. "But Lucrine was after her. And it sounds as though Cilia's come with him. We must learn what they wanted with her."

"Too late for that, mate." Jaq spat excess venom at the ground. "She's already gone. How're we gonna find her again?"

Lindel was a bigger city than the last two we'd visited. It could take days to find her again if she was a fast runner and a good hider. But why would she run?

I glanced back at the Stonedragon we'd killed. Its feet were still trapped in those spikes that had jutted out of the ground.

And that Terravoker from Nulani was here also, helping us. Where had *he* gone? And what was he doing here at all?

Priorities. Aside from my stinging shoulder wound—for which I quickly sought an on-duty Healer to seal—there were many bodies lying dead on the streets. But there were also wounded survivors. Unlike Nulani, *all* of these souls seemed to still be tied to their bodies, not a single chest disturbed. *Why are the Fera acting so strangely?*

I shook away the question, joining the Footrunners and Rockraiders in searching for those still alive, helping to cart them to the Healing clinic as quickly as possible.

25

A DEMON'S MEMORY

MACARIUS

Venom leaked from my fangs, the bitter taste pooling over my slitted tongue.

I scowled at Cilia, my back against the moldy wall of this flat we'd procured last night. The place wreaked of death and mildew, the previous owners' blood crusted on the table in the next room and attracting flies. It smelled worse today than it had yesterday, somehow. I hoped to Gods Cilia wouldn't stay here long.

My scaled fingers drummed irritably over my folded arms, awaiting a much-owed explanation of why, for Iri's sake, three entire districts of Lindel had been destroyed by Stonedragons.

Stonedragons, of all things! Never mind that Cilia's Necrofera had slaughtered citizens without my allowance. That had been far less unexpected than rock-hided reptiles barging in.

How in the five realms could such a mistake have festered? Venom flooded faster, despite my long fangs being folded to the roof of my mouth. *I expect Cilia to give the mongrel responsible a fitting punishment.*

Lucrine leaned against the wall beside Cilia, smirking in amusement at the callous sneer she was casting at our third Sentient.

Her subordinate knelt before her, cowering in the darkened room of the small home we hid within.

"What are you doing here, you worthless idiot?" Cilia's grey cat ears grew, glaring at her rookie soldier. "I recall ordering you to collect others on the *opposite* coast. Lindel is not the opposite coast. It's not a coast at all."

"I-I'm sorry, Mistress." The underling's face was pressed to the floor. "I was only doing as ordered. G-gathering any stray Reapers. I was following the girl, I didn't know she would come here."

"Then why is she yet alive? She's a blasted apprentice, not a seasoned knight. It ought to be as tedious as picking tulips."

"I thought the same at first, Mistress..." He hesitated. "But she is more skilled than she seems. Our small numbers weren't enough. But I, I'd gathered more soldiers this time—"

"You could have killed the wolf boy." She yanked the underling's feathered hair, lifting his face to hers. "Macarius wants him alive for now, and you almost cost us any chance we had at finding his brother."

"I-I'm sorry, Mistress!" His voice shook. "But I-I-I collected others for you! Much more than before! And one of them had an Evocator's mark, he'll be one of us in another three days...!"

Her brow raised. "Oh? Well, that changes things. Where is this Evocator?"

The underling pointed a shivering finger to the other room.

Cilia released him, his head *thunking* to the floorboards, and she rose to inspect the room. Curious myself, I craned to peer inside as Cilia pushed open the door, the hinges groaning slowly.

A corpse lay there, bleeding on the floor, flies scuttling over the victim's hollow face. *Ah.* So that's why the stink was so repugnant today.

"A Land mark, is it?" Cilia hummed, noting the golden sword of petal-like diamonds on the man's shoulder. "I suppose that could be useful, if he is a Terravoker... Well done, newborn. It seems your little slip-up was of some use after all."

Lucrine gave a disappointed groan from the wall. "What? So he's suddenly off the hook now?" He pushed off. "Come on, give him some kind of incentive to follow orders. How's he going to learn to respect ya if he keeps disobeying ya, Cili?"

She shot Lucrine a vexed glare. "I believe I asked you to cease your spewing of that irritating pet name? Perhaps it is you who is in need of a lesson in respecting your superiors?"

"Aw, come on." He folded his arms behind his head and grinned, horse ears twitching. "You and me? We're not like these Bloody newborns. We got brains, we got power, and best of all, we got our charmingly good looks left." He made an ostentatious gesture to himself and then to Cilia. "That gives us more things in common than... well, anyone else."

I chuckled, amused. "Does it now?"

Lucrine flicked me a piqued look. "What's so funny, Clean One?" During my time with Cilia, I learned that 'Clean One' was how they referred to the living shifters.

"I'm afraid I must disagree, Lucrine." I hid my hands within my deep maroon cloak. "Currently, I am the only one in this room who shares anything in common with your queen—"

Lucrine squeezed my throat with hoof-textured fingers and *slammed* me to the floor, pinning me by the neck. My skull swelled painfully, and I had a moment of panic when my spectacles clattered to the floorboards, the blur of his fist hovering at my nose.

"Ya got some nerve, Clean One…!" he growled, white pupils burning bright. "Let's get one thing straight! You're a twig under my hoof, got it? A little, tiny, *puny* ant who wandered into the wrong hive and thinks he can play with the birds."

He didn't lift his hand from my chest, but he sighed, his tone pensive now. "Maybe I should have done ya a favor and squished ya the second your scaled foot stepped into my nest? You've been an annoying little thing. I wonder if I should just get it over with now, and save both of us time—"

Cilia seized *his* throat. Lucrine gasped as her claws dug into his neck.

"Lucrine." She lifted him with a single arm and pinned him to the wall, holding him high. The horse squirmed frantically, but she was far stronger than he.

Fool, Macar, I thought, retrieving my spectacles and calming my pulse. *I should have prepared a phantom copy. I've been careless… And around demons, carelessness could very clearly be my end.*

Cilia's hand wavered with smoke, and Lucrine screamed in pain as she evoked her fire Hallows, burning his throat. "I thought I'd made myself clear that no one was to touch Macarius?" she rumbled.

Lucrine shrieked as her fire burst hotter. The smell of burnt flesh permeated, and Lucrine's skin flickered with black sludge, the tendrils squirming like thin worms from his pores.

Cilia's gaze staled, her tone dull and placid. "You believe we are alike, you and I? You think us equals?" she chuckled. "Poor, little Lucrine. Such hubris. You think yourself a match against an Ancient?"

Lucrine choked, his throat burning to a crisp as black liquid fizzled across his now trembling limbs.

"You've been in far more danger than you expected, little one," Cilia cooed. "I hate to crush your fragile bubble of misplaced confidence, but we are not equals."

He could only scream and whimper.

A patronizing smile rolled over her lips. "Piteous. It's almost not even fun. It certainly isn't fair; a cat playing with a roach. Disgusting… but hardly threatening."

She dismissed her Hallows, the fire extinguished. Cilia released his throat and the horse flopped to the floor, wheezing as he waited for his burnt neck to heal itself with black, slithering syrup. Grotesque…

"Remember this, Lucrine," she said, her back to him. "To defy me is to sentence your death. Consider this a royal decree: Macarius is under my protection. Those who so much as glance his way will have their Seam torn to shreds, by my own claws."

My scaled lips stretched into a smile. "My thanks… Queen Cilia." The title spurred entertained chuckles from me. *Cilia, a queen of demons. To think, a whore in life, and royalty in death.*

I clapped my hands, still chuckling, and produced a large, mirrored sphere from the Storagebox strapped to my belt. "I should think such obedience is worthy of another reward."

Cilia's gaze snapped to the sphere, staring hungrily at her bulbous reflection.

"Lucrine," she hissed. "Newborn. *Leave us.*"

Her last command crackled like fire, so hot that Lucrine and the third Sentient sprang to their feet at once and fumbled out, slamming the door behind them.

"That is a curious trick," I mused, striding to Cilia. "What I wouldn't give to have such power…" I inspected her with a considering hum. "It's amazing, what's become of you. You were always a strong soul when you were alive, but never like this. Death has treated you well."

Cilia waited in silence as I circled her. I slid open the lid of the spherical, hollow mirror, where a cluster of wispy lights shone in the dim room. "Now let's see here… which memory would you fancy this time?"

Cilia rasped a whisper. "All of them."

"Of course, of course… However, such an order is too dangerous, I'm afraid. One memory at a time is safest, else you'll find yourself in an eternal sleep. And yours is such a sad story…"

"Then…" She hesitated, then held her chin high. "If only one memory, I wish to know who the Voice is."

I paused my pacing and frowned. "Voice?"

"Yes," she said, "I wish to put a face to his voice." Her eyes flicked away, tone draining hollow. "Before I… became this way, there was a voice, in the darkness… It called me. And it calls even still…"

A voice, calling her? My lids narrowed, anger simmering.

"I wish to know who it was," she said. "If I only had a name, or a face, even…"

It was odd to see her so desperate. So vulnerable. The new demon queen I'd grown accustomed to was hardly one to show weakness. The 'voice' must have stirred her terribly.

This will not do.

I barred my teeth, venom leaking from my fangs yet again. She oughtn't have *any* memory of him left. How had I missed this one? How many more may yet be out there? *The Shepherd see that those are eaten by the Golems swiftly.*

"That…" I calmed with a slow inhale. "Will be for another time."

I stopped behind her and wrapped my scaled arms over her warm shoulders, holding the sphere of memories before her face and murmured in her ear. "I think, for now, I should remind you of a… fond memory. One that we share, together."

I reached into the sphere, singling one ball of light. It was a small memory, barely the size of a marble between my fingers. As my Dream mark lit with an azure gleam from my chest, the ball in my hand floated upward. It glided wistfully to her brow, sinking into her pores.

Soon, her eyes opened. "Land's Blade," she whispered, shaken and blushing. "You were there. When I was alive…"

"You thought me a liar?" I smiled, grip tightening ever so gently around her shoulders as my breath brushed the flesh of her neck. "Once, Cilia, the blood in your veins beckoned me on solitary nights… Nights much like this one. You were a vision; the finest in the brothel… do you remember?"

"Remember…?" She pulled away, beguiled yet fascinated as her white pupils gleamed in the darkness. "You claimed you were a Clean One. If you aren't a demon, how have you lived this long?"

I chuckled. "Does it matter? We're here now, both of us. It cannot be coincidence, don't you think? Fate has brought us together again, Cilia, and I believe it is for a purpose."

She ground her sharpened teeth. "And what purpose is that?"

"To build a sanctuary. One that will protect us from the world's destruction." A laugh slipped from my lips. "We will kill the Relicbloods, before they kill us all."

Her brow creased with wrinkles. "You… think the Relicbloods will bring the world's destruction?"

"It is written in the Shepherd's Sands," I said simply. She doubted me? Laughable. This was perhaps the only truth I'd confessed all night. "They will be the end of us, unless we end them first."

She laughed but once. "You're a strange man, Macarius. And a fool. You wish to kill the Relicbloods? Not even I could gather enough of these little goblins to form an army that large. There are Reapers in all the realms. If they knew they were facing war, they would gather and exterminate us."

"Ah, but therein lies the beauty of it." My grin peeled further, fangs gleaning from their gums. "It is true, only a fool would strike all realms at once… but we, no such fools, are only targeting one. And we will not be the ones to do it."

She gave me that usual, stupid look, as though my words were too complex for her.

"Do not doubt me, Cilia," I said. "I've had much time to design this strategy. The Relicbloods will be terminated. After all, I'd already seen that one Bloodline was killed." My chuckles clicked and trembled. "Now, only four stand in my way."

26

HAUNTED HISTORY

LILLI

The sun had long passed the horizon, the night sky twinkling with bright stars and a full moon as I heaved the colossal doors of the Harmonist temple closed, collapsing back against the wall.

I found him! This afternoon replayed at a gleeful speed. Those eyes, that mark… Gracious Death, it was Xavier!

After six years of believing he was dead, I found him very much, undeniably alive. I would have cheered, but instead felt a pang of failure. I'd fled after the danger had passed, panicked when the Raiders came.

My heart sank and I slid to the ground. He was there, but I… I let him slip away. Now I had a slim chance of finding him again. I'd spoiled my best opportunity, all because I was paranoid of being caught by the Raiders. If they threw me in that same blood-spattered prison where Linus slaughtered those men… I shuddered.

Oh, what now? If I returned to Grim, I'd be executed. If I stayed here, I'd likely be killed by the demons or die of hunger. *Wise Shepherd, is this truly my fate? To die a cold, starving, hopeless death alone…?*

Despair crushed my heart and I curled into a ball. Mixed with the hunger pains, there was little else I could do but weep. I doubted I was even in my right mind anymore.

Yet my depression was interrupted, something catching my eye.

I wiped a straggling tear and glanced up. A ray of blue light filtered over the altar. Through the ceiling's stain-glass window, moonlight spilled into the temple, dust floating in the glow.

Entranced, I rose, drifting down the aisle between pews. When I stepped into the cool, radiant light, I knelt. *Perhaps if I pray for Shel and Nira to give me luck? Or, at the very least, guide me back to Xavier, to complete my mission?*

That was all I wished. He was here, he was still alive. As long as I remembered that, there was always hope, wasn't there?

I produced the amulet from my Storagesphere, clicking the case open and turning the dial with delicate clicks, setting it on the floorboards. The music began to play, its slow tune ringing through the temple.

Then someone's gentle touch warmed my shoulder.

I would have jumped in fright, if not for the soothing wave that washed over me. I turned to look, but no one was there.

I'd felt the familiar warmth many times before. The touch wasn't from this plane of reality. It was comforting, loving, draining my worry and filling the cavity in my chest. I didn't need to see Her to know it was Nira. She was here beside me, the Mother Goddess Herself, here to support me during my trial.

Then a second warmth came to my other shoulder. This touch gave me strength, a heat that powered me like a flare of light, bringing a surge of courage and resolve. Was this Shel? The Father God, come to watch over me while I traveled in His domain?

"Thank you," I whispered to them both, taking a breath and began to sing along with the amulet's melody, in the language of my people.

Kris la vheh, weh shae'beahl hu'leigh…

XAVIER

"*No…!*" I gasped awake, hand thrusting out to snag the cliffside.

But there was naught to grab. I was no longer drowning, the sea beneath my legs had been replaced with a feathered mattress and tousled, silken sheets.

Willow was gone.

My thudding heart dulled, relief draining to see the uneventful, elegant wallpaper of the inn's bedchamber staring back at me. Mal's head cocked from a chair's back, the raven grumbling in annoyance that I'd disturbed his rest.

I swung my legs over the bed, dabbing the sweat that beaded my face. Through the terrace window, the clock tower displayed the time: it was nearly eleven. I played with the idea of returning to sleep, but the memory quickly smothered that plan, and I drifted out the door.

Sleep wasn't appealing if it meant having to relive that same Gods damned nightmare.

Why can't I remember anything more of her? I slipped on my boots and promptly left the suite, Mal alighting on my shoulder, as though to 'escort' me in case his true Reaper awoke later. He bit at an itch on his wing as I took the lift to the lower lobby. *Why only her?*

Over the years, I'd regained many memories of my family; of Jaq and our Healing friend, Bianca; of Alexander and our lives, when we were separate brothers. Yet Willow, and anything during my time in the Death Palace, was gone. There was nothing still, after so long. The only memory I had of Willow's face was one sullied with terror and destruction.

And that, I brooded, fists balling as I crossed the abandoned lobby, *was no way to remember her.*

I stepped out to the empty streets, leaning against a lamppost and blew out a controlled, even breath.

This kingdom's air was still incredibly warm, even at Dim Light. The breeze gave a brief shield from the spring heat, the full moon blanketing the road with soft, blue light, circling clouds forming a glowing ring around it.

Beside the moon, as though to match, loomed the glowing clock tower. The hands hung just shy of the twelve and eleven, its glass face displaying the gilded Nirussian Crest. It was the same Crest as the birthmark on my hand.

I compared the two side by side curiously.

Crunch!

Mal had hopped off my shoulder and snatched a scuttling beetle next to my boot, crushing it in his beak before swallowing it whole.

I hummed. "Had you only followed me to find a midnight snack?"

Mal croaked up at me, then fluffed his feathers and found a second beetle to crunch into, fanning his tail as if to block my view of him.

I sighed, scratching my bristly face. "It's not as if I asked to be a parasite to your Reaper, Mal—*ow!*"

He bit my shin, squawked, then took off to fly up the length of the Howler's Inn, heading for our terrace on the top floor.

I angrily kicked the inn's wall, calling after him. "Your Reaper will feel that in the morning, you feathered bastard!" My wolf ears grew. "If your brother-messenger ever shows up, perhaps he'll feel inclined to repay all your 'endearing' sentiments over the years…!"

I puffed futilely, glaring after where Mal's tiny figure had disappeared. *Where IS your brother, Mal?* I thought, my anger leaking away dismally, my wolf ears drooping. *Does he even exist…? Should I have existed at all?*

I lowered to the stones and leaned against the inn's wall, pulling up a knee. Another beetle crawled over my fingers, and I lifted the insect to my face.

"Am I a mistake?" I asked the beetle. "Should Alexander and I have been one person, and the Gods decided to correct their mistake and rid the world of one of us?"

The beetle's horned snout turned to me, its wings twitching. Then it buzzed out of my hand and dropped to the stones, scuttling into a sewer drain.

I rubbed my eyes vigorously.

Kris la vheh, weh shae'beahl hu'leigh, Neschalist p'laven ash kemn mea la schae…

My wolf ears perked, hearing a voice singing behind the temple doors.

Heist, e spell du'beahl hu'dohn, Yechet heme kraveshahe trist kohn…

The tune was familiar. It was in Grimish, the language of our people, before the adoption of Landish had become primary. Only certain regions of Grim still spoke it today. Though, being of a higher education, it was required that I become fluent in the tongue from an early age. So, the song's meaning came immediately:

'Still and cold, winds running slow; be reborn from trailing ash which blows… Listen, a voice cries with sadness over the names engraved in stone'.

But who is singing? I pushed to my feet and crossed to the temple, climbing the steps. I quietly pushed the doors open.

A'speles speles la a'hoh hoh, Tatacha veben shelic'u nahohko…

Nira veilla ke halaa pievf, Necrotha myel'u dohn la sheft…

'Breathless breath, and sightless sight; embrace the silence of hollow life. Nira appears to ease your trouble, and destroy your sadness and blight'.

When I slipped inside, I could hear twinkling, as though from a music box. A songbird accompanied the voice as well, and I crept between pews toward the front.

Waiting before the altar was a girl, sitting in prayer on the dusty floor while she sang. Her charcoal hair was tied with a black ribbon lined with butterflies, a silver bell hanging there, and a hair-stick held it all in place.

I almost laughed. *The Sister Reaper? From this morning?* Had she been a mere street away all this time?

An amulet lay beside her, resembling an opened pocket watch. There was no clock inside, but a revolving platform that shone with white specks as it played the twinkling music. The notes crept from the back of my memory, marching mechanically like musical ants. Where did I know it from?

O myel heist timbriw lahla'beahl? Murrderes craw hellacha lola'beahl...?

'Do you hear the bells ringing? Many crows that begin singing?'

Heist craw'u lole fret myel ena, Yechet wuw kmen droh la wuw kemn thal...

'Listen to their song as you lay to sleep; it is for those who are honored and those who are blessed...'

Yechet wuw kemn droh la wuw kemn thal...

The watch's music slowed, and soon, it came to a gentle stop. She hung her head in prayer as the light from the roof's window extinguished, the moon shielded by passing clouds.

The new silence smothered the temple, shocking me sober. *Death, now what?* Should I speak to her? No, surely that would startle her.

I was suddenly aware of how dark it had become, she likely wouldn't recognize me from this morning. All she would see was a shadowed figure lurking behind her, and the glow of scythe-spheres dangling from my neck. They were scarcely bright enough to reveal my face.

She continued her silent prayer. My stomach fluttered nervously. *I suppose... if she's staying here, I could return in the morning?* Perhaps it was best to leave quietly while I could. Yet—

Fool! My head shook, banishing that ludicrous idea. I couldn't leave her here for the Necrofera to slaughter her in her sleep. She was far safer with reinforcements, small though we were. Bringing her to the inn was the best course of action.

But my legs wouldn't move. *How do I know her…?* The question gnawed my brain raw. If I could only remember her name… It was right there, teetering at the edge of my memory. My head throbbed, straining to yank the name out—

GONG!

The bell tolled above, striking the hour and shaking the temple down to the last floating speck of dust.

GONG!

The girl twisted, starting when she noticed me standing behind her.

My throat iced. *What in Bloods…?*

I swore my eyes were seeing phantoms. Moon rays speared through the clouds and glittered over her from the ceiling's stain-glass window, her face framed in wispy strands of grey hair that tumbled to the floor in playful curls. Her sharp, onyx eyes were deep voids of pure blackness, my mind drifting the further I stared through those orbs.

She seemed so… surreal. Nostalgia prickled my brain and seemed to… to *change* her. Instead of the dirty tunic and trousers she wore, I could remember her in a more splendid, black gown, its sheen subtle yet brilliant, a butterfly broach sparkling from the collar. The grease on her face was forgotten, replaced with a time when she was clean and radiant.

The new image was clear in mind, as though she were a manifestation of my blotted memories. *But what is her name…?*

She squinted at me, uncertain. "Who's there?"

Belatedly, I realized I wasn't under the light with her. I was left in shadow outside of it, there must have been a glare where she was sitting. I tried to answer, but my throat dried, words slipping away. Her stare was dizzying.

GONG!

Neither had moved. Neither had blinked. In the light, I saw something there; something in her face, her eyes… Scenes played in my memory, colliding rapidly and archiving like sparking links that had been severed.

I remembered a bustling city in Grim. Alexander and I spent time with a little girl, a bell jingling from her grey hair as we ventured the town and shared candied sweets in the market.

GONG!

We were a year older, sneaking into the city at nightfall. The girl and I were alone, Alex hadn't come with us.

GONG!

She and I stared at the trampled carcass of a wolf pup that'd wandered into the edge of town. A trio of boys had thrown stones at it. I'd chased them off, but the pup was already dead. I hadn't realized I was crying until the girl dabbed my cheek with her sleeve. We gave a prayer for the pup and buried it in the forest together.

GONG! GONG!

I didn't know where these memories sprouted from. They were so clear, so vivid…

Now, in the present time, the girl's crow gave flighty twitters from a lamp. The girl snapped out of her daze, turning to the black bird. She looked frightened as she slid her feet along the floor.

GONG!

She bolted for the back doors.

"W-wait!" I fumbled after her, rushing out to the temple's graveyard. I thought to call her name, but it still wouldn't come to mind.

I weaved between plots and lanterns, making certain not to step on the gravesites directly. It was disgraceful to stand atop the dead, if you didn't know them personally. Best to tread around, if you could.

As I neared the girl and reached for her shoulder, she skidded to a halt. I staggered, straining to see her in the darkness. I couldn't tell if her expression was welcoming or hostile. *If I could just remember her blasted name…*

The white light of her Death mark gleamed from her collarbone suddenly. Her fingertips brightened with a sparkling violet light, and she murmured a quick prayer, asking forgiveness from Nira for her violations.

The surrounding graves trembled.

P-pop! went a root underground. The dirt shifted and cracked. A shriveled, boney hand wriggled up, clawing from the dirt, fingernails caked in mud and squirming with maggots.

Three corpses pulled themselves from their plots, sluggishly lifting to their decayed, clumsy feet, their bones tethered by violet lights which strung their clattering skeletons in place.

Death. I swallowed. *I'd forgotten she was a Necrovoker.*

Why was she exhuming these vessels? She didn't have their ghosts' permissions, that sort of sacrilege was only excused if the caster was using self-defense. *She must think I'm attacking her,* I realized, dread sinking.

In a vicious grunt, she thrust her shining hands forward, dragging the corpses with them and commanding her puppets to apprehend me.

One grabbed my arm with thin, cold fingers. I kicked it away, but another groped for my side. I shoved it back, bones breaking as they hit the ground. I whispered my own apology to Nira, wincing as they cracked. I was left with little choice in harming the corpses. I couldn't control the vessels, and Alexander wasn't awake to help.

I caught a glimpse of the girl running back into the temple.

"Wait!" I shoved away another corpse and stumbled inside, leaving them behind in the graveyard. The Evocation would wear off in time, I knew. The Hallows could only be retained for so long.

I dashed for the girl as she sprinted toward the altar. She crouched over an item she'd left behind: the amulet.

My footfalls startled her.

She growled, leaving the amulet, and pulled the black ornament from her hair. Her scythe materialized, and she swung its hooked blade at my neck.

"Death!" I drew out my own scythes and deflected her blade with a *clang!*

She swung again, this time from the side. I ducked, then thrust upward to stop her next strike with my other blade.

She struck and she struck, leaping and dodging, her grunts growing agitated the longer I blocked and evaded her swings, the clash of metal shrieking through the temple.

I knew I should be concerned about the girl trying to kill me, but something felt… too familiar.

My feet seemed to move on their own. I would step to one side, she would mirror to the other. She would swing for my head, I would bend back and spin upright in time to jump over a swing to my feet. I would block a horizontal strike while she would spin and strike the other way.

I knew the patterns, I could see them before they happened. I remembered… sparring with someone years ago. It was engrained there in my subconscious, flooding back and reminding my muscles where to go.

Giving a final, furious snarl, she leapt backward and crouched low, her weapon cocked behind her. "What are you after, Sentient?" she demanded.

My expression fell flat. Was *that* what this was about? "I'm not a Sentient," I said.

"I'll have none of your lies. My messenger would know if she sensed a demon or not—" Her little crow fluttered to her face and chirped sharply. It grabbed a strand of her hair in its beak and tugged her toward me. She blinked, remaining rooted where she stood. "Jewel?"

"My apologies for the confusion." I put away my scythes, raising my hands to show her I was unarmed now. I only hoped the temple wasn't dark enough to hide this gesture, but I was confident the glow of my scythes, in their spherical form, would be enough to show I meant peace. "Perhaps I should have announced myself," I said. "We met earlier today. I'm an apprentice Reaper as well."

Her messenger still tugged her hair toward me, but she was silent.

I cleared my throat. "I, er, didn't mean to offend—"

She ripped a guttural scream and drove her knee into my stomach, shoving me to the floor.

I fell hard on my back, coughing as she snatched my tunic's collar and held her blade to my throat, the metal cool against my dangerously close skin.

"Death, woman!" I choked, her knee pinning my gut. "What is wrong with—?"

"Where is your messenger?" she barked.

"That's… complicated…" My breath squeezed out in slivers. I could hardly see her features in the darkness. Her scythe illuminated my throat, but dimly. I supposed only my neck was visible now. "I… I'm not going to do anything…" I croaked. "You have my word…!"

"Do you take me for a fool?" she scoffed. "I've met others in this horrible realm who've promised me no harm and they… blast it, Jewel, will you *stop that*?" The crow was still tugging her hair. She shooed it away and grabbed my collar again, pulling my neck closer to her blade. "Now, you've followed me here. Why?"

"I heard you… singing that prayer." A chuckle slipped, seeing the crow was now whizzing circles over her head. It was a faint outline, since there was hardly any light, but it was clear enough from the crow's chirps and the sound of its buzzing wings.

"What do you want with me, *Fera*?" she sneered.

"I've already told you I'm… not a Sentient…" I failed to stifle a short laugh. The little bird pulled her hair again, the girl's irritation bubbling, my laughter worsening.

"Do you find something amusing?!" Her blade kissed the risen hairs on my neck.

My snickers dampened into quivering chuckles. "I… I'm sorry, it's only… I can't seem to recall your name?"

"I don't recall offering it."

"Oh, you didn't… but I can't help but feel like you've… tried to kill me before."

She sang a high, condescending note. "Yes, that seems likely. I do make a point to kill any demons that dare to cross me."

"There's been a drastic misunderstanding… Could you perhaps… put your scythe away? I'd rather like to… keep my head."

"I'm sure you would! But I'd rather like to keep my soul—!"

"When you were a little girl," I sputtered, desperate. "You were trapped… on a high wall…! And you couldn't come down!"

She blinked.

Thanking Nira this made her pull the blade away from my throat, I went on. "You said you would die if you jumped. And I…" More from that memory flooded back, and I breathed a laugh. "I said I would catch you."

Her confidence faltered. "L… lies. You're just another Seer."

"We once buried a wolf pup together. Gave it a stone grave in the woods. You stayed with me until Dim Light."

Her throat sounded tight. "I-I…"

I carefully placed my left hand over her heart. "Do you remember what you told me? That the pup would live again, and meet a better fate, simply because its memory was there in my spirit…?"

My Death mark shone with a white light and I drained the Hallows from my soul, evoking it into hers. She lurched back in a yelp, her scythe clattering to the floor.

"What…!" she stammered, dumfounded. "What did you do?"

"I made your soul feel as though you were lying on a bed of down feathers." I smiled, though I doubted she could see. "I thought it'd be calming. Was I wrong?"

She seemed to be at a loss for words. "You're a Necrovoker? Not a Seer…?"

"Yes," I said, then amended, "partially."

"What do you mean 'partially'?"

I rested an arm over my knee and grinned, thankful she'd finally taken to having a civilized conversation. "I only evoke the Hallows of souls. I have no power over vessels."

"Then," she began softly. "You're *half* a Necrovoker?"

"Yes," I said, eager. "That is precisely the case. I take it you remember me after all?"

She was quiet for some time. I strained to see her expression in the dimness, but couldn't glean much. Then a light filtered through the overhanging window, the clouds finally parting outside. Our faces lit, and her gaze widened, glimmering dust drifting between us in the subtle, blue ray.

Whatever she found in my eyes left her mute. Shaking, she rose, drawing back in a sickened expression. "Gods," she barely whispered, her back *thunking* the wooden altar. "It can't be that simple. I… Bloods, I almost killed…" She swayed, looking faint.

I hefted to my feet. "Are you all…"

She dropped like a sack of flour.

I lunged to cradle her head before it hit the floor. Her skull was saved from the collision, but the rest of her fumbled over the floorboards in ungraceful *thumps*. Her eyes had fluttered closed.

"Er…" I carefully slid my arm free, gently shaking her by the shoulder. "Miss?"

No response. Her breath remained even and slow. *Bloods, she's fainted.*

Her little black bird fluttered onto my head and nestled in my hair, perfectly comfortable, as if it were habit.

"You're an odd one, aren't you?" I chuckled to the bird. "'Jewel', was it?"

The bird gave a confirmative twitter and I glanced at the unconscious girl. Why couldn't I remember her name?

Sighing, I retrieved her things and scooped her up. I supposed it couldn't be helped—I'd have to take her back with me. It was either that or leave her here where she could be mauled by the Necrofera stalking this city.

I carried her out of the temple and started across the street, but staggered midway when I noticed a shadowy figure lingered nearby.

There was a lion-tailed man down the road, watching me. *That same Terravoker?* The Healer woman was with him also, the one from Nulani. She clung to his back by the belts of his scabbards, shying behind him when I swung my gaze at her.

"Why did you help us with the dragon today?" I called cautiously, keeping hold of the Sister Reaper. "Who are you?"

The Healer woman whispered something to the warrior, who shook his head and walked away, falling out of sight as the woman trailed behind him.

My eyes narrowed after them. I thought to follow, but decided I had more pressing matters. With a sniff, I let them be and carried the Sister inside to find her a bed.

27

SECRET OBSERVERS

ANABELLE

"I could swear I recognized that girl." I whispered to Kurrick, clutching the belts of his scabbards while he led us back to our inn. "The one he carried. She almost looked like Myra, I could swear."

Kurrick grunted softly, keeping his amber eyes forward. "It has been some time since Myra left us. Perhaps your memory has dwindled."

I murmured absently, "Perhaps…"

"I don't understand this boy," he rumbled, suspicious. "All this observation and we've yet to find answers. Our monitoring has offered naught, there has been no sign of the second brother. You're certain you haven't made a mistake?"

I nodded, gripping his scabbard's straps tight. "Dream was certain. They are the ones we seek."

"Oracles have known to be wrong. Even Dream."

"Yes… but we'd observed the two in their youth. Dream showed us."

"Yes, I recall the pampered misfits," he muttered, unimpressed. "They were a strange pair, even then. Your sister was run ragged from chasing after them, dragging her daughter into their mischief."

I paused, pressing a ponderous knuckle to my lips. "My sister's daughter…" I drew in a surprised breath. "That's it. That's why I recognized the girl. I'd forgotten Dream had sent Myra's daughter after them as well."

Kurrick halted abruptly, shock wrenching his scarred features. "Land's Blade! *That* was she?"

"I'm sure of it," I said. "Dream mentioned his plan to send her, but I hadn't expected her to arrive so soon."

Kurrick's throat vibrated. "It's likely the Fera chased her to this location… This changes plans. Safeguarding the daughter of Myra exceeds all other priorities. Those twins can take care of themselves for all I care, Shadowblood or not."

"What's this?" I hid a giggle behind a hand. "Why Kurrick, could you be taking the role of a concerned uncle?"

He snorted. "Hardly. I fear if anything befalls the girl, your sister will hang my balls on her fir tree next Rebirth Day."

I chuckled. "Yes, that sounds likely. And she would do so with a smile, I'd imagine." I gave a nostalgic sigh. "My, it's been some time since we've seen her… And the Artist bless her, her daughter is as stunning as she, when Myra was that age. She's inherited her Hallows as well, it seems."

"Yes," he murmured, pensive. His lion tail twitched behind him. "While I understand her need to hide herself, one must wonder why she'd worn prisoner garb… Something must have happened before our charge found her. I pray her identity was not compromised."

My lion ears folded in a shudder. "That would make matters difficult, for all of us. Not a soul must learn of her whereabouts. Shel forbid her father discovers she has left Grim."

"It is not her father who worries me." Kurrick's lion ears began to sprout, curling back in a snarl. "It is the cobra I fear."

My gaze fell to the stones. I took a breath to reply—

Clattering sounded behind the corner building.

Startled, Kurrick swept his arm over me, ducking into an alley and crouched behind a stack of crates. I peeked round to look, one lion ear perked.

Two Footrunners strode past us, their lances resting lazily on their shoulders and Shotri holstered at their belts.

"Hold, Ana," he hushed, drawing one of the shortened claymores at his back with a quiet scrape. He pressed the Sealing Rune on the hilt, causing the blade to radiate with golden light and extend to its full length, ready to strike if the need came.

The Runners crossed the alley and fell out of sight, proceeding with their nightly route. Kurrick loosened his lungs and had his blade shorten in a golden gleam once more, sheathing them as we snuck away in the opposite direction.

We were in sight of the inn… But more clatters came behind. I stole a glance over my shoulder, whispering to Kurrick. "Rockraiders."

He stiffened slightly, but kept an even pace. "Do not acknowledge them. Do not run. You will draw suspicion."

We reached the *Stonebed Pub and Inn*, and Kurrick shoved open the door. I clung to his leather scabbards, hiding behind him while we made our way through the smoke-peppered pub toward the stairway in the back corner.

The rickety tables were thinly filled tonight, the pub dim with flickering lamps. One table kept a scrutinizing eye on Kurrick: Bounty Hunters. Their stares followed us as we crossed, and I tensed.

They are focused on Kurrick, I assured myself, my eyes plastered to his muscular back, biting the panic spiking my lungs and threatening to squeeze them shut. *Kurrick draws their attention. Not I. Not I.*

My pulse calmed, gripping Kurrick's scabbards and resting my brow on his back as we strode toward the stairs. *Nearly safe… nearly alone.*

Squeee!

The pub door swung open.

The troupe of Rockraiders had followed us inside. One knight stomped toward us, his gauntleted hand reaching out.

No! I released a frightened squeak and wheeled around Kurrick to shield myself from the stranger's fingers, my chest thumping as I pressed against my warrior's chest.

The knight clasped Kurrick's shoulder.

"Hang on there, mate." The man said. He had more detail to his armor than the rest of his company, a purple stripe adorning his chainmail. He must have been their captain. "Ye two were out there pretty late, and I didn't see anyone escortin' ye. Had some errands to run?"

Kurrick grunted and drew away from the captain, starting up the stairs with me trailing behind—

I gasped when the captain snagged my wrist.

"Breakin' curfew's a crime here," he growled, his leaden fingers crushing my skin. "If ye don't have an escort, either pay the fine or be brought in."

Kurrick didn't face the man, but paused on the steps. "Return my companion. She does not like to be touched."

Chair legs scuffed the floors suddenly, the Bounty Hunters rising from their seats. The barmaid stiffened behind the counter, carefully setting down the glass she had been drying.

The Raider yanked me closer, causing me to stumble. "Don't like bein' touched, hm?" His hawkish gaze drifted over me, hot breath brushing my neck as he pulled back my curly hair and laughed in my lion ear. "Maybe ye just haven't been touched by the right man… Eh, pretty one? What d'you say to that?"

I flushed, my throat cinching closed. I stared at the fingers clutching my wrist like snakes, my breath straining into rapid wheezes, the world shrinking away and focused only on the intruding hand burning my skin.

"Well, lass?" he barked. "Ye going t' say something when spoken to?"

I trembled under his hold, producing naught but a whimper.

"She does not speak with unfamiliars." Kurrick climbed down the stairs, his glare fixed on the captain. "I will ask again: restrain your hand. Else I remove it from your wrist."

The captain grinned a laugh along with his men. "Oh, ye will, eh? And I s'pose ye have permits for those swords as well?"

"Let the lass go," one of the Bounty Hunters spat behind him.

The captain whirled, and I peeked around him to see there were four Hunters, fully armed and stacked with muscle, coming to surround the captain and his men. The lead Hunter rapped his fingers along his sword's grip, but kept it sheathed. An intimidating gesture.

"They showed us their permits last mornin'," the lead Hunter explained. "An' they're Hunters. Hunters be excluded from curfew, so's they can catch their targets in the act."

I blinked at them. We hadn't shown them anything—not even spoken with these men. Though we did indeed have forged permits and Hunter's licenses, they wouldn't have known of those. Why were they lying for us?

The captain hesitated, but after Kurrick produced our forged licenses, the Raider grudgingly released me. I scuttled behind Kurrick, pressing against his back and fighting to regain control of my breathing.

The captain muttered an insincere apology, and the tension lessened as the Raiders went to the bar to order whiskey and ale. The Hunters who'd assisted us tipped their heads to me before returning to their seats.

We hurried to our room upstairs, and Kurrick bolted the door.

I calmed now that we were alone in the safety of these solitary walls, and removed my cloak and boots. I found an oil lamp by the bedside table with a box of matches beside it. Striking one ablaze, the acrid smell of sulfur swelled as I lit the wick and adjusted the flame.

The orange glow danced in the darkness as Kurrick slid off his swords, armor and numerous daggers hidden underneath.

"Why had they lied for us, do you think?" I asked, lowering to the ratty mattress, its worn springs squealing under my weight.

Kurrick moved to the window, drawing back a small corner of the curtains to peer outside. "They're not Hunters either," he said. "They are with the rebellion… I heard them through the walls last night. It would seem this whole establishment is dedicated to hiding those who follow the rebel leader—the one they call 'Land's Servant'. I suspect they only helped us because of their vehemence for the Raiders harassing us."

"Should we say anything? Perhaps they will aid us further if they know our goals intertwine?"

"No." His answer was definite, declining to pry his gaze from the window. He was always this way, when we'd leave Aspirre. Always alert, always awake in case we ran into danger… Or if someone discovered us. That was his greatest fear.

"We both may wish to see the Old Kingdom restored," he said, "but they follow a different path toward it. If we involve them, we may change the outcome of Dream's prediction."

Though he'd discarded his swords and armor, Kurrick was still cautious, ever attentive. I admired his sense of duty, but Bloods was it frustrating. We were alone here. *Finally* alone, away from eavesdroppers and unwanted eyes. That was a rarity for us. I always looked forward to time outside Aspirre, but this time was different. He was spending more time fussing over danger than enjoying time in the sun—the *real* sun. The danger was gone for now, would there be no time for leisure, this trip?

I sighed. There was at least some celebration due. The Necrofera had gone, and we'd survived again. Though, we hadn't come out unscathed. I'd finished healing my wounds, but Kurrick had yet to let me mend his own.

I slid off the bed and went to join him by the window, my lion ears flicking back. "Kurrick." I lightly touched his shoulder. "Your cut is bleeding again."

He drew a finger over the slice on his cheek, streaking the blood. "It will not end me."

"Please." I reached for the cut, evoking my golden Hallows. "For me?"

He hesitated, but eventually conceded, glancing away as I sealed the wound. Another scar appeared on his face, accompanying the many others he'd garnered over the years. A sadness came as my fingers traced the lines over his broad, stubbled jaw.

He was not what many considered a handsome man, even before the scars. His brow was naturally set in a scowl, his nose was long and crooked from beatings, his ears were proportionally too small for his skull… but he was still beautiful.

As my Hallows finished its work on his wound, I found my lips drifting to his…

He seized my hand, stopping me. "That is enough."

He turned back to the window to ignore me as he often did of late.

I bristled. "You cannot stay awake until sunrise. We can survey tomorrow."

"I do not trust this place," he rumbled. "Everland has become a dry wasteland, whose self-acclaimed 'ruler' is keeping the people ignorant and spiteful toward the other nations. That was not the way of the Old Kingdom. These people could be capable of anything—or perhaps the Necrofera will decide to strike again?"

"Then you should be well rested to better prepare for battle. Please, if you fear an invasion, I will stand watch tonight. You have yet to sleep in two days. How do you expect to observe the Shadowblood if you collapse from exhaustion?"

"The Shadowblood." He gave a scoffing laugh, lion tail swishing. "I am still skeptical of the choice. The legend says the champion was to be one wolf. Not two. Will their chances not be fractured, with the split?"

"You must have faith in them."

"Forgive me if my faith is overshadowed by fact. And currently, I see no evidence pointing to them having influence over anything."

"That is why we must guide them. You must trust in Dream's prediction, Kurrick."

"Those two are as vulnerable to corruption and death as we are. Even if they live long enough to see their fate—as they have done so terribly in the past, since one of them was thought dead for years—how will we know they will not turn against us? What if they become an even worse threat? Who is to save us from them?"

"The Gods would have considered this…"

He laughed. "Gods? If they even exist, why should we trust Their decision? Many say Everland's new ruler was chosen by the Gods. And look what happened. I have said it once, Ana, and I will say it again: trust only in yourself. Place too much faith in others, and it will only hurt more when they betray you."

"Then should I not place trust in you? Is that what you're implying?"

He kept his eyes on the window. "Go and sleep, Ana. I will keep watch."

I shrank away, lowering back to the bed. He would not join me tonight, it seemed. Or, I feared, any night from this day on. I'd known it would happen someday, but I'd hoped that… in the end, he would ignore our differing classes and…

"Yes, Kurrick," I whispered hollowly, sinking into the raggedy blanket. "Good night…"

28

THE NEW REAPER

XAVIER

SIX YEARS PRIOR

"It was somewhere over this way, I think," I told Alex, holding my lantern ahead to better see in the misted forest.

A single speck of cold light bounced in the fogged glass, and I rubbed a sleeve over it to clear a path for the light to get through.

The dark overcast swirled with more of these lights at the cave's ceiling, and a chilled wind swept past, rustling the willow leaves surrounding us. We were in the Weeping Woods tonight, hunting for a Fallen Light I'd seen gliding down here not half an hour ago.

I'd convinced Alexander to come along, but he didn't seem as enthusiastic. He crossed his arms, holding his own lantern and fidgeted in the confining fabric of our white suits. Tonight was Death's Festival. We'd left the ball for a time to get this light.

"You *think*?" Alex scowled. "You didn't drag me all the way out here simply to get lost, Xavier."

"We're not lost," I assured, though I had been doubtful for the last five minutes. I swore we'd seen that same crooked trunk three times now. Best not to divulge that to Alex.

I patted my vest pocket, feeling the solid edges of the long box hidden within: Willow's gift. I blew out a nervous breath. This was the real reason I'd decided to explore these woods, to get away from the Death Palace for a time. Away from Mother and Father. Away from the scrutinizing eyes of the other barons. Away from the Death King and the azure-haired queen.

Away from Willow.

This must be done, Father had said. It was meant as an encouraging sentiment, but it only squeezed my stomach tighter. *Willow will be thirteen today—the proper age to receive her vines and declare the engagement official.*

For four years, Willow and I had been arranged to be wed. And I discovered it not a week ago. Granted, I wasn't outraged. Why should I be? The future Queen of Death was to be my wife, when we came of age. I was only fourteen now, so the wedding wouldn't come until much later. That was comforting, at least. And I knew Willow accepted me as her husband-to-be.

But that did nothing for the stress.

Tonight, I was expected to seal the arrangement by presenting her with these custom engagement-vines. I was sure she would like them. But to perform such a private ceremony in front of the entire court? Perhaps even broadcast to the whole nation, to both continents?

My hands shook. What if I made a mistake and chose the wrong design? What if she had second thoughts? I… I felt so unprepared. Why hadn't I been told about this earlier?

That's why I'm getting that Fallen Light for her, I reminded. *To have something else to offer, besides the vines.*

It felt like a silly idea, but the Fallen Lights were seen as good omens. If I gave her a light *with* the vines, it would signify a long, joyful marriage for the rest of our lives. *The rest of our lives.* My arms shook again. There was no telling if I could keep her interested that long.

Alex took out his silver pocket watch, craning back toward the blackstone palace, whose tall spires stretched behind the woods.

"It's getting late, Xavier," he said. "Lilli wished to meet with me about something, and Mother wanted you in the ballroom at exactly eight-thirty. We need to return now, if you're going to do… er, well…"

I sighed, lowering my lantern. "R-right… you're right. I suppose I can give her one of these older lights…"

"Just give her the vines. Old lights don't have any luck left in them, it'd be pointless. Let's just…" He trailed off, head cocking. "Do you hear something?"

I listened, noticing a faint twinkling in the distance, like wind chimes. "Is that…" I began, frowning at the familiar melody. "The Requiem?"

Alex yelped in fright suddenly, dropping his lantern and held up his right hand to gawk at it.

His Crest of black diamonds was shining with a strange light. One of the diamonds was pointing in the direction of the wind chimes, and they switched when he would change orientation. I saw my own Crest was also glowing, shifting toward the music.

Exchanging a glance, we started toward the sound of the wind chimes, following our gleaming Crests, specks of ash fluttering around us in the mist.

PRESENT DAY

I woke from the dream in a groan, groggily floating upright.

I was in the psyche. Alexander must have woken before me. I floated to the circular window where light spilled in from the conscious world.

Alex was staring at the door to our inn's bedchamber. He didn't move. He only stared, like a madman.

"Watching the lacquer crack?" I inquired, my voice bouncing around this empty void.

If Alex had been startled, it hadn't gleaned through his placid gaze. He only hummed. "I was wondering, Xavier. Could you explain something for me?"

"I can try," I offered.

He quietly pushed open our door and peeked inside. "What is *that* doing in our bed?"

There was a grey-haired girl lying on her side, faced away from us above the plush comforter. A tiny black bird snoozed on the pillow beside her head.

"Ah!" Memory flooded back, and I cleared my throat as Alex clicked the door closed again. *"The Grimlette. Yes, I found her in the temple across the street last night. She'd fainted, and I couldn't leave her there as a demon meal."*

"And why is she in our bed?"

I shrugged, though I knew he couldn't see. *"It's only polite. I took the chaise down in the lounge."*

"I noticed," he muttered, cricking his neck in a wince.

"—What happened?"

Alex whirled at the new voice.

Vendy had appeared behind us suddenly, her drooping eyes heavy with grogginess. Her usual braid had been untied to let her frazzled, tangled locks tumble like a crazed animal over her shoulders, one mass rising over her head in a comical swoop.

She yawned, her rabbit ears folding back as she rubbed her lids. "What's all the fuss about…?"

"We have a new guest, apparently," Alex muttered, tossing his head at the door in a gesture. "That Reaper girl from yesterday is here. Xavier found her last night and said she'd fainted for whatever reason. She may have been injured during the Fera raid. Vendy, could you watch over her? Alert us when she awakens?"

Vendy nodded absently and yawned again, shuffling into the chamber. "Sure, sure… I'll keep an eye on her…"

Vendy lowered into a chair by the bed. Then her head rolled forward like a boulder and *puffed* into the fluffy mattress. She broke into a deep, snoring slumber.

Alex smeared a hand over his face. "Not a morning-soul. Noted…"

The sound of a lavatory being flushed came from the next room over, and Octavius soon emerged, stretching his neck. He found us in the hall and paused. "Uh, hey. What's going on—?"

"The Grim girl is here," Alex informed for the second time this morning. He did not sound pleased for it. "She might be injured. Since you have that 'sense' for feeling ailments, why don't you do some… scans or something to check on her?"

Octavius looked overwhelmed, gulping. "I… guess I'll see what I can do?"

"Good man." Alex patted his shoulder and crossed the upper hallway toward the chamber at the end. "Go and get started. I suppose we have to tell Jaq and Henry, as well."

29

A COLD WELCOME

LILLI

Something soft nuzzled my nose, like a ball of gentle feathers.

My eyes fluttered open. Jewel cocked her head at me, nestled on a silken pillow by my head. I belatedly realized I wasn't sleeping on a bench. This was an actual bed, with silk sheets and a warm comforter.

I jolted upright. Behind the velvet canopy, I found myself in an extravagant room, the morning sunlight filtering through a terrace window to my left. There was a private washroom opposite the bed, a few finely-furnished chairs and a vision-gem that was powered off on the wall.

There was also a young girl drooling on the comforter at my feet.

The rabbit girl was slumped over the mattress halfway, the rest of her nearly falling out of a chair. Her nose ripped with a snore, and she breathed it out through her open mouth atop my feet.

I cleared my throat, hesitant. "Erm… miss?"

Another snore, like an engine rattling with a loose bolt.

I awkwardly squirmed out of the comforter and slid off the mattress. *Wasn't this that rabbit girl from yesterday? The Terravoker?*

"Jewel?" I whispered to my songcrow from my shoulder. "Where are we?"

The croak that replied wasn't from Jewel. It came from outside the terrace window. I nervously slipped out of bed and went to check.

Through the glass, a jet-black raven cawed at me from the stone railing, cocking its head to look at me with one eye. Its feathers held a bluish sheen in the sunlight, and it pecked its beak against the glass.

Another messenger? Could this be…?

"You're Xavier's!" I squealed with joy, unlatching the glass door.

The raven grumbled in annoyance, as though it had been waiting all this time for me to let it in, and it soared to the front door. The large bird perched on the handle and cawed, as if commanding me to follow.

I thought my heart would explode as I fumbled forward, throwing open the door, the rabbit girl undisturbed as I followed the raven down the hallway and trotted down the stairs after it.

The raven led me to an expansive lounge with cushioned seats and couches huddled in front of a large vision-screen. The screen of light was tuned to a news station, the reporters chatting away about the wreckage left behind by the Necrofera yesterday.

On different chairs were perched three black birds. One was a crow with soft, slightly tattered feathers, its tail fanned flat; the second was a larger raven with white cheeks; the third was the raven that led me here, waiting at the arm of a chair near many cartons of… dearest Death, was that *food?*

My eyes bulged at the glorious bounty. There was glazed meat, grilled vegetables, numerous drinks, bowls of fruit… I didn't wait to sit down and help myself. My stomach demanded I eat it all immediately.

The raven fluttered on the chair's arm beside me, cawing in expectance.

I threw my arms around the bird, hugging it to my chest. "Thank you, thank you, thank you!" I kissed its head, and it squirmed angrily, screeching.

This was Xavier's messenger! His very own! Where his messenger was, I knew it was only a matter of time before Xavier appeared himself. After all, that had been him last night before I blacked out, of course he'd take me to where he was staying. Such a gentleman, as he always had been.

The raven pried himself free of my hold, huffing irritably and flapped upstairs, disappearing. I was too drunk with glee to worry over how I'd annoyed the bird.

I returned to my feast and watched the reports with happily-kicking feet, spying a teapot on the cart and poured myself a cup. I drank it heartily as the warm liquid drained down my throat like silk. It tasted of apples and cinnamon.

Odd, I thought, pausing to stare at the steaming drink, *this is my favorite… could Xavier have remembered after all?*

Given the circumstances, I'd assumed he'd forgotten me completely. But this…

"Oh, um," a meek voice came behind me, almost making me choke. "I guess you're up."

I fumbled to put down the tea and wheeled round, heart fluttering.

Oh. My excitement waned. It wasn't Xavier. It was a black-haired boy with lime green eyes, his skin a golden-beige. The white-cheeked raven to my left flew off its chair and alighted on the boy's head, nestling in his hair.

Another Reaper, I noted as the boy scratched his messenger's neck with a small smile. *That's right, I recognize him from yesterday. He was part of Xavier's company… but then, where was Xavier?*

Behind the boy was a burly man in dirtied overalls and a stained work-shirt. He saw me and smiled amiably, his rabbit ears perked as he chuckled. "Ah, awake at last! See you beat my niece to the punchline. She's never good at rising in the early hours of the morning."

"Your niece…" I regarded the man's rabbit ears curiously. "Ah, the girl upstairs? I tried waking her, but she seemed too far gone to hear me."

The man guffawed. "Sounds like her, all right! Come, sit down, sit down. Help yourself. We got that food for you, little Grimlette." He nudged the black-haired boy with a grin. "This one here says you're starving. Best if you got something in your belly right quick."

The boy laughed shyly. "Y-yeah… Land, you were in so much pain I'm surprised you woke up already."

I had to take a moment to register that. "How did you know I was in pain?"

"Uh… let's leave it at, 'I had a feeling'." He blushed and coughed into a hand. "A-anyway, um, me and Henry are supposed look after you. They told *me* to make sure you weren't hurt or anything. I kept telling them you didn't have a concussion, but you know, they just kept saying to check anyway. You'll be fine as long as you eat enough. Oh, but don't eat too much in one setting, you'll just get an ache, since your stomach shrivels up after fasting for so long."

I stared at him, then glanced at Jewel from my shoulder. "You know much about this sort of thing, don't you?"

He smiled proudly. "My mom was a Healer. She told us a bunch of stuff as kids, so… uh, anyway, you can go back to eating. I just want to make a few scans to see how you're doing, as far as injuries go."

"Very well…" Cautious, I lowered into the chair again, reclaiming my tea.

The rabbit man, Henry, hummed to himself and moved to a table in the back corner, grabbing a rag and polishing cream before scrubbing at crusted blood-stains on several sets of armor.

The black-haired boy shyly shuffled around me and began waving his hands around my head. He never touched me, he only glided his hands in the air. I raised a brow at the strange gestures.

"Okay, nothing there…" the boy mumbled in inspection. "Your inner ear's a bit off, so you're a little dizzy, but you seem to have gotten enough rest. Lacking a few vitamins and nutrients, but you'll get those back after eating."

I skeptically sipped my tea as he kneeled and waved his hands around my leg, which was still recovering from the bite wound. But my wrinkled trousers covered the scar, he wouldn't be able to see the marks unless he rolled it up, and he seemed much too flustered to touch me.

"Your bite's still tender," he said, making me blink. "Try to keep off of it if you can. It'd be a good idea to clean it too, when you get the chance—"

"Pardon," I interrupted. His behavior was just so familiar, I had to ask, "Are you an Infeciovoker?"

He recoiled as if I'd struck him. "I-I'm not going to do anything, I swear! I was just asked to look after you, so…!"

I set down my cup and stared at him, amazed. "Nira Below. I didn't think there were any left… You needn't worry, I'm familiar with how infection Hallows works. I have a friend who evokes that Hallows—but, well, she also evokes five other elements… I didn't know there were any Evocators left with *only* infection."

His cat ears perked up. "You know another Infeciovoker?"

"A few, actually," I amended. "But again, they don't have the Hallows alone. You're one of the first I've seen with the lone element. My friend isn't nearly as strong with hers anyway, since her magic is diluted from her other elements. She isn't even able to feel wounds in others, as you can."

He went starry-eyed, the raven on his skull cocking its head with interest. He cleared his throat. "She, um, didn't happen to come with you, did she? Your friend?"

I suppressed a wince, seeing I'd gotten his hopes up. It must be a lonely life, being the only one of his kind up here… after all, Infeciovokers hadn't been seen in over five hundred years.

"Well, technically…" I tried to word it as best I could, giving him as little information as possible. "She *is* up here. But she isn't with me at the moment. We haven't had a chance to, er, meet up, you could say. But I didn't expect Xavier would be traveling with an Infeciovoker."

He was forced out of his daydream. "Er, wait, what? Who?"

"Xavier," I hummed absently, eyes narrowing at the boy. "Besides the obvious fact that your Hallows is extinct, I would have thought he'd avoid that Hallows altogether, given the circumstances. I suppose it's possible he doesn't remember… Well, it doesn't matter now. Where *is* Xavier, speaking of?"

He glanced back at Henry from the corner, and the man shrugged. The boy swallowed. "I, er… hang on a sec."

He turned and sprinted up the stairs, leaving me and Henry alone in the lounge.

Oh, good. He went to fetch him. I smiled at Jewel, anxiousness bubbling as I drank the rest of my tea.

XAVIER

"… and he's looking after her now," Alexander informed the viper as Jaq rubbed the sleep from his eyes.

We were in Jaq's bedchamber, explaining the situation and planning our next course of action. Now that a Sister-in-arms was to stay with us, we had to be sure certain secrets weren't divulged.

"According to him," said Alex. "She's starved and mildly wounded. Obviously Grimish, probably visiting the surface, as we are. Based on her raggedy clothes, I'd normally think she was a peasant, but I looked in her Storagesphere and found nothing but noble gowns and expensive items. Either she's higher class and ran out of money, or she's a thieving peasant pretending to be a Howless."

"Splendid…" Jaq scratched his scaled nose, abandoning his peasant persona. Either he felt this was too important a matter, or he hadn't fully woken and wasn't in the mood. "Let me see if I've gathered all this: We've either come to the aid of a Howless in need, or brought a kleptomaniac into our living space and could potentially be robbed of our scythes and our finances?"

Alex tipped his head. "Essentially."

"Mmm. I see…" Jaq gave a yawn, displaying his fangs, and scratched the sparse hairs at his chin. "And *whose* idea was it to bring her here again?"

Alex pushed a thumb to his brow. "Who else?"

Jaq grunted, unsurprised.

"She isn't a thief," I muttered from the psyche. *"I had memories of her, from our childhood. You knew her as well."*

Alex lowered into a chair and grumbled. "That explains why she seemed familiar… In any case, I suppose we ought to give her the benefit of the doubt. She's a Sister Reaper, of that we can't deny. And I must admit, having another soldier with us gives me more comfort, after yesterday's disaster. We need reinforcements just as well as her."

Jaq nodded, considering. "True. And Bloods, despite her injuries, she fought well. We could use someone of that skill right about now."

"Yes, we could." Alex paused. "However, there is one caveat: she's a Necrovoker. Which means she can see Xavier. We don't know who she is or what she's capable of, and I for one don't wish to risk her going to the Death King about our circumstances if she finds us out. That being said, Xavier…" He sucked in a hesitant breath. "I'll have to take control from now on. At least until we find another way to keep her from seeing your eyes."

I muttered. *And right after being done with that for Octavius. Brilliant.*

"Sorry." He hunched in his seat, massaging his temple. "We need to know why the Fera were targeting this girl. And we need to learn what she knows. We may be able to find their nest and report its location to Master and Mistress. They'll send troops to exterminate them all before any more disasters happen."

Jaq folded his arms. "So, call them now. We agreed we could use the reinforcements."

"We've already contacted Mistress about the girl, and about the attack," Alex reported. "She's ordered us to seek refuge at the capital as soon as we speak with Maveric Liste. If the demons follow us, there will be more of our soldiers to fend them off. In the meantime, she's ordered a guard of Reapers to meet us halfway, as escorts to the capital."

"Good," said Jaq. "But, er… I'm still confused about the Sister. If she doesn't have any money, how did she get to this city?"

"According to the reports, she's been hounded by the demons since she was in Mimeir, which is near the opposite coast of where we started— which means there was at least one other Sentient following her, while *we* had two following us. So now, we have three commanding demons to deal with, one of which we haven't seen yet. We'll have to ask the girl about the one following her—"

Octavius burst inside.

"Guys!" The cat shut the door behind him, letting Shade and Mal flutter inside first. Mal went to Alexander's shoulder, seeming aggravated. Octavius came to meet us. "We might have a problem."

"I assume she's awake?" Alex rose. "Unlike Vendy…"

"Yeah, but that's not the problem. She's asking for…" He swallowed. "For Xavier."

Alex stared at him, his voice edged. "She asked for him by name?"

Octavius nodded hurriedly.

Alex groaned and looked to the ceiling. "I thought you said you didn't tell her your name?"

"*I didn't.*" I assured. *"As I said, I'd had memories of her. She must have recognized me after all."*

My window went dark as Alex shut his eyes. "Well, isn't that wonderful. Now we'll have to deal with those questions also."

Jaq heaved to his feet, stretching, and switched back to his peasant-dialect while in front of Octavius. "So, wha'da we do? Kick her out or what?"

"What good would that do?" scoffed Alex. "We'd lose any information we'd hoped to gain on the Fera. *And* we'd be back to the three of us against an entire army of them."

Octavius lifted a finger. "She said she had a friend up here somewhere. Maybe we can take her to where *she* is and ask her all that before dropping her off?"

"That could work," Alex considered, but shook his head. "Let's see what we can glean from her, first. You said she was awake?"

"Yeah," Octavius threw a thumb over his shoulder. "She said she's, um, waiting downstairs with Henry. She probably thinks I'm getting Xavier."

Alex cracked his knuckles. "Right then. It's a fine morning to crush someone's hopes."

Alex stormed out, striding down the upper hall and stopped at the top of the stairs, sliding his hands in his pockets. "Who is asking for my dead twin?" he yelled down, his tone impertinent.

Below us, the girl jumped from her seat in the lounge. She scrambled to the stairs, panting when arriving at the bottom step.

Alex gave her a strict glare. "You're a bold one, if you think I'd find that little joke funny. Shall I tread on your grief, as well?"

The girl's face fractured with shock. "Alex?"

"My, aren't we brave? Daring to speak to a High Howllord so informally." He strode down to meet her, eyes cold as he gripped her chin and turned her head in examination. "You do look familiar… are you a peasant or a Howless?"

She swatted his hand away. "I don't have time for this, Alex. Where is Xavier?"

He replaced his hand in his side. "Since you haven't started screaming, you must be from Low Neverland. No one there was afraid of us, like they are here… I'll forgive your insult and assume you were unaware. My brother has been dead for the last few years. Pay more attention to the news."

"Xavier isn't dead." She protested. "I found him yesterday. He helped me with the Fera—and helped me kill one of the Stonedragons."

"Miss, I think Octavius has neglected to check your eyesight. *I* had done that. I'm flattered you remember."

"My vision is fine," she insisted, grey fox-ears growing from her head. "I know what I saw."

"And I suppose it was him who received these scars while helping you yesterday?" He rolled up his left sleeve, showing her the dragging marks of raised skin on his shoulder. We'd had them healed after the attack, but they still pulsed and burned.

She gasped at the scars and grabbed his arm, incredulous. "No…! But this hand had the Crest… I-I had the blood on my fingers from holding it, it was *this* hand!"

Alex ripped his arm away and shoved past her, Jaq and Octavius following stiffly. "Then perhaps have your memory checked. Or better yet, have your head looked at entirely. You were imagining it."

The girl stood gaping. "But… That was his messenger earlier, wasn't it?"

My window's view circled when Alex rolled his eyes. He gave a whistle. "Mal?"

Mal croaked from upstairs before soaring down to Alexander's extended forearm, giving an annoyed screech at the girl.

"Do you mean this messenger?" he asked, presenting Mal. "Who is mine?"

"But I…" She didn't seem sure what to say. "But last night… That must have been him, he had the Hallows of souls. Which you don't have."

Alex growled under his breath to me. "You Bloody idiot."

"She was trying to kill me," I reminded.

The window went black as Alex pinched his nose. "All right, I've had enough of this. Miss, *who* are you?"

The girl straightened, clearing her throat.

"My name is Lilliana Tessinger," she said haughtily, cupping her hands. "I am the daughter of High Howllord Daniel Tessinger, the Hand of the Death King. And," she added, her chin lifting tall and proud. "I am the appointed Aide of Her Royal Highness, Death Princess Willow Ember."

OLD ACQUAINTANCES

XAVIER

Not a soul dared to speak.

Alexander was frozen where he stood; Jaq and Octavius exchanged nervous glances beside him.

Lilliana. The name rang in my memory, screaming at me. I did know the name. But something was wrong. It sounded unnatural. *Lilliana… No! It was…*

Lilli!

Yes, that was it. I vaguely remembered calling someone that, years ago. She always went by the shorter name.

"L…" Alex's eyes narrowed at her, recognition dawning. "Lilli…?"

The girl, Lilli, gave a satisfied smile, her small crow fluttering cheerfully. "So, you do remember me?"

"Good Gods." Alex cupped his mouth, sounding horrified. "*Lilli?*"

"You sound so shocked," she mused flatly. "I haven't changed that much, have I?"

"What are you trying to…" He weakly pointed an accusing finger, but bit his knuckle instead, stifling whatever curses I could hear him muttering.

He glanced at Octavius, then at Jaq. Henry had abandoned his work on the armor and stepped beside the two, his stare equally questioning at Alex, awaiting an explanation.

Alex shook his head and turned to Lilli again. *"Onet ysch choft ul myel trenn, Lilli?"* he demanded in Grimish.

Lilli staggered. Either she was puzzled by his sudden change in language or by the profanity in the question. She peered at the three lingering men behind us, all of whom now looked lost as Void since none of them spoke Grimish—Jaq only knew a few words and common phrases—and she seemed to understand: Alex wanted this conversation to be private.

She put a hand on her hip and replied. "*Onet ul* ma *trenn?* <Why are *you* here, then?>"

"<We're following an assignment.> He threw a hand at Jaq and Octavius. "<Our *last* assignment as student Reapers, I should add. Since when were you given leave from the Death Palace? You're supposed to be on the opposite Undercontinent with your father.>"

"<And you're supposed to be underneath *this* continent with yours,>" she countered. "<I think I deserve an explanation as well. Why are both you and Xavier in the same town, in the same kingdom? You can't possibly have me believe you know nothing of him?>"

"<For the last Bloody time, Xavier is dead. And you damn well know it, you were there with us when it happened.>"

"*A gegt a'ul!* <He's the one I saw in the temple last night, he must have brought me here. Now where is—?>"

"<How would you like it if I asked where your mother went?>"

She stopped cold.

"<Ah, that's right.>" He strode to the beverage cart and poured himself a glass of gin, snorting. "<Her soul was destroyed. Like my twin.>" He knocked it back and sank into a cushioned armchair, propping his feet on the matching hassock. "*Hu'choft Necros, a'hu'fett…*"

Lilli had lapsed into a long silence, her face hollow.

Behind us, I heard Octavius whisper to Jaq. "What's going on?"

"Ya got me," Jaq muttered back, his head shaking helplessly beside Henry.

Lilli slowly lowered onto the ottoman next to us, her voice soft as she switched the language back to Landish. "That… wasn't what I meant, Alex." She sucked in a pained breath before letting it go in a swallow. "I'm sorry. You must not have known."

Alex cocked an eyebrow. "Known what?"

"Xavier is alive," she hushed. "One of his memories was found in the Dream realm."

—my mood made an incredible leap from the psyche. "*A memory?*" I blurted, my voice bouncing in the void. "*MY memory?*"

Alex gave a mocking laugh, ignoring me. "I fail to see how that's relevant."

"*What was it of?*" I asked franticly and watched keenly through the window. "*Where was it set?*"

He muttered through clenched teeth to me. "It isn't relevant…"

"Damn relevance, I want that memory!" I laughed. *"Ask her how we can get it! Or what year it—"*

"Lilli," Alex sighed. "Just because you found a small memory, which may or may not be his, that doesn't mean anything."

With the baffled look she gave him, you'd think he'd decided to dye his lashes purple. "It means *everything*," she said. "Every soul's lost memories are scattered across Aspirre. And when that soul is either destroyed or disappears from Nirus, the memories disappear with them. Yet Xavier's memory was found." The smile that split her face brightened any sour mood she'd had before this. "His soul still lives… He's *alive*, Alex."

He touched his now ice-only glass to his brow, sighing. "Then, this is why you came here, is it? To… to find him?"

The little crow on her shoulder twittered before she answered shyly. "Er… Indirectly, yes."

"What do you mean, 'Indirectly'?"

"King Dream was the one who entrusted me to find Xavier," she admitted. "But only because he wished for me to reunite him with *you*."

"Dream?" Alex scowled at the name. "Why would he want that?"

She sang an exhausted sigh. "Oh, I don't know. I rarely understand the man. But, er, that isn't the *only* news…"

Alex waited for her to expound.

"After I left," she began, biting her lip, "Willow overheard where I'd gone, and what I'd planned to do. Recently, I'd gotten word that she…" Lilli blushed. *"Ma yeyt kes mea…"*

Alex's stare splintered at her. *"Yeyt kes O?"*

"Willow is here." She said in Landish, pulling her knuckles anxiously. "In Everland…"

Another wave of silence fell over us all.

"Willow is…" I didn't need to breathe in the psyche, yet I found myself suffocating. *"Willow is here?"* The room had grown distant and fuzzy, a swell of… of *something* thumping my incorporeal chest. Whether it was fear or incomparable thrill, I wasn't certain.

Jaq whistled and rubbed his nose. "Well, damn. Didn't see that comin'."

Octavius sheepishly agreed beside him. "Um, yeah… wow much?"

SLAM!

Alex hit his glass onto a table nearby, his throat ripping a growl. "Willow can't be here. She *can't Bloody be here*."

Lilli snatched his glass and poured her own shot of whiskey, glugging heavily and slamming it down with a *clack*, grimacing darkly. "She *shouldn't* be here, of that we agree… Yet here I am: tasked with finding a man who's come back from the dead, *and* returning my runaway charge before her father discovers she's left." She collapsed into the seat and hid her face in her hands, groaning despairingly. "Oh, what am I to do, Alex? I've lost the Gods damned heiress of Death! I'll be held responsible if anything happens to her, since I… Death, I wasn't supposed to leave her side in the first place! Oh, I'm ruined, Alex, *ruined…!*"

Alex breathed through his nose harshly, trying to calm, but his tone still flared. "What is your plan, then?"

She grumbled and folded her arms with hunched shoulders, crossing her legs in thought. "I suppose… since you're up here as well, we could find her and Xavier together?"

Alex shot up an impatient finger. "Oh, no, no, no. Firstly, I don't want to hear another word about Xavier. Who is dead."

"Thanks," I grunted dully.

He ignored me once again and went on. "Second, I'm not helping you find anyone. I have my own 'missing persons' assignment to handle, and I'm not failing my last test because you slipped up yours. Third." He rose, glaring bolts at her. "I think you need to leave."

She remained seated, perplexed. "What?"

"You heard me." He went to open the door, gesturing sharply to her. "It's time for you to go."

"Alex, I really don't think separating is wise," she said, fumbling to her feet. "Did you already forget that horde from yesterday? Those demons are still out there. And right now, we're the only Reapers this city has, apprentices or not. I'll… I'll leave if you wish, but *after* reinforcements arrive, which I'm sure your mother has already deployed, knowing her."

"Which is precisely the point we'd agreed on ourselves," I reminded from the psyche. *"We needed her help yesterday, and we'll surely need it again if another attack happens."*

"And…" She blushed, rocking on her heels as she cleared her throat. "I'm, er, also out of money. I can't afford a room of my own anywhere, let alone here…"

Octavius interjected meekly from the back. "She's also malnourished, remember? Feels like she's been starved for days."

She blushed further, rubbing her arm. "Yes… and that."

Alex ran a hand through his hair. "Gods dammit…" He relented and closed the door. "Fine! But listen here. If Willow has run away up here, I could be blamed for kidnapping her simply by being in the same kingdom. Right now, this entire continent thinks I want to rip off their heads. I don't need Willow's 'abduction' added to that. If I let you stay, you have to swear never to tell the Death King I was here. Is that clear?"

She nodded, her crow hopping from her shoulder in agreement. "I'll not say word. I promise."

"Good… but once those reinforcements arrive, I'm giving you enough Mel to go on your own."

She nodded again, solemnly this time, but I saw her shoulders relax nonetheless. "Thank you… I'm in your debt, truly."

"Don't blather on about debts," he muttered, going back to the cart to fill himself a new glass of whiskey. "Blasted woman, coming up here unprepared… *murrderes duxuth…*"

He stiffened when she snagged him in a hearty embrace.

"Thank you, Alex!" She squeezed tighter, overwhelmed with relief. "Bloods, am I glad Nira sent me to you of all people…!"

"All right, all right!" He wriggled free, tugging his jacket and scowled. "Death, you haven't changed… you're still annoying."

"And you're still no fun at all." She chuckled and folded her hands behind her back. "Oh, and you'll be happy to know Xavier doesn't seem to have changed either, from what I could glean last night."

He chewed on a string of curses, taking his drink. Then he nearly choked, catching the time from the clock tower outside.

"Death, it's almost noon!" He hustled to the table cluttered with half-polished armor, throwing on a set in a hurry. "Lilli, for your sake, Maveric had better still be there!"

The other three men followed Alexander's example and hurriedly donned their own armor, the viper man hopping on one foot as he pulled on his last boot and scrambled out the door behind us. After yesterday, we weren't about to take a single step outside unless we were fully equipped this time. Dirtied plate or not.

"Who had better be where?" Lilli called after us, she and the others rushing to keep pace behind us.

"Don't concern yourself with the details," he clipped, stopping at the lift and jamming the call button. "We have information to acquire. We're to meet with our contact in one of the Healing Clinics in town, and we'll be late if we dawdle any longer. This is *not* an appointment I wish to miss—the shock of your sudden arrival can wait."

The lift arrived and the cage folded open. The attendant within froze at the sight of us, paling. Alex jerked his head in a curt gesture, and the man scrambled out of the box.

Our company shuffled inside, Lilli hopping in quickly, and Alex cranked the doors closed and maneuvered the lift to descend, leaving the liftman shaking on the top floor.

Alex tapped an impatient finger on the lever, and an awkward silence swelled in the cramped box.

Lilli timidly peered at Jaq and Octavius on either side of her, then turned to Alex. "If we're going to a clinic, I don't suppose…" She cleared her throat and gestured to her boot. "I've nearly run out of my previous Healing tonic for this bite and… well, as I've said, I don't have the, er… funds for…"

"We'll purchase you another vial," Alex said. The lift stopped at the lower lobby and he led the way out, crossing the floor and stepping outside. "Irritating as you may be, I scarcely want the only extra soldier we've gained to fight with an old wound. And I have no desire to face the wrath of your father if you die up here. I'm trying to avoid him at all costs and…" He clicked his teeth shut, as though regretting that last bit.

I heard her limping steps behind us, her tone suspicious. "So I see…"

"Quickly, quickly!" he encouraged nasally, hastening his step. "And for Death's sake, keep alert. I'd like to go one Bloody day without any damned Necrofera, but given our luck thus far, I'm not fool enough to count on it—"

"aaaaaaAAAAAAAAAAHHHH!!!" A terrified scream erupted above us as we crossed the front of the Howler's Inn building, and a figure came flying down at top speed—

Squrrlsch—crack!

The rabbit-eared figure splattered into a mess of bones and pulpy, bloody muscle at our feet, dead as a sack of rotten cabbage.

Alex smeared a hand over his face and groaned. "Gods damn it, Vendy…"

Lilli screamed and rushed to the broken body, frantic. "Good Nira, did she *jump* down here?! Oh, Bloods, if I'd known she was suicidal, I wouldn't have left her up there—!"

"Lilli, be calm," Alex muttered. "She was already dead. Meet our vassal, Vendy." He gestured to the leaking chunks of what had once been Vendy.

Lilli relaxed, breathing in relief, though she kept a skeptical hand against her chest. "Oh, thank Death… er, but why did she jump?"

"I suspect she was too lazy to take the lift," he grunted, then waved a violet-glowing hand over Vendy's pieces to put them back in place, restarting her heart.

Vendy gasped awake and bolted upright, panting, her clothes now covered in blood. She looked around, everyone staring at her.

Vendy gave her illustrious, crooked-toothed grin. "Hah! It worked!" She stabbed a finger toward Lilli, exclaiming, "She's awake, *Da'torr!*"

Alex sighed.

31

NEW ALLIES

LILLI

She's a strange one, that vassal of his.

I skeptically watched Alexander muttering to the rabbit girl, Vendy, walking ahead of our makeshift squad. There was Henry taking up the back, the Landish, blond viper taking the left flank, and the skittish Infeciovoker taking the right flank. I strode in the middle of their formation, not sure where my position should be. I felt like an unwelcomed wart, having shoved myself into their troupe and now wasn't sure where my place was among them. I was also the only one lacking armor. They seemed to have prepared for only their group and no others.

Something is certainly strange here, I brooded, my gaze narrowing at Alex. Bloods, he was so much taller than I remembered. *But I remember more about him than he seems to remember about me.*

How could he believe all of that nonsense from earlier? I knew it had been years since we'd last seen one another, but after everything we'd been through, how could he have forgotten something so crucial? *Either he's playing along, or he's mixing up everything.*

I decided it must have been the latter.

Faint rumbles crackled from the sky. That accursed sun had thankfully been blotted out by encroaching clouds this morning. Oddly, the scene reminded me of Grim's ceiling mist, only darker and rupturing with distant bursts of… something. The sound was familiar, but I couldn't quite pin what it was or where it was coming from.

Alexander's Grimish comrade, the Infeciovoker, lifted his gaze to the sky and grimaced. "Land. I guess the Stormchasers are scheduled to bring this town rain today. I should've brought an umbrella…"

I frowned at him, puzzled. "What do you mean, 'bring the rain'? I thought rain appeared of its own accord up here?"

"It usually does," the Grim boy hummed, shrugging. "But we've been in a drought for a while. During those times, the Sky Knights go up there and bring storms to the driest places, kind of on rotation, in a way. It just takes them a while to get to the other cities, since their roosts are only allowed in the capital, like the Reapers."

I stared bewildered at him. "How do you know so much about this realm and its scheduled rain storms? Do you surface often?"

He laughed in a blush and rubbed his nose. "Actually, I live here."

"Oh! An immigrant?" I tapped a ponderous finger to my lips. "Then perhaps you could offer me some advice regarding this 'sun'? How did you adjust to the brightness? How long did it take for the stinging to subside?"

"Um." He squirmed, embarrassed. "I'm not an immigrant. I was born here."

I paused, gaping. "What? But your hair is…" I pointed weakly. "You're not a Grimling?"

"Nope," he said proudly. "Everlandish, born and raised. These two are the Grimlings." He waved to Alexander, then to the blond viper walking at my other side.

I stared at the viper now, craning to see the tall man's scaled face. "*You're* Grimish?" I questioned.

The viper grinned, his long fangs visible as he pushed up his rectangular spectacles and reached a hand to me. "You bet, Howless. Name's Jaq."

"Jaq…" I took his offered hand thoughtfully. Hadn't I known that name? "Oh!" I gasped. "You're *that* Jaq, aren't you? The twins were always on about a viper friend from overseas when they came to the palace. You must be him?"

The viper, Jaq, laughed cheerily. "Yep! That'd be me alright. Autographs start at twenty Yln… And however much that translates to Landish Mel."

I chuckled. "They did call you a jokester. While I'll humbly decline a valued autograph, I'm honored to finally meet you in the flesh. They'd told many stories of you, along with the Healer girl… what was her name again? Bianca?"

"Yeah," Jaq confirmed, folding his arms behind his head in a snicker. "But I bet Alex talked about *her* more than my ugly scales."

At the front, Alex inched his gaze back at us. I thought I saw the hint of a blush on his scowling face before he snapped his attention forward again.

"From what I recall," I began, "they seemed to speak of you both equally. Is she here as well? I'd love to meet the *master chemist* they spoke so highly of."

Alex chewed on a growl from the front. "Bianca left Grim three years ago. She's been here on the surface, studying to be a Healer. It's been... some time since we've seen her, outside a com call."

"Oh," I said. "Then, will you visit her while you're here? Could I meet her?"

Alex grumbled. "Provided we survive long enough to get our information and get the Void out of this Fera infested city, sure. Why not?"

"That would be ideal..." I sighed and turned to the Infeciovoker, humming. "Now, if you're a Landish local, does this mean you're a recent addition to this troupe? Sir...?"

Octavius laughed bashfully and waved his hands. "I-I'm not a Sir yet, I just started this Reaper gig... I just, um..." He flushed scarlet and started again in a flustered smile. "I-I'm Octavius. They came up here to look for my mom's ghost, she's missing from Grim."

"Oh." I blinked, turning to Alex. "This is the assignment you mentioned?"

Alex grunted in reply. "Yes. This doctor we're meeting was her old Healing Master and may well know where her ghost has gone."

"Dearest Death, I hope she hasn't been eaten!" I fanned an aghast hand to my collarbone. "With the Fera's outrageous numbers, I see why you're so urgent to find her. Being an exposed ghost in this environment is extremely dangerous."

"Precisely," Alex said, turning a corner and stopping before the steps of, what I assumed was, the Healing Clinic he sought. "This is the one... And it's only five minutes after noon. He'd better still be here."

He stormed up the steps and shoved open the gnarled, wooden doors.

Jaq hurried at his heels, followed by Vendy and Henry, yet Octavius lingered beside me, watching me limp up the steps, my wound swelling at the pressure.

"U-um..." He blushed, wincing in sympathy as I took another determined step. "Do... do you want some help?"

"I'm perfectly fine," I assured, climbing with a straight face, though the wound burned and thudded dully under my boot. *Perhaps I'll ask the doctors for an anesthetic as well...* "Nothing more than an annoyance."

"Um." He gave me a twisted look. "I can feel it burning."

Ah, yes... the Infeciovoker. I sighed and reached the last step, walking inside. "I've been through worse, believe you me," I said. "I'll simply add this to my arsenal of sensory-illusions. A combative Necrovoker's training involves inflicting oneself with such pains, it will be all the better if I make my enemies hurt to this degree in the future."

Octavius staggered, his shoes squealing softly over the tiled floor of the clinic's lobby. "You... *hurt* yourself?" he asked skeptically. "For *training?*"

"Of course." I cocked an eyebrow, not sure why this was shocking. "It's standard practice, for Necrovokers who follow a martial career path. If one is to expect dangerous combat, it is prudent to add the self-torture regiment to one's training, to collect painful sensations to later give to your adversaries."

He looked ill. "That just sounds so... I mean... you at least heal afterward, right?"

"Of course. Though, most inflictions leave scars that can't be healed." I swept my bundled hair away from my neck and pulled down the back of my tunic's collar, showing him the tail end of hardened scars, tribute to my early years of training. "You'll find most Necrovokers with these scars, typically on their backs."

"But Alex doesn't have any," Octavius protested. "I've seen his back, and it's pretty clear except for a couple claw marks. But he said those were from a Fera attack on a ship, when he was younger."

"Alex is a... curious exception," I explained. "Has he told you of his twin?"

Octavius's green eyes flicked away for a brief moment. "Uh. Y-yeah. Kind of... what about him?"

"Xavier and Alexander are oddities in the Necrovoking community. While Alexander is indeed a fellow Necrovoker, he lacks the soul-half of our Hallows, which holds the sensory-illusions. *Xavier* was born with that half, so it had been he who underwent that training with the rest of us in the Death Palace. Alexander underwent different training instead... which seemed to have paid off, if that truly was him who'd raised that enormous dragon-corpse yesterday..."

Now that I thought on it, perhaps I *had* been mistaken after all? Xavier could never raise a single bone, let alone a dragon corpse that colossal.

But the Crest had been on his left hand. Of that, I was certain. And when I'd spoken to him in the temple last night, he referenced how we'd met during the disaster... *Could Xavier have stepped in unbeknownst to Alex?*

Something very bizarre was happening here, and I intended to get the bottom of it. Swiftly.

Whispers began to rise in the clinic's lobby, and I belated noticed many eyes flicking to me. They were murmuring about my clothes. What was so interesting about my...

I gasped when I looked at my raggedy garb, the brown tunic and matching trousers wrinkled and stained with dark splotches from unknown substances.

Nira Cleanse me! I blushed and stiffly wrapped my arms around my front, as if this would hide the greasy garments from their watchful gaze. *I'm still wearing the prison clothes!*

Alex had rushed out of the inn so quickly, I hadn't thought to look at my wardrobe. I should have changed—what if someone calls the Raiders, thinking I'm an escaped prisoner?

I AM an escaped prisoner, I reminded, panicking. *Death, Death, Death, Death—*

"He hasn't arrived?" Alexander barked from the clinic's front counter, irritated at the male nurse behind the window. His booming voice drew the attention of the awaiting patients in the lobby, their focus no longer on me. "We'd arranged a meeting with him for noon today! How could he not be here?"

The nurse shook behind the counter, his bear ears growing in fright. "I-I-I'm sorry, High Howllord! We haven't heard a word from him today...! He-he may arrive soon though!"

Alex let out an aggravated breath. "Fine... we shall wait until he arrives." He glanced back at me, muttering to the nurse. "In the meantime, we have a comrade in need of medical attention. See to it that she is cared for immediately."

"Y-yes, High Howllord!" The nurse squeaked, calling back to me. "P... p-p-please follow me, miss! I'll have one of our doctors see you in room 3...!"

I rushed out of the lobby and dashed into the backrooms, my laughter nervous. "Ah-hah, yes, thank you!" I reached the nurse and leaned in to whisper in his bear ear. "And, er, I don't suppose you have any spare garbs I could borrow...?"

32

A FERRET ONE STEP BEHIND

RINGËD

The train whistled in the echoing station, and I scarfed down the sandwich I'd ordered from the built-in eatery.

Kurn's furry head dipped and twisted at me, the feral ferret snickering like he was the saddest Gods damned thing on the planet. "<Awful butler…!>" he cried in his breathy language, rolling onto his back and flailing his stubby paws in a pathetic tantrum. "<Sadistic, terrible, cruel, ruthless, callous…!>"

"oo had 'oor haff," I said between chews, waving the sandwich at the discarded crusts and lettuce pieces the little bastard didn't even finish. I swallowed. "That was more than enough."

"<I'm a growing exiled-emperor!>" he complained and rolled on his belly, flopping flat onto the table in a pout. "<I need to keep up my energy if I'm going to keep living on this bi-pedal rock long enough to find my home planet and take back my empire!>"

I snorted a laugh. "Right. Well, in the meantime, you can wait another five hours like a normal feral."

He squeaked. "<Horrible, selfish, ugly…!>"

I rolled my eyes—

—*I know her.*

I froze in my seat, my Third Eye opening as a vision slammed through my brain.

My point of view fell away, and I now looked through someone else's eyes, the station disappearing, the chatter and train whistles dimming into silence. They were replaced by terrified screams, Necrofera scrambling through the streets like skeletal globs of tar.

I Bloody know her…! The thought was a mix of elation and panic. The narrator's feet spurred into motion as he sliced the demon pinning down his Sister Reaper.

The vision faded, my point of view coming back.

The tiled floors and echoing ceiling of Lindel's eastern train station dripped back to my attention, and I let my shoulders relax, exhaling hard.

That must have been yesterday. I'd seen that on the news earlier. But this had been through *his* eyes. Again.

I buried my head in my hands, groaning. "Bloods, Kurn, I have to find them before something else happens. Maybe these visions will leave me the Bloods alone when I actually *meet* them in…"

I paused, touching my face with my fingers; my fingers that had been empty after I came out of that vision; my fingers that *hadn't* been empty *before* I went into it.

"Kurn…" I growled, looking for the furry bandit and not seeing him on the table anymore. "*Where* is my sandwich?"

I swung my head under the table.

Kurn was huddled at my feet, chewing on the last of my deli ham, a piece of lettuce laying between his ears like a hat of shame. He noticed me and squeaked, scurrying away.

"Oh, no you don't!" I grabbed him by his long belly and yanked him to my face. "What did I Bloody say about stealing *my* food?"

The ferret squirmed and wriggled in my hold, frantically blubbering. "<Y-you usually don't come out of those visions for another five minutes!>"

"This was a short one." I kept hold of him and slung my bag over my shoulder, storming out of the station. "Come on, you fat little bastard. We've got to find that Grimling."

33

THE WILLOW OF ASHES

XAVIER

A torrent of dripping water doused us when we left the clinic.

The storm had arrived, and I spied several winged shifters flying above us. They wove in and out of the rolling clouds, dressed in scarlet, rubbery uniforms and wielding archer's bows, the Stormchasers whooping and laughing in a thrill as they soared over our heads in the distance. Perhaps they were preparing to harvest the lightning within the storm? I'd heard these were part of a Stormchaser's duties. It was fascinating to watch.

Though, that curiosity soon dripped into gloom, the reminder of today's failure creeping back to mind.

Maveric hadn't shown. We'd waited until the clinic closed, and still, he never came.

We consigned to try again tomorrow, hoping his absence today had been a fluke. Though, I doubted we would be so fortunate.

If he's left the city to run from us, I thought in the psyche, a sinking pit curdling in my floating spirit, *I'll have lost the one lead that may know where to find my body.*

I gazed solemnly out the window of my brother's vision, watching as Alexander and our company ran through the rainy streets back to the Howler's Inn. When they entered the shelter of the expansive lobby, their boots squealed and creaked over the marble floor, dripping puddles in their wake and drenching the carpet of the lift as they climbed the floors and made their way back to our master chambers.

Once Alexander shut our door, he asked if I wished to take over. I'd been inside the psyche all day because of Lilli, and now that we were alone and away from her, I jumped at the chance to switch.

I took Alexander's place in the physical world and breathed in deeply, stretching and curling my fingers, the touch of chilled rain prevalent on my skin.

I shivered, my clothes soaked and sticking uncomfortably. The coldness I could ignore, living in the freezing, underground caves of Grim all your life acclimated you to cold weather. The wetness, though… that was different. I've only experience 'rain' once before this. But I hardly wished to relive that memory.

Regardless, I was glad as Death to be in control again. The day may have nearly been over, but I'd take any chance I could get at being out. There was no telling when the next opportunity would arise these next few weeks.

I shuddered. I'd go mad if I were forced to spend so long trapped in that Bloody void, never feeling, never touching… not existing. Perhaps I really would disappear, after so long.

I peeled out of my soaked garments and changed into dry clothes, dropping into one of the cushioned seats and propping up my feet on a hassock before flicking on the vision-screen.

A flattened square of projected light brightened along the wall where the crystal was planted, and I set down the controller to watch the news station, twisting a finger in my ear in an effort to rid it of water. *Let's see what these people are reporting about us that has them talking so damned much.*

Our rising publicity had me worried. What if this footage reached the Death King? Would he ask why Alexander was in the Uppercontinent?

And, I shivered, half from my wet hair that chilled my ears and half from a new realization, *The Death King has soul-sight. Were he to notice my eyes compared to Alexander's, would he piece together our crime?*

My focus returned to the reports, deciding to banish that worry for another time, and I sank further into the chair's plush cushions.

Though, there was something strange about these reports. I picked up the controller and flipped the channel to a different station. Bloods, *everyone* was discussing the sequence of attacks over the last few weeks.

The attacks only occurred where Lilli and our company had visited. There were zero sightings in the other cities. Everywhere we *weren't* seemed to be left alone. Were Cilia, Lucrine and this third Sentient only focusing their attacks in locations *our* groups stayed?

"I know what I saw," a tiger-eared man clipped on the screen. He was being interviewed as a witness to the most recent attack here in Lindel. *"The Reapers were left alone. They were talking with the demons, commanding them. They're friends with the things!"*

"That's quite a bold claim," the interviewer hummed, looking intrigued. *"What exactly did they say to the Necrofera?"*

"Probably something about where to hit next, I bet. I have a friend who saw that Grimlette in a different town, too, when his place got attacked. Same thing—she wasn't hurt. And now they're all together here. I don't know about you, but I'm moving before anything else happens. Gotta warn the other Everlanders listening out there, too. If you see any Reapers, get the Void out of town. It means demons are coming."

I watched the rest of the interview in disbelief. He expressed his opinion on what must be done: either banish us from the kingdom or sentence us to death for our 'crimes'. If we weren't careful, it seemed Everland might not be safe for us… With or without demons.

My gaze moved to something on the wall then. Below the screen, there were many dots of sparkling light on the wallpaper, holding brilliant colors as if from a prism.

I searched for the source of these lights… and found Lilli's amulet on the table beside me.

Ah, that's right. I'd almost forgotten I'd put it there for her to find. She must not have seen it.

Its diamond-encrusted case glittered with brilliant white crystals and blue stones, a beauty fit for a noblewoman of the highest standing. I lifted it by its thin, delicate chain, admiring the intricate design.

There was a knob above the amulet's dial. I pressed it with a thumb and the casing clicked open, revealing an equally breathtaking inner-framework that trailed with small diamonds and azure gemstones. The frame bowed on either side of the circular watch, one side taking the form of a stylistic fox and the other taking the form of a wolf. The fox had an azure gem placed where its eye would be and the wolf had a clear diamond. Underneath the two silver creatures was a disc made of ebony, speckled with white jewels in the shape of diamonds.

These jewels were strange, though… They flaked with some sort of dust, dull and soft as if they would rub away at the slightest touch. Almost like… ash.

Curious, I wound back the dial, feeling the soft ticks of clockwork gears tinkering within. When I released it, the disc inside began to spin, and the twinkling music from last night echoed from the watch.

Just as the melody played its first line, the white specks of dull jewels began to glow, giving off an ethereal mist as the soft flakes came to life in a sparkling dust.

Wondrous Artist… I couldn't look away. The beauty of the lights was something I'd never seen before, the powder frosting the ebony disk like an icy wind as it revolved under the silver framework. And the music…

What was it about this song? There was something there, nagging at the back of my memory…

"Do you hear something?" I recalled Alexander asking me in the Weeping Woods years ago.

I'd listened to the faint wind chimes twinkling in the distance. It was the same, solemn song that always played from that amulet…

A soft glow glared at my vision, distracting me. I glanced at my hand—

"Bloods be good!" I yelped in a flinch.

My mark of black diamonds was *gleaming*, pulsating a faint, violet-and-black light, like a shadow misting through purple lamps.

Startled, I shut the amulet.

Once the music halted, the shadowy light faded from the diamonds on my hand, and all was normal once more.

"Wh… what was that?" I whispered to Alex. So, so cautiously, I opened the case again. When the music started and the sparkling dust swirled—

My mark shined as it had before, the shadowed light of black and violet pulsing again.

I stared at my glowing mark, terrified yet… fascinated… "Are you seeing this…?" I hushed to Alex, mesmerized. "Or am I hallucinating?"

Alex gave a hum from my head. *"No, it's real. It did that back then, also."*

"Did this happen last night…?" I turned my hand over in dazed observation. "I must have been too distracted to look…"

"Oh!" someone gasped, making me whirl.

Lilli lingered under our suddenly-opened doorframe.

I shut the watch. The light faded from my mark while I hurried to hide my left hand from her. "You should knock first before barging in here." I tried to sound stern like Alexander, my eyes locked on the floor.

"Oh," she said, hesitating. "I'm sorry for the intrusion… May I come in?"

I quickly fell back into the psyche to switch with my brother. "What is it?" Alex growled, hostile. "I allowed you to take this room for one night, but we've arranged for you to share Vendy's chambers across the hall. Henry's agreed to share a room with Octavius, so you needn't worry about—"

"I was only looking for my music watch," she explained. "Could I have it back?"

He gave a scoff and held the amulet out for her to take. She approached with light steps. "Thank you… I was afraid I'd lost it."

He handed it back and looked at the black diamonds on his right hand. "I… see it plays that same song."

She slid it round her neck and flicked her eyes at him in suspicion. She seemed to be debating something in silence, but after a moment, she shook her head and gave a separate breath. "Does your mark still glow to it?"

She clicked open the watch to test it. The music played like before, the lights glittering with a frosted mist again.

Alexander's mark began to gleam from his right hand, just as mine had done, the shadow pulsing black and violet. He and Lilli stared at it.

"Apparently." He muttered, scratching his neck.

She closed the watch. "Always so strange… we never did find out what it meant, did we?"

"No." He said, perhaps a little too quickly. His tone had me suspicious.

It grew silent, and the vision-screen's reporters chatted in the background until Lilli spoke again. "Your friends are rather interesting."

Alex gave an indifferent shrug. "Jaq may seem brash, but he means well."

"I was referring more to your cat friend," she clarified.

"Ah…" Alex cleared his throat. "Octavius is rather new to us, as he mentioned."

She raised a speculative finger to her lips. "There's something I wished to ask you regarding… Octavius. Why have you taken him in, yet not explained about… well, about that man?"

He flicked away his gaze. "I hardly see how that's necessary…"

She snorted. "Spare me. He's a black-haired cat shifter *and* an Infeciovoker? That Hallows is extinct. For you to be traveling with one at all is outrageous. But why are you hiding the assassin from him?"

"How does it concern you?" he sneered.

"Because if you want me to keep this from him as well, I think I should know the reason."

He kept his stubborn gaze on the wall. After a moment, he answered, "He's… not only here to train with us. He's looking for his mother's soul and… also hoping to find his father."

"And his father…?"

"Left their home six years ago."

"Infeciovoker?"

He nodded. "We don't want to worry Octavius over a suspicion."

"But what if he *is* the one who killed Xavier?"

He rubbed his shoulder, looking at the clock along the wall. "We don't know."

"'We'?"

"It's getting late. I think you've stayed long enough."

"Oh… Of course." She stepped back through the doorway, seeming either embarrassed or annoyed to be so offhandedly dismissed. "I'll stay silent, if… that's what you wish?"

His gaze flicked to her, both in request and appreciation. "It is. Thank you, Lilli."

She nodded, then quietly closed the door behind her. There was silence behind the door for a time, then we heard her soft footfalls retreat on the carpet, and the door to the next room clicked closed.

Alex lifted his right hand, examining his mark. It wasn't glowing anymore. "Same as before, then…"

I gave a low mutter. *"You knew about that amulet? And our Crests?"*

His head tilted in a half shrug. "It's always done this, around it."

"And you failed to mention this to me over the last six years because…?"

Another shrug. "I suppose I… forgot."

I laughed. *"Forgive my skepticism, but our marks glowing to some piece of jewelry hardly seems forgettable—"*

"I had more pressing concerns at the time, Xavier," he snapped. "After the assassin slaughtered everyone, and you ended up *trapped in my body*, you expect me to give a damn about my Crest?" His teeth barred and he shut his eyes. "I wasn't hiding it. I suppose… I still forget sometimes that you lost your memories. I hadn't even considered that you may not remember what we found that night."

"What do you mean?" I asked, a dark feeling gripping my spirit.

He hesitated. "The night you disappeared… before the assassin… we found something, in the woods. Our marks had the same reaction, gleaming as it did."

Woods… my dream from this morning came to mind: Alexander and I wandered the Weeping Woods, searching for a Fallen Light. Our marks gleamed that same, shadowy light, ash swirling in the mist around us…

"I… think I remember," I said, hushed. *"Or, part of it. Our marks were leading us somewhere. I don't remember the rest…"*

"We didn't think it actually existed." He glanced out the window distantly. "It was supposed to be a myth."

"What are you talking about? What did we find?"

His stare glazed out to the Harmonist temple across the street. Rain applauded over the clear glass as a silent streak of light burst from the grey sky.

"The Lost Relic of Death," he whispered. "We'd found the Willow of Ashes."

34

HORRIBLE HOLIDAY

UNNAMED

"*Adrial Station,*" the train's speakers announced pleasantly in the first-class compartment, snagging my attention. "*Now arriving at Adrial Station.*"

I straightened in my seat, stretching my bat wings in a yawn.

Finally. Between the ferry ride from Low Neverland to the next Undercontinent, Surfacing to *High* Everland, and taking this train into the city, I was exhausted. It'd taken me weeks to arrive here, it was about time I was drawing close to my quarry. *And Nira knew she was in for a sharp reprimanding after having me run around the whole Bloody realms.*

I reached into my Storagesphere and plucked out my compact powder and mirror, patting my nose and smoothing down a stray strand of my silky, black hair, checking to be sure the sparkling hairpins and jewelry were in their proper places, keeping my hair in a twisted, perfect bun that was tied with a pink ribbon.

I rose and smoothed the short skirts of my rose-pink gown, turning to the crow perched on the back of my seat.

"Come, Dusk," I huffed, presenting my pink-sleeved arm to her. The crow fluttered and alighted on my offered arm, puffing her feathers and holding her head high. "We've that Bloody girl's mess to clean up."

Dusk gave a prim caw and twitched her head, and I followed the other noble passengers out to the echoing platform.

An attendant was blathering on about 'curfews' and 'escorts' to the crowd. I rolled my eyes and strode around the mass, seeing myself to the exit.

"Escorts," I muttered to Dusk on my arm, scoffing as I stepped out to the dark streets and headed for the towering building in the distance, its glowing, silver letters spelling *Howler's Inn*. "As if I need the protection of those who are ill-equipped to save anyone from Necrofera."

I fiddled with the glowing scythe-spheres dangling from my neck, assured that I had my weapons in case such a scenario were to find me. The news reports on the train certainly made one cautious to even surface at a time like this—what was that blasted girl thinking, coming here with such a disaster waiting for her?

I yawned and stretched my arms over my head, leathery wings flexing stiffly. Having them folded so often during my traveling had left them rigid. Perhaps once they'd regain their circulation, it would be prudent to fly and give them a good stretch… but for now, I would make do with walking to the Howler's Inn.

Perhaps now that I've arrived, I ought to call Mother Alice. I reached into my Storagesphere chained round my waist and pulled out my silver communicator, its exposed gears and springs glinting in the lamplight as I passed under it in the street. *Perhaps she can arrange a last-minute reservation for their family's inn here?*

I dialed the appropriate number, adding the extension to bypass their corresponding servant so I could make a direct call—

"Miss…!" A beggar shuffled in front of me, his beady eyes gleaming under matted hair and a grimy face. "Miss, please…! Some Mel, any will do…!"

"Ew!" I leapt back in a gag, plugging my nose as Dusk ruffled her feathers from my arm. "Gods, that *stench*! What a hideous creature!" I promptly rounded him and quickened my pace, flapping my wings to speed up their circulation recovery.

"Please, Miss…!" The beggar scuttled after me, his voice a strained wheeze, teeth brown and crooked. "Please…! Just one bead of Mel…!"

Disgusting! I hurried on faster. *Just ignore him and he'll go away.*

He didn't fall behind. Instead, the bug whirled in front and dropped to his knees, sweaty hands clasping my fingers. "Please, miss…! Just one bead!"

"Ew, ew, *ew*!" I shook his dirty presence from my hands. "Don't touch me!"

Desperate to wipe the slime off my hands, I hurried around him. He kept following. "Please…! Just one…!"

"Fine, *fine*! Just get away from me!"

I fumbled for my Storagesphere and pulled out a pink, velvet sack of Mel beads, scooping up a handful and scattered them on the street. "Here! Bloody parasite. Now go—"

He snatched my Storagesphere, breaking the delicate chain around my waist, then grabbed my com and bag of Mel.

I gasped as he ran off into the shadows, only leaving behind the beads I'd thrown at him.

"He—hey!" My voice was shrill, bat ears growing. I took flight, ignoring the icy prickles in my wings as I soared over the buildings, searching frantically for the disgusting thief. "Come back here at once!" I called down, but I couldn't see him from the shadows. "That has my passport…!"

My fangs gritted furiously, and I touched onto a building's flat roof, puffing. *Well, that settles it.*

I'd only been in High Everland for two hours, and I already hated the place.

35

THE DREAMCATCHER

XAVIER

I squeezed a breath through my cinched throat, panicking, my windpipe crushed by leaden fingers.

I grabbed the arm holding me up, grip slipping from the rain, and my feet kicked above the threatening waves. Through the storm's chaos, I looked past my captor.

Willow lay on the rocky ground. She was older this time, her face undefined and blurry. I struggled to reach for her, trying to break free of the man choking me—

His fingers snapped open.

I rushed down the cliff, the ocean's waves foaming below as I shut my eyes and prepared to hit the water—

A hand suddenly snagged my wrist.

"You again, huh?" a new voice muttered. I was yanked up to safety. "Do you give all the Catchers this much trouble?"

My lids flew open. I was on my feet and standing on a roped bridge tied to either side of two cliffs. When had this appeared?

The man who'd saved me wore a hooded azure cloak with white, velvety trim. Many silver chains dangled between parallel buttons that trailed down the length of the garment. His face was hidden by a white fox mask.

He held some strange metal pole in his hand with a dome-shaped fabric on top, which was hoisted above both our heads and shielding us from the cold rain.

I stammered, "Who… who are you?"

"Name's Jimmy." The fox-masked man extended a gloved hand to me. "Central Lindel's Dreamcatcher: Department of sleeping travelers." He gave a short shake when I took his hand. "What's your name, kid?"

I hesitated, still bleary. "I… er, Xavier…"

"All right," he hummed thoughtfully. "So, uh, are you the son of Lucas Devouh, or is that the other kid I keep seeing?"

"It…" I rubbed my head, my brain rushing to sober. "We're both…"

He scratched his chin when I couldn't finish a coherent sentence. "Guess you're that twin, then… Weird, I kind of thought you were… aw, never mind. You guys traveling separately or something? Haven't seen you both on the screens, it's always just one of you."

"You're not… afraid of us?"

"Nah, the new Eyes is a Reaper, right?" He gestured to me. "We've got the same goal in mind, Reapers and Catchers. We just want to make sure no one's soul gets hurt, so I figure if the new Eyes was chosen to be a Reaper, there's no way he's anything like the last guy." He laughed. "But I gotta say, never had many problems in my district 'till you showed up. You've got some dangerous dreams, kid. Giving me a run for my Mel."

"You've been watching my dreams…?" I hushed, straining to grasp what was happening. Was this a dream, or…?

"It's my job to watch your dreams," he said, pounding his chest with pride as his fox-mask lifted to the dripping sky in a gloating laugh, "We're knights of the Dream realm. If you die in your dreams, your soul does too. Where'd you go to school? They don't teach you that?"

"I… I'm sorry, I can't…" I rubbed my eyes hard. Ah! Yes, that's right: the Dreamcatchers. Slowly, awareness was returning, my dream-like fog dissipating. "I'm sorry," I began again. "I'm admittedly not familiar with seeing you all while on duty. Our Catcher at home doesn't show herself in our dreams."

"Bet you give her a lot of trouble," he muttered. "So, what's your deal? You have the same dream of being thrown off a cliff two nights in a row? You got some problems, kid, way down in your subconscious."

I wasn't really sure how to reply to that. "You saved me yesterday, also?"

He began walking along the rope-bridge, bringing his rain-shielding item with him. I followed after him, watching as he waved a glowing blue hand and created a set of stepping indentions in the cliffside.

"Yeah, you're sleeping in my district of town," he explained as we climbed the steps and stopped at the rift I'd fallen from. "I'm in charge of travelers around here, during the night shift. Had to wake you up before you died and all that… What's with the girl, by the way?"

He nodded to Willow, whose flickering figure was still lying on the ground. The Catcher's fox-mask tilted. "Old girlfriend?"

Willow was frozen in time as the rain sprayed around her, soaking her ashen hair and dripped down her cheeks. She phased in and out of focus, like a scratched vision-gem with a faulty signal.

I didn't answer his question, staring at Willow.

"Well, anyway," Jimmy began in a separate thought, "I'd be careful on the streets if I were you. People are starting to talk about you Grimlings. They're saying you probably brought the demons here yourselves. Might want to stay out of trouble."

"Why have you shown yourself?" I finally regained more clarity again. "It's not usual for Dreamcatchers to approach someone in their dreams. Why are you speaking to me?"

"It's not usual, sure, out of privacy. But you seemed interesting. Nothing ever happens in this part of Aspirre. The most I get is some kid dreaming he's gone to school in his nickers. You're the most work I've had in a long time."

"But why do you hide your face?" I questioned. "I don't think our Catcher wears a mask."

"She must be a hired Catcher. Most barons have them. With us local Catchers, most people don't like the idea of someone spying on their dreams when they're sleeping. We keep our face hidden so people don't come after us in the conscious world."

"And you didn't think I would come after you?"

He circled me, teetering the domed cloth and pole over his shoulder. "Like I said before, Reapers and Catchers have the same goal in mind. And, uh, most of the Landish shifters dislike the Reapers as much as us Catchers right now. So like I said, be careful... Is that the Death Princess, by the way?"

He gestured behind me. "That is her, isn't it? Hah, bet my king would be pretty interested to know you're dreaming of his granddaughter."

I started to protest, but he held up a pausing hand. "Hey, it's fine, I'll keep it between us. I actually wanted to show you something real quick. Just wanted to make sure you were the right twin."

He gestured for me to follow and walked away. I staggered behind, asking, "Where are we going?"

"To get something that, I'm pretty sure, belongs to you."

We headed up to the barren craters along the other side of the plateau.

Then the rain stopped, and the ground vanished beneath our feet.

I gave a startled yelp and dropped several feet below, only to catch myself on a floating piece of... what was this, a road? It was made of bricks, which were plastered together in a perfect square just big enough to hold me.

I straightened, feeling the cool brick beneath my bare feet. There was naught here save the floating square I stood upon. Now, I was in an abyss of nothingness.

"Watch your step, kid," the Dreamcatcher's voice sounded above me.

My head snapped up. He was on his own square of bricked road, crouching over the edge and looking down at me behind his fox-mask. His rain-shielding item had vanished.

"People who can't evoke my Hallows usually can't leave their own subconscious," he said, "so stick close to me if you don't want to be falling for the rest of the night. It'd be a real mess for me if you jumped into someone else's dream. I'd have one confused client."

The Catcher weaved a set of stairs between his brick square and mine, and waved for me to climb up. I shivered on my way, skin cold from the previous rain.

"Here," the Catcher began, noticing my chilled skin and soaked garments. He lifted a hand to me, and his fingers gleamed blue. "Let me help with that."

The water peeled away from my skin, then was sucked out of my clothes and hair. The extracted water waved into a massive ball in midair between us. I watched in awe as the sphere of rainwater began spinning into a whirlpool within its center, and the water drained into itself before disappearing with a small plink!

I was dry, and no longer freezing.

"All right." The Dreamcatcher rubbed his hands together. "Now that that's all taken care of, let's hurry on. We're wasting moonlight here."

He continued along the path, one hand out before him that glowed with a blue light as the brick at our feet pieced themselves together. They formed a safe path for us to follow in the void.

Then something changed. The darkness became lit with a strange, ethereal light and the void soon filled with objects.

The floor appeared first, made of cluttered wood and creaking planks. Then the walls came into view. The paint was peeling from old age and a strange smell permeated. It was the scent of rubber and aged leather.

The floors were now scattered with shoes; some worn, some unworn, some unfinished and some coming apart. The faint tinkling of a shop's bell sounded around the corner behind me.

Voices murmured up ahead. They were muffled at first until we rounded the corner of this unkempt hallway, and there I saw an opened door.

The room inside was covered in clothes scattered about the floor, and even the small desk was hidden under crumpled textbooks and papers. A single bag rested against the wall beside a black, stringed instrument, and the walls were covered with indecent posters, wall-scrolls with various band names and a single, tattered calendar with circled dates in red ink.

I already knew whose room this was before spotting the lone figure on the bed.

Jaq sat with one leg hanging over the tattered mattress, scratching a confused hand over his blond hair as his brow twitched under his rectangular glasses. "So, uh… Sorry about tryin' to eat ya, Alex," he said.

"You'd better be sorry!" a toad croaked from the edge of the bed. It had my brother's voice. "You don't start eating anything that moves!"

Jaq's arms folded. "Well I'm hungry. We don't have enough money to get groceries yet, what else do I get? And where's Xavier, anyway? Are you both in there or what?"

"No, I'm right here, Jaq," my own voice called beside him. Yet I hadn't spoken.

Jaq flinched when he saw his messenger crow sitting on the mattress suddenly. He gapped. "B-Bridge?!"

The crow laughed in my voice. "No, it's me! Can't you tell?"

The last I saw of the scene was Jaq scuttling back and letting out a terrified yell. I tried to stifle my laughter, but couldn't help myself while I caught up to the Dreamcatcher, who'd walked on without me.

"What was that?" I chuckled as the cluttered hallway disappeared and was replaced with the same black void as before. We started on the brick path the Catcher weaved for us. "Where are we?"

"Aspirre," he said from behind his mask. "These are shifters' dreams. We're traveling through your friends' right now."

"So, that was Jaq's dream." I grinned. "Are all of his dreams that entertaining?"

He chuckled. "Most of them. He's the weird dreamer of your group."

"What am I?"

His fox-mask tilted in consideration. "The most trouble."

We entered through a much nicer, carpeted hallway. The only source of light came from a small crack of a partly opened door.

"Whose dream is this?" I asked, observing the smooth walls beside me and recognizing the scents of spiced blossoms and candle wax perfuming the carpet. "This looks like our manor in Grim."

He let out a dismal grunt. "This is the depressing one."

A boy sat against the wall outside the parted door. He looked like an adolescent, hunched over his folded legs, his face buried in his knees. His shaggy grey hair fell over his eyes while he listened to the voices murmuring inside the room.

"What will we do, Lucas…?" a woman asked, and I realized it was my mother. Her voice was so shaken, I almost hadn't recognized her. "We don't know why this is happening. What's to become of them if we don't find a cure?"

"Is there a cure, Alice?" my father's voice snapped. "We've looked through every damned book there is on soul theology and history—this isn't written in any of

them! Are they trapped like this for the rest of their lives? Will one of them slip out suddenly without warning? Will it KILL Alexander like a disease—?"

"Hush! You'll wake them and frighten the boys with that sort of talk."

The voices faded when we passed.

I stared at the boy sitting against the wall, his hands balling tighter as he listened.

"So, you're that twin that supposedly went missing," the Dreamcatcher hummed. "Man, I can't tell you how confused I was when you first got here. I kept getting your dreams mixed up. Then I figured out yours are the only ones with the Death Princess."

I pried my gaze away from my brother, turning to the Catcher. "Where exactly are we going?"

"It's right here." He came to a stop, gesturing forward.

At first, I saw nothing. But then I noticed a ball of light was floating in front of us.

I leaned closer to examine the light. "What is that supposed to—?"

The ball zipped round and shot at my forehead, sinking into my skull with a startling, cold wind.

The Dreamcatcher vanished.

Soft grass sprouted under my feet.

I was twelve now, somehow I knew this. I sat down and rummaged through a wicker basket of apples, autumn leaves scattered over the ground in pastel colors of orange, yellow and red. The orchard hushed when a breeze swept past, the looming clouds bright with morning lights that floated within their mist.

This was the royal orchard, in Grim's palace.

Crisp smoke from the castle's hearths pleasantly spiced my nostrils while I plucked a bruised apple from the basket and tossed it aside. I shuffled through the pile and found a bright red fruit, crunching into it, leaning back and watched the clouds overhead.

Someone pushed against my back.

"When do you think they'll return from their hunt?" A girl sighed behind me.

Spread over the grass at my feet were long strands of white, ashen hair. My head craned to look at her. We were leaned back to back, a second basket of apples waiting by Willow's bare feet.

She sorted her fruit into two piles: those with one color, and those with mixed splotches. She had a silver tiara atop her head engraved with small skulls, and her long strands hid her face from me.

I swallowed the piece of apple I'd bitten off. "They oughtn't take long. You know how they are when hunting demons in the forest. 'A swift and efficient extermination', that's what my mother prefers if they find a nest."

"My father says the same thing." She singled one apple from the rest, inspected it, then took a bite.

The fruit she'd chosen was an exact mix of red and green, the colors meeting halfway at the center. I grinned. "Why do you always pick the half-colored apples?"

She gave a questioning hum, chewing.

"In the two years I've known you," I said, "I don't think I've ever seen you eat a full-colored apple. What is so special about the halved ones?"

She took a moment to swallow. "Nothing, really. I suppose I fancy the colors. They're more… interesting, being two things at once."

"Two things at once?" I laughed. "I wonder, do they remind you of a certain someone, dear princess of Death and Dream?"

"I… supposed they do…" She sounded flustered, hiding her face behind her hair. "I like halved things. Half-colored apples, my halved blood… You and Alexander are halves of each other, also. And Lilli is even halfblooded. She's like me, though by different means."

That caught my interest. "Even Lilli? In what way?"

Willow hesitated. "Perhaps she'll tell you one day, but at the moment, she's… not fond of her 'halved' status. Though, that trait is part of why I chose her as my Aide. She may not accept that part of herself yet, but I hope she'll know that I won't judge her for it, when she does. After all, I know what it's like to be looked at like a diplomatic mistake. It's… lonely."

My gaze lowered, looking at my bitten apple and turned it in my hands thoughtfully. "Alex and I…" I began, pondering how best to word myself. "We know, also. That feeling. We were fortunate to be born together, though. It helps when there's someone to share the burden with you."

She gave a quiet chuckle. "Yes… It does help, doesn't it?"

The scene disappeared, and Willow's weight lifted from my back. I was left alone in the darkness, older again and sitting over the empty floor.

"Yeah, thought it was yours," the Dreamcatcher said from behind.

I dumbly turned and stared at the emptiness, hoping to find her there again.

Finally. I finally remembered something else with Willow; something where her face wasn't sullied with horror and dripping with blood. This had been… pleasant. Relaxed and gentle…

"Where did you get this?" I whispered, fingers balling, feeling that the apple had vanished from my hand.

"Weirdest thing, actually." The man threw his thumb over one shoulder. "This other girl was carrying it."

He had gestured to a thicket of misted trees, suspended in the black void of Aspirre.

It was a forest of willow trees, their branches drifting in the chilled wind that swept past. I knew this place… it was the Weeping Woods, found near the Death Palace.

A grey-haired figure peeled away the branches, her breath fogging in the cold air. She searched left and right, uplifting more branches and vanishing into the woods again.

"Lilli?"

"So, that's her name, huh?" He folded his arms as we watched her search in circles through this isolated forest, floating in the blackness. "Not sure why she had one of your memories, but I found it floating around in her subconscious tonight."

My brow furrowed. "She's dreaming of the Weeping Woods?"

"Looks like it. Haven't been paying much attention to her. She keeps having this same dream, so I don't have to do much. You're really the only one that keeps having problems."

"Er, I see…" I cleared my throat. "Well, I suppose… thank you. For every-thing… Especially for the memory."

He gave a shrug. "Don't mention it. It's part of my job. Oh—looks like you're fading."

My gaze shot to my now translucent hands, flinching when they began to disappear.

"Guess it's morning," he hummed. "See you around, kid."

He vanished, along with everything else as I woke.

36

BAD ACTORS

XAVIER

"Will you take those ridiculous things off?" Lilli glowered, walking backward along the sunlit street to scowl at me with hands on her hips. "Is this how you wish to be seen in front of this doctor we're trying to visit?"

I adjusted the blackened glasses Octavius had lent me. He said they were called 'sunglasses'. Rather useful things. They not only blocked out some of that blistering sunlight, but also hid my heterochromia from Lilli—which I needed greatly, since Alexander hadn't yet woken. *Damn her annoying soul-sight…*

"If Maveric cared," I said dully, "he wouldn't have agreed to meet with us at all. If he's willing to give us information, he'd give it if I wore a jester's uniform, pied stripes, bells and all."

Beside me, Jaq peeled off a layer of snakeskin and mumbled. "If nothin' else, give *me* a turn, will ya? My eyes are stingin' just the same."

"I, er…" I frowned at him. "Would they even fit over your eyeglasses?"

Jaq blinked, fingering the black frames of his rectangular glasses, then dripped depressively. "Aw, damn it… Maybe they got bigger ones somewhere?"

Lilli rolled her eyes and gave an indignant snort, turning forward. "You both wish to look like fools? Fine. See if this doctor gives you your information looking like that."

"You realize these 'sunglasses' are being worn by most of these surface-dwellers?" I pointed out, gesturing to the crowd around us. "I hardly think we'll be judged for wearing something so commonplace. What say you, Vendy? Henry?"

"They're normal," the two answered in unison, striding some paces behind us.

Lilli flushed over her shoulder, scowling angrily as her grey fox ears sprouted. She hadn't a retort to that.

I had a suspicion my appearance wasn't the problem. Her surreptitious glances made it more likely she hated how the glasses blocked my eyes from her. *Is she having trouble remembering 'Alexander' is behind her?* I wondered.

Beside her, Octavius rubbed his neck, offering Lilli a nervous smile. "S-so, um, Lilli…" he began, flicking his gaze away bashfully. "I guess that, um, Infeciovoker friend you mentioned was, um…"

"Her Highness Willow," Lilli confirmed. She bit her lip. "I, er… expect you'd like to ask her of her infection Hallows, don't you?"

"W-well, I've never met another one other than my dad, and…" He kicked at a loose stone in the street. "I don't know. I guess it sounds kinda dumb…"

"Not at all," Lilli disagreed cheerfully. "I'm sure Her Highness would be most interested to meet a true Infeciovoker. She and the royal family may have your Hallows, but as I've said, they don't have that element alone. Most shifters are born with one element—at rare times, two—but none have more than this. None save for the Relic Bloodlines. All who carry the immediate Bloodline are blessed with all three of their home-realm's Hallows… though even among Relicbloods, Her Highness Willow is a unique case, as she has *six* elements, being the first child born of two Relic Bloodlines."

Octavius scratched his chin, where sparse, black hairs had begun to sprout over the week. "I kinda remember hearing about that."

"Yes, it was quite the popular news topic," she grimaced, sounding irked. "I *still* have to bat away the reporters from Her Highness when they come snooping into the palace. They always want to see how her powers are progressing. Though I don't see how it's any of their business…"

"How *are* they progressing?" Octavius asked. "I mean, I don't want to pry, I'm just curious, since she's an Infeciovoker and… and what else?"

She began counting on her fingers. "On her Death side, Her Highness is a Necrovoker, Pyrovoker, and Infeciovoker… and on her Dream side, she is a Somniovoker, Decepiovoker and Seer. She's most practiced with the first set, however. Being the heiress of Death comes with certain priorities and expectations, you see."

Octavius rubbed his neck. "That's a lot of elements… I can't even imagine how I'd go about training with it all."

She laughed. "I'm sure she couldn't imagine how a real Infeciovoker ended up on the surface. Wait until I show her you, she'll be so curious."

She started asking Octavius about his life, now. He spoke of his siblings, his mother and father…

I stopped listening after the father. I had no desire to hear any falsely endearing stories about my killer. The picture he'd shown us was like being face to face with the man himself. I felt sick, remembering that we might have to face him again soon…

"Bloody dirt crawlers," a woman hissed from the crowd as we walked by, catching my ear. "What do they think they're doing, coming back here like nothing happened? The nerve of it."

It was a waitress from a nearby café outside, whispering to a co-worker. They snapped their heads away after meeting my gaze. The women hurried inside, but I could still see them glaring at us through the small window.

They weren't the only ones whispering such bile. The more attention I paid the people around us, the more sneers I heard, of the worst sort.

Something is not right.

The city was crowded, yet the roads became empty wherever *I* walked. Many hissed 'dirt crawlers' when we passed and spat at the ground. Some even shoved into Jaq and grumbled 'traitor' or 'Grim lover' at him, staring at his blond hair and scoffing at the greyness of his scales.

Lilli and Octavius didn't seem to notice the whispers. They were watching a theater troupe performing a small play for the crowd up ahead.

"Xavier," Jaq hissed under his breath, walking at a stiffer pace. The sneers around us grew more fervent. "I don't think I like this town…"

"The sentiment seems mutual," I muttered.

We hurried to Lilli and Octavius, whose eyes were glued to the play.

"Vile monster!" one of the gold-robed actors shouted, a wooden sword raised threateningly at the pretend-villain before him. "You dare stain my palace with the blood of innocents? Your treachery ends here!"

The brunet villain *hmphed*, rapier waving in a gesture to the 'dead' kings and queens who cluttered the street. "These others were no match for me, Land King Adam! And you'll be no different! I was trained well within the honored knighthood you trusted so dearly—and that trust will be your demise!"

They clashed swords, wood clunking as the accompanying accordion player puffed frantic notes. The villain stabbed for the king, who leapt back and drew a startled gasp from the crowd nearest him. The rogue knight charged, wood meeting again as the two pushed against each other, glares sharp with false hate.

"You planned this all along…!" the king sneered. "When I swore you into my honorguard, you meant to kill me from the start, didn't you? I knew your skill with the sword was too great for a lowly farmer—you were a warrior, to the bone! An assassin! I should have seen the signs!"

The assassin laughed. "A shame that your fellow Relicbloods were just as blind! And now they've paid the price! As will you!"

With a deft swivel of the villain's rapier, the king's sword flew from his hands, landing on the street with wooden clunks. Opportunity open, the assassin thrust his blade under the king's armpit—and the bearded actor pretended to cry in agony, crumpling to the floor.

The assassin spat in his face, towering over the 'dead' king. "And thus ends your Bloodline, Your Majesty Land! I've already done away with your wife, and the child she carried. You've no heir to take after you. My master will be most pleased. Send the Death Goddess my regards…!"

The actors transitioned into the story of how the current king's ancestor took the throne. How the treacherous Arborvokers and their queen split the land in two. How the strength and hope their new king sewed the Everlanders together once again, after such a terrible loss…

I found Lilli frozen at the edge of the audience.

She stared at the actor playing the Death King. His black robe was covered in fake blood as he lay slumped in feigned stillness, his skull-crown toppled next to him on the street, scythe broken in two at his side.

Outrage smoldered her onyx eyes.

I stepped beside her. "Lilli, come. We haven't time to watch this drivel."

"They're wrong." Lilli's fox ears grew fully. "The Death King was the only survivor of that assassination. The Death King and… King Dream…"

A child actor, wearing a gaudy blue wig and an orange robe far too large for him, stepped onto the wooden platform.

"Tank yew, King Seffick," the gap-toothed child said to the actor playing King Setthick, shaking his hand in a giggle, his blue wig falling over his eyes. "Wiffout yew, the kingdum wud be in… in…"

The director hissed the child's line from the side.

"In wu-in!" the child finished, his confidence rekindled. "I giff yew my bwessing! I know that Ev'rland is in good hands, as I haff Seen so wiff my Thurd Aye! May I…"

"May I…?" A man's voice hushed in my memory.

My head throbbed, images flitting. I remembered a chilled night in Grim, a palace ball, a garden with a trickling fountain... a man on the fountain's wall, crouching to me and asking to see my hand, the man staring at the Crest of black diamonds under my knuckles...

In the present time, I stared at the little actor's blue wig; at the child's round, bronze face.

It's wrong. The man's face blurred in my memory, but his azure hair and eyes burned as clear as breath. *Dream wasn't a child. He was...* What had he been? A teenager? How long ago had that been...?

Lilli snorted beside me, ripping me from my distraction.

"You're quite right, Alexander," she huffed and strut away from the acting troupe. "We oughtn't waste our time on these simpletons. If they think *that* passes as an accurate representation of His Majesty Dream, they'll find no admirers here."

"Yes..." I murmured absently, following her alongside the others. Vendy whined why she couldn't see the rest of it, but Henry hushed her and dragged the girl along. I turned back to Lilli, hesitating. "Wasn't Dream... older? Not a child?"

"Of course." Lilli spun on her heels to walk backward, putting fists on her sides. "Oh, don't tell me you've forgotten him as well? I know he only visited so often, but he always made sure to see you and Xavier when he did."

I rubbed my chin. "That's right... Dream is Willow's grandfather, isn't he?"

"Yes. Ooh, perhaps we shall tell Dream of that rendition, when next we see him?" She giggled and clasped her hands mischievously. "Do you remember when we would call him the "Little Blue King"? Oh, how he hated it! I even made his ears grow once."

"Little Blue King..." I stared at my hand; at the Crest. The memory of Dream's face dissipated, falling away like a Fallen Light dimming into inexistence. "Yes, I... vaguely recall the name..."

She sighed and turned forward, wafting a dismissive hand at me. "Honestly, Alex, between you and Xavier, I'm beginning to worry your memory loss is a collective effort."

I chuckled, a grin tugging my lips. "I suppose it does seem that way, doesn't it?"

She paused, twisting to me. Her brow furrowed suspiciously.

"You're awfully pleasant today..." she murmured. "I expected a less *polite* reply..." She reached for the sunglasses on my face. "I've decided I want a turn with those things after all. Could you take them off for a moment—?"

"I-I think not!" I sidestepped round her and hastened my pace, my laugh nervous. "You denied the chance when you had it! *Khmm-hmm!* Now. Let's not dally. We've a doctor to meet."

MACARIUS

I watched the theater troupe with stale amusement.

This was what became of that day? This was all that was left? The turning point of history, the disaster that triggered everything…

Watered down to a laughable tale of an unnamed 'rogue knight' and his evil plot?

Disgusting. Strange, that Land King Adam was seen as a marvelous idol. Strange and infuriating.

Adam had been a dimwitted brute, arguably the worst king Everland had seen. And here they thought this 'rogue knight' was the villain, instead of the victim?

Absolutely disgusting.

Woefully, it seemed no one from this era would know the tale of the heartbroken surgeon who sought retribution for his murdered wife. His love who was slaughtered by Adam himself, after the surgeon failed to save the queen during her fruitless delivery of their unborn son…

I turned away from the horrible acting, seeing that the Grimlings were leaving. I took care to follow close behind. My quarry, the twin boy, glanced over his shoulder, meeting my eyes. He noticed naught and continued on his path.

A grin peeled across my scales. *Good… my 'imposter' Evocation is working.* After so long, my skill with illusions still amazed even myself. It mattered little who I was posing as, I simply picked a bystander at random; taking his image, memorizing his features and clothing, replicating the man's visage and created an illusion of him to use as a full-body cloak around me.

To most with my Hallows, the 'imposter' Evocation was tricky. Creating authentic, believable illusions took a great amount of skill and memory. Both of which, I prided myself, I had a great deal of. Centuries worth of practice didn't hurt, either.

Curious, though. I hadn't stopped to consider this, but now, with so much experience behind me, I dared say I was the greatest Decepiovoker of this era. Perhaps of all time, if I excluded my old friend, Dream.

I chuckled at the thought and strolled through the streets after the Reapers, observing their little group, unnoticed. Decepiovoking may not have any physical use, but illusions could certainly help one gather well-needed information. And the information I currently sought was that of this boy with heterochromia.

The viper called him 'Xavier' a moment ago. I was sure the boy introduced himself to me as 'Alexander' in Nulani.

Could this perhaps be the missing twin? The one Kael assured me had been killed years before?

I would have words with Kael. The half I'd thought was already dead is still alive after all? It seemed Kael had been too incompetent to do what was needed, the fool. His slip up may well be the death of us.

Though, if this 'Xavier' was the missing half, where has the other gone? My arms folded. *And why does the girl call him 'Alexander'?* Were they deceiving her?

In any case, I couldn't afford to make the same mistake as Kael. I'd have to wait until both halves were together and take care to witness their deaths myself.

I let out a gruff breath and strode away from the crowd, heading back to where I knew Cilia and Lucrine awaited.

I must speak with Kael, I decided. *The twins were an unexpected part of the plan's first stage. I cannot let our deaths run free.*

But Kael still waited within Everland's capital, and I had to watch over Cilia as well, to be sure she stayed away from him at all costs. She and Kael must never meet. Everything relied on their ignorance. No, I'd have to create a copy to watch Cilia here while I went to see Kael myself. Even if the twins were not dealt with now, I had to be sure we could proceed as planned.

I will tolerate no more mistakes. Venom dripped from the fangs folded in my mouth. *Not from Kael, and certainly not from Cilia.*

37

A FERRET CHECKING INN

RINGËD

I rang the bell at the front desk of the Howler's Inn, drumming my fingers over the smooth marble counter, waiting for an attendant.

Oscha, this place was enormous. I never in my life thought I'd step foot in a fancy inn like this. Artist paint me stunned, there was a Bloody *fountain* in the lobby, and a bar and a classy restaurant with a bunch of random grapevines sprawled over a pergola.

Something rummaged in my bag, dipping my shoulder. Kurn popped his head out and sniffed the air. "<My word,>" the feral ferret snickered in his language, tapping excited paws. "<What a delectable scent…!>"

"Don't get any ideas," I warned. "This is a fancy place. They probably don't take kindly to feral pets. Well… maybe feral hounds or something, but I doubt they'd be into a rodent crawling around their clean floors. Not unless I had some serious Mel."

Kurn swung his head left and right, his round ears dipping. "<Where is everyone?>"

"You know, Kurn," I said and took out a smoke from my pocket, lighting it to take a puff. "That's a damn good question." I hit the calling bell again.

Kurn was right: for all its space, there was no one here. Did the Necrofera scare everyone out of town? *Those Grimlings better still be here.*

I rang the bell again, then again.

Nothing. Was everyone on break or something?

Oscha, I don't have time for this. I reached over the counter, finding a book of names listed for the hotel guests.

Devouh, room 5000.

"Top floor." I crossed the lobby and hit the call button for the lift. It took a little while for the box to drop down to me, but when it did, the cage unfolded and I stepped into the carpeted box.

The liftman inside cringed when I walked in. Then he blinked, gasping in relief.

"Bloods, mate, I thought you was the High Howllord again," the guy said, patting his chest like he almost had a heart attack. "He's been the only one coming up 'n down, other than the cleaning maids. Harry 'n I've been debating to just get outta here 'n find a new job if he don't leave soon."

So, he's still here after all. I took a hit from my smoke and gestured with it to the empty lobby. "Where's everyone else? They do the same and high-tail it out of here?"

"Right on it, mate." He adjusted the little, square hat on his head. "They was the smart ones, getting out early. Harry 'n I should've left already, the Howllord can use this thing well enough on his own."

"And Harry is?" I asked.

"Night shift. Sometimes the guests gotta come down and up afterhours for things. Harry does that shift when I get me some shut eye." He grinned and reached for the door levers. "What floor, mate?"

"Top."

He liftman stiffened. "B-but that's where the—"

"I know." I flashed him my Footrunner badge inside my vest. "Official Seeker business. I'm, uh… running an investigation on the Howllord and his associates."

He went bug-eyed at me. "Oh, Gardener sow me, mate, you're doing a great service, you are."

He eagerly cranked the doors closed and took us up to the top floor, letting me out.

"It's right round that corner there," he directed, pointing. "I'll stay right here in case you need to make a break for it… best luck, mate." He saluted with two fingers to his brow and a toothy grin.

I waved back awkwardly, hurrying around the corner he pointed to, counting the doors numbers. "5003… 5002… 5001…"

5000.

I reached the right door and pounded on it, calling. "Howllord?"

No answer.

I pounded again. "Tavius? You in there? It's Ringëd!"

Still nothing.

"Gods damn it…" I knelt and set down my bag, prompting Kurn to scuttle out. "Kurn, time to execute plan B."

Kurn rose on his back legs and snickered dutifully. "<Roger, Ringëd.>"

"If you find them in there before I do, you can eat whatever you want for a whole day. A meal all to yourself."

His round ears perked straight up. "<To victory!>"

He scurried to the nearest ventilation unit and tapped his paws against it impatiently, looking at me.

I patted my pockets, then grumbled. "I don't have a screwdriver… but maybe I can…" I went over and pried the slits apart, just big enough for Kurn to climb into.

He squeaked when he got stuck half way.

"Kurn, you fat little weasel…" I gave him a push, and he was in.

I heard his tiny paws clatter away in there, and when he gave confirmative scratches on the other side of the door to tell me he made it, I pushed to my feet, blowing out a breath.

While he waits for them in there, I thought, going back to the lift around the corner. *I'll keep an eye out for them outside.* If I happened to miss them for whatever reason, Octavius would see Kurn and know I was here looking for them.

I swear to Bloods, if this doesn't work, I'm going to be so pissed.

38

DIRT CRAWLER

UNNAMED

Clack-cl-cl-clack! Clack-cl-cl-clack!

The lopsided dragon-skeleton rattled and clattered under me, violet lights stringing from my hands and tethering the boney joints together as I rode through the dried wasteland into Crinkbend-Tain.

My leathery wings flexed in a yawn, my messenger crow, Dusk, gliding at my side, my skeletal mount dipping and bounding over the cracked dirt of this new city's road.

I'd started my journey by flying, since I hadn't the money to travel by train after that blasted beggar robbed me in Adrial. But I thanked Death I'd spotted this Landragon skeleton lying in the wastelands. My wings had suffered enough abuse after an entire day of flying, *any* other means of travel was appreciated.

I wasn't the most talented Necrovoker, but I could at least raise this much of the foreign beast. Though, it would have been a less… *shaky* ride if I could resurrect the dragon in its entirety. If it had its living muscles and skin, and a fully, breathing function, I wouldn't have to sit on its sharp spine, with naught but a pink pillow tied with a scarf to save my rear from bruising.

But a full resurrection required a general knowledge of the creature's anatomy. Of which I unfortunately lacked. The best I could do was tether the bones and pray they were in the proper order. Judging from my mount's lopsided steps, I supposed I'd failed somewhere along the way. But how was I to know where a Landragon's bones went? I'd spent my training years of Necrovoking by studying *shifter* anatomy, not dragons!

When I reached the outskirts of Crinkbend-Tain, I slowed my skeletal beast and dismounted, pushing my Hallows into the bones to keep the flow of magic burning for another ten minutes, at best.

Now on my own feet again, I arched my back in a wince, audible *cricks* zippering as I flapped my wings in a stretch.

I took out the map of High Everland I'd acquired in Adrial, smoothing out the creases over my dragon's ribcage, and searched for my next destination.

My crow flew onto my shoulder, perching there with a delicate caw.

"All right, Dusk," I said, eyes narrowing at the map. "Those reports in the last town claimed she was in High Lindel. We're just between High Drinelle and there. If we leave now, we may arrive by nightfall."

Dusk cooed lightly, a refined, yet tired grumble. She was just as exhausted as I. Our Bond pulsed with the same frequency of fatigue, and I stroked her feathers drearily. "We'll take a small break here… don't worry."

I walked through this dustbowl of a town. It was the poorest city I'd visited thus far. Their carriages even had wheels. *Wheels!*

I'd never seen those on carriages, outside of museums. Apparently, this place couldn't afford any Levi-stones to make their vehicles hover. I felt like I'd traveled back in time a hundred years.

Patches of mud littered the dirt road, and I was sure to keep away from them. I didn't wish to soil my rose-pink boots.

The locals were an odd bunch. Their chosen language seemed to be more of a clucking prattle. But what was it? An indigenous dialect, separate from Landish? I supposed this place could have been its own country, in a time before the Relicbloods claimed their lands and sanctioned their territories… Still, I at least hoped they could understand me if I ordered a meal.

"'Ey, bat lady," a man called behind me, as if to answer my thought. I found him sitting on a wooden porch. "Yer in the wrong town, Grimlette. Yer dirt crawler friends're in the next town over."

Dirt crawler? Was that some sort of insult?

The man was anything but handsome, his gut drooping over his belt like disgusting blubber, his shirt too small to cover his hairy belly. He gave a hideous snort and spat at the ground. I shuddered and strutted onward.

"So, the dirt crawlers came here, ah?" a woman questioned from a window on the second floor of a building. "It's an omen, I says, time to leave a'fore the demons come 'n eat us next." She closed her shutters with a loud rattle.

Many townspeople mimicked the gesture. Suddenly finding myself alone in the streets, I turned to Dusk. "What does 'dirt crawler' mean?"

"It means *you*, Grimlette," a small choir of voices chimed behind me, making me start.

Five mud-faced children stared at me with fixated, beady eyes. I cringed away from them, delicately pinching my nose at their stench. "Eugh… Why use such a horrible name?"

The tallest boy crossed his arms. "'cus that's what ya are—a no good, demon lovin' worm that crawls in your dirt-caves."

I bristled, wings bowing in outrage. "Excuse me?"

"Ai, ai, ai!" A woman ran to the children, shepherding them away. "Lads, lads! Go inside, all of ye!"

I stamped a foot in an exasperated huff. "Did you hear what they called me, ma'am? I demand they be reprimanded—!"

"They don't owe ye anythin', dirt crawler," she sneered. "Leave us be 'n get outta here before we drag ye out tied to a hog."

She shoved me back—and I tripped into a large mud pit, splashing in the slimy muck.

"Augh!" My voice was shrill as I tried to fling off the mud in vain. "L-look at this dress! It's ruined…! You miserable peasant!" I rose, mud glopping back to the puddle. "My Spirit Father can have you all punished for such abuse…! I will remember this, and you'll wish you'd never—"

A shower of rotten food fell over me. I gasped in disgust, quickly brushing off the apple cores, banana peels, spoiled meat and rotten lettuce.

I glared up at the scullery boy who had emptied the bucket of scraps, the little brat laughing.

"Ai, look!" He giggled. "She *does* crawl in dirt! She misses home so much, she can't stop 'erself from jumpin' in the mud!"

It sounded like the whole town was laughing, cackling 'dirt crawler' and spewing rough syllables in their own clucking language.

I flushed, tears welling, and ran back to my skeletal dragon that I'd left outside the town, quickly mounting and rushed around the city, away from its horrible people. Dusk followed close at my side as my sharpened fangs gritted, bat ears curled behind my head. "I am not a dirt crawler…!"

39

HOSTILE HOSTS

XAVIER

Alex, will you hurry and waken? I brooded in silence, anxiety bubbling as I tapped a nervous finger within my coat pocket.

I hustled along the streets of Lindel, keeping pace with Lilli, Jaq and Octavius as we huddled in the mass of shifters who muttered hostile curses at us. *I have a dreadful feeling no good will come of this if you aren't with us soon.*

We turned a corner, crossing the damaged section of the market: the section where those Stonedragons and Necrofera had laid waste, days before.

Merchant booths and shop windows were broken along the streets, buildings crumbled in fractured chunks that trailed the ground under our feet.

The smell of decay was thick here, flies swarming around aged blood stains that were smeared across walls and splattered on the cobblestone. I silently gave the fallen a prayer, and heard Lilli whispering her own peace beside me.

She flicked me a suspicious glare, glowering at my borrowed sunglasses.

Alex, I thought in a panic, *hurry and wake before she decides to rip these things off.*

Of all the times he could have decided to have one of his damned episodes, why did it have to be now? Every so often, he would sleep late like this. I couldn't help but think there was something wrong, but he denied it when I'd ask. I learned to leave him be over the years, but right now, he had the worst timing.

We passed an aisle of wrecked booths, and the vendors gave us rueful looks while setting up their merchandise as best they could, the phrase 'dirt crawlers' thrown about their tongues.

Octavius and Lilli stopped ahead of us to observe a large collection of newly hung posters. The papers cluttered the wall with pictures of missing people, old and young, of all different shifts.

"What's all this?" Lilli stared at the faces on the posters.

Henry's brow furrowed at the wall. "Is this from the raid?"

Vendy craned her neck to try and gaze at them all at once. "That's a *lot* of missing people."

"Yeah," Octavius agreed, leaning closer to read all the names. "They didn't find all the victims?"

"Uh, mates?" Jaq's gaze shifted to the many eyes watching us from the crowd. "Am I the only one gettin' creeped out that everyone's staring at—?"

Lilli gasped suddenly, a stranger snagging her wrist. The man barked. "So it *was* you, little thief!"

Lilli paled at the belligerent merchant and jerked her arm free, fleeing behind me. She tugged my arm, urging us to leave.

The man stepped forward, stabbing a hard finger at Lilli. "Give that one here, Reapers. She's a damned murderer. Killed seven men in cold blood from her jail break."

"That wasn't my doing!" cried Lilli, voice shrill with panic, fox ears sprouting.

"One of those Raiders was my friend, ye Bloody whore." His teeth sharpened. "*I* had to explain to his kids why their Da wasn't coming home."

She ducked behind Jaq when the merchant grabbed for her again. "It *wasn't* me!" she insisted, yelping when her hair was seized with a stern yank. The bell tied to her strands jingled as he dragged her from Jaq's guard, making her trip to the ground.

She quickly pulled out her hair ornament and had her scythe materialize, kicking the man's stomach and rolling back, using her scythe to propel herself upright. She panted and held the blade between them.

"It wasn't me," she puffed. "It was the man in the next cell, the goat shifter. I… I couldn't stop him."

"Like ye couldn't stop the Fera from killing everyone after ye led them to my street?" He glared a safe distance away from her weapon.

Jaq and I came between them, as did Octavius. "She wasn't leading them anywhere," I said.

"Y-yeah, they were just chasing her." Octavius didn't seem as confident, perhaps due to his lack of weapons. Still, he went on with a swallow. "We helped her kill them. At least you're alive, right?"

"It's your fault they came here in the first place!" a voice shouted from the crowd. "Our town's never had an attack until you all showed up! Some 'protection' you all provide!"

We shuffled together as the voices rose.

I swallowed. "We're only apprentices…"

"And we were just passin' by," added Jaq. "If your king didn't ban the actual knights from the other cities, ya prob'ly wouldn't have had this problem—"

"So that's what this is about?" someone shouted. "You're trying to *give* us a demon problem so you can be the 'heroes' and fix it? Well, you won't get our king to lift the ban on your kind, we're better off without your 'help'!"

"And your king forbids our own knights from having your special weapons at all," someone else pointed out. "That's why King Galden banned your kind, so your Death King would see how much his laws were hurting us."

"Maybe that's just what he wants?" another piped. "The Death King wants the demons to kill us so he can have our souls, doesn't he?"

A woman stabbed a meaty finger in the air. "It's true! I saw it on the news this morning, they were conspiring with the demons themselves!"

"I saw it too," a young boy added. He was a skittish child, all skin and bone with blond, feathered hair and wings sprouting from his back. He tugged on his mother's skirt, who scooped him up as he continued. "The Fera even left them alone. They were right in front of them, but they didn't do anything. They even said they were going to keep the Reapers alive, like they were friends."

This caused an uproar.

We couldn't get a word in without being drowned by the booming voices.

"It is no surprise that this behavior is coming from Grimlings," I overheard one Roaress sneer to her husband. "You can't trust those dirt crawlers, not the way they do business down in their dirty hole."

"Why would anyone live in such a disgusting place?" another Roarlord drawled as a few passing nobility gathered in their own respective groups. "It's a dark and slimy din, filled with mud and bugs. They'd have to be worms to welcome that sort of environment."

"I hear they're repelled by the sun."

"They're scared of our storms as well, a little rain makes them absolutely craven. They must have dirt in their brains as well as their claws, if you ask me."

"I'm not surprised they want us gone. It's simply part of their culture to think everyone's more appealing when dead—"

"Stop!" a small voice bleated over the noise. "Stop it, stop it, those're lies! Mum, tell them! Make them stop!"

A young girl with curling sheep horns was tugging at her mother's skirt, red faced and stamping her feet in a tantrum. "Stop it, Mum! It ain't true, none of it! Liars, all liars, tell them…!"

The mother reached for her daughter, but the girl ran to Lilli instead, hugging her.

"She's good, I know it!" cried the girl. "I saw it on screen! She helped all those people 'n everything. And-and…"

A black-feathered head popped out from the girl's orange hair. The small crow emerged and hopped over her shoulder, causing the crowd to gasp.

Lilli stared at the girl's crow, transfixed. "Your messenger! It came?"

"She did!" the girl wailed, holding Lilli's waist tighter. "She came this morning, just like you said! I love her, 'n she knows you're good, too!"

Lilli seemed at a loss for words, kneeling to the girl and smiled at the new messenger. It was a small crow, bigger than Jewel yet shorter than Jaq's Bridge. The bird nuzzled the little girl's cheek, and Lilli murmured congratulatory breaths while brushing back the ewe's hair.

"Milann!" the mother shrieked and yanked the girl back. "Get away from that thing!"

The mother lifted her handbag and gave the crow a swift *thwack!*

The bird dropped like a stone, and with a disgusted kick, the woman's foot met the messenger's head, crunching its skull under her shoe and cracked its neck.

The cry that split the silence shattered my ears.

The girl's scream echoed hauntingly as she clutched her chest and doubled over, dropping to her knees when her mother continued smashing the crow under her foot.

"Stop…!" she sobbed, gripping her chest as if to keep her heart from bursting. "It hurts…! It hurts, stop it!"

The mother finally ceased her cruelty, her glare curdling at us. "What in Land do ya think you're doin', lettin' those feral rats touch her?" she demanded. "You wanna brainwash our kids with your scum?"

The crowd began closing in, gathering rocks from the broken street. The girl's wails rang on, pained and blubbering over her trampled messenger.

Lilli stood in shock beside me, her eyes trapped on the grieving girl. "What have you done?" She trembled, gaze snapping to the mother. "When you break the bond…"

"Listen here, ya little worm." The mother's throat gave a guttural click. "Ya ain't takin' Milann down to your shithole caves, not a chance—"

"Stand down!" I commanded, my voice shaking, the girl's sobs twisting my chest. I stepped beside Lilli, my sharpened teeth barred. "You've broken the Sixth Law of Death! To kill a Reaper's messenger is a crime of great consequence…! In the name of my father, and His Royal Majesty Death, you will be tried and sentenced by the courts of Low Everland—!"

Lilli cried in pain when a sharp rock scrapped her cheek, drawing blood. She clutched her face, sticky crimson leaking through her fingers.

The silence broke into chaos.

The crowd chucked rocks without mercy, brick and fractured stone hurtling from all directions.

Lilli screamed behind me.

Three men were dragging her away, led by the disgruntled merchant from before. One man had grabbed her scythe and the other two shoved her to the ground, stones pelting her as they strapped dampening gloves on her hands.

"Death!" I bounded after the men, shielding my head from the new volley of rocks. I released my soul Hallows through violet-shining hands, preparing a sensory-illusion.

I concentrated on the feeling of burned skin, the memory plucked into focus: a small flame licking a finger. Pain, like chilled wind melting the nerves, hot and intense in that split second. With the feeling set in mind, I added to it, multiplying that one burn into a thousand. They were tiny pinpricks alone, but a swarm of agony when combined.

I shoved my black-and-violet hands over the men's faces. They wailed in pain, stumbling back, gripping their heads as though to stop their skin from melting off their skulls. In their distraction, they staggered away from Lilli.

"Stay back!" My voice crackled, wolf ears curled in warning and…

I stopped, static fuzzing my brain. Something felt off.

No, not off, but… familiar.

"*Stay back…!*" I remembered a younger version of my voice barking at another man: the yellow-eyed assassin. In the memory, I had clutched someone's hand behind me. *Willow's?* No… It was a girl with charcoal-grey hair.

In the present time, I stared at Lilli, numb.

"You," I began, my tongue feeling limp. "You were there?"

She didn't seem to hear me, shouting Alexander's name.

Two men came from behind and seized my arms. The first three of Lilli's assailants had recovered, confused but enraged, and ran for Lilli again. One of them yelled, "Tie the bitch to the gallows!"

Mother of Death! Most of this mob was keen on seeing Lilli's head served on a platter. They didn't seem to care nearly as much about the rest of us.

I wriggled free of whoever was dragging me back, and I darted for Lilli and the men coming after her. Her scythe was lost in the crowd, and she struggled to pull off the gloves they'd put on her. She was shackled now, they must have hurried with the chains while I was distracted.

Jaq and Octavius found us in the anarchy and rushed to meet us, the rocks still spraying.

Then, somehow… the number of stones dwindled.

The crowd was thinning, but not because they were leaving. They were collapsing to the ground. One by one, shifters dropped until there were only two men left standing, along with the young sheep girl still crying over the ground.

One of the men, wearing a blue-billed cap with holes in it to make way for his curling elk antlers, clasped a hand over the last man's shoulder. An azure glow brightened under the antlered stranger's palm.

"Come on, people," the stranger spat as the last man collapsed, unconscious. "Have some dignity."

He slipped his hands into his pockets and let out an aggravated breath. "I told you to be careful out here, didn't I, Howllord? Look at this Bloody mess, I had to put everyone to sleep. I just pray to Iri no one saw me, they'll be stoning me next in the morning."

I squinted under my sunglasses, recognizing the voice. "Hang on. You're the Dreamcatcher from last night?"

Our rescuer had a narrow face, speckled with stubble that trailed down his slender neck. His brown skin was smooth, save for his hands, which were hard and coarse like hooves. His antlers bowed behind his head and shot up at the ends with brown-tipped spikes.

The Dreamcatcher glanced up, brown eyes unveiled from the shade of his cap. "I told you my name's Jimmy," he said. "And I'm here every night. It's my job."

"Thank you," I panted. "Bloody Nira, thank you…"

He saluted with two relaxed fingers, walking to Jaq and Octavius to make sure they were all right.

I turned back to Lilli. Bruises burdened her skin and face like the rest of us, and a few gashes split at her arms. She caught my gaze and inched back, shaking. "I didn't kill those Raiders," She said. "I didn't kill anyone. I…"

She cringed when I reached for her shoulder. "I believe you. You didn't kill anyone."

Her head sagged in relief, and she rubbed the blood from her cheek.

The antlered Dreamcatcher came round, holding the stolen key to her shackles, and returned the scythe she'd lost. She unlocked the cuffs and took her weapon, reverting it into her hair ornament and slipped it into her tangled strands. The Catcher offered her a hand and pulled her to her feet.

"You probably shouldn't stay here," the Catcher warned. "They'll be out for a few hours, but they have to wake up eventually. Maybe it'd be best to go back to your inn for today?"

Lilli smeared her hands on her face, a streak of blood trailing on her cheek. "Yes, I… I think that would be best…"

The Catcher eyed me next, trying to see behind my sunglasses. "Which one were you again?"

I made a note to remember I was supposed to be my brother, who was still asleep. "Alexander."

The man's head cocked. "Really? I don't remember interrupting your dream last night. How'd you recognize me?"

I tried to think of some lie—

"Sorry?" Lilli cut in shakily. "Who… whose dream did you interrupt?"

"The other one," the Catcher said. "Uh, Xavier. Right."

She inflated. "You've talked with Xavier?"

"Briefly."

"But he's still here?" she pressed. "In Lindel?"

The Catcher's brow raised skeptically. "You saying you're not with him?"

Her head shook. He waved a finger at both of us. "So, he wasn't with you when you were killing those Necrofera yesterday?"

I hastily replied before Lilli could open her mouth again. "That was me. You surely confused us."

"Mm… well, all right, then." He shrugged, then turned to Lilli. "I went ahead and showed him one of his memories you were carrying. Thought you should know."

"He has it now?" She flushed with a smile. "I was beginning to think I'd lost it."

"No, but I want to know why you had it in the first place. It wasn't your memory, so how'd you end up with it?"

"Ah…" Lilli's face reddened. "My name is Lilliana Tessinger—"

He stopped her with a hand. "Back up. Tessinger? Like High Howllord Tessinger?"

"Well, yes… He is my father."

His eyes narrowed, and he fell silent for a while, as if debating something. After a moment, he started again. "Aren't you supposed to be at the Death Palace?"

"I was," Lilli affirmed. "But, you see, the princess's grandfather—er, your king—found that memory and asked me to give it to Xavier. I had to put it in this special holder, though, since I'm not a Somniovoker." She reached into her Storagesphere and pulled out a tiny, mirrored ball, with a sliding lid that opened into a velvet compartment. "But now, I also have to find Princess Willow. You haven't seen her up here, have you?"

He cocked an eyebrow. "Why would she be up here?"

I snagged Lilli's wrist and pulled her down the street. "We really should be going. We don't want to run into another mob. Thank you for your help, we'll, er, see you tonight, I suppose."

Jimmy kept pace with us. "You saying Willow Ember's up here on the surface?"

I growled. "We're not saying any—"

"She left the palace to look for Xavier," said Lilli, prompting a piqued look from me. "I need to locate her before the Death King finds out and has me punished. And I need to find Xavier, also. Do you think you could help?"

Jimmy rubbed his stubbled chin. "Well, I'm not much use in the conscious world, but I'll keep an eye out in Aspirre for them… Guess I should start looking, huh?"

He strode the opposite way, twisting back to call, "Try not to get into any more trouble! I don't like using my Hallows in public, people hate my kind just as much as yours right now… well, whatever. Business as usual, for me. See you tonight. And for the love of Iri, be careful!"

When he was finally out of sight, I threw up my hands. "Fantastic." I started for the inn, gesturing to no one in particular along the way. "That won't come back to bite us in the backside later. Not at all. No repercussions lie ahead for us, not one. Splendid day we're having, just splendid…"

Everyone followed behind me, save for Octavius, who hadn't moved.

"What about Maveric?" The cat asked. "We're not going to try and meet with him?"

I craned back to look at him flatly, exhaustion sagging my lids and welts pulsing painfully. "We can try again tomorrow. That Dreamcatcher was right, we need to get the Void out of here."

Octavius looked disappointed. "But what if Maveric *does* know where my mom is? We've already waited long enough to see him, what if tomorrow's too late to help Mom?"

I stifled a groan. "Octavius, I want to see Maveric just as much, but if we stay out here another minute, we risk running into this absolute disaster again. I'm quite confident the rest of us would elect to leave."

He breathed out through his nose and wiped the sweat from his brow, then spun on his heels. "Then I'll go... Just to see if he's there. I'll see you guys at the inn."

"Bloody Death..." My gaze moved to Jaq and Henry, muttering. "Will you two go with him? Vendy, come with me to watch Lilli. I'm not about to let her or Octavius stroll around without someone watching them. This is not a good time to have Grimish hair."

Jaq wiped blood from his nose and started for Octavius alongside Henry. "I suppose my general visage *is* less Grimish," Jaq said, his peasant dialect gone for the moment. I suspected this last incident had drained him... but not for long. The peasant speech returned when he hollered to Octavius. "If we see anyone holdin' rocks, Tavius, we're leavin'! Got me?"

Octavius nodded, and the three walked off as we parted ways.

Lilli, Vendy and I walked past the still-crying sheep girl, all of us stopping to watch the girl mourn. Her tears dripped from her chin, beading over the dead crow's remains.

I'd heard that the bond between a Reaper and its messenger was exceptionally strong... As if both souls were linked. If one life ended, the other would crumble in an unseen pain... Clearly, that was no lie.

I whispered sadly as we hovered over the girl. "She won't be a Reaper now, will she?"

There was a long silence before Lilli answered. "No. And since she lives in this Gods damned nation, she'll never know that she would have been."

I hung my head, kneeling to the girl and clasping her shoulder. "Nira bless your fallen companion," I hushed. "Take solace that ferals, even messengers, do not have a NecroSeam as we shifters do... Their souls are free to return to Nira without aid. Your messenger will find you again, in your next life. Your souls are forever bound in the cycle."

The girl didn't reply, choking on pained sobs.

Lilli wiped away the water welling in her eyes as I rose, and we left the crying ewe behind.

40

CAPTURED

JAQ

"Well, that sucked," I muttered, wiping blood from my nose. "These people have gone ape-shit. Is everyone on the surface insane?"

"Most of them," Henry grunted to my right. "There's a reason our rebellion exists."

Octavius stepped over a snoring civilian splayed on the cobblestones. The mate's hat had fallen off, and Octavius swooped down to grab it, sliding it over his black hair. That was probably a good idea, since these Everlanders apparently didn't like Grimlings, and Octavius looked more like one than I did.

"That was *really* bad though." Tavius adjusted the bill of his new cap. "I mean, I've been beaten up before, but not by so many people at once."

I spat venom off to the side. My fangs were still leaking, even though I had them folded. I guessed I was still tense, the adrenaline hadn't faded yet.

"It looked like Lilli got the worst of it, though," Tavius mumbled. "They really wanted to hang her… She didn't actually kill anyone, did she?"

"I don't Bloody know," I snorted. "Looked to me like she was traumatized from whatever happened. Probably watched 'em die, is my guess."

Henry rubbed at his beard thoughtfully. "Why was she in prison at all?"

"Beats me," I said. "Guess ya can ask her later."

A series of Wanted posters hung on the brick wall next to me, showing four masked faces of bird shifters. They were labeled, *The Carter Siblings: Dalen, Carrie, Herrin, and Rolen Carter.*

"So," Octavius began, pulling my attention away from the posters. "Did you hear stuff about Lilli from the twins at all? Before all this. She came in out of nowhere and started acting real familiar around them quick. No one mentioned her to me before, but I'm new. Even you looked surprised."

"I was," I admitted. "This is the first time I'm meetin' her. Void, I never even heard of her till now."

"They never mentioned her?"

I shrugged. "They might've, once or twice… I can't 'member too well. But Xavier forgot everything from the palace, and Alex doesn't talk about those times, anyway."

Tavius frowned. "Why not?"

"It…" I sighed, staring at my feet. "It's just too painful. I stopped asking a long time ago—"

"—*huah!*"

I snapped back to Tavius. He was gone. Thinking he tripped, I spun around to look. "What in Death?"

Henry jabbed a hand upward and shouted. "Up there!"

Octavius had been snagged by a winged shifter, flying him higher and higher—

I flinched when someone tried to grab me from behind. I instinctively dropped down and elbowed them in the gut before they could get a good hold of me.

"Just leave those two!" A voice said overhead.

What the Void is going on? There were three winged shifters, two teenage boys and one woman, flying over my head. The woman was struggling to grab Shade from the sky and put him in a netted bag, and one of the teen-agers had Octavius.

I'd hit the other boy, who gave a small groan and glared at me behind a mask. They all wore masks. They looked… really familiar. Kind of like those people from the Wanted post—

Death.

"Help me with this one," the boy who held Octavius called to the other one. "He's heavy enough as it is!"

Tavius flailed as they flapped him upward, out of my reach.

I unwound the chain from my wrist and drew out my scythe, but Henry pushed my arm down.

"Don't," he warned, his rabbit ears folding back furiously. "You might snag Tavius."

Venom seeped out of my fangs, and after a cursing minute, I wound back my chain.

The bird-shifters flew over the rooftops and out of sight as I pulled out my com and jammed the buttons to call the others.

41

ACCUSATIONS

XAVIER

Lilli and I walked back toward the inn in silence, Vendy stalking behind us with a stern expression, hand resting on the hilt of her sword. That girl could be goofy, true, but Bloods did she know when to stay alert.

Lilli still seemed rattled from the mob, keeping her hood drawn to hide her face while she stared at her boots. She was hauntingly blank beside me.

"Lilli," I began, uncertain. "I don't suppose… Well, what was this prison business about?"

She wiped at a bloody streak on her cheek, smearing the red on her hand. "I didn't kill anyone."

"I know," I assured, keeping my voice soft. "But what *did* happen to those Raiders?"

"The man in the cell beside me killed them," she said. "I was only there for stealing apples…"

I gave a light laugh. "Apples? Was that all?"

"They weren't very good apples," she grumbled, blushing. "But… well, I was so Bloody hungry, I feared my stomach would collapse." She buried her face in her hands. "Oh, I've never *not* had money, Alex. And the times I *had* run out, I could simply walk home and crawl into *my* bed, under *my* blankets, sleep under *my* roof and awake the next morning with no troubles…"

I gave her a sidelong glance. "You didn't want to come here, did you?"

"I…" She pulled at her knuckles. "I needed to. To learn that Xavier was alive—to have true *proof*, after years of no one believing me—knowing that he would surely never return on his own without his memories…" Her tone quieted. "I had to find him. To help him remember."

Remember…

That last memory on the cliffs came to mind. Lilli had been there, standing with me at the ledge.

"Could you help… *me* remember something for a moment?" I asked cautiously. "I feel as though I've mixed something up, about those times."

She tensed, her hands balling. "M… mixed what?"

"The night of the assassination." I tried to word it in a way Alexander would have put it. "Why did you go with Xavier and the princess, when they surfaced up to the canyons?"

Her features twisted at me, puzzled. "What?"

"The princess fled to the surface with Xavier. But I remember you went with them, didn't you?"

Her eyes focused forward in thought. She was silent for so long, I worried she suspected me. Had I made a mistake?

"You *are* mixing things up." She looked perturbed. "Xavier wasn't with the princess that night. Willow was with you, Alex."

"I… what?" I halted. "I saw her leave with him."

"No, *I* was with Xavier." She lifted an eyebrow. "You forget Willow is a Decepiovoker. She had enchanted a bracelet with an illusion in it, on my request. I knew we needed to distract the assassin away from her, so I asked her to give me a decoy illusion, which would give me her white hair and blue eyes."

I stared dumbfounded at her. "Why would you do such a thing?"

"You could say it comes with the job. As her Aide, it is my duty to protect her any way I can." She held herself higher. "So I offered to serve as a decoy. She was disguised as *me*, so others wouldn't think twice if she slipped away in plain sight. I went with Xavier, and the princess went with you. We'd split up, and the assassin went after Xavier and me instead, which in turn protected Her Highness."

I struggled to process this, my head pounding. "So then… *You* watched him fall from the canyons? Did he know it was you?"

Her head tilted, sullen. "It was he who volunteered to accompany me. He said he wanted assurance I was safe… I watched that man poison him, watched those veins cover his face, blacken his eyes…" She shivered, then banished the memory in a huff, walking on. "Well, it doesn't matter now. He's still alive. I just have to find wherever he's hiding in this Gods forsaken realm and be done with this mission."

I was silent, my feet rigid as I followed several paces behind, joining Vendy in the rear. *If it hadn't been Willow that night…* My breaths grew ragged, temples throbbing to wrap my head around this mess. *Who have I been trying to remember?*

"How has Xavier been faring up here, anyway?" Lilli pondered, arms folding. "This place is a nightmare for anyone with grey hair. I miss Grim… I'm tired of almost getting killed, always fighting off demons, being imprisoned… I want to go *home*."

I muttered absently. "I thought you'd be punished if you returned home without Willow?"

Lilli rubbed her shoulder, her tone heavy. "Well… truthfully, I… may be *executed*, if I return."

I gawked at her. "Executed? For losing the heiress?"

"No, no, Father Serdin would never allow that of his Spirit Daughter. No, the one who wishes me executed is my cousin."

I scowled. "Why would your cousin want you executed?"

"My uncle doesn't think I'm worthy of my title," she explained dismally. "He hates my very existence, and has taught his son to hate me as well. I'm afraid my cousin will kill me upon my return."

"But *why?*" I demanded, snagging her wrist. "What reason would your own flesh and blood have to wish you dead?"

"Because my blood is mixed," she said. "I don't know if you remember, Alex, but… well, you know my father is a High Howllord. But my mother was a… a scullery maid in the castle. Only a peasant. I'm only half nobility, by blood. My uncle doesn't approve… When my mother died, Uncle said it was a blessing. That now, my father was rid of the dirt on his boots, and the only thing left to do was wash the stain he left behind on the rug."

"That's sick!" I cried.

Vendy grimaced in disgust. "Yeah. Ew."

"Yes, well, that's my uncle," Lilli sighed. "He never liked anyone with half-anything… He detested you and Xavier, also. He thought you were weak without each other, since your Hallows were split. And he calls Willow the king's vermin daughter, that mixing the Bloodlines was a mistake." She shook her head, the bell in her hair jingling. "My uncle simply prefers everything to be pure."

It fell silent for some time. Cicadas screeched around us, a warm breeze rustling.

"Then…" I finally said. "I'd stay away from him. Even after you have Willow. Tell her of your concerns, perhaps the king could offer you protection."

Lilli smiled wanly. "I'm not sure the king can do anything, in this case. It's possible my cousin has designed his plans for my demise the very moment I return—"

"Then don't return," I growled, my wolf ears sprouting and curling tight to my skull. I clutched her wrist, pleading. "Don't return. Please. We'll talk with our father, he'll help you, he…" My grip tightened. "Please. Let us see you safely home, if nothing else?"

She stared at me, stunned. Then her lashes fluttered. "Did… did you say 'our' father?"

I stiffened, and Vendy snorted a laugh.

Lilli's gaze slitted. "Could I see those glasses?"

I swallowed, shuffling back. "I, er, but the light…"

"The light affects me as well as you, now give them here—"

A disoriented breath sounded from my head suddenly, and I perked. *Alex!* Thank you *Death*, he was finally awake!

Alex grumbled in my thoughts sluggishly. *"What…"*

I threw my soul backward into the psyche, forcing Alex into the conscious world.

"…Time is it?" Alex stopped after realizing he was outside, stumbling. "Where—?"

Lilli plucked the sunglasses from his face.

"Hah!" She gave a triumphant laugh, but it drained into disappointment when she saw Alexander's eyes. "Bloody Death!" She shoved him and threw the sunglasses at him, my brother fumbling to catch them. "You're acting too strange, Alexander! I swear to Bloods, it's like you keep swapping personalities with Xavier, it's infuriating!"

Alex fumbled for a reply, blinking at her, Vendy chortling up a storm. Then he gapped at Lilli. "Bloods be good, what happened to your face? You look like a beaten plum!"

Lilli blushed under her dark welts and turned up her nose. "What do you mean 'what happened'? We were just there."

"Just wh…" I hurriedly explained the mob, and his mouth shut. "Oh. Er, yes, sorry… what are these?" He slipped the sunglasses back over his nose curiously, the world darkening behind the shaded lenses.

"Octavius lent me those," I explained from the psyche. *"Lilli can't see my eyes behind them. Apparently, it also dampens that blasted sunlight."*

Alex tapped the frames experimentally. "How clever."

"What's clever?" Lilli questioned. "Alex, are you ill? Did one of those stones rattle your head loose?"

Vendy rolled us a sidelong glance, whispering in amusement, "You really suck at this don't you, Sirs?"

Alex glowered at our vassal, muttering under his breath, "We've spent the last six years confined to a mansion whose occupants *all* knew of us, we're not exactly practiced with how to regard unknowns…"

Vendy hummed. "Might want to work on it quick."

"Advice noted—"

"Hey!" a new voice shouted from down the road. A man was running toward us, puffing and tossing aside a cigarette he'd been smoking. "H-hey! Howllord! Wait up…!"

Alex sidled back a step as the man fumbled to a stop in front of us and puffed over his knees. Vendy clutched the hilt of her sheathed sword and slid in front of me and Lilli protectively, a guarded growl reverberating her throat.

The stranger was a flat-nosed man, his cropped hair a creamy blond with brown tips, rough stubble dotting his jaw. He wore an indigo vest and short trousers, sandals strapped to his feet. Alex's eyes snapped to the Shotri holstered to the man's belt, and he tensed.

"I…!" the man wheezed, bending backward in a wincing stretch. "I've…! I've been trying to… catch up with you for a… a *long* time, Howllord…!"

Vendy exchanged a coiled glance with us, securing her grip on her hilt. "Who're you?" She spat. "Say what you want or beat it."

"My name is Ringëd Fleetfûrt," he said, regaining his breath. "You left Brittleton before we could meet, Howllord. I know Octavius."

"Er… oh." Alex twisted to Lilli, then to Vendy. Both girls only shook their heads, Lilli's bell jingling from her hair. He cleared his throat, addressing this Ringëd fellow, "And, er… how do you know him, exactly?"

"He's my brother-in-law," Ringëd explained, amending, "Well, almost. I'm engaged to his sister, Mikani Treble."

"Ah," Alex relaxed. "All right, then. Stand down, Vendy."

Vendy blew out a breath and hopped aside to allow Ringëd through.

"You'll have to forgive the suspicion," Alex said. "It's been a hectic day. But why do you carry a Shotri?"

"Oh, I'm a Footrunner," Ringëd said, patting his holstered Shotri and showing us his badge. "Brittleton Beach, Seeker Department. Didn't mean to cause a scare, I just figured I should be careful, with all these demons running around, you know?"

"Yes, that seems wise…" Alex rubbed his neck. "I'm afraid Octavius isn't here at the moment. But I suppose we can wait for him inside. Perhaps you can explain why you came all this way for him, in the meantime?"

He laughed. "I didn't come to find Tavius, Howllord. I came to meet you—"

Alexander's com rang.

"Er, excuse us." Alex answered the call.

Jaq's face appeared on the screen of light, his voice fuzzing from the speaker. *"Mates!"* Jaq sounded panicked, it looked like he was running. *"Mates, you gotta get back here, quick!"*

"What's wrong?" Alex started. "It's not another riot, is it?"

"Not exactly!" He shoved through a crowd of people. *"Some birds picked up Octavius! We have to get him back!"*

OCTAVIUS

The ground shrank under my kicking feet, cat ears sprouting in panic. I groped at whatever I could get my hands on, but the Bloody *air* wasn't going to keep me from cracking my head open on the street. I was forced to rely on the two thugs hauling me away, flapping higher by the minute.

The wind rushed by and blew off my hat, and I watched it spiral to the city below. "What in Land are you doing?!" I yelled at the masked bird shifters carrying me.

"Shut it, Grimling!" the kid holding my left arm ordered. He sounded like a dumb teenager, but I couldn't see his face under his mask.

"I'm not a Grimling!" I shouted over the wind. "I'm Landish! I-I live in Brittleton!"

He snorted. "Black hair means Grimling! Can't fool us, Bloody dirt crawler—"

"Actually, Rolen," the kid on my right interrupted. He looked at least sixteen or seventeen, like the other kid, his eyes also covered by a mask. He wasn't as muscular as the first, but had a sharp chin framed in a feathered goatee.

"His hair is black, but his skin's too dark to be from Grim," he observed. "And look at what he's wearing. I'd say he's telling the truth, and he's from a beach on the surface."

I heard Shade crying to my left. A masked, winged woman had my raven slung in a bag. "This stupid feral is so noisy," she complained over Shade's screeching. "Why's it followin' him anyway? Weirdest thing I've ever seen."

The muscular kid, Rolen, gave a shrug. "Probably a Reaper thing, every-one in their group had one of 'em."

"It's called a messenger," the smart one said, his voice analytical. Obviously, he was the nerd of the three. "They're companions to the Reapers."

"Aw, who cares!" Rolen snapped. "Just get rid of it! It's makin' too much noise. Bloody annoyin', that's what it is."

The scholar rolled his eyes under the slits of his mask. "If we let it go, it'll just follow us—or more likely, leave to find reinforcements. They're called messengers for a reason. If you don't want his friends busting down our door, just bring it with us."

The woman shook the bag, and Shade squirmed inside. "Bloody pest… Can I just kill it?"

"No!" I kicked harder, making us lunge down. "Look, whatever you want you can have it! Just let him go!"

"Then tell us where all those missin' shifters are, Reaper," the woman sneered.

I threw my head back and groaned. "*Argh*! Look, just let me and my bird go, and… and I'll make sure you guys aren't hurt or anything!"

The woman scoffed. "If ya mean you'll get us protection from the High Howllord, save it! We know we're prob'ly gonna get our heads cut off for this, but we gotta risk it."

"I meant protection from *me*!"

They all laughed.

Rolen pulled my cat ear painfully. "Ya think just 'cus we're birds that means we gotta fit the stereotype? We ain't scared of you, cat."

"Not because I'm a cat! I'm an Infeciovoker!" That usually got people to leave me alone, maybe it will work in my favor this time? "I can kill you guys right now just by touching you!"

Their laughter subsided.

"Oh, sure," Rolen mocked. "Extinct Hallows aside, ya don't even have an Evocator's mark."

"My mark's right here!" I kicked my left foot up, though I knew they probably couldn't see my mark where the straps of my sandals hid it. I was cursing my own, stupid insecurity. "I-I hope you can keep flying for a *really* long time! Because as soon as I know I'm not going to fall to my death, I'm going to cripple all of you!"

I wasn't actually sure if I could gather enough Hallows' strength to crip-ple anyone. I probably just got lucky when I put that one kid in a coma years ago. I didn't want to destroy their Seams or anything—and what if I wasn't strong enough to destroy *living* shifter's Seams?

I don't know a lot about what I can do, I realized with draining confidence. I was always too scared to test it, since my Hallows never did anything good for me… Well, not till recently.

The birds chortled again. "Sure ya will, Reaper," the woman chuckled. "Just keep still, we ain't gonna hurt ya so long as ya don't try nothin'."

"Uh, Carrie?" The scholar glanced at the woman meekly. "It might be a good idea to put dampening gloves on him… I mean, Infeciovokers are dead, but there's still a chance he's a Pyrovoker, since his ancestry is Grimish. If you don't want to risk him getting away…"

The woman reached for the gloves and thin slippers strapped to her belt. "All right, fine. Hold 'em tight, boys."

After an excruciatingly long flight, they finally landed me in an old, rickety building.

The violent kid and his bookworm cohort had my arms spread out so I couldn't touch anything, and they carried me to a dimly lit room with creaking floors and molding walls. It smelled disgusting.

Did they live here? I saw four worn out mattresses laying around the room, not really in any specific order. My brow furrowed. *Why are there four beds if there're only three people?*

There were papers all over the walls, drawings—no, diagrams and blueprints. One of the most recent ones looked like a weaponry here in Lindel; exits and escape routes were labeled all over the paper.

Oh, Bloods.

I remembered last week before the twins picked me up… On the news, there was a break-in at a weaponry here in Lindel. They said a bunch of Reaper scythes were taken.

Land, I realized in horror. *I just got kidnapped by the Bloody Carter Siblings! Wait till Ringëd hears about this…*

I waved my fingers in annoyance, the gloves they put on me chaffing. They'd put dampening shoes on me, too. They were wet on the inside, the Yinklît gel slimy and gross.

The two boys, the Carter brothers, Herrin and Rolen, still had my arms spread so I couldn't take off the gloves or try to run. They tied my hands behind my back and bound my feet, throwing me to the creaky floorboards. I squirmed, the ropes scratching my wrists raw.

I hung my head and groaned. "All right, what do you want? I don't know where the missing shifters are, and neither do my friends." I paused, a faint screech blurting from a different room. That sounded like Shade. "Hey, can you at least bring my bird out here so I know he's—?"

"Shut it," Rolen snapped, removing his mask. His teenaged, freckled face came into full view now, and he turned to his older brother. "Go get a blindfold or somethin' yeah? We don't want 'im to know where we are."

Herrin took off his own mask and grimaced at his brother. "We flew him over here without one, idiot. He already knows where we are."

"Oh. Damn it… Then how do we keep the Raiders from stormin' the place later?"

Herrin gave him a sharp look. "You're worried about *Raiders*? We'll be lucky if we aren't strung up by High Howllord Lucas himself for kidnapping his son's friend!"

Rolen gave a shudder. "Good point… The Eyes would pull somethin' like that, wouldn't he?"

"Can you blame him right now? We shouldn't be doing this. We've never done a kidnapping before. We steal things, not—"

"Times have changed," Carrie grunted, pulling up a chair in front of me. She swirled it backward and sat, sliding off her mask.

She had the same brown eyes and feathered hair as her brothers, only hers were grown longer and tied back. Carrie was older than the brothers, I'd have to guess in her late twenties.

"All right, Grim cat," she said as Rolen came behind me.

Herrin did the opposite and backed away, leaning against the far wall and looking nervous as Carrie went on. "Now either you tell us what you and your Reaper friends did with those shifters, or Rolen here starts findin' incentive."

The muscular teen gave an anxious grin, *cracking* his knuckles.

I swallowed. "I-I already told you I don't know anything. Go ask the Sentients, they're the ones who took them all, probably."

"Sentients?" Carrie's nose scrunched as if smelling a cheap ruse. "What the Bloods is that supposed to mean?"

"It's a kind of Necrofera." I repeated what Alex and Xavier told me before. "They look like normal shifters, something about an Evocator dying and having their soul rot, or eating enough souls… I don't know, I've only seen one of them. We think there's three, and have no idea what's going on—look, I'm not the best person to ask! I'm new at this Reaper thing, my friends would know more."

She took a minute to think, looking at her brothers. "You guys buyin' this or what?"

Rolen spat a glob of saliva on the floor. "No way. Demons lookin' like us? That's just a myth parents tell their kids to make 'em behave."

"A-Actually, they *are* real…" Herrin disagreed, rubbing his fingers nervously. "Not commonly reported, but real. I've read about those things, in a demonology study. They say Sentients can look and think like the rest of us, and there've been cases dating back thousands of years on them… If I had to guess, I'd say he's right about them abducting the shifters… I guess that means the Reapers *aren't* working with—?"

"Don't fall for it, Herrin," Carrie warned, then looked back at me. "So, where's this Sentient thing now, Reaper?"

"How the Void should I know!" I shouted. "We don't know where any of them are! We're trying to kill them, not work with them!"

Rolen snorted. "Bullshit! We know your kind. You're all a bunch 'a schemers and murderers. We saw what that one Reaper did to our brother—"

"Rolen, we didn't even clarify if he was one of their knights," Herrin interrupted. "Even Dalen himself said he wasn't sure."

"Well, *I* saw 'im, and *I'm* sure! Bastard didn't even give Dalen a second glance when he did 'im in, it's no wonder they get along so well with demons. I say have this one tell us where his minions took everyone, right Carrie?"

"Couldn't agree more." Carrie flicked her eyes at the younger teenager. "Well, Rolen? Why don't ya give our little crawler here some talkin' persuasion?"

He jabbed me in the gut.

I gasped, curling over and sucked in the sickness.

The sister went on. "Don't try 'n protect your demon friends. If ya don't know where the other shifters are, then tell us where the Sentient is. We'll let ya go if ya cooperate."

I coughed over my knees, the pain slowly—real slowly—subsiding. "*Almost* the worst day of my life…" I muttered. First people threw stones at me and now this?

Well, at least it was better than the night Mom died. Or when Dad left—
Another fist sank into my gut.

"If ya don't talk," Carrie began. "We'll make it the worst day of your life."

I swallowed a grimace. "The bar's set pretty high… That's going to be hard—*khouh!*"

Another jab by Rolen. *Damned little punk.* I was going to have a dark bruise after this.

"I think we'll manage to kick it up a notch or two." Carrie pulled out a switchblade. "Now start talkin', unless ya think ya don't need all your fingers."

My gloved hands reflexively balled, stock-still.

What if I lied about being guilty? Would they let me go?

Wait, no. They wouldn't be that stupid, would they? I've seen their faces and knew where they were staying. I was a loose end—and as Ringëd always said, criminals didn't like loose ends. *Bloods, what do I do...*

"All right then," Carrie sang. "Let's start with the little finger and go on from there, uh?"

Crap!

She and Rolen pulled my bound arms under my legs to bring them forward. They dragged me onto my stomach and pinned my wrists to the hardwood, prying out the finger I tried like Land to keep curled.

Rolen held his own knife to my cheek, tilting the blade at an angle, the glint blinding me.

"Come on, Grim cat," Rolen growled. "Your fingers, or your face. Or maybe an ear?" He pinched my cat ear and tugged hard, pressing the knife's edge over the skin.

Carrie finally got my finger isolated and drew her blade over the top knuckle, making me grunt between teeth.

"All right, all right!" I shouted when she cut deeper, blood soaking the glove.

She stopped, looking at me expectantly. I drew in a deep breath, heart drumming. The two maniacs stared at me and fidgeted with their switchblades.

"I... I give," I panted. There was still a chance to get out of this, right? If the others found me, everything would be all right. I just had to stall for time... "You're right—we're working with the demons. We were just hoping no one would notice."

Carrie folded her arms over the chair's back, her grin satisfied. "Thought so. Bloody dirt crawlers thought ya could get away with it? We ain't stupid."

"Yeah, really surprised us there..." I muttered.

The two interrogated me about location and drop-offs, and I pulled each answer out of my ass as fast as my brain could think. Herrin frowned from across the room, his feathered wings bowing nervously. I sent him a sharp glare, pouring every shred of *follow-your-gut-and-help-me-out* message into it.

If Jaq or the twins didn't find me in time, then Herrin was, annoyingly, my safest bet. He knew something was up, didn't he? Something the Bloody reporters were missing? He totally believed me, he knew about Sentients and whatever...

Please, I thought furiously, my sharpened teeth gritting as I flicked the bookworm panicked glares. *Get. Me. OUT OF HERE.*

Herrin swallowed and stole a glance at his brother. His way more *muscular* brother. Herrin shuffled back and rubbed his arm, his wings dipping and giving me a 'sorry' look.

Dammit... the ONE thief who believed me had to be the weakest one...

"B-ad!" Shade screeched from the other room. "B-ad! B-ad! Help!"

Herrin's wings perked, his fingers snapping. "Oh!"

Carrie and Rolen stopped questioning me to crane back to him. "What's 'oh'?" demanded Carrie.

"I—uh, nothing," Herrin coughed, shying out of the room. "I was just... fed up with that bird. You were right... I think we should kill it."

Rolen shrugged. "Fine by me. Noisy thing, makes my ears ring."

Carrie didn't care either, and Herrin hurried into the other room, out of sight.

—*Crack-clack-CLACK!*

Clatters burst behind the door, and Herrin let out a sharp yelp.

Carrie and Rolen leapt to their feet—

Shade flew through the room. My raven ducked out the window, and Herrin clambered after, sucking on a finger.

"The damn thing bit me!" he cried. Then he snuck a grin at me. "Guess we have to move him, Carrie. Those birds always send reinforcements."

His sister cursed, stabbing her knife into a table with a hard *ku-thunk!* "Gods dammit, Herrin...! Fine! We'll move 'im... But we ain't gonna be caught off-guard. If his friends do show up." She dug her knife out of the wood, growling, "We'll get more answers outta *them.*"

42

GHOST STORY

XAVIER

"This was them," affirmed Jaq, stabbing a finger at a series of Wanted posters. "They just came out of nowhere and grabbed him."

"*Oscha!*" the Footrunner, Officer Ringëd, punched the wall. "That's the Bloody Carter Siblings! Are you kidding me?! *Taeux l'ïce, Ôlyowest flouflusé Rin, Gingette...!*"

Lilli leaned toward Alexander in a mumble. "Why is an Everlander spouting Marincian curses?"

"I don't know," Alexander muttered, his brow knitting at the Runner. "But more pressingly... Officer, do you know these birds?"

Ringëd grabbed a box of cigarettes from his pocket and lit one between his lips, sucking furiously. "They're a band of arms-thieves. We had some trouble with the siblings in Brittleton before they high-tailed it out of there and moved here."

Henry grunted and folded his burly arms. "Yeah, the siblings have all of us Blacksmiths leery of new customers these days. They're a load of trouble, no doubt."

"Gods, Bloody *damn it!*" Officer Ringëd hit the wall again. "Mika's gonna kill me...!"

"*Why aren't the officer's ears growing?*" I asked from the psyche, skeptical. "*He's clearly irate.*"

"Not the time." Alexander combed his fingers through his hair, turning to Ringëd. "I don't understand. What do thieves want with Octavius?"

"Void if I know." Ringëd said, rubbing his eyes.

Jaq smeared a hand over his face. "Bloods, I feel like it's my fault… By the time I realized what was happening, he was already too high for me to catch, I could have…"

"Lament on hindsight later," said Lilli. "We must focus on *finding* him first."

Vendy snorted. "And how do you plan to do that? They could have taken him anywhere."

Alex's gaze drifted to the fourth poster on the brick wall. "Wait," he began, "Jaq, I thought you said there were only three of these birds?"

"There were." Jaq came beside us to look himself. "This one wasn't with them. It was just the first three—"

The fourth man's face suddenly turned white on the paper, and we jumped back when it rose off the page altogether.

"That's 'cus I went to follow you three," the translucent face muttered.

A ghost?

The specter peered at Lilli and Alexander. "Sorry about your friend. I told those idiots not to do nothin', but it sounds like my sister couldn't listen for more than two seconds, like usual."

A wispy, white body came with the head as the ghost phased through the wall, floating in front of us.

His wings fluttered in silence behind his back as he crossed his arms. "Bloody girl thinks she's the captain, now that I'm outta my body. She's usually just our distraction, on a project. Dumb as a sack 'a rocks sometimes, I actually ain't surprised she did this."

We all stared at the ghost.

Jaq was the first to throw an incredulous hand at him. "What the Death?"

Officer Ringëd frowned, sweeping his soul-blind gaze over our shocked faces and scratching his head. "What? What's everyone staring at?"

Henry looked just as perplexed, looking to any of us for an explanation.

Lilli hesitated. "There's a… a *ghost* here." She pointed to the specter's Wanted poster. "This man's ghost."

Ringëd's face wrench in bewilderment. "Uh… what?"

Alex kept his eyes on the ghost, but rumbled off to the side. "Lilli, would you give Henry and the officer soul-sight for a moment? I don't have that Evocation."

Lilli nodded and touched either mans' shoulder, her hands gleaming violet as her Death mark brightened at her chest.

Ringëd and Henry found the ghost and leapt back in a jolt. Lilli stretched to keep contact with their arms, to keep the Evocation burning. Without an item to hold the Hallows, the men's soul-sight relied on her touch.

Ringëd pointed a shaking finger at the bird-shifter's floating soul. "Wh-wh… what the Void?! You're dead?!"

"No." The ghost sighed, putting fists at his sides. "I know, I know, ya want an explanation. It's a long story that I ain't got time to tell right now. Let's just say my crew went on a heist in this town, things didn't go well, and I ain't in my body no more. The important thing right now is findin' your friend before my sister does somethin' really stupid."

Alex waved back a hand. "But where are we going to find him…" Alex glanced at the poster with the ghost's face, reading the name. "Dalen?"

Dalen rocked his head to the left. "Our pad's down that way. My guess is they took him there. Come on, we better hurry—"

A raven's croaking came from the sky, and Shade soared down to us, screeching.

Lilli gasped. "Shade! He's free!"

Shade took to the sky again, flapping in the opposite direction Dalen had gestured to. We sped after the messenger on foot.

"Hey—wait a sec!" Dalen floated after us. "I said they're *this* way!"

The others went ahead as Alex craned back to him. "Don't underestimate a messenger's connection to their Reaper. They'll know better than anyone where they are. Now hurry up, you're coming with us to talk to your siblings. And stay close, in case there's another Fera raid." Alex rushed after the others. "They'd better not have hurt him, or there will be consequences."

"You're telling me!" Ringëd panted as we sprinted, the officer taking out his Shotri. "Bloods, Mika's going to kill me!"

43

A RUINED RESCUE

XAVIER

S hade beat his wings furiously, his feathers fluttering off as he led us through the wastelands outside the city.

Over the horizon, towering canyons loomed like a rocky fortress, the setting sun burning their cliffs in a piercing splash of orange and pink fire. Long shadows barred the many crevasses and nicks in the rocky formations, stretching across the wasteland's barren floor toward the east.

Feral lizards scuttled under rocks as we barreled past them, the parched ground cracked under our boots and skulls of decayed Landragons buried by the blowing dust. Buzzards pecked at fresh carcasses.

We followed Shade into the canyons, stopping at the ledge of a cliff and examined the terrain. The jagged formations loomed over us, striped with yellow and red cliffs that pulled into wide plateaus at their tops.

Shade alighted on a rock beside Alexander, flapping wildly and dragging his talons over the rough surface with dull *scrriks*.

Alex scanned the canyons' terrain. "He must be in here somewhere."

The raven flew up to perch on a boney branch of a dead tree, its head dipping and rising. Shade hopped and bounced, thrusting his beak upward in a gesture.

"Higher?" Alex asked.

All the messengers went to the same tree, screeching furiously.

"Uh," Jaq began, his scales paling when his gaze fell down the cliffside under his feet. "Mates? You, uh, might wanna see this."

Alex peered down. "Blood and bones."

Huddled in the canyon's bowl-shaped floor below us, their inky skin slithering with blackened sludge, were hundreds of Necrofera. Their squirming skin surged restlessly, though the beasts were snoozing soundly.

Finally, I thought from the psyche, *these nocturnal creatures were acting normal for once.*

It'd been beyond bizarre to see them awake during daylight before this, but then again, with a powerful commander such as Lucrine leading them, it was a small wonder they went against instinct.

"Tell your messengers to quiet down." Alex looked at Jaq and Lilli. "We don't want to draw attention."

They did as asked, and soon, Jewel and Bridge hushed, Shade and Mal following suit.

Shade lifted off the tree and soared into the canyons, settling on a rock beside a slope that led to the second level plateau. He fluttered, as if telling us to join him.

Alex was the first to follow the bird. "Come, the Fera seem to be staying down there. So long as we refrain from disturbing the nest, we can worry about them later."

Ringëd kept his Shotri close to his cheek, the Shockspheres in the cylinder lighting his skin with a bluish glow. "Either way," the officer muttered, "if Octavius *is* here somewhere, I got to get him out of this death trap."

"Indeed," Lilli agreed. She waved to the ghost. "Sir, come up here with me, if you would. You'll be safer around a Necrovoker."

The winged soul floated beside her in a mumble. "My name's Dalen… I ain't a 'sir'."

Vendy hissed to the ghost. "Why the Bloods would your siblings come here? Didn't they see those things down there?"

Dalen shook his head. "They have wings, they obviously didn't walk here. More likely, they flew 'im to the top so they could find a place away from Rockraiders. If I had to guess, I'd say they don't even know 'bout these things, Bloody idiots. Ya know, I've been tellin' them for years to always check their surroundings, ya never know who or what's gonna be there. Idiots never listen to a word I say, I swear—"

"Quiet down," Henry muttered gruffly. "The last thing we need is to wake up that swarm. Do you want them to climb up here and maul us to death?"

That shut him up, along with the rest of us.

We finally reached the top plateau after a long hike. Here, two winged boys stood beside a similarly feathered woman. They all wore masks.

At the woman's feet, his hands bound behind him and strapped with dampening gloves, sat Octavius. He looked like a miserable whelp, his cat ears grown and folded down his neck, face bruised with purple splotches, and his lip was cut open and seeping red.

His exhausted, green eyes flicked to us when we trotted toward them, and his cat ears perked. "G-guys! Thanks Bloods…!"

The masked woman yanked him in front of her and held a knife to his throat. "So, ya finally showed?"

"Tavius!" Ringëd shoved in front and cocked his Shotri.

Octavius blinked at the officer. "Ringëd?" he called. "What in Land are you doing here?"

"It's a long story." Ringëd aimed his Shotri at the woman, flashing his badge. "Carrie, Rolen, and Herrin Carter!" he bellowed. "You're under arrest—!"

"Not yet we ain't, Runner!" Carrie snarled, her wings wrapping around Octavius as she backed away with him in tow, his neck beading red under her knife. "Ya ain't takin' us nowhere till *after* those Grimlings tell us where this Sentient thing is!"

Alexander frowned at her, exchanging a baffled glance with Ringëd. "You…" Alex began, his brow raising at the woman, Carrie. "You expect *us* to find the Sentients?"

"Don't ya play dumb with me, Grimling! We know all about your demon friends—"

"Carrie," the ghost of Dalen interrupted, phasing through Ringëd to float between us. "What in Land's name are ya doin'?"

Behind her mask, Carrie gapped at the ghost, the two brothers beside her stiffening.

"Dalen!" Carrie gasped. "What're ya doin' out here?"

Those masks must have a soul-sight Evocation seal into them, I thought from the psyche, *like Jaq's eyeglasses… where had they acquired those? Had they stolen them?*

Dalen glared at his sister with scolding, white eyes. "I'm away for one day, and ya suddenly think you're in charge? I might be as solid as ale-vapor now, but I'm still the captain. Now let him go."

Carrie's confidence faltered. "But… but they have the shifters!"

"No, they don't." Dalen's spectral arms folded. "I've been keepin' tabs on 'em all day. They ain't got nothin' to do with the demons. Far as I can see, they just came to the wrong place at the wrong time."

One of the teenaged brothers beside her gestured curtly. "There, see? Even Dalen says they're clean. Will you let him go now?"

Carried growled. "Shut up, Herrin—"

"No!" The lanky boy, Herrin, stamped a foot and flapped his wings defiantly. "Why do you ignore everything *I* say, and when Dalen says the same damn thing you actually listen? If you just Bloody listened to me before this happened—"

"I said shut up, Herrin!"

"*Carrie*," Dalen's ghost warned, his tone void of patience. "Listen to your Gods damn brother and let the Reaper go. Bloods, Herrin's the only one of you with any sense left, I swear."

Herrin shot a smug grin at Carrie. She glared at him, then stifled a scream and threw her knife at the dirt by Octavius's feet, shoving the cat to Ringëd.

"Fine!" She hollered, red-faced with rage. "If they ain't part of this, then the Howllord better not tell his Da nothin'! Or about what we did in that armory…! We didn't steal no scythes, we caught someone else doin' it!"

Officer Ringëd swept Octavius behind him, hesitating to holster his Shotri. "Someone else?" he echoed.

Alex scratched his head helplessly. "Er… Who did what now?"

The bulkier teenager, who must have been Rolen, dragged an indignant foot over the dirt. "We didn't get to see the guy's face exactly."

Herrin added, "But the real thief was wearing one of your Reaper cloaks."

Carrie finished with an accusing finger. "So it was *you* guys that stole those scythes, not us!"

"I…" Alex began, straining to piece together whatever nonsense they were spouting. "No, I'm not following. Could someone grant me some Bloody context?"

Officer Ringëd muttered, "They're talking about the armory here in Lindel. The reports said the Carter Siblings stole some Reaper scythes recently, after they left Brittleton. But you're saying it was a Reaper who stole them?"

"We don't know why he did it," Carrie rumbled. "But we know what we saw. Things were goin' good at the start, we got in nice 'n quiet, no alarms sounded… Problem was, there was someone already there. *They* had the scythes, and when they saw us sneaking in while they were sneakin' out, they used one of the scythes on Dalen here 'n cut his Seam early… but he was still alive. Herrin guessed it was a pure-crystal scythe, or whatever."

"The guy snuck out while we were tryin' to help up Dalen," Rolen said. "But someone called the Raiders on us and we had to leave. We don't know who that other guy was, but he was definitely a Reaper. We've been tryin' to get Dalen's soul back in his body since, that's why we need that doctor back, the one the demons took."

Alex paused.

I hesitated from the psyche. *"Did he say doctor?"*

"The doc said he was gonna take Dalen's body someplace where there's others like him." Carrie started tearing up. "He gave us these masks so we could see 'n hear him, said they were gonna find a cure… But now that Maveric's gone, I guess *that's* hopeless. It's all that damned Reaper's fault! If he wasn't there, this never would'a happened!"

"This Reaper," Lilli began, suspicious. "Did you happen to see if he had… wings? Black wings?"

"No wings," Herrin answered. "Mammal, I'm guessing."

Lilli seemed relieved. "Well, at least that rules out Sir Janson—"

"Who cares about his damned shift!" Alex barked, storming to Carrie and grabbing her shoulders, shaking her vigorously. "Is Maveric one of them now?! Is he a demon?! Damn it, we don't have time for this! We need him alive!"

He stamped a foot on the dirt, summoning a puff of dust. His hands were shaking, wolf ears grown. "We spoke with Maveric mere days ago! He knew something…! He knew…!"

Alex punched an angry fist at the rocky wall, recoiling from the rebounded shock and seethed. "Gods damn it…! Why did they take *him* of all people?!"

Herrin rubbed his fingers nervously. "I kind of don't think Maveric should be your main problem right now. These Necrofera have been acting off, lately. Ever since the massacre in the valley, things have been getting worse and worse… If the Reapers aren't responsible for all that, then *someone* else has to be."

Carrie snapped her head to the boy, her nose scrunching. "What're ya yappin' about, Herrin?"

He sucked in a breath, seeming a bit scared of his sister, but held strong nonetheless. "I'm not saying it's definite, but look: they're coming out during daylight, huddling in large groups led by commanding Sentients who've gathered together, killing civilians but not eating their souls, taking their kills after a raid…" His shoulders dropped. "They're building an army. Now why would they do that?"

Lilli gasped as if remembering something. "I've heard of Sentients who've gathered armies before. Yet their numbers have never grown to this scale in such a short time."

"Their new leader is probably pretty strong." Herrin flicked his gaze away in thought. "But that still sounds too simple, a bunch of demons gathering an army… I mean, I still want to know why they want you Reapers alive. What use are you to them?"

Octavius gave a flat laugh. "If you count taking the blame for their raids, we're super useful. Everyone hates us, thanks to them."

"Sorrowed Death," Lilli hushed. "He's right. They do hate us. And as consequence, they hate the Death King. What if enough Everlanders come to despise our king? Would they demand to go to war against him?"

Alex rubbed ponderous fingers over his chin, murmuring, "If the Death King and his Reapers fall at the hands of someone else, the demons would be free to do as they pleased… Nira Cleanse me, they want to overrun the realms. And to do that, they need the one king that manages their deaths to die. They're building an army to prepare for war."

I muttered from the psyche. *And we walked straight into it. If a war happens, it will be our fault.*

Jaq cursed and smeared a hand over his face. "Looks like we all picked one Death of a time to visit the surface."

Alex spun on his heels. "Come, we haven't time to waste. If Maveric is truly gone, then there's nothing for us here. We must report this to Mistress and correspond with the reinforcements she's sending immediately. Perhaps with their help, we can stop this war before it gets out of hand—"

The ground shook, making us stagger. Dirt rumbled beneath our feet and a slow moan echoed through the canyons, scattering the surrounding buzzards.

Alex inched his gaze to the others. "What was that?" he asked, stiff.

Grinding rocks sounded behind. We twirled, seeing the wall was sliding upward in two places, like a pair of doors lifting. But they led nowhere. Instead of dark caverns inside, there was a white wall, sticky and slimy as if made of soft tissue, red veins littering its surface.

Then two brown irises revolved to the middle, black pupils slitting into focus sleepily.

Another moan grumbled at our feet, and the ground shuddered when the cliff jerked off and crumbled away from the canyons entirely. We stumbled at the resulting tremors, sliding down as the cliff leaned to one side.

We all clung to whatever secure gripping we could find, Alex snagging the branch of a sparse tree. Vendy and Henry jammed their swords into the dirt, clinging on for dear life. Lilli was nearly thrown over, but Alex caught her wrist.

"Alex!" Lilli screamed, her eyes fixated on the bottom of the canyons far, far below her dangling feet. "I don't think this is a cliff…!"

It wasn't. What we thought had been cracked rocks were actually scales of the largest Stonedragon we'd seen yet.

A Stonedragon that, we realized, we'd just woken.

44

COLOSSUS

XAVIER

The colossal dragon flipped its head back and swung us in the air. Alex lost grip of the branch, flew up, then tumbled down. Lilli flew past us, screaming as we came down. Alex grabbed her arm to pull her in before his back hit the dragon's rocky brow.

I heard a loud *crack* as my brother's head slammed against the stone—

I inhaled the dusty air, gasping as I was forced out of the psyche. My head swelled with a sharp pain and I winced, clutching my head.

"Alex…?" I called weakly, coughing.

He didn't respond from the psyche. *He must have blacked out.*

Something else was wrong, though. I couldn't move. It felt like something was pinning me down. struggling, I lifted my head.

Lilli huddled over me, pinning me under my already-heavy breastplate, clutching my neck with shivering arms.

"Lilli…" I wheezed, trying to pry her off, but her grip wouldn't yield. She looked like a crazed thing with her tangled hair wild and frayed over her face. "Lilli…! Get… off!" I managed to wheeze from my constricted throat.

She was sobbing like a child now, hiccupping. "No, no…! Don't—don't you dare drop me, Alex! I-I-I don't want to die…! Not like this!"

The memory of her as a little girl came back, where she was crouched over a wall and spouting the same nonsense.

Ah, so that's what it was? She was afraid of heights? *Of all the things this woman had to be scared Deathless of…*

"Dares to face a Sentient demon who could kill her with a flick of his wrist," I muttered under her sobbing figure. "Yet drop her on a cliffside and she turns into a simpering wretch… Blasted woman, doesn't make a lick of sense."

I wrestled her arms open and sucked in a reviving breath, pushing her off so I could sit up.

She wiped her eyes and runny nose. Then she stiffened, gawking at me. "X… Xavier?"

I froze, patting a hand to my face. Nothing was there. The fading sunlight wasn't muted by the sunglasses anymore. *Death, they must have fallen when Alex was thrown!*

I fumbled for an explanation. "I, er—"

"Oh, thank the Seamstress Below!" She latched onto me and crushed my windpipe again. "It is you!" she cried with joy, her grip tightening painfully around my throat. "I've been looking—*hic!*—looking everywhere…! Oh, I can go home now—!"

The dragon trumpeted under us and threw its enormous head to the side. We were propelled over the edge, spiraling to the ground, and Lilli shrieked and clung to my neck, strangling me—

I was suddenly seized by the stomach, hoisted to a stop in midair.

One of the winged brothers had caught me. It was the lanky teen, Herrin. He only had enough hands to lift *me*, so Lilli lost her grip on my neck and shrieked when she dropped. I grasped her arm in time, swinging her back up as she took a secure hold of my neck once more. This time, I held her waist to save my windpipe from any more abuse.

"Don't drop her," Herrin warned, eyes intent under his mask. "There's only three of us, physically. Dalen can't grab anyone as a ghost."

His winged siblings were flying behind. Carrie lifted Jaq—who had snagged Ringëd's arms, the officer flailing frantically—and Octavius was held by Rolen. Octavius had been freed of his bonds and dampening gloves, probably by Ringëd before we were thrown, and was now holding Dalen's spectral wrist. Thankfully, Octavius had that infection Hallows, otherwise he wouldn't be capable of touching the ghost.

Below, I found Vendy and Henry still clinging to their sword hilts, their blades jammed securely in the beast's rocky hide. They stayed crouched on its wide nose as the enormous Stonedragon crunched through the canyons with its mountainous steps, crumbling the rocks at its feet.

The noise made the horde of demons stir from their slumber.

The Fera funneled out of their nest, the rocks teeming with the creatures like black water pouring down an anthill. The Necrofera scattered round the Stonedragon's legs in startled annoyance.

The dragon stomped southward, bleating a deafening, guttural roar as it left the canyons. The demons followed, scuttling over its legs as if trying to pry through its rocky scales. They weren't successful, and hopped off the dragon, scrambling after the giant as if curious where it was going.

I glanced ahead at the horizon. Bloods be good, it was heading for the city, with Vendy and Henry stuck atop it.

I tapped into Vendy with my mental connection, a fuzz of static washing over my brain. "Vendy, are you both still on that thing?"

Yeah! Her reply came in my thoughts, frantic. *Um, what should we do?*

"Hold fast, for now," I said. "And whatever you do, *don't* jump off this time! That is a direct command!"

All right, all right!

The static in my brain faded, the connection ending as I focused on my present distress, taking a count of our party to be sure we were all still alive. I was relieved to find we were.

"Did you see the size of that thing?!" Octavius hollered to me, panting from Rolen's arms as he kept a secure hold of Dalen's ghost. "It was practically the entire canyon!"

"It's going to destroy the whole Bloody town if it gets there!" I yelled from Herrin's arms.

Lilli sniffled from my neck, straining to keep hold of me as Herrin's flapping wings dipped and bobbed us in the air.

"W-wait," she said, lifting her gaze to mine. "Xavier... What happened to Alex?"

"He'll be back later!" I shouted, then muttered under my breath. "I hope."

No word came from the psyche. *Alex must still be unconscious.*

Lilli frowned, looking at my dented armor. "Why are you wearing the same clothes as him?"

"Coincidence." I craned my head to Herrin, whose arms were quivering to keep us lifted. "How fast can you get us to the city?"

Herrin peered after the Stonedragon and swarm of demons, estimating. "N... not fast enough. You guys are *really* heavy in that armor."

"You even have the same bruises," Lilli continued, eyes narrowing at my face.

I ignored her. "Jaq, get your com out and call the local emergency num... Jaq?"

Jaq's eyes were shut while Carrie held onto him, his breaths hard and methodical. He looked like he was in deep thought, wrinkles prevalent on his scaled forehead.

"Death, right, you also hate heights… Er, Lilli. Can you grab my com?"

She blinked. "Hang on. What did you call m—?"

"For the love of Gods, enough with the questions! Will you get my Bloody com?!"

She finally focused on my request. Her eyes searched me frantically, patting me down with constrained arms that I'd pinned to her sides to keep my hold. "Well, where is it?" She asked desperately.

"Trouser pocket. Er, no, the other side. The other—not there! *Not* there! That's not a pocket!"

"Sorry!" She blushed, finally finding the pocket with my com.

"Good!" I panted. "Now call High Everland's emergency line!"

She blinked at me. "How would I know the number for that?"

"It was in the informational pamphlet!" I groaned. "Does no one read the Bloody pamphlet?!"

"WHAT NUMBER?!"

"3315!" I shouted.

She fumbled with the buttons, but managed to dial them properly. A screen of light projected from the device, and after a moment, a woman's face appeared. *"Everland Emergency, how can I—"*

"Evacuate the city of Lindel!" I yelled over the rushing wind. "The whole city! There's a swarm of Necrofera heading straight for town, and a Stonedragon the size of a Bloody mountain is with them! Connect to whatever line you must but do it quickly and get everyone the Void out of there!"

Lilli ended the call and I shouted at Herrin, "Get us back there now!"

45

THE SWARM

CILIA

Sirens rang through the city, and a low, powerful rumble shuddered the building Lucrine and I waited within. The quake only lasted a few seconds, but quickly picked up again. Then another came, and another, the tremors rising in strength.

I went to the window, lifting the glass pane to peer at the dusk-lit horizon. "Odd…"

Lucrine came beside me, though he kept a safe distance, perhaps not wishing to provoke me a second time. "What is it?" he asked.

"It seems another Stonedragon is heading this way. And our budding army is following."

"Again? I thought ya told that idiot to keep 'em away from here?"

"I did," I muttered, cat ears growing. "Apparently, he's disobeying me a second time."

The door squeaked open behind us, and a shadowed figure lingered behind the wood, hesitating. "I-I'm not responsible this time, Mistress…" My second underling said. "I've been here since morning."

I frowned, peering out the window again. "Even odder… I can send back the Fera, but there is naught I can do with that dragon. It's far larger than those others that came yesterday."

I sighed, watching the enormous Stonedragon break its way through the buildings, screams of terror ripping down there, citizens fleeing the streets. My ink-covered minions scuttled after the people, tearing into the ant-sized carcasses and peeling off limbs… It was utter chaos, Rockraiders and

Footrunners trying their best to shepherd the men and women to safety. It didn't do them much good, too much was going on for them to handle.

Bloody mongrels, I brooded in silence, envy burning. *Why did they get all the fun?*

Here I was, the queen of these stupid things, and I was the only one who hadn't *any* time to stretch her legs since getting our third Sentient, who now waited behind the door. Oh, the valley was so invigorating… I hated staying locked up in here. I was tempted to join the raid myself.

But what would Macarius think?

He'd gone elsewhere for a time, as he often did. He'd promised to send a copy of himself shortly—a doppelganger phantom of some kind, a Somniovoker trick of his—but it hadn't yet arrived. The cobra had only left this morning.

"What're we supposed to do?" Lucrine questioned, sliding his rough hands in his pockets. "Stop 'em, or let 'em at it?"

I combed my fingers through my grey hair, humming longingly. "Well, I don't see why we can't have a little fun ourselves… Macarius only wanted the wolf boy alive to find his brother. If we find him now, he wouldn't mind if we killed his friends, would he?"

Lucrine's lips tugged in a vicious grin. "As ya wish, Mistress…"

46

PRINCESS OF EMBERS

XAVIER

Nightfall had nearly arrived by the time we made it to Lindel.

The Carter siblings landed us in the graveyard behind the familiar Harmonist temple. Fortunately, our district hadn't been hit yet, and was the farthest from the destruction uptown.

"Thank you," I said to Herrin as he set me and Lilli on the ground. It felt odd to thank someone who'd kidnapped our friend, but there was some credit due. They could have left us to die in the canyons while they flew off. I supposed their brother, Dalen, had great influence on their moral standings.

I turned to the temple. "It looks like the town's evacuated, thank Death. There isn't much we can do without reinforcements. We'll gather a few things and leave."

I spun back to Herrin, hesitating. "I, er, know there's not much reason for you to stay, but… Is it possible for you to fly us out of here?"

"We got ya covered," Dalen's ghost answered instead. He was being set down by Octavius, who was set down by Rolen.

Octavius shied away from the teenager and stood beside Ringëd after Carrie came to put him and Jaq down.

The cat still looked rattled from earlier, and for good reason. But it seemed he was willing to tolerate their help for the sake of making it out of this city alive. Good instincts.

The ghostly brother came to meet me, waving at his siblings. "They'll wait as long as ya need," assured Dalen. "Whatever ya ask."

Carrie gawked at him. "Screw them, Dalen! Let's just get outta here and—"

"We're *stayin'*." He shot her a cutting look, silencing his sister. "It's you three's fault this mess happened. Especially you, Carrie. I've just about had it with you. You ain't in charge, you ain't the captain, and you better make sure ya follow my orders, or I'm kicking ya out of the crew."

Her face soured. "Ya can't kick me—"

He stabbed a spectral finger at her. "What do I always say? 'Ya make a mess, ya clean it up'. That's how it's always been, and that's what I expect ya to do now. How many people have died today 'cos of your misjudgment, Carrie? How many?"

She fell quiet, her eyes dropping to her feet. "I… just wanted to help ya, Dalen…"

"And what a Bloody great help you've been. Now shut it and do what I say. We're helpin' them outta here."

Rolen interjected meekly. "What about your body? It's still at the clinic."

Dalen cursed under his breath. "Land, I forgot about that… Howllord?" He turned to me. "We gotta get my body. We'll meet ya back here."

My lips pursed, and I looked at Lilli, Jaq and Octavius. "You can't go out there alone," I said. "With demons running amuck, you'll want Reapers to escort you. We'll stay together."

Officer Ringëd snorted and cocked his Shotri. "Damn right we're staying together. I just ran over half this damned continent looking for you Grimlings, I'm not about to split up and lose track of anyone now."

Dalen's white lips tugged an appreciative grin. "All right then. Herrin, you take the lead. If we get separated, you're in charge."

The lanky brother's wings perked. "R-really?"

Rolen looked envious, grumbling. "Why does Herrin get to be in charge?"

"'Cuz even though Carrie's in hot water for startin' this mess, she wouldn't have been able to pull off that kidnappin' without your help, Rolen. Herrin's not stupid enough to go against my orders unless you two bullied him into it again, so *that's* why Herrin. Now shut up and follow your brother."

With Herrin eagerly at front, he waved everyone onward as we started out of the graveyard.

But I only took three steps before Lilli grabbed my arm. "Xavier, wait! There's something I…"

"It can wait." I dragged her forward. Most of the others were leaving us behind. "We have to get out of this death trap."

"Xavier, please!" She yanked me to a stop, standing her ground. The group disappeared around the buildings, but Dalen's ghost lingered to wait for us, looking impatient.

"I know you've lost your memories," she said. "And I don't know how much you remember, but this may very well be my last chance to say this!"

I hesitated. "I… look, we don't have time for this! We have to go!"

"I have come too far and risked too much to let it all go to waste now!" She nearly crushed my arm, making me wince. "I almost had my guts splattered not a few moments ago, and now we're about to head straight into the middle of the biggest Bloody demon army I've ever seen in my life, with a colossus none of us are equipped to kill! My execution is undoubtedly waiting for me when I return home, so even if we do manage to survive, *I'm* running out of time anyway! The least you can do is help me feel like my mission was worth something, and to do that, *I need you to remember me!*"

She was puffing when she finished, exasperated.

I frowned. "Er… Lilli, I actually remember more than you might—"

"That is exactly what I'm talking about!" She groaned. "That's it! I've had enough of this blasted game, and I don't even know how you heard about it, but Nira help me, you are remembering me one way or—!"

"Well, well, *well.*"

We jumped at the new, drawling voice. It'd come from above. Tensed, Lilli and I twisted our gaze upward.

Perched on a nearby tree, staring down at us with piercing, chartreuse eyes, was a bat-winged girl with silken, black hair.

She didn't look pleased, her leathery wings rising as she grumbled. "Why am I not surprised to find you in the middle of a disaster like this?"

Lilli stiffened at the sight of the new girl. "Bloody Death…!"

"Oh, you'll certainly be bloody when I'm through with you," the young woman snapped. "Do you have any idea what I've been through because of your stupid little holiday?"

Her black hair was tied in a bun by a pink ribbon, and I noticed her pink dress was caked in dried mud. She wore a thin, silver chain round her neck that had a second layer beneath it, two metal scythe-spheres dangling there. She flicked a short glance at me before glaring bolts at Lilli again.

"I see you've found Xavier, as promised in your runaway note," the new girl huffed as a crow fluttered to her shoulder and gave a haughty caw. Her bat ears grew and curled back, sneering ruefully. "How good for you. And while the blessings are throwing themselves at your feet up here, the Death Palace is in an outright panic. And *I'm* being blamed for it! Oh, you'd best count yourself lucky your father hasn't come back from the Sky realm, otherwise he might have my head."

I stepped between the two girls, cautious. "Who are you?"

The bat girl's sharp eyes snapped to me. "What do you mean 'who am I'? Don't you remember me?"

Death, I was getting tired of everyone demanding me to remember things. "Remind me."

She looked insulted and hopped down, hands at her sides. "I am High Howless Lilliana Tessinger! Daughter of the Death King's Hand!"

I paused, craning back to the girl I was shielding. "You're… *both* Lilliana?"

The first Lilli cringed, the other glaring bolts at her. "What have you been telling him?" the bat huffed.

The first cleared her throat. "I, uhm… may have said a few things I shouldn't have, I admit… But I did find him! He was alive after all."

"Yes, that's all well and good, I'm inexpressively delighted. And that isn't sarcasm, Xavier, I am glad to see you, it's just that I'm in a hurry." She glared at the other Lilli. "You. Pack your things, we're going straight back to Grim—"

"Will someone explain what is going on?" I demanded, irritated.

The bat stabbed an expectant hand at the *other* Lilli, who ducked her head. "Go on," the bat encouraged. "Tell him. You've gone on with this silly charade long enough."

The first Lilli sucked in a breath, opened her mouth to speak…

"Hey," Dalen's ghost interrupted instead, clearing his throat behind us. Blast, I'd almost forgotten the ghost was even there.

Then I realized the messengers were screeching from the tree. I'd apparently tuned them out in the confusion.

"I don't mean to be rude or nothin'," said Dalen crossly. "But we ain't exactly alone here."

The ghost pointed to a tall monument nearby. Our eyes followed his translucent finger.

Sitting daintily atop the monument was a young, grey haired girl.

Cilia.

"Please, don't stop on my behalf," she called, her smile amused. "I can wait until this famous brother of yours appears next. That would be splendid."

None of us spoke.

Cilia sighed, lifting a hand. "Oh, fine. Ruin my fun right when things were getting interesting…"

Her hand ignited in a burst of fire. We leapt back as the flames were sent flying at our feet. The messengers were sent away as the tree caught ablaze, along with the grass and wooden structures around it.

Cilia slid down from her monument. Her smile was crooked with thrill, licking flames circling her hands, as if she were molding the fire into a wavering shape. The form became clearer with time, and soon, she'd summoned a hound made of flames. Then another. And three more were drawn from her palms, her Death mark gleaming from her neck.

"Shall we play a bit of fetch with your friends, wolf boy?" Cilia's head cocked, giggling. "Perhaps your brother will see our fun and play himself?"

With a swift wave of her arms, the fire hounds crackled after us, fumes trailing their blazed path.

I snagged Lilli's wrist—the Lilli I'd come to know over the week—and pushed her back to get her away from the flames. I almost turned to lead her, Dalen and the other girl away from the incoming fire, but my foot caught a low stone and I stumbled to the dirt.

The hounds sprang for me, and I scuttled back, shutting my eyes with a yell.

… nothing happened. My lids slit open.

The hounds were snapping at my feet, struggling to reach, but were held back by what looked like orange-flamed leashes. And on the other end of those leashes was Lilli—the first Lilli—who grasped the enflamed ropes with her bare hands. Smoke rose from her blouse, and the smell of burnt cloth simmered as the material opened at her midriff.

"Lilli…?" The certainty had gone from my voice. "How are you doing that?"

She heaved the dogs round and flung them away. They all splashed into the temple's wall. Smoke curled between the stones, and it looked like the wooden framework underneath had caught fire.

Cilia hummed with interest. "Another Pyrovoker? Strange… I was told you were a corpse-raiser."

I lifted a beguiled finger at Lilli, eyes fixated on the place her blouse had been burnt. Her skin was pale and smooth there, no burn scars visible.

Instead, an azure Dream mark was displayed there.

"Wh… why do you have *two* marks, Lilli?" I asked skeptically.

"Oh, will you stop calling me that?" She slipped off a silver piece of jewelry from her ear—some sort of small cuff—and threw it to the ground.

Her charcoal hair began to bleed white, the ashen color trailing up her scalp. Her onyx eyes shifted to an icy azure, and her Death and Dream marks suddenly displayed crowns above them, creating the mark of a Relicblood.

My brain dimmed. "Willow…?"

The Death Princess sucked in a resolute breath, straightening in a calm exhale while she slid out her black hair-stick.

"Lilli," she addressed to the bat girl, tone draining to a more commanding tune as her scythe materialized. "Go with Xavier and find the others."

We both stared at her. Lilli—the real Lilli, apparently—was the first to protest. "You can't fight a Sentient alone!"

"Watch me." Willow glared back, azure eyes committed. "I'm the only one here who can stand against another fire-thrower. Find the others and stay together. That is an order."

"My, isn't this convenient?" Cilia clapped excited hands. "Now Macarius won't have any objection to this little game!"

I was still lost in shock when the *real* Lilli pulled me to my fumbling feet, telling me to grab Dalen's ghost as she spread her leathery wings and took flight.

"Wait!" I shouted as she hauled me and Dalen into the sky, my fingers gripping the ghost's arm tight. "Willow…!"

My betrothed's ashen hair weaved in the wind beneath me, then disappeared as Lilli flew us above the veiling smoke.

47

A DUEL OF ROYALS

WILLOW

The Sentient giggled when I cocked my scythe behind me, feet sliding wide and knees bent low.

Fire raged around us, burning the temple and trees as the smoke thickened. Wind blew past, jingling the bell tied to my ashen hair as my gaze grew intent at the opposing Pyrovoker. My white fox ears curled.

"How considerate of Her Highness!" The demon girl clasped her hands in delight. "Coming all the way to the surface so that we needn't retrieve you down below?"

"So, it's true." I tried to sound confident, but my hands still shook. Hopefully, Xavier and Lilli hadn't noticed. I'd never killed a Sentient before. The last time I tried with Lucrine, it hadn't ended well. How was I going to fair against his superior? "You do intend to kill the Death Bloodline so your army can overtake the realms, don't you?"

"You'd be correct, had you not assumed your family was the only target."

One of my fox ears lifted. "You mean to destroy another Bloodline?"

"Oh, dear girl!" She giggled. "We mean to destroy all of them."

"Then it's even more imperative that I kill you now." From my hands sprouted black, crooked veins, my Death mark gleaming from my collarbone as I evoked infection Hallows onto my scythe.

The veins slithered around the weapon, stretching and creeping round its length until my scythe was completely coated in the black poison. *All I need is one slice to her chest*, I thought, *and her Seam will disintegrate.*

I fought back the bile rising in my throat, steadying my legs before I was tempted to sway. I was terrible at Infeciovoking. Octavius was obviously more practiced with it, since he hadn't a need to use most of his energy to evoke it. Having six elements depleted my magic's strength significantly.

The demon's eyes glazed at my blackened scythe. "Infection Hallows? How nostalgic…" She tapped a prim claw to her lips. "It's been some time since I last saw that element… I'd nearly forgotten the Death family was the last to survive that extermination, wasn't it?"

I held my scythe before me in caution. "What extermination?"

"The riddance of the Infeciovokers," she explained with a breathy gesture. "You hadn't wondered why there were none left in Nirus? I was there for the hunting. Of course, I suppose genocide like that was too… horrid to be placed in the history books. And five hundred years can prove to diminish the memories."

"They were… hunted?" questioned, baffled. "By whom?"

"The Everlanders, of course. Though, this was a time before the continents were separated, so I suppose you can say the Neverlanders were equally as responsible."

"Why would they hunt the Infeciovokers?"

She made a pouting face, her mouth twisting. "Didn't you know? It was an Infeciovoker who killed the last Relicblood of Land."

What…? Was she bluffing? I'd never heard of such a claim. *Grandfather Dream said nothing of this…* "Why would an Infeciovoker kill the Land King?" I asked.

She set her hands at her waist. "How would I know? I was killed before then. Macarius says I Changed after the hunting had already begun."

"Macarius?" My brow furrowed. "Who is Macarius?"

"That." Her eyes flicked away. "Is a very curious question… Regardless, he wanted you alive. So, if you cooperate, this will be beneficial for everyone."

My grip tightened on my blackened scythe. "You can have me once I've taken my last breath, Demon. But your rotten spirit will have gone to the Void before that happens…!" I propelled forward, cocking my poisoned scythe behind me.

I swung for her chest, but she twirled to the side. I revolved the weapon round my neck to strike for her throat, but she bent back with an unnatural crack of her spine. She pushed her feet off the ground and flipped backward away from my third swing, chuckling while her joints popped back into place with black tar crawling over her skin.

"You're certainly brave for a maiden your age." Her musing tone was low and guttural. "Intentionally fighting a demon as old as I?"

"You and I look to be the same age physically," I muttered, noting her young face and grey hair. "Under normal circumstances, you wouldn't dare challenge me, as a Grimlette under my rule."

Her smile twisted. "I am ruled by no one, Your Highness Death. Haven't you heard? I am royalty myself, here on the surface. You may refer to me as Queen Cilia, the Grim Killer of Everland."

A Demon Queen? I tried not to look fazed, but my heart pounded sickly. *I can't kill a Necrofera queen!* The Land King died five hundred years ago, she must have been the oldest Sentient I've ever heard of. If I couldn't scratch a mere Class 2 Sentient, my odds looked terrible against Cilia.

Fire blazed from the temple beside us, smoke clouding the yard and clinging to my lungs. The air was becoming suffocating, my head growing dizzy as I continued to evoke my infection Hallows.

I must retreat. I realized. *Even if I wished to fight her, this was not the place to do so.*

I may have been immune to fire burns, but the smoke would asphyxiate me eventually. Cilia must not have been affected because she was already dead. Breathing was not an issue, to her.

Plan set, I shifted my stance and sprinted out of the graveyard, heading away from the smoke with Cilia following close behind.

48

TEST OF COURAGE

XAVIER

"Idiot!" I held Dalen's ghostly wrist with tight fingers, the bat girl flapping us high over the clock tower as I cursed my own stupidity. "Bloody idiot! She was right in front of you...!"

It all made sense now. The fragmented memories rushed back in a blur. Willow would always change into her disguise before we snuck into the city together, outside the palace walls where she was forbidden to go unescorted. They weren't two separate people—she was the same girl. Gods, this was confusing...

I craned back to the bat girl, who was concentrating on keeping me lifted, chewing on a string of obscenities. We'd barely gotten anywhere, but she looked exhausted, as if she'd been flying without break for days and my added weight wasn't helping.

"I remember you now." Memories flashed back, many scenes of a little bat girl playing, always there in the palace with Willow. She must have been the half-nobility, half-peasant girl. Yes, that clicked, somewhere. *So, Willow had been jumbling facts about herself and Lilli...*

"I really wish you'd have come days ago!" I hollered up to Lilli. "It would have saved me a lot of—"

"Xavier, will you shut up?" Lilli's face was red with exertion. "I have been flying all over this damned continent looking for Willow, my father is furious with me for losing her, I haven't slept, I've been robbed, humiliated, disrespected, threatened, and now I come here to find out a blasted army of demons is destroying the town! While I'm thrilled you're alive, forgive me if I am in no mood to rekindle past relationships!"

Lowering to the roof of the Howler's Inn and setting us down, she collapsed to her hands and knees, coughing the smoke from her lungs. Behind us, the city was in shambles, sirens whining and buildings crumbling to rubble in the Stonedragon's wake.

With every step the gigantic creature took, the town quivered. And it was headed straight for us. I only hoped Jaq and Octavius were all right.

I pivoted to the temple across the street, horrified. The building was in flames, fumes pluming to the sky as if to drown the stars. I peered over the edge of the roof with frantic eyes, hoping to find Willow.

"We shouldn't have left her," I said as Dalen floated beside me. "We must go back—"

"Willow has more of a chance against that Sentient than we do," Lilli said, coughing from the smoke. "Trust me. Provided she doesn't exhaust herself with her Hallows, she should fare well against such a demon."

"And if she *does* exhaust herself?"

Lilli covered her nose and mouth with a pink sleeve. "Then she'll run. She knows when to accept defeat, at the very least. She's clever, if hardheaded and spoiled."

She went into a coughing fit, leather wings bowing at her sides.

I went to clasp her shoulder and stifled my own coughs. "Don't worry about flying us anywhere more. I'm too heavy for you. We'll go on foot, but we have to hurry. The first thing we need to do is find—"

"All right Clean Ones," a voice sneered to our left.

A horse-eared man was leaning against the concrete wall of the roof's stairwell, his red-shaded glasses falling down his large nose. His white pupils gleamed against the dark smog, and he *cracked* his hoof-textured knuckles.

"Well?" he spat, looking between Lilli and me. "Where's this damn twin 'a yours?"

My face drained at the horse-shifter. *Lucrine is here? Now, of all times?*

"Dalen!" My head snapped to the ghost behind me as I plucked my scythe-spheres off their chain, having my weapons materialize. "Fall!"

Startled, the ghost complied and phased downward through the roof, disappearing to safety.

"So?" Lucrine inquired, pushing off the concrete wall of the stairwell. "All I've been hearin' for the past few weeks is 'brother' this and 'twin' that and 'get both of them'… but I ain't seen a second one this whole damned time. So, ya want to help me out? Fill me in on where the Void he is? I'm getting real tired of waiting around."

Lilli flapped to my side, plucking her own spheres from her neck-chain and had her dual scythes materialize. "Why does that concern you, Demon?"

"Like I said, my queen wants both of them before the cobra gets back," Lucrine grunted.

My footing shifted. "Then I'm sorry to say she'll have to be disappointed. You won't find my brother."

Especially since he's not even conscious at the moment, came the afterthought.

Lucrine shrugged, giving a long sigh. "Well, I tried giving ya a way out…"

He lunged forward and whipped a hooved-hand at my side. I crossed my scythes in a reflex, and they *clanged* against Lucrine's hand.

My feet skidded back from the force, and I staggered as Lucrine dashed round and slammed a fist into my spine. I yelped and nearly dropped my scythes, but not before biting down the ache and spinning round to deflect another strike.

Lucrine came again, I was barely able to evade, forced to shuffle back to keep distance.

Lilli sliced her double-edged scythes at Lucrine's head. She managed to pierce his skull and forced him back, then flapped beside me, glaring at the Sentient as he took a pained moment to heal his wound with pulsing tar.

"Don't forget he isn't alone." Her throat clicked.

Lucrine spit at the ground, the wad rotting black and slithering back to him as he cracked his neck to one side.

In a yell, we charged.

49

BOLSTERING WARRIORS

ANABELLE

Kurrick sped ahead through the crumbled city, Necrofera scrambling in the rubble and feasting on the poor souls who hadn't evacuated in time.

I tried to keep pace with my warrior, but he was far too quick.

Kurrick broke the creatures' dripping bones with his two heavy claymore blades, but they hadn't much effect. With every crushing swing he landed, the demons would glop back together.

"Damn it all!" He whipped his gaze back at me, finding me trailing behind. His eyes splintered, looking past me, and he ran back. "Anabelle!"

A snarl came behind and I whirled. A hideous, liquid beast leapt for me.

With a panicked grunt, I evoked my Hallows—hands glittering with golden light—and *ripped* the ground up from under me, stone cracking at my will, shaping into a high wall.

Pushing more energy, I forced three other walls to shoot up from the ground. Their jagged tips crunched into each other and trapped the demon on all sides. I could hear the beast screech from within, scratching its new prison, shoving itself against the stone. The rock fractured under its weight, crumbling. *That would hold it for now,* I thought in a pant. *But not for long, it seems.*

"Ana…!" Kurrick threw down one of his swords and came to help me to my feet, searching me for injuries. "Are you hurt?"

I brushed myself off, head shaking.

Relief flushed his breath, and he retrieved his second claymore. "Come, arm yourself! And stay close!"

I nodded, evoking my Hallows into the road. The stone tore free, and I molded it into a heavy, wide blade as tall as a man, the rock solidifying in my hands. The weapon gleamed with golden light as I used more of my Terravoking to lift the heavy stone with more ease.

"I'm ready," I announced to Kurrick, hefting the blunt blade over a shoulder, only able to lift such a weapon due to my many years of strength training with both muscle and Hallows, and dashed through the streets at his side.

A cluster of Fera shrieked for me, and I gave a guttural roar and *cracked* my enormous sword over their bodies all at once, ribs and skulls fracturing into bits, the blade breaking at its head when it slammed into the ground.

I used my rock Hallows to re-fasten the broken fragments, grunting as I swung horizontally at a second cluster who bounded for me. The slice left a golden afterimage.

Kurrick had pushed back another pair of demons with his two steel blades, then ran to my side.

"We must help the Shadowblood escape!" I panted.

He turned to me, still sprinting, his lion ears grown. "If they are as skilled as the legend claims, they will escape by their own means! My priority is to the daughter of Myra!"

"Either way leads to the same path!" I puffed in a chuckle—

A small scream came from an alley.

A young, winged boy was trapped under a pile of rubble. A goat-horned man was helping to pull him out, but he couldn't lift the heavier rocks to free the child.

Kurrick and I rushed to their aid. I evoked my rock Hallows onto the rubble, lifting it off of the sobbing boy, and the goat-horned man picked up the child in relief, eyeing me appreciatively as I lowered the bits of rock to the ground again.

The boy attempted to unfold his wing, but winced. It looked broken and mangled, blood soaking his chestnut feathers.

He was a skinny thing with dark skin, clothed in nothing save a pair of shorts and a red-and-black striped scarf. A crow flapped from the boy's head, hollering ceaselessly.

I blinked at the bird. *This boy is a Reaper as well?* Why was he not with the others? *Perhaps they were unaware of one another?*

"Pray, let her see the child," Kurrick said to the goat-shifter. "She will attend to his wounds."

The man hesitated, but before he could protest I set down my stone sword and approached them.

The child's wing twitched in pain when my hands lightly touched it, and he cried out. I fished into the satchel at my waist for a cleansing cloth, wiping the wound of bacteria. With that finished, I took in a slow breath, drawing my second element of Hallows from my soul, and evoked it onto his wing.

The wound glittered with gold light, his broken bone fitting back into place. It was positioned correctly, but with any movement, it would slip back out. *I must push further.* Broken limbs required more difficult Evocations.

I intensified my Hallows, concentrating, until the fractured bone quivered and began mending, connecting back to its rightful place. Once it was finished, I had his skin seal over it, leaving a small scar on the wing.

"You mustn't move it too drastically," I whispered to the child. I was never comfortable speaking with anyone I didn't know, yet this child was a patient now—and the goat shifter his acting guardian, for lack of any others in sight. I breathed to the goat-shifter now. "I've only reconnected the bone at the edges… It will take time to mend at the core. Pray, do not allow him to fly for a time."

"Yes…" The goat-horned man raised an eyebrow at me. "A Dual-Evocator? How rare…"

I hurried back to Kurrick, hiding behind him. Kurrick nodded to the two. "You may come with us if you wish, but we will not leave immediately. Personally, I suggest you do not follow our example."

The child touched his protector's shoulder, shaking his head. "Don't— *hic!*—don't go with 'em, Linus!" He sniffled and wiped his lids dry.

The boy's eyes had glazed in deep thought for a moment, but just as quickly as the look had come, it vanished, his panic returning. He tried to regain some composure, though he was shaking profusely. "It ain't… it ain't gonna end well for us otherwise…! We survive if we go—*hic!*—the other way, but *just* that way!"

The goat's eyes had also glazed with a similar stare when the boy touched him, and he gave a hum. "Curious. You and I seem to have something in common, little owl."

The goat glanced back at Kurrick. "Thank you for the offer, sir and miss, but we have our own path to follow. Best luck to you, and pray the Gods deliver you safely."

He bowed, then hurried off, following the directions given by the child he carried.

Kurrick frowned after them. "Strange pair."

I whispered a mutter. "Indeed…"

The ground shook under us. The Stonedragon had destroyed another building in the distance.

I took hold of my enormous stone-blade once more and hefted its blunt edge over a shoulder, grinning at Kurrick. "What say you to bringing down the giant?"

50

PSYCHOPOMPS

OCTAVIUS

Jaq, Ringëd and I huffed through the streets behind the Carter siblings, taking alleyways to avoid the swarming Fera.

We lost track of the twins, Lilli, and that ghost guy a while ago, but Jaq said we had to keep up with these birds and not worry about them for now. With all these demons running around, I was at least glad as Bloods Ringëd had come—out of nowhere—with that Shotri. If any of those things found us, it was good knowing we could at least slow them down long enough to let us get the Void away.

Stupid thieves. It was their fault this was happening at all. Why should we care what happens to them?

We stopped at the corner of a main road, the ground quaking when the Stonedragon lumbered around the block. We pressed ourselves against a wall, panting.

"There's the clinic," Herrin puffed, taking charge of his siblings like Dalen's ghost told him to. For good reason, too. The bookworm was the only one of these three that tried to help me earlier.

"Good," Ringëd puffed, "it's still in one piece. Let's get in and get out quick."

We waited for a few straggling demons to clear, then rushed inside and barricaded the door.

The place was empty and dark, the only source of light coming from Jaq's glowing-blue scythe. It didn't give off much light, but it was better than nothing. The power must have been cut off in this part of town—and probably the other districts where the Stonedragon came by.

I sidled next to Jaq, muttering under my breath so the birds couldn't hear. "Why are we helping them?" I asked. "I mean, Herrin I get, he's reasonable, but the other two almost slit my throat an hour ago."

Jaq kept his glowing scythe in front of him, and he carefully stepped around a fallen chair. "We're Reapers, Tavius. We help everyone with a soul."

"Even people who tried to kill us?" I glared at Jaq, annoyed. Why was he siding with them? Wasn't he supposed to be my Brother, or whatever? They almost killed me! Did that matter to anyone?

Jaq pushed up his glasses, the lenses glinting dimly. "Yep. Even them."

"That's stupid. They could have left us in the canyons to die."

"But they didn't. When their brother set 'em straight, they helped us outta there."

"They got us there in the first place! Do they even deserve 'protection'? I say we get out of here with or without them—"

Jaq halted, making me bump into him.

"'I'll not let actions souls once took deter me from my duty'," he recited from the Reaper's Creed they taught me, and I could see in the light that his fangs had unfolded, his tongue slitted and wavering. "'I will forgive old histories, and never show one cruelty'… Do you understand what that line means, Octavius?"

I blinked. Why did he sound so angry? "Well… I guess it means… If someone did something bad, it doesn't mean we should get back at them?"

"It means no matter what someone has done, what they've said, how we've felt about them—whether we hated, cherished, loved, or loathed them—we do not allow their souls to suffer. We're escorting these siblings to make sure they aren't killed by demons, and that they don't *become* demons. We are not judges for their souls. We are their guides and protectors. Psychopomps. Nothing more, and nothing less. That is what it means to be a Reaper."

Another thought hit me, and I frowned at Jaq. "Wait a minute. You're talking weird. And how do you know about some random book by some old writer I've never heard of?"

He coughed and scratched his nose guiltily. "There… might be a few things I haven't mentioned about my education… and heritage."

My eyes went wide. "No way. You're a noble?"

"Half-blooded," he said humbly. "My father is a cobbler, but my mother was a Roaress from the surface."

"But I thought you were poor?"

He shrugged. "My mother denied her inheritance when she married my father… it's a long story."

"But why don't you talk properly all the time?" I demanded.

He stopped at a door labeled 'coma ward' and pushed it open as I followed him inside. "'Cos." He grinned and switched back to his slang talk. "It's more fun that way."

The ground shook from a colossal footstep of the Stonedragon. It felt close, the rumble making the whole building shake. Things clattered to the floor, metallic and wooden utensils clunking and clanging from tables, and it sounded like the siblings were shouting from a room a few doors down. When did they get so far ahead?

Hurrying, Jaq and I found them in room 127, crowding around a patient bed and fumbling with plastic tubes that were stuck into the winged man who was sleeping there. Jaq hovered his scythe over the man, showing the face of that ghost called Dalen.

His siblings were panicked, trying their hardest to untangle the tubes and pick him off the bed. He was still alive, breathing steadily in his sleep.

Carrie and Rolen argued about what tubes went where, their fingers trembling, voices rising as the tremors got worse. Herrin flipped through a medical book he probably found on a shelf, muttering to himself and studying the machine that kept Dalen alive. It was a bulky thing with gears and non-working Shockvials. Rolen was cursing, messing with levers and buttons, twisting copper wires and coils, then gave up and kicked the thing.

Herrin flung the book to the ground. "Forget it! Let's just grab him and go!"

Jaq and Ringëd helped them take out the tubes and dragged the body out of the bed. I locked my jaw and went next to Herrin, deciding I should help, too.

Across from me, Rolen glanced my way, scowling. But there was something else in that sour look. He looked kind of… sorry.

So, he's just an immature kid… Who panicked when his brother needed help.

I guessed I could understand why they freaked out. They were scared and desperate, probably looking for any person to point fingers at. Bloods, if it'd been *my* brother, I'd want to do everything I could to help him, too.

We lifted Dalen off the bed and headed for the door—

A giant, stone foot *crunched* through the roof, brick crumbling and dust puffing in the new light. We were thrown off balance and dropped Dalen, chunks of ruble partially burying him. We tried to shovel him out, but had to lurch away from another giant foot.

Jaq grit his teeth, looking up at the enormous dragon. "We have to get rid of that thing!"

I gawked at him. "How?!"

"Let's see how strong your poison is—you three!" he addressed to the siblings pulling their brother out of the rubble. He reverted his scythe into a sphere and wrapped the chain around his wrist. "Get him out of there! We're going to see if we can't bring this guy down!"

They shouted shocked questions at him, but he grabbed my arm and rushed toward the dragon.

Ringëd jolted and hustled behind us. "Tavius, wait! Where are you going?!"

"I don't know!" I hollered, following Jaq.

The three of us went to the dragon's tail. Jaq waited for it to swing low enough for him to leap up and grab it. I followed suit, then Ringëd, finding a good footing between the dragon's scales.

"Now what?" I yelled to Jaq above me.

Jaq hesitated, clinging to the scales until his knuckles turned white. "I-I'm not going to like this, but… climb!"

We did. It was hard, with the tail whipping back and forth, but we managed to reach its back and scrambled to its neck. Jaq and Ringëd made sure not to look over the side, but I didn't take the same precaution. The streets under us looked so small—we must have been nearly forty floors up. Just its head made it an even fifty, I betted.

"All… A-all right, Tavius!" Jaq hollered over the wind, trying to keep the panic out of his voice and failed. "Go and do your stuff!"

I blinked at him. "What stuff?"

"I don't know! Just poison the thing!"

"*That* was your plan?!"

"That's all I could think of! Just try it already!"

Cursing, I tried his stupid plan. What else were we going to do up here?

I evoked my Hallows, hands festering with black veins, and shoved them between the cracks of the dragon's armored scales.

The dragon shrieked, throwing us all off balance. I fell on my back, and Ringëd caught my wrist before I rolled off. He pulled me back up after the dragon calmed down, and we exchanged stiff looks.

"Okay." Jaq's small voice cracked as he clung to the dragon's scales. "Maybe that wasn't such a good idea…"

"You think?!" I shouted. "This thing is way too big to do anything—!"

We braced when the dragon's weight shifted, its head craning back. Its large mouth creaked opened and came down at us, like it was trying to bite at an itch.

Its teeth barely missed Jaq, and the viper yelped and scurried up to me and Ringëd.

"Move!" Jaq screamed, all of us scrambling up the dragon's neck to avoid its next bite.

We ended up on its head and Jaq drew out his scythe, digging it between two scales to hold his place. The thing's head tilted, and I tumbled down, fumbling to grab something—I got Ringëd's legs.

Ringëd grunted at my added weight and reflexively kicked, his shoe catching my chin and made me bite my tongue. I cried out in pain, but held on anyway, both of us screaming as the dragon whipped from side to side, trying to fling us off while we headed away from the clinic.

—Two rabbit-eared heads suddenly popped up from the dragon's snout, Henry calling over at us, "A'hoy, gentlemen! Welcome aboard!"

51

UNITED

XAVIER

Lilli and I exchanged blows with Lucrine, the Sentient struggling to focus on both of us at once.

For every slice he would dodge from her, he wouldn't be quick enough to avoid me. Lilli's wings gave us an advantage, where she could parry his attacks from above and lunge away in time to evade.

But we were running out of time. The Stonedragon was approaching and the air was coated in smoke from the fire at the temple.

Lucrine backed me to the roof's ledge, my foot slipping, and my head snapped to the street fifty stories below. Vertigo had my vision tumbling, and the smoke clung to my eyes, the hot sting making my lids sticky. I rubbed them with a sleeve, coughing.

Lucrine stepped forward, keeping distance from my scythes. But he was still close enough that a quick sprint could shove me off the ledge.

"Look, I ain't playing games here," he said. "Where's your broth—?"

Lilli sliced his shoulder from behind.

Lucrine snarled, his oozing wound healing with black ink, and he swiped for her.

With him distracted, I jammed my scythe into his stomach and ripped him open. He howled and jabbed my chin hard, and I felt something *crack!*

The taste of blood trickled when I spit a glob of red saliva.

Lilli tore into his back, hooking him by the shoulder blades as she heaved and flapped him up, struggling with his weight. "Get… away from him…!" she growled, her bat ears curled and fangs sharp as razors.

Lucrine *slammed* a hoof-textured fist to her temple, and her wings faltered, limply spiraling both of them back to the roof.

Lucrine recovered faster. He kicked Lilli in the stomach and sneered over her. "I'm getting *real* tired of you, girl."

I ran to Lucrine and drove my blades into his neck, putting all my weight into shoving him away from Lilli. He stumbled and whirled on me, his shoulders hunching to prepare a counter as he waited for his neck to heal… but a cough rasped out of me, and he paused.

His image was shifting direction, wavering like a water ripple. His flickering face broke into a wicked grin. Lilli hacked alongside me, the haze growing too thick. Everything spun… Lilli dropped to her knees, blinking her watering eyes and wheezing.

I tried to hold my balance, but the ground suddenly tumbled upward, and I found myself kneeling on the roof, scythes vanishing from my fingers.

"Lilli," I wheezed, steadying myself with a hand on the ground. "We have to… get lower. We can't keep this up…" I coughed up spittle, tasting ash on my tongue.

"Nnnmn…" A groan suddenly mumbled from my thoughts. My coughing nearly drowned Alexander's voice. *"How long was I…"*

I lost control, feeling myself slip into the psyche… Then everything went black.

… I came-to seconds later, floating within the psyche.

Through the window, I saw Alexander staring wide eyed at Lilli, whose soot-coated face was cracked with shock.

"What…" Alexander barked at her between coughs. "The Void… Took you so GODS DAMNED LONG, LILLI!?"

Lilli was at a loss for words, gaping. "A—*khauh!*—Alex? But you were just… Your eyes just…!"

She had soul-sight? I realized in the psyche. *Death's head, another Necrovoker…* Well, it didn't matter at this point.

Alex crawled to her, shaking her shoulders irritably. "Have you any idea how long I've been waiting for you to pick up Willow?!" he shouted. "Did you know she was pretending to be you? Bloods, I—*khauh, khauh!*—I can't believe you let her leave at all! You should have heard her pathetic excuses!"

Now that I was safely in the psyche and out of the smog, my hazy mind cleared at last, and I paused. *"Hang on. Alex, you knew it was Willow?"*

"Of course I did, you idiot!" he screamed at the sky. "I only played along with her ludicrous story so *you* wouldn't give us away!"

"Alex, what—*Krhmm!*—what is going on?" Lilli questioned, baffled beyond measure. "What happened to Xavier?"

"Never mind!" he groaned. "Let's just get out of this damned smoke—!"

Lucrine returned, bending down and grasped Alexander's neck, pulling him up. "That's it, twerp." He kicked Lilli's stomach again when she tried to push up. "Now, I don't give two shits how I find your twin. All I have to do is chuck ya off the edge, and you'll go splat like a bowl of spaghetti. I can find him *after...*"

Lucrine's gaze narrowed as Alex sputtered under his grip. "Wait a sec," the demon muttered. "Weren't your eyes the other way a minute ago?"

That's right, Lucrine is dead, I realized. *He can see the difference in our heterochromia.*

The Stonedragon's quaking steps were deafening now, it must have been right beside us. Alex strained for breath, coughing under Lucrine's stranglehold. Then he lost consciousness from the lack of air—

I was forced outside.

Damn it, Alex!

Lucrine jumped back, pulling me back onto the roof. "Holy shit! They just... What the Void is going on?"

"You won't find... my brother..." I wheezed. Alex finally mumbled back awake from the psyche, giving a weak apology. I took another strained breath. "It's... impossible..."

Lucrine *hmphed* challengingly. "Bullshit. You're *both* of them, ain't ya? Ho, *ho,* this is Bloody beautiful—"

He screamed when a new, poison-infested blade sliced off the arm holding me.

I dropped to the roof, gasping for breath in the haze and scrambling for the scythes I'd lost earlier. I found one, but the other was still missing.

My gaze drifted upward. Octavius, who had appeared out of nowhere, was wielding my missing scythe. He'd been the one who cut Lucrine.

Lucrine wailed in a startled pain, waiting for his arm to reattach, his glare furious as he backed away to heal himself.

"Where the Bloods..." I panted, hacking smoke. I found Jaq and Ringëd standing behind Octavius as well, Henry and Vendy accompanying them.

Confused, I gave them an incredulous look. "Where the Bloods did you all come from?"

Vendy shrugged, tossing a thumb behind her. "Hitched a ride on the dragon's head. It's tall enough to reach up here, and when the thing passed by, we saw you guys were—"

"Ya damned little *brat*!" Lucrine spat, his arm fully healed now. He was glaring bolts at Octavius. "I don't know what kind of trick ya just pulled, but that's the last time you're gonna get so lucky!"

He rushed Octavius—

Jaq's chain-scythe caught the demon's shoulder, the links wrapping around Lucrine's arm, and our friend *yanked* the Sentient away from him. "They're not the only ones you should be worried about anymore!" the viper shouted.

Lilli gave a soft grunt from the ground, the bat's lashes fluttering into consciousness. When she pushed herself upright, she tore off a long piece of her sleeve with a claw and wrapped it around her nose and mouth to block the smoke, then rose to her feet.

Lucrine wriggled one of his arms between his metal binds and was now clutching Jaq's chain. He pulled Jaq toward him with incredible strength, the viper's feet skidding forward.

I dug under my chainmail and pulled the collar of my tunic over my face, blocking out the worst of the smog before running over to help Jaq pull. Octavius followed suit, and Ringëd and Henry gripped the chain alongside him, Vendy grabbing the last of the links and yanking with all her might, Hallows included. Our added strengths evened out the match, but it brought us to an impasse. We were all stuck in a terrifying game of tug-of-war.

My knuckles cracked over the chain, and when my fingers began to numb—

Lilli ripped a ferocious snarl from the air, dropping from the sky with her leathery wings fanned outward. She landed hard on Jaq's taut chain, the links acting like elastic as she not only threw all of us toward the center— the Sentient included—but simultaneously launched herself back in the air.

Her wings tucked tight to her body as she arched and spiraled into a dangerous dive toward Lucrine, her scythes plunging into his skull and knocking him on his back.

She landed knee first on his throat, and he squirmed under her pinning weigh, black blood surging from the deep wound at his temple.

"Alex!" Lilli barked at us behind her tattered mask. "Or, Xavier! Whoever you are!"

I quickly grabbed my second blade from Octavius and charged for the pinned demon. Lucrine cursed and forced himself up, throwing Lilli aside and plucked her blade out of his head. He used her scythe to come at me, swiping it back and forth like a clueless amateur.

I smirked and ducked under one of Lucrine's sloppy, horizontal strikes, spun away from a vertical cut, rolled behind him and raked my blade over his spine.

Jaq came next, his chain reeled in and scythe in hand. He tore into Lucrine's side while Ringëd fired Shockspheres at the Sentient, lightning snapping over the demon's limbs and paralyzing him long enough for Lilli to reclaim her scythe and land a stab at his neck.

Octavius hurried beside me, afraid to be so close to the demon, but wanted to help somehow. He came behind Lucrine and gripped his head by his ears, evoking his infection Hallows.

Lucrine shrieked in agony, writhing, flailing, jerking aimlessly to get away from the pain Octavius caused. He tore away from us and fumbled back, clutching his blackened head.

"What the Void did you do?!" he screamed at Octavius, overwhelmed with pain as black veins pulsed over his skin. His breath burned hot, voice curdling. "What is this…?!"

"Your death!" I sprinted for him, crossing my blades and *ripped* them through his neck.

Lucrine's head dropped like a stone, still screaming, teeth snapping mindlessly as the stubbed neck tried to slither back in place. I kept it down with a foot, drawing back one of my scythes and aimed for his heart.

"Or," I added in an afterthought, "I should say, your *second* death. Alex? Would you like the honors?"

"*Gladly.*" He grunted from the psyche.

We switched control, and I watched from the psyche as Alex's blade *cracked* into Lucrine's chest. Alex slit it over the Sentient's heart, his NecroSeam snapping apart.

With a small, sputtered curse from the disembodied head, black tar vaporized under Lucrine's skin. The poisonous veins that infested his wound fizzled and crept across his chest until all the black mist that was his rotten soul vanished into the air.

His body collapsed, skin decaying into aged bones. Lucrine's skeleton laid over the roof in the same position he fell. His clothes flattened over the bones, red-shaded glasses clattering to the ground.

And thus ended the hundred-year-old beast's rotted afterlife.

Alex hacked, limping back toward the others. He clasped a hand over Octavius and Jaq's shoulders, nodding to Ringëd, Henry and Vendy as well. "Nira, are we glad to see you all. What happened to the siblings?"

"Not sure." Jaq wound his chain along his arm. "We'll have to go back and find them."

"Great." Alex rubbed his eyes, which were probably stinging from the smoke. "Let's retrieve a few things from here and find them."

They nodded and started for the roof's door. Alex hurried after them, but another thought hit me, and I quickly told Alex to scoop up Lucrine's bones and clothes. Alex was confused, but gathered them with his Hallows nonetheless and piled them in his arms before we made our way to the roof's door, which led to a stairway inside.

Everyone followed us in, tremors shuddering the walls, the Stonedragon parading outside. Now that we were out of the choking smog, Lilli ripped off her mask and Alex unzipped his jacket, tossing it aside. They all hacked out the rest of the toxins.

"All right." Alex dropped the dead Sentient's bones, putting fists at his sides. "Why did I bring these inside?"

"You have to resurrect him," I said from the psyche.

He cocked an eyebrow. "Why?"

"Just do it, I'll explain as we go."

Jaq and Lilli sat to rest atop the steps, and she murmured to the viper. "Who is he talking to?"

Jaq shook his head, wiping his apparently-bloody nose. "It's a long story." He paused, befuddled, and eyed her with a contorted expression. "*Who* are you?"

Alex dismissively waved a hand. "Jaq, this is Lilli—Lilli, Jaq."

"Wait." Jaq's brow furrowed. "You mean there's two—?"

"We'll explain later." Alex raised his hands to Lucrine's brittle bones, evoking his Hallows.

The violet magic spread to Lucrine's remains, and his bones began reconnecting. Alex pushed his energy further, summoning tendons, muscle, skin and hair over the skeleton until Lucrine stood before us again, his heart jumpstarted at Alexander's command.

He was also stark naked, since Alex was still holding his clothes.

"Done," Alexander announced, seeing Lilli turn away from the nude corpse in a blush. Vendy, however, stared with a shameless grin. "Now why did I do that?" Alex asked.

"Dalen needs a temporary vessel," I said. Alex had been unconscious since the canyons, so he hadn't known what happened between then and now. *"It'll give him more protection while we find the others. Now, let me out. It's my turn."*

He switched inside, and when the physical air touched my skin, I inhaled deeply.

"Dalen!" I shouted, my voice bouncing down the long stairwell. "If you're in here, come up! It's safe now!"

A few moments passed before the winged ghost floated up the stairs. He had to go one step at a time, since it was a myth that ghosts could float higher than a few feet. We weren't sure where that rumor started, honestly.

Dalen's ghost drew back after seeing Lucrine's newly risen vessel.

"How's it safe?!" The specter demanded. "That thing is standin' right there!"

"He's dead," I said bluntly. "We cut his Seam. Now come, I have to sow you into his body."

Dalen's eyes splintered in horror. "Like Void—!"

I shoved my hand into the ghost's chest, my Death mark gleaming as I evoked my soul Hallows.

From my fingers, violet lights strung together, forming a temporary NecroSeam for the soul. I clutched the thread inside his chest, then dragged Dalen's protesting soul toward Lucrine's empty vessel.

I shoved the ghost inside and tied the NecroSeam to the heart.

Lucrine's eyes shot open, and he gasped awake.

"Bloody Land!" He inspected his new body with a shudder, cupping his indecency when Vendy giggled. "Gods, this feels weird! At least give me some damn clothes!"

I handed him Lucrine's old clothes and let him dress, the thief muttering something about wishing he'd had wings.

Lilli gapped at me. "How in Death did you do that?" She demanded. "Alex, you've never been able to even touch a soul! How did—"

"We don't have time to explain, Lilli," I snapped.

Her mouth shut. She was staring at my eyes. "W… we?"

Octavius clutched my shoulder. "Guys, we still have a problem. That dragon's still out there."

I pursed my lips. "Well, we've killed one Sentient, I'd say that's enough for now. Let's help Willow and those siblings, then get the Death out of here."

Octavius paused. "Willow? Wait, you found the Death Princess?"

Everyone followed as I trotted down the stairway and slammed open the door to the top floor of the inn, running toward our chambers. "I'll explain on the… way…" I opened our chamber door.

Inside, heaps of trash and nibbled-on vegetables lay scattered on the carpet.

And on the food cart by the chairs was a long-bodied weasel, rubbing its protruding belly and snoozing with its head rolled back, a chewed-on loaf of bread acting as its pillow.

Behind me, Ringëd groaned and smeared a hand over his face. "Damn it, Kurn."

REINFORCEMENTS

WILLOW

I sprinted away from the Sentient queen, scrambling onto the street that divided the burning temple and the Howler's Inn.

Both structures disappeared into the smoke far above, the result of Cilia's reckless fire tossing.

Gripping my scythe, I veered left and ran in front of the burning temple.

CRASH!

The enormous Stonedragon crunched its foot into the street with a vigorous tremor. I had to leap away from its heavy step, rolling back as another foot almost crushed me flat.

Ash and embers swirled in the blackened smoke, the flakes blanketing the road. I coughed, covering my mouth and nose with a hand. At least the haze was thin down here. I hoped Lilli hadn't flown too high into those suffocating clouds.

Skriririririiii!

A flurry of Necrofera screeched and scuttled into the street, beginning to swarm. It was all I could do to not trip on my own feet while jerking away from their claws.

There were so many, I'd taken to a shameless hacking frenzy, aimlessly slashing my blade at whatever moved. There was no time nor space for artful techniques or skilled showmanship. The thinning oxygen was too dizzying regardless.

I made a misstep—and cried out when a creature hooked its claws into my thigh. It ripped a large gash in the muscle, reopening my previous bite wound on the same leg, and I stumbled to the ground, dropping my scythe—

Hollers sounded, followed by gushing noises and distinct snaps. The shouting wasn't of fear or pain. They were determined, like an army charging into battle. My neck craned behind me, and the breath caught in my throat.

Staring down at me, surrounded by the corpses of the now dead Necrofera, were a pair of brilliant, sapphire eyes.

The man before me was grey-faced, his black and grey beard thick yet well-groomed to frame his broad chin and square jaw. His brow was furrowed low, either furious or concentrating as he towered over me, his staved scythe cocked behind him.

I let out my trapped breath. "Father Lucas?"

Lucas Devouh peered down at me with a scrutinizing gaze. "Is that Willow?" he rumbled with a deep, powerful voice that scratched like a river of glass.

His white cloak fluttered in the chaotic wind, draping hood waving from his head. Pinned to his collar were six silver skull-emblems, my father's sigil etched on the right shoulder plate of his armor while a black-and-silver Reaper's badge was placed over his left breast. His intense stare made me shudder. "What in Death's name are you doing here?" he demanded.

My head ducked, white fox ears folded to my neck. "I—"

A beast burst forward and shrieked at me.

But a large, rugged man with bear ears suddenly slammed into it with his shoulder, summoning a vortex of flames from his hands and sent the demon hurtling away.

The newcomer turned to me, his bear ears flicking as he grinned under his black beard. "Careful there, Yer Highness," he said in a gruff, though pleasant, tone. "*Da'torr* Lucas didn' haul me all the way up here to see ye get ripped to shreds, did he?"

Da'torr? Was this a vassal of Father Lucas's? *Hang on, I think I remembered him…*

"Thank you, Nathaniel." Lucas Devouh nodded to the bear. "Keep them back. We seem to have stumbled upon an unexpected treasure. Don't allow anything near her—*especially* my sons, if you find them in this mess."

I peered behind Father Lucas, seeing hundreds of other Reapers were engaged in combat, squads taking their formations against the demons and ripping them to shreds.

It was a true battlefield. Demons were cut down, Reapers fell at the claws of the beasts, shouts and screams crying out in the smog… A few squads even went to the Stonedragon, trying to wedge their scythes between the creature's scales to get to its soft underbelly.

In the distance, I caught sight of one Reaper in particular. He had black, feathered wings protruding from his back, and I gasped to see Sir Janson among the ranks. *He WAS still following me! Did he lead these reinforcements here to us?*

I blinked, noticing two other figures were running toward us.

One was a lion-eared woman with curly brown hair and crimson eyes, hefting an enormous stone blade over her shoulder. She crushed the demons in her way with powerful swings as she and her burly companion, who wielded two steel blades of his own, sprinted for us.

Weren't those two in the market the other day? I thought. *The ones who spoke of Grandfather Dream?*

"High Howllord," the man said, his voice scratched as he and the woman trotted to a stop before us. "I suggest you get your troops away from that dragon. When it falls, it will crush anyone beneath it."

The woman behind him flicked her gaze to me, her lion ears swiveling and causing her looped earring to waver. She swung her blade off her shoulder and dug it into the ground, clasping the stone hilt, and bowed to me.

"Daughter of Myra," she said in a thick voice. "It is an honor to meet you in the flesh at last. Allow us to offer you protection in this devastating hour."

Befuddled, I glanced from her to Father Lucas, who frowned at them.

"Who are you?" asked Father Lucas. "State your names."

"Those who will slay the dragon," replied the warrior, darting toward the dragon with the woman trailing behind. "Call back your knights! When the beast is dead, we cannot direct its fall!"

Father Lucas watched them sprint away, their blades cocked behind them as they charged for the colossus.

The woman's bare feet glittered with gold Hallows, and I gasped as rock and stone ripped from the ground around her toes. She made stepping platforms with the hovering boulders, leading up to the dragon's back to allow her burly companion to climb ahead of her.

When he reached the top, she slammed her feet at the ground and pushed her Hallows onto the road, *cracking* the ground as she propelled upward at a blinding speed. She lithely landed on the dragon's back alongside the man, hefting her giant blade as they raced for the beast's head.

Who ARE those two?

The High Howllord's lips pursed into a thin line, and seeming to debate the matter in silence, he finally began calling orders for the Reapers to fall back.

"Come, Willow," he grunted next, grabbing my arm with a strict hand. "I don't know what in Void you're doing here, but it seems we'll have to address that another time."

"Father Lucas," I began, finding my wits again as my Spirit Father dragged me along. "I can explain…"

"Lucas is correct, Willow," a woman chided behind me. "There will be time for explanations later."

I whirled, watching a wolf-eared woman dance with her chained dual-scythes, killing the stray Necrofera that came for us. She wore a silver skull-helm, which had holes in the sides to make room for her wolf ears. There was a flap at the lower-back section of her Reaper's cloak, where a tail waved freely.

"Mother Alice!" I cried in relief and surprise. *Both my Spirit Parents had come?*

Alice Devouh killed the last of her threat, then ran beside us while lifting her helm's visor.

"Willow," she greeted, voice urgent. "I'm afraid we cannot risk you being at the heart of the threat. Go with my vassal, Aiden, to find shelter elsewhere. You should be safe with him."

"Aiden?" *Why did that name sound familiar?* "Hang on… You mean that same vassal you had in the palace?"

My waist was seized by a new pair of arms.

"Your Highness Death," a boyish voice greeted cheerily. My head craned back to find a feather-haired, brown face smiling warmly at me. He wore a pair of goggles over his eyes, and strapped to his back was a quiver of arrows and a curved bow.

"Lovely to see you again!" He gave an amiable chuckle. "I'm not sure if you remember me, but my name is Aiden. I am here by request of my *Da'torr*, the High Howless Devouh. Please hold tight, and do not flail about, else you may fall!"

I paled. "No. You can't mean—"

I screamed when Aiden jumped, and the sound of flapping wings whooshed behind. The ground shrank under my kicking boots, the Devouhs turning to ants as Aiden flew me higher and higher, until we were level with the clock tower's glass face.

I sobbed in the bird's arms, tears streaming down my face as I gasped for breath.

"Put—put me down!" I demanded shrilly. "If you drop me, I'll... I'll tell my father! Put me down, oh please, for the love of Death...!" I choked off, the world swirling nauseatingly.

Aiden gave a calming laugh, as if trying to ease the tension while he flew above the clock tower's coned roof. "Still sore with heights, eh? Don't worry, Your Highness. You're safe with..."

He made a pained grunt and dropped me on the rooftop. My claws clung to the shingles, breath frazzled.

A winged Fera withdrew its long talons out of Aiden's shoulder.

Aiden ignored the wound and readied his bow, drawing back an arrow from his quiver. On his left elbow, a scarlet Sky mark shined bright, and from his fingertips came a rush of compressed wind, launching the arrow at a blinding speed.

It went right through the Fera's skull. It hadn't killed the thing, but it did push the beast away several yards.

"A—an Aerovoker," I remembered suddenly, quivering over the roof as Aiden nocked another arrow, evoking his wind Hallows to create a whirl-wind around him. "That's right... You used to be a Stormchaser."

"Guilty as charged." He turned back and winked. "Get it? *Charged?* Like lightning? Keh, heh!" He chuckled at his own joke and adjusted the goggles over his eyes. "Please hold on, Your Highness! I'll retrieve you right after—"

A long, black claw split through Aiden's adams-apple.

The creature had returned and come behind him. It slid the claw out of Aiden's throat, and a dark spurt leaked from the hole like a fountain. The vassal gurgled and choked on his own blood until his breath ceased com-pletely, and he spiraled to the ground fifty stories down.

The beast screeched at me next, and I cried while carefully lunging away on the tower's coned rooftop. My hair-ribbon and bell slipped out of its knot and fell after Aiden, letting my long, ashen strands wave in a frayed tangle past my feet.

Gods, it was all I could do not to sob at the sheer sight of the distant, distant ground, the gash at my thigh burning as I strained to keep balance on the roof.

Dear Nira, it was definite now.

I was going to die.

53

CLOCKTOWER

XAVIER

"Kurn!" Ringëd barked at the rodent snoozing on the food cart. "Wake up!"

The feral ferret jolted awake, its head popping up. Its round ears swiveled to us in fright. It spotted Ringëd and quickly rolled onto its tiny paws, skittering on the cart in a panic, snickering quiet, but frantic, breaths.

"Yeah, yeah, I'm sure," Ringëd muttered at the long-bodied rodent, crossing his arms. "Did you clean the place out? Yeah, well, while you were in here helping your greedy self to this little banquet, we've been out there fighting demons. How does that… you know what? It doesn't matter. It's not like you…"

He continued to argue with the ferret, the rest of us staring blankly at the bizarre exchange.

I scratched my nose. "Well, er… I suppose we know Ringëd's shift, now?"

Octavius hummed in a shrug. "Sort of. Ringëd's a little weird in that case, though."

Jaq frowned at him. "How?"

Octavius began, "Well—"

"Oh, for the love of Death," Lilli groaned and rolled her eyes. "Do we plan to take what we need and carry on? We've wasted enough time in this death trap."

I exhaled. "Yes, agreed. Take whatever you can carry, then we'll grab Willow and—"

"Uh, that might be harder than you think," Octavius interrupted. He pointed out the large window, unlatching it and pushed it open.

A plume of black smoke flooded inside, and we covered our mouths. Once the cloud dissipated, I saw a stream of long, white hair flapping in the wind.

Willow!

She was clinging to the clock tower's roof, ducking away from a winged Necrofera.

"Bloody Death!" I rushed to the window beside Octavius. "How did she get up there—!"

Jaq squeezed my shoulder. "Mates," he said, pointing downward. "Look there."

I did, staring at the chaos below. The streets were now cluttered with the tiny dots: the demons and armor-glinting Reapers who'd broken into an all-out brawl.

"Reinforcements!" Lilli breathed when she came to look herself, her bat wings fanning in relief. "Thank the Goddess!"

"That isn't going to help Willow," I muttered, turning to Lilli. "Can you fly to her? Bring her here?"

Lilli nodded, hopping onto the windowsill. "Of course. You all wait here." She flexed her bat wings, jumped off and dipped down before her leathery sails caught air and lifted herself with a sharp flap, taking off toward Willow.

WILLOW

My claws strained to keep hold of the shingles, fingers growing sore and cramped.

I didn't dare look down again. My foot slipped over the edge, making me shriek and skid down an inch. My knuckles screamed with pain, growing numb with exertion.

The Fera flapping on the other side of the roof circled behind, and I scuttled the other way to keep distance. This wasn't very productive. I had nowhere else to go but where I started. I took several ragged breaths, carefully tearing off a shingle while evoking infection Hallows over it.

If Octavius can do it, I thought desperately, *so can I!*

I'd seen him throw those knives on the screens enough times, why couldn't I give it a try? Granted, I didn't have anything sharp, but I could improvise.

Resolute, I summoned as much strength as I could muster, took aim, and hurled the shingle at the demon.

It missed horribly.

The flattened square didn't even fly more than half a foot, it simply fluttered downward the moment it left my fingers.

Brilliant.

"Willow!" a familiar, relieving voice called ahead.

My fox ears perked, seeing my faithful, brilliant, *beloved* Lilli dive feet-first onto the demon's murky face. The force of her kick sent it tumbling backward, and she stabbed into its chest to cut its NecroSeam.

Thank the Goddess and all her loving mercy! I cheered to myself. *I'm saved!*

"Lilli!" I cried in both glee and terror. "Lilli, get me down!"

Three more winged demons soared to us, and my Aide released a guttural snarl. "Hold fast, Willow!" She sliced at one Fera and dodged away from another. "This won't take long!"

"Lilli, for the love of Nira, get me down this instant—!"

An ear-splitting *CRACK!* sounded below, and the tower rumbled under my claws. Terrified, I looked down.

The enormous Stonedragon had finally been killed, its head cut open wide and bloody.

The pair of lions from before leapt off its head, the woman evoking her rock Hallows onto the cracked street below to summon a piece of road upward, catching their fall and providing a safe landing back to the ground.

Although it was a relief to see the beast dead, its place of collapse couldn't have been worse.

The dragon had fallen onto the temple, its blistered, oozing head whipping around and smashing into the clock tower. It began to lean forward under me. To *really* lean.

The structure moaned, flames charring the support beams. The tower leaned farther forward, taking me with it.

CR-CRACK!

The tower dipped and lunged down a foot.

"LILLI!" I screamed, voice fracturing. Lilli was too engaged with the Fera to hear my pleas. "Lilli, get me down from—!"

CRACK!

The final beam had given way, and I screamed as the clock tower toppled toward the Howler's Inn in a slow, powerful rush of wind.

XAVIER

"Holy Bloods!" we all cursed, watching the clock tower hurtle toward us in a slow, colossal moan.

Willow clung desperately to the tower's roof, her ashen locks wavering behind her like an icy waterfall.

"Vendy!" I shouted, pointing at Willow and the tower heading toward us. "Rip off a piece of this balcony and navigate us to Willow! Like that Terravoker had done with the Stonedragon down there!"

Vendy's rabbit ears dropped and she swallowed. "U-um, I'm not really sure if I'm strong enough to—"

"Direct order."

She stiffened at the command, her limbs bursting into action on their own thanks to our Bloodpact, and the stone floor under Vendy and my feet *cracked* off from the rest of the balcony and clumsily lunged into the air toward the tower, leaving the others behind.

Vendy chewed on a string of curses, but kept her Hallows active as ordered. We dipped and jerked unsteadily, Vendy clearly not as trained as the Terravoker below, but she was at least able to reach the falling tower in time.

We leveled with Willow, who still clung to the tower's roof. "Willow!" I shouted and reached for her. "Grab hold!"

She looked beguiled at me but quickly grabbed my hand, then I yanked her off the falling tower and onto our floating piece of stone.

SMASH!

The tower fell beneath us and crashed at an angle into the side of the inn, a few floors down from where the rest of our party hollered in terror.

The top floors—including our floor—began to shudder and lean over the tower like a broken candlestick. Our company dangled from the sill, and I saw Henry copy Vendy's example as he ripped the balcony off its perch, struggling to keep it and everyone on it lifted over the fallen clock tower.

"Xavier…!" Willow gasped for breath, hyperventilating. She latched onto me for dear life, her fox ears glued to her neck as she stared down to the distant street below. "Get…! Get me…! *Down….!*"

"Right!" I called over the wind. "Vendy, bring us down!"

Vendy panted with exertion. "Where?"

"Anywhere! Perhaps back onto the tower!"

Vendy obliged and lowered us to the tower, her floating piece of stone lurching to a sputtered stop as we were thrown off the piece and stumbled through the gaping hole in the wall of the Howler's Inn.

My boots crunched over the glass shards scattered over the carpet, remnants of the broken windows, and I helped steady Willow's limping figure.

"Are you all right?" I asked, looking at the blood seeping out of her right boot. "Can you walk on that leg?"

She panted, regaining her wits. "Not as quickly as I'd like, but well enough."

"Good… Vendy, how are you faring—?"

Vendy collapsed in a groan, flattening to her back. "Bloods…!" She gasped. "That was…! That was really *hard*! How'd that girl… make it look so… so *easy*?"

I rubbed my chin. "Perhaps she's better practiced… thank you for your help, Vendy, you did well. Rest for now. We'll have Alex replenish your stamina shortly.

Willow eyed me in confusion. "Vendy is both yours *and* Alexander's vassal?"

"Twin blood," I said with a weary shrug. "Who knew?"

"Who indeed," she muttered, pulling her long hair away from her face.

I watched her for a moment, staggering. Her new, azure eyes were a strange sight. Shocking, when this close.

"Willow," I began, thinking an apology was due, but wasn't sure where to begin. I steeled myself and took her fingers. "I'm sorry… For not recognizing you. I should have known from the start and…"

She stopped me with a gentle hand squeeze. "Do you remember now?"

I nodded, hoping my stare properly relayed my sincerity.

"And have I lost your hand, after so long?" She asked.

I took her free hand in mine and placed it over the captured one, trapping it. "You have it now, don't you?"

She smiled, gripped my hand one last time, then freed me. "Then reunions can wait. Last I checked, we had a war raging beneath us."

"Yes, yes, the war… Priorities." I cleared my throat and hobbled toward the broken gash where the wall collapsed, where the fallen clock tower was still leaning like an enormous bridge toward the burning temple.

"We left the others up there," I said, realizing Henry must still be straining to lift the balcony above us. "When we get them down—"

"On second thought." Willow seized my shoulder. "I realized you've just rescued your betrothed from a blood-splattered fate at Shel's floor. I believe protocol demands that I give my thanks before we charge into battle and meet our *dismally* likely demise?"

I blinked. "Oh. Well, you're welco*mmn…*" She caught my lips.

Lovely Death! I wasn't sure if it was the fire across the street or the adrenaline prickling my blood, but her flesh *burned*.

Attention horribly abandoned, I reeled her in, drinking in her fire—

The warmth vanished.

"*Mnf…* Death!" I heard my brother bark, his voice echoing around me.

Bleary and drunk, I found myself surrounded by blackness. Sobriety hit like a boulder on glass, snuffing my bliss when I found the window of the psyche behind me.

Alexander had taken my place, having pulled me into the void while I was distracted. I watched through the window as he shoved Willow off him, wiping his mouth and spitting. "What the VOID do you think you're doing?!"

Willow stumbled to the ground and brushed her hair out of the way, startled. When her head snapped up, her eyes widened. "A… Alexander?"

He stiffened, his mistake dawning.

"*What…*" Willow growled, red faced and incredulous. "Is going on here?"

54

OUSTED

WILLOW

Am I delusional?

Alexander sat before me where Xavier had just been, in the same clothes and holding the same wounds.

"Alexander?" I said again, uncertain. "How… what happened to Xavier?"

Alex gave a harsh cough and turned his head away. When he faced me again, I gasped. It was Xavier again. The blue eye had switched back to the left side.

"Ah—er, Alexander?" Xavier choked in a nervous laugh. He gave a vigorous scratch at the base of his neck, obviously trying to act nonchalant, though his voice was still panicked and his wolf ears were grown. He coughed into a fist. "I, er, should hope you weren't thinking of my brother…! I mean, it's, *khm-hmm*! only us here!"

My gaze narrowed at his mismatched eyes, which were swimming with dread. "What is going on, Xavier?" I asked, standing.

"Nothing!" He cringed when I stepped closer. "You must have hit your head!"

My head was fine, that much I knew. But if I wasn't imagining it, then what else was happening? It was almost like…

Like they're the same person. My fox ears grew, teeth sharpening. *I at least know one way to get to the bottom of this.*

Before he could flee, I grabbed Xavier's collar and jerked him down, crushing my mouth against his. I kept my eyes open this time—and saw Xavier's eyes switch places.

I was shoved away in an instant. "Will you stop doing that!" Alex demanded, wiping his lips like before. "Death, woman, that burns…!"

I staggered back. "Nira, it *is* true…! But how…?"

Alex groaned and pinched the rim of his nose. "Great. Brilliant Bloody job, idiot."

"Alexander!" I shrieked, dumbfounded. "What is going on?"

His tongue clicked, and his gaze jerked upward as if hearing something I couldn't. "Yes, well, no one said you could *kiss* her, either," he muttered. "I'll not be blamed for it."

My fox ears folded back in disbelief. "Are you *talking* to him?"

"*Argh!* I don't have time for this!" He rubbed his temples furiously. "Willow, distract yourself and help the others down or something… I'm afraid I've a *pest* to deal with."

I gawked as he turned round and started away. *Like Death I'm about to let that go!*

I snatched his wrist and jerked him to a stop. "Alexander, you will not speak to your future queen with such disrespect!"

That made him rigid. I decided it was time for me to assert my authority—something I've had to hide this whole blasted week from him. "I demand to know what is going on! And you will answer me this instant!"

"Oh—um," a different, hesitant voice interrupted behind me.

Octavius stood outside on the fallen clock tower. *Where had he come from?* I'd been so distracted with Xavier, I'd nearly forgotten about the rest of them.

"Sorry." Octavius ducked his head while helping Ringëd down from… Bloods be good, was that a *floating balcony*? "Don't want to interrupt, but we kind of have to go."

Henry, whose hands were glowing golden to keep the balcony—barely—steady, hopped down next, followed by Jaq.

Then *Lucrine* followed them.

I gasped and shuffled back at the sight of Sentient. "What is *he* doing here?" I stabbed a finger, pausing. "Wait. Why are his pupils not white?"

Octavius shook his head. "It's just Dalen, now. We killed Lucrine, and then Alex and Xavier put Dalen's soul in him and—*ow!*"

Alex swatted his head. "Will you shut it?! Just tell her everything, why don't you?"

My glare moved to Octavius now. "You knew about this…! *Whatever* this is?"

Octavius gave a petrified swallow. "I… um… sorry…"

Alex groaned. "You can at least pretend not to know anything!"

"Why'd you change in front of her in the first place?" Octavius snapped. "I thought you said *she* definitely couldn't find out?"

"It wasn't my fault! She kissed him—me—whatever! *Twice!*"

Jaq muttered flatly. "That's a really stupid reason to give yourselves away."

"Yeah," Vendy snorted from the floor. "You really *do* suck at this, Sirs."

Alex threw back his head. "For the last time, we—!"

"EVERYONE SHUT IT!" I bellowed, startling the men as my hands ignited into bursts of flames. Once I had their attention, I extinguished the fire, fists shaking. "I've had enough of this nonsense. Someone had better tell me what's going on, or I'll…"

I trailed off. What would sound most threatening? I stared at Alexander narrowly. *Why would they want to keep this from the Death Princess?* I had an inkling, but it was a blind one. I blurted, "If you don't tell me the truth, I will go to my father."

I grinned when Alex bolted upright. "You can't!"

"Like Death I can't." I raised my chin in triumph. "Now I would know what's going on, and you'd best tell me everything, from the beginning."

Alexander's wolf ears began to grow and he glanced away, grumbling to himself—

A loud *CRACK* sounded overhead. We craned to look at the teetering floors of the inn. The structure was leaning at a more extreme angle. The broken roof gave an ominous moan and it leaned ever farther directly over our heads.

CRACK!

The structure gave way. Pieces of the building crumbled as the tower shook beneath us, and the rest of the broken floors came crashing down.

Everyone scrambled ahead of me down the neck of the fallen clock tower, heading for the burning temple.

I thought they were daft for going that way, but then, the only other way was crumbling behind us. There wasn't much choice…

Swallowing, I set my sights ahead of me and limped after the others down the tower, the war between demons and Reapers roaring faintly below.

I hadn't fallen too far behind the others, and sped up my hobbling, wishing like Death I had my scythe to use as support.

If only I hadn't dropped it down in the battlefield before Aiden flew me up here! I brooded.

Behind me, debris crumbled from the inn above, large chunks smashing dangerously close. I hurried on as fast as my hurt leg allowed—

A strong wind rushed by, snagging my long hair, some strands tangling round my ankle. I accidentally leaned on my hurt leg, giving a small, startled yelp as I dropped to the stone. The cut on my thigh burned horribly.

Alexander was at the back of the group and spun when I'd cried out. He rushed back to me, muttering hurried curses before heaving me to my feet.

His eyes had changed back to Xavier. *What was with these two and their… oh, never mind, there isn't time!*

Xavier slung my arm round his shoulder to help me balance on my good leg before we rushed—well, limped—down the tower.

CRASH!

The top of the inn broke off and slammed into the clock tower. Gears and springs cracked out of place, the clock's face shattered, stones crumbling. The impact sent us flying a few feet in the air before falling back down. We skidded down the tower, which was now deteriorating in our wake.

We were headed for the burning temple, its wooden roof collapsed and splintered with wooden parapets and crumbled buttresses, coated in black smoke and orange flames.

"Vendy!" Xavier shouted ahead, "Henry! *Now!*"

The two Terravokers evoked their rock Hallows one last time, summoning what little strength they had left to *rip* the final, still-intact piece of the tower upward with all of us on it, the stones rumbling clumsily under our feet as our new vehicle skipped over the flaming temple, slammed into a tree, and crash-landed into the graveyard.

We were thrown to the dirt, coughing from the potent smoke. Xavier came to help me up, and when I hobbled onward with him—

A sudden gasp sounded above, and Lilli fumbled to the ground from the sky, her bat wings entangling round her figure.

Her scythes clattered to the ground, her shoulder seeping blood. My Aide gripped her wound with clenched teeth and staggered to retrieve her weapons while a flock of winged demons alighted on several graves.

"Lilli," I puffed in relief. I didn't know what'd happened to her after the tower fell, but I thanked Nira she was still alive.

Lilli turned her head to me slightly, but didn't remove her gaze from the beasts. "Are you hurt, Willow?"

"I'll be fine—"

"How wonderful!" a girl's eerily soothing voice cooed behind us. "For a moment, I feared you'd lost interest and quit our little game."

Cilia emerged from the smoke, strutting beside one of her minions and stroked its head like a skeletal house pet. "You're all here, are you?" she mused dully. "Yet still, this twin is not to be seen... Does he even exist, I wonder?"

A commanding Reaper's voice bellowed somewhere from the streets, and the distant cluster of militant soldiers could be seen all around the burning temple. The troops pushed their way toward us, some wielding scythes and others bearing shields in tight formations as they wadded through the demon scourge swarming the yard, claws and blades clashing in the smoke.

Cilia's cat ears grew, teeth sharpened. "Damn it... Bloody Reapers always coming in packs..." Her white pupils flicked to Xavier. "I'll need some compensation, if Macarius is to excuse my depleted army... Come here, boy—we'll find your brother one way or another later. He obviously doesn't care if you live or die, if he hasn't come out to play yet."

Her hands burst into fire, which shot straight for Xavier in a steadfast blaze of incredible heat.

"Get down!" I ordered, biting the pain in my leg and skid in front, evoking my fire Hallows.

A wall of white flames leapt from my palms, drowning her cooler, orange flames in a steaming sizzle.

It was a risk to raise my strength at this level. *But after everything I went through to get him back, I'll be damned if I let this bitch lay a single ember on my betrothed!*

When I was sure her fire was gone, I extinguished my burning wall, swaying, coughing, my vision spotting. I'd been evoking too much of my Hallows today. I could manage the colder fire before, but the hotter flames took more stamina.

My throat scratched painfully, but I was determined to stand my ground, shivering from the sudden cold or not.

Cilia lifted an eyebrow. "White flames? Curious... You seem exhausted only doing that much. I wonder, how long can you last with such heat?"

She sent a stream of blue flames this time, hotter than white, summoning a magnificent wave of splashing fire that threatened to wash away our entire group.

Nira help me...!

I sucked in a long breath, throwing my hands up and poured a dome of blinding, purple fire around everyone, growling as I felt my stamina drain with each licking flame produced.

Cilia's blue wave splashed into my dome the moment I had it explode outward, bright flames crackling in a furious cyclone of fire. I let the scorching storm rage around me, draining the last of my stamina, my inner heat turning cold until I… couldn't hold…

The colossal flames puffed to smoke when my hands dropped and I fell to my knees, panting.

It was so cold… My skin shivered. The ground swirled, and before I realized I'd fallen to the ground, my vision went black.

55

REAP THE REWARDS

XAVIER

The impressive display of blazing, purple flames disappeared into smoke, and Willow dropped to her knees, falling to the ground, her white hair wafting after her.

"Willow!" I rushed to her, shaking her avidly and hoping she would wake, my voice trembling. "Willow…!"

Gods, she was cold as ice, her lips turning blue.

Cilia cackled. "Oh dear, she doesn't have much heat after all? How sad…" She stepped forward. "Now that that little distraction is gone, I believe our game is… Lucrine, what are you doing there?"

She was looking at Dalen, who glanced round with a puzzled expression winding his face. "What, me?" asked Dalen.

"Stop standing there like an idiot and bring me the wolf boy," she clipped, waving an impatient hand at him.

Dalen gave a flat stare. "Why in the five realms would I do that?"

"What is this defiance?"

"Lucrine's dead," I spat. I gently laid Willow down to pluck my scythe-spheres from their chain, a growl spilling from my throat. "We killed him. And we'll do the same for you…!"

I leapt up, charging as the others followed suit behind me.

Cilia made to move away, but Jaq wrapped his chain around her, immobilizing the demon. Lilli took to the sky, coming behind her and ripped her dual scythes over the creature's spine, a scream gushing from her lips.

I swiftly cut off her hands before she could throw any fire at us, kicking the squirming, ink-infested appendages away. The fingers crawled over the ground, trying to reattach themselves like disgusting worms.

Dalen, using Lucrine's body, gave a brief shudder before picking up the hands, gagging as the black glop dripped in large chunks over his bare, hoof-textured feet.

I drew one blade to Cilia's throat and drove the other into her chest with a satisfying *squish*.

"Congratulations for your grossly extended life," I growled, beginning to draw my scythe toward her heart, the she-beast screeching. "Rest in peace…! And may your soul be Cleansed by the Goddess!"

I gave a final heave—

"*NO!*" She broke free, leaping back in a scream and pulled my scythe out of her chest.

Jaq jerked his chain, trying to reel her in, but she let the scythe cut through her body in a spiral, black blood whirling round her, unheeded.

Finally free, she crouched like a feral creature, cat ears curled in a vicious hiss. "You dare think you can send me away so easily?"

Dalen gave a disgusted gasp when the detached hands he held wriggled furiously, curling toward his arms and drew sharp claws down his skin, making him yell and drop them. The hands obediently slithered back to their places on Cilia's stubbed wrists, black sludge sealing the wounds.

Her joints cracked and popped, slinking around us as a lynx stalked its prey. Her lips stretched into a hungry smile, voice unnervingly playful. "Amusing little game you had there… I'm afraid you won't be so fortunate a second time. A team effort, is it? Why don't we see what happens when I pick you off one by *one!*"

The last word ripped from her throat, and in a flash, she pounced for Octavius, grabbing his shirt collar and igniting her hands with fire.

"How about you first, little cat?!" Cilia giggled, mad with fury. "I'll enjoy tossing your entrails to my horde and add your soul to my collec…"

Her breath caught, stopping when their eyes met.

Her fire extinguished, white pupils wide and cat ears folded down her neck. Octavius stumbled to the ground when she dropped him, and he shuffled back, face flashing with shock at her.

"You…" Cilia staggered, looking sick. "Who are…"

Ringëd stiffened behind Octavius, his gaze splintering at Cilia. "*Oscha.*" Ringëd stumbled on the words. "M… Mika?"

Cilia's brow furrowed as though pained. "M… Mika… ni…" She held an absent hand to her head. "That was my… mother's name…?" She took deep, jagged breaths. "No… No, it was *his*…"

A Reaper yelled out a command in the distance. The knights charged through the haze of smoke toward us. The demon army had been thinned to a mere few dozen, by the looks of it.

Cilia hesitated, sobriety rekindling in her green eyes. Her confusion dripped into fear.

Yet her retreating step faltered, stealing another glance at Octavius. Her fists balled, and with a sharp shake of her head, she fled, disappearing into the smoke.

The Death Knights finally came to our aid, calling out orders to search the perimeter for the Sentient. But I had a feeling she'd already vanished. I doubted it'd be so easy, after all this.

There were a few Reapers running to the burning temple with hoses, perhaps having found the nearest fire station and taken its supplies, and began dousing the fire. It was a small help, but there wasn't much else one could do for this rubble. The entire town had either been leveled or broken beyond repair. The Everlanders who'd once called this place home were either dead or reduced to wandering vagabonds now.

The troops gathered in their individual squads, reporting to their captains. Some, however, were mourning the loss of their Brothers and Sisters. We hadn't won this battle free of casualties. Watching Reaper after Reaper being carried away on stretchers, covered with white cloths, their friends wiping tears and speaking prayers to the Goddess…

My fists tightened on my scythes. *Cilia would meet her end before even stepping foot in our caverns.*

Behind me, there was a circle of knights, and I put away my scythes before pushing through the crowd. Jaq met my glance and followed.

In the center of the gathering, Willow lay where I left her, slumbering. One of the higher ranked Reapers, with brown bat wings, was checking her pulse, announcing in relief that she was alive. He noticed me then and shuffled to his feet.

"High Howllord." He saluted with a fist to his chest, wings tucking behind him. "I am Trixer Mauve, captain of squad 243 C. It is an honor to meet you. First Fangs Alice has tasked us with escorting your group out of the area."

I nodded, crouching over Willow to brush away a stray hair from her face. I muttered absently. "Send my Mistress our gratitude…"

"Gratitude received."

I jolted at the sound of my mother's voice. My head snapped up to find her looming over me.

Her helm was tucked under an arm, the other placed expectantly at her side as her wolf ears curled tight beside her head. Her tail swished brusquely at her ankles, a delicate brow cocked in my direction.

Alex cursed from my head, Jaq gave a respectful bow to my left. I floundered to speak. "Moth… Mistress? You came as well?"

"I did," she said, tone rough. I saw she had a split lip and a few bruises on her cheek. "We thought it was time to retrieve our students ourselves."

My breath faded. "Our…?"

A new shadow cast over me from behind, large and imposing, followed by a strict, grating voice. "I see you haven't grown out of your habit for finding trouble, boys."

My legs sprang straight on their own, pivoting to face the Death King's Eyes, hands clasping behind me at a hastened attention.

Jaq followed my example verbatim, both of us reciting our pre-programmed greeting in succinct unison. "Master Lucas, my liege! You honor us with your gracious presence."

Jaq and I saluted with fists to our chests and bowed, remaining low.

"At ease," Father permitted.

We rose, but still stood at attention. Neither of us, it seemed, could help our conditioned training, especially not when staring directly at those daunting, sapphire eyes. Even the messenger raven that'd flapped to my father's shoulder was the image of authority, Barrach matching his impeccable posture and intent gaze.

"Status report," Father rumbled, his calm tone even managing a commanding resonance. "Any fatalities among your team?"

"No, Master," we said at once. "All accounted for."

"Injuries to be treated?"

I spoke separately this time. "Few and minor, to my knowledge." I paused, flicking my gaze to Willow. "Though, I wish to request immediate medical attention for Her Highness. Her pulse is strong, but she may have suffered a head injury, or perhaps severe fatigue."

He nodded. "Our field Medics are coming as we speak, Her Highness will be well looked after. Now tell me what's become of the Sentients."

Jaq answered that one. "One killed, the other retreated, my lord, after seeing her numbers thinned."

Another nod, this time impressed. His gaze scanned the smoky destruction around us. He seemed to smell something foul in the air and took a sniff. "I expect an explanation of what's transpired here the second you and your team have been tended to. Understood?"

"Understood, Sir," we said, saluting again.

"Good. Now…" Father blew out through his nose, the stone-cold glare suddenly softening. I cringed when he laid a hand on my shoulder.

"That aside," he said, chuckling. "You've made this old man unbelievably proud."

I froze under his grip, seeing his bearded lips offer a rare, endearing smile. "You've fought well, tonight. Especially considering the circumstances. Not many apprentices would have survived this without reinforcements. Perhaps even *with* them."

He released me and straightened, folding his arms behind his back. "And for that, I'd say you've passed your final examination. Your induction into the Brotherhood will henceforth be accepted without question."

"As of this day," Mother announced, stepping beside him. Her eyes had a twinkle of smug pride. "I am pleased to declare you are no longer our apprentices. As far as we're concerned, you are our Brothers-in-Arms. Congratulations on your graduation."

A roar of cheers came from the surrounding knights, voicing their approval with goodhearted whoops and metallic clangs with their scythes and shields. Even their messengers were croaking and screeching from the sky, Mal and Bridge cawing jovially at our feet along with them.

Jaq and I stood there, exchanging shocked glances. We broke into thrilled laughter and clasped hands, then saluted and bowed to Mother and Father, this time profoundly lower.

"Thank you, Mistress," we said in unison. "Master… We are honored to have called you our teachers."

"And you our students," they replied together, chuckling with congratulatory nods.

Jaq and I broke our stance and pounded each other's shoulders in a laugh… but my cheer soon dulled when I glanced back down at Willow, who was still slumbering at my feet.

The crowd kept to their chatter around us while moving on with their duties, but their voices faded from my attention when I crouched beside her.

Jewel fluttered down to Willow, alighting on her collarbone. In the crow's beak was Willow's black hair-ribbon, the silver bell jingling as Jewel set it down and chirped in concern, rubbing her head against Willow's smooth jaw.

I picked up the ribbon and bell, clutching it. Lined along the black silk were grey butterflies, and my eyes traced them nostalgically. *Now I remembered.* I gave this to her as a gift, years ago. It was the first gift I ever gave her. Butterflies had been her favorite…

From above the mirth, the mourning and commotion, a familiar face came soaring toward us. My mother's winged vassal, Aiden, flapped beside my mother. He handed her what looked like Willow's scythe. She must have dropped it during the battle.

"Ah, thank you, Aiden," Mother said, examining the bejeweled weapon with an admiring eye. "I'm glad you weren't killed the second time I revived you."

She reverted Willow's scythe back to its hair-stick form, the black rod glittering with gems as Mother turned it in her hand. She gave the ornament to Aiden. "Please inform the lady Yulia she has been assigned to look after the Death Princess in her dreams, and to report any concerns to me, should they arise. And make it clear that only *she* is permitted to even glimpse at Her Highness's subconscious. Discretion is preferred."

Aiden nodded, adjusted his goggles, and took flight to do as asked.

My mother and father looked down at me, flicking their gazes at Willow. Father lowered his voice to avoid eavesdroppers. "Now then… Xavier. I don't know what Willow is doing here, but I'm sure you can guess what my next question is."

Oh, I could guess, all right. The difficult part would be answering. Bracing, I started with, "It hasn't been… clarified."

Mother's lids turned into slits at me. "Meaning?"

"—Mother Alice!" Lilli called from the crowd, pushing her way through with her leathery wings. "Father Lucas!"

When the bat stepped up to them, my mother blinked. "My word, is that little Lilli?"

"I should hope I'm not little anymore," Lilli grumbled, arms crossing. "Mother Alice, there's something I wished to ask you."

"That certainly makes two of us," Mother muttered, her tone smoldered with suspicion. "What are both my Spirit Daughters doing on the surface? Has the whole blasted castle gone on holiday?"

Her head shook tiredly. "It's a rather long story. But I wished to ask about my arrangement…"

Both Father and Mother seemed to remember whatever she was talking about, and the High Howless breathed. "Oh. Yes. It's still ongoing, if you were worried."

"Well, yes, but..." Lilli looked conflicted, glancing at me. "How is their... *condition* going to affect it?"

I cringed when Mother's stare iced over, her voice scratching. "Condition?"

Lilli gestured to us uncertainly. "Well, this... er, I'm actually not sure what it is... What's happened to them, exactly?"

Father's glare bore down at me while Mother pinched the rim of her nose, drawing in a slow breath. I knew that meant she was barely containing her fury.

Mother kept her voice calm and level when addressing Lilli again. "Dear, I'm sorry, but it will have to wait. We'll explain in private... Until then, I beg you: do not, under any circumstances, speak a word of this to anyone else. Not a soul."

Lilli's wings bowed in bewilderment. "But why?"

A scream cut through the air.

It was Lucrine—er, Dalen—on his knees, reaching for his chest as if in great pain. "*Argh...!*" He gripped his shirt, gasping between agonized grunts. "No... Gods damn it, no...!"

Jaq, who'd been off to the side wiping ash and dirt from his face, rushed over to see what had happened. I could hear him from where I was crouched, the viper asking. "What's wrong, Dalen?"

Dalen doubled over his knees, wheezing. "I'm... dead. My body's dead, I can... feel..."

Mother turned suspicious. "Your body is standing here in front of us."

"It isn't his." I looked up at her. "We'll explain later, but I think we should find his body. We at least owe him that much, for helping us."

Mother straightened with a low grumble. "Very well. Debts must be paid, when rightly due..."

She stopped, glancing at Octavius and Ringëd. Both men were still sitting in the dirt, staring dazedly off in the distance, looking to where Cilia had fled. Neither had spoken a word since the battle ended.

"Isn't that the new apprentice?" asked Mother.

"Yes..." I squinted at the two, concerned. Ringëd had called the Sentient *Mika*... Wasn't that the name of Octavius's sister? *And Ringëd's betrothed.* What did this mean?

I stood as Jaq followed me toward the pair. When we loomed over them, they didn't seem to notice us. That feral ferret of Ringëd's curled round the officer's neck and desperately patted its paws against his cheek, as though trying to rouse him from his shock.

I put a hand on Ringëd's shoulder, hesitant. "Officer…? Was that truly…?"

He whispered. "I… I don't know." He swallowed, voice shaken as he finally looked at me, haunted. "I don't *Bloody know.* I-I'd be able to tell the difference, right…? I-I'm marrying her, I know what she damn well looks like, I…" His throat tightened, and he clenched his jaw, storming off. "Tavius, come here!"

Tavius snapped out of his haunted daze, gaze trembling at the officer. "Wh-wh… what?"

"Give me your com," Ringëd rumbled, his gaze Deathly determined. "I have a call to make."

56

A NEW DAWN

XAVIER

With solemn steps, Dalen led us to the ruined Healing Clinic.

Not much was left of the building, its rubble scattered on the streets in a crumbled mess of bodies and blood, desolated like the rest of the city.

I'd let Alexander take control and watched from the psyche as he hobbled alongside our steady-striding father, followed by a guard of armored Reapers. Vendy marched blithely at our other side, her arms folded behind her head, sword rattling at her hip and braid wavering over her back.

The others had left for the last train station that wasn't ruined by the destruction. We would meet them there later. The concerns of Octavius's incident with Cilia would have to wait until then, since there were still loose ends to tie here.

We found Dalen's siblings in the destroyed Clinic, standing over his breathless body. They were in tears, masks peeled off to rub their red-rimmed lids.

Dalen went to them, first explaining it was he, and not a strange horse-shifter. He cursed when looking at the wreckage.

Dalen's body, looking much like his ghost, was laid on the cluttered floor, motionless and pale.

"I Bloody knew it." Dalen wiped his eyes. "I knew it. I… I'm dead…"

Our father stepped up to them, demanding an explanation. In hushed whispers and choked hiccups, they told him their story. They spoke of the robbery in the armory, the stolen scythes, the traitorous Reaper, Dalen's ghost, Maveric Liste, *our* involvement…

When they'd finished, Father rubbed his beard ponderously.

"Everyone," he commanded gruffly to the Reapers escorting us. "You are dismissed."

They saluted with fists to their chests and obeyed, respectfully taking their leave.

Father waited until we were alone, then turned back to the siblings. "For your crimes, you all should be tried and imprisoned. The evidence against you in regards to the stolen scythes is too great, however, so you will be sentenced to hang instead. No council will believe that a Reaper would steal their own weapons."

"But we didn't do it!" Carrie sobbed, her freckled face red and eyes blurred with tears. "We swear, it wasn't us…! We didn't…!"

Father raised a pacifying hand. "The council will not believe you… but I do." Father cleared his throat and tugged on his gauntlets. "Your grief for your brother is proof enough for me. I understand the pain—the desperation of wanting to abandon everything to bring him back… And I'm honestly impressed at your bravery for coming before me instead of fleeing. Anyone guilty would have ran at the first sign of getting caught. Death, even if they weren't guilty, they would have run."

Carrie rubbed an arm over her eyes. "Th… thank you…"

"Unfortunately," Father sighed, "this is not evidence enough for a court… Since there were too many witnesses for me to let you run, I must apprehend you, as is my duty. Thus, I see two options before you." He lifted a hand. "Either stand trial and face death, where your ghosts will be imprisoned in the afterlife…" He lifted his other hand toward Alexander and me. "Or have your ghostly brother serve my sons under a Bloodpact."

Dalen swallowed, sniffing. "Wh… what's a Bloodpact?"

"It is the Pact made between a Necrovoker and a ghost, which would bind them in a vassalship," Father explained, giving a nasally hum. "A Bloodpact is highly respected in Grim. Even those of the council honor this. Such a contract will be seen as an act of atonement for you, Dalen Carter—"

"Tesler," Dalen's ghost mumbled. "Carter's just a name to throw off the Runners…"

Father nodded and began again. "Yes, well… if you accept the Bloodpact, the court may pass judgment in your favor. As for the rest of you, I will have a better chance of getting an appeal to pardon you if you agree to pay for your crimes by serving my sons as well, for a time."

They all took a long pause, then after exchanging resolute glances, the siblings quietly agreed.

Father folded his arms behind his back, satisfied. "Very well. A Bloodpact it is."

Vendy shot us her famous crooked-toothed grin. "Looks like I get a friend. Hey, am I older than him in dead-years?"

In the night-darkened ruins of the city, I strode beside Father and our accompanying guard of armored Reapers. The Tesler Siblings huddled between them, tears still stale on their cheeks and sniffles still sounding between sobs. Dalen had formed the Bloodpact with us, and now walked with his physical feet alongside his family, having been resurrected before we left.

I relayed our findings of Sirra-Lynn—or lack thereof—to Father, as well as Maveric Liste's disappearance. Father listened with impeccable intent, nodding slowly as I explained the arduous turn of events.

We reached the train station, echoing with shouting Reapers and clattering footsteps, the whistle blowing as steam hissed from the hover-train's chimney at the front.

"And what of your new members?" Father rumbled in a hum, rubbing his peppered beard. He stopped at the platform. "The cat and the officer? They say they... *knew* the Sentient?"

I shook my head. "We've yet to gain clarification, my lord. It seems this Sentient *resembles* Octavius's sister... And, I suppose, Officer Ringëd's fiancée."

"Could this woman have Changed since they'd last seen her?"

"Unlikely, my lord," I said. "We had seen Miss Mikani ourselves not days ago. It would have taken her three days after death to Change, and this Sentient we'd faced was far too sure of her convictions than a newborn Necrofera would have been." I crossed my arms and drummed brooding fingers. "Though, it's uncanny... she did look much like the woman. Alexan..." I paused, craning to the many Reapers buzzing about the station, then began again. "*I*... thought the Sentient looked familiar when we'd first met her in High Nulani... but why would a demon as powerful as she look like a modern, living shifter?"

Father considered. "Perhaps this Mikani woman is a descendant of the Sentient?"

I grumbled. "Perhaps… I admit, I hadn't considered this."

"It is wise for a Reaper to consider all possibilities in the matter of demons," Father said, wrapping his arms behind his back. "Do not be so quick to ignore these possibilities, no matter how slight they may be."

"Yes, my lord," I said, my spine straightening from habit.

Bloods, this is unnatural, I thought in a shudder, stealing a sidelong glance at Father's intimidating visage.

Though, oddly, I found little difference in our heights. I remembered when he towered over us, yet now we seemed to match his eye level. I wasn't sure when that had happened, but I supposed such details were expected to be missed: we'd barely spent more than ten minutes with Father these past few years. It wasn't as if I had time to pay attention to these things. *Which makes this long-drawn interaction all the more unnatural.*

"My lord," I began, clearing my throat. "What is our next objective? With Maveric Liste missing, and likely a demon now, where do we start from here?"

Father stepped onto the hover-train, answering over his shoulder. "We go to this land's capital. Where miss Bianca's master will, with luck, have more information to offer."

"We?" I echoed, stepping aboard behind him, Vendy and the Tesler siblings following after. "You're coming as well?"

"Your mother and I have business with Everland's king there," he said, striding through the empty car and crossing to the next one. "Which, if I'm not mistaken, is where Miss Bianca is studying as well. It seems only prudent that you join us in the king's quarters if our separate missions meet at the same location. Once you have a new lead to Sirra-Lynn, you may be on your way as per your preference."

"Ah," I said. "And, er, how long will it take to reach the capital?"

"A month," he grunted. "We plan to make multiple stops along the way, to give you and yours proper treatment for your injuries as needed, and to search each city for signs of our retreated Necrofera. One cannot be too careful with a horde that size. If they regain their numbers, we must be prepared."

He stopped and turned to the Tesler siblings behind us, nodding. "You four are permitted to stay in this cart at your leisure. To discuss future plans and such, and perhaps take time to grieve, if you wish." His gaze turned sullen at them. He clasped Dalen's rigid shoulder. "I truly am sorry this happened. But I believe my sons will provide you a safe transition to your afterlife. My wife and I raised them to respect the deceased with great care."

Dalen's nod twitched, seeming unsure how to respond. "Th… thanks, High Howllord…"

"Please." My father curled his hand behind him once more, a broad smile stretching his face in a chuckle. "You are my sons' vassal now. Along with dear Vendy, here. You may both call me Lucas, if you wish."

Dalen's face wrench into stunned shock, and Vendy smiled excitedly.

Father bowed respectfully, murmuring a Grimish prayer to Dalen and his siblings, then left.

Vendy and I followed him through the connecting, accordion tunnel to enter the next car.

This one had many, feathered beds instead of seats, all empty save for one… One where Willow lay covered in layers upon layers of blankets. Her ashen hair fell over the bolted frame, her blue lips warming slowly.

Sitting in a chair beside her slept a second woman, with short, white hair and a velvet-azure cloak. The cloak trailed with silver buttons down the middle, opening only for the hood, chain dangling between the buttons. A blue and white patch in the shape of the Dream King's sigil was sewn at the breast.

Father nodded to the sleeping woman, seeing her hands were gleaming with an azure light. "I see your mother has asked Yulia to watch Willow in her dreams," he said, moving his gaze from the Dreamcatcher to turn to me. "Now. You say Willow knows of you both?"

"Yes." I touched Willow's cold brow. She was warmer than earlier, thank Death, but it was still far cooler than her usual warmth.

Her usual warmth… I brushed my fingers over my lips, remembering how they burned, though sweetly. *That's right. It had always been that way, hadn't it?* Vague memories resurfaced, but they refused to focus.

"Father," I began, "What will happen to Willow?"

Father's gaze dripped into a creased, troubled expression. "That, I'm afraid, I do not yet know. Come. We will discuss such things with your mother."

He strode to the next car, leaving me behind with Willow.

I traced my fingers over her smooth jaw, tucking a strand of ashen hair behind her ear—

I was pulled into the psyche so swiftly, I found myself tumbling in circles in the psyche. When I'd regained my wits, I righted myself and saw through the void's window as Alexander tugged his coat and stormed after Father, muttering. "Bloody pest. This is *my* body you're using…"

57

EXPECTATIONS

XAVIER

Wendy and Alexander followed our father into a private compartment, where we found my mother, Lilli, Henry and Jaq in the midst of discussion.

"… And then I was robbed by a beggar!" Lilli explained to my Mother, exasperated, waving her hands in sharp gestures to fully illustrate the audacity of such an action, her wings smacking Jaq in the face beside her. "And then I tried to have the Inn receptionist call you and Father Lucas, but they wouldn't even do that much if I couldn't afford a room there, and…!"

Father and Alexander slid the train's compartment door shut as Lilli continued her story.

Octavius wasn't present.

Alex lowered into the seat beside Jaq, muttering. "Where is Octavius and Officer Ringëd?"

Jaq flinched when Lilli's flapping wings smacked him in the face again, his glasses thrown askew. "He's in a different compartment," Jaq grumbled in annoyance, glaring at Lilli and her obliviously flailing wings while she told the tale of her adventures. "They're trying to get a hold of Tavius's sister on com."

Alex slid a hand through his tangled hair and eased back in his seat, wincing at a scrape on his shoulder. "Octavius seems to have the worst luck with family, doesn't he?" he sighed.

Jaq flicked his eyes at me. "You really think it was his sister?"

"Master brought up the possibility of some sort of ancestry. A Sentient that controls that many demons can't be less than a hundred years old, at the least. But if she *is* an ancestor, it seems Octavius has two murderers in his bloodline."

Lilli's prattling died at the mention, and it fell silent suddenly. Father lifted his prominent brow as Mother's wolf ears perked in question at me.

"Two?" she asked, her grey tail curled delicately round her leg. "Who is the second?"

Alex took a deep breath, then explained, "Octavius's father. He is the one who threw Xavier from the cliff, those years ago… He was the assassin."

All were silent.

The train whistle blew, and the ride smoothly pushed forward, the train departing. The ruined city fell behind us through the window, and the night sky painted our view with stationary stars.

Father was the first to break the silence. "Then… you've befriended that assassin's son?"

"Octavius isn't like his father," assured Alex. "He'd fought beside us in that battle and risked his life on more than one occasion for us. He's as much our Brother as anyone deserves. And keep in mind, he passed both Mother's entrance and graduation examinations in a matter of days. If that doesn't ensure his place among us, then I question the validity of those tests."

Mother snorted. "My tests are highly respected. If he passed, then he deserved it, no one is questioning that. However…" She flicked her gaze away in thought. "With the assassin's son on our side, this could be an incredible opportunity. Perhaps with his help, we may finally find the man and bring him to justice."

Alex pursed his lips. "He doesn't know where his father is, I'm afraid. Neither is he aware of what the man's done."

Father hummed low. "And do you intend to tell him?"

Alex's gaze fell.

Father breathed out through his nose. "I see… if he knows nothing, then it seems that is what we'll discover with questioning. But I feel I must warn you: you *will* have to tell him eventually. Secrets of this nature are detriment to a soul, if discovered too late. You can keep him ignorant as long as you wish, but the truth will find a way to surface in the end. I suggest you don't prolong it."

Alexander gave a slow, grim nod. It wasn't so much Father's warning that felt eerie, it was the fact that our father was giving us advice that sounded… well, fatherly. No commanding decrees or militant orders, no cold tone that separated blood ties and kept formalities in check… Bloods, was that rare.

Father nodded back to us, resigned, and turned to Lilli next. "Now, for the real question… What do we do with *you*, Lilli?"

Lilli's bat wings folded beside her, stretching taller. "I follow wherever Willow goes, of course," she said. "I must return her to the palace before Father Serdin learns she's gone."

Mother's wolf ears dropped. "It will not be that simple, Lilli. Willow wasn't meant to discover the twins. Now that she knows, we can't simply take her back to her father. She may very well tell him everything. As may you."

"I wouldn't…"

"We cannot risk you *accidentally* letting it slip," clarified Mother.

She and Father stared at Lilli with deep consideration, the bat growing rigid.

After a few finger rolls on his arm, Father sighed. "I suppose there's nothing for it… Lilli, you and Willow will have to stay with us. I'll speak with an illusionist about providing Willow with a more convincing disguise. She could only change the color of her hair and eyes, but a professional Decepiovoker can give someone a new face entirely."

Mother approved with an impressed frown. "I see. So, when Serdin returns to Grim and discovers his daughter is missing, he won't know she's with us. Though I suppose *you* should remain as you are, Lilli. We'll tell your father you're traveling with us in hopes of finding Willow. That shouldn't be difficult to believe, being our Spirit Daughter. Daniel will understand. This will last until we find Xavier's vessel."

Lilli grumbled and sank in the bench, her wings folding. "Oh, very well… I suppose I can't marry a man who shares a body with his twin, regardless."

Alexander shocked straight at that. He started to say something, shut his mouth, then clipped. "Sorry? I must have misheard you. Marry whom?"

Lilli chuckled. "Very humorous, Alexander, pretending you've forgotten… Oh, and speaking of, do you have my vines? I think I've been unspeakably patient, considering it's long past time I received them."

"Are you mad, woman?" Alex scowled at her. "I'm not marrying you."

She bristled. "If you keep up this silly jest, then you'll be correct soon enough! Now I'm serious, Alex. I want my vines. You've taken so long to come back, my patience has worn thin already. So, where are they? And don't you dare say you left them back in Grim, I'll scarcely believe such an excuse."

Befuddled, he turned to Mother and Father and threw a thumb at Lilli. "What is she babbling about?"

Mother seemed wary. "Didn't your father tell you?"

"Me?" Father cleared his throat behind a fist, his voice dropping to an uncertain mutter that I've never heard spill from his lips. "I'd told Xavier of his arrangement, I thought we agreed *you* would tell—?"

"Excuse me?" Alex's wolf ears sprouted. "Are you telling me I'm engaged?"

They both looked away toward opposite ends of the compartment. Their usually flawless posture now faltered and squirmed. *What in Void was happening? Were these even our parents anymore?*

"What!" Alexander barked in outrage, "When in Death's name did this happen?"

Mother fidgeted, her tone accommodating. "Well, er, Alexander… When you and Xavier first came to live in the palace, there were many lords hoping to arrange you both with their daughters. After you met with all of them, we let you choose who you preferred—"

"I don't remember choosing such a thing!" Alex cried.

Mother rubbed her temples. "Yes, well, we discovered later that neither of you were aware *what* you chose the girls for… But it'd been years until that was brought up, and you were already promised by then. Xavier was arranged with Willow, and you with Lilliana. Of course, your weddings aren't expected until you come of age."

Anger clipped. "We come of age in a few *weeks*! I wasn't given any prior warning! You honestly don't expect me to concede, do you?"

Lilli wilted, her hurt expression dripping her delicate features. "You… don't wish to marry me?"

Alex clicked his teeth shut. "I didn't mean… You can't actually expect me to…" He gave up and groaned. "*Argh*, forget this!"

He stormed out and slammed the door, forcing himself into the psyche as I stumbled out.

"*You deal with them!*" he fumed. "*I can't believe they'd do this—I should have expected it…! Of all the Bloody times to tell me, they…*"

I took a deep breath as he prattled on furiously, and I reentered the compartment, bowing to Mother and Father and hoping to Gods Alex hadn't condemned me to a painful backhand by father.

"He, er," I began, ignoring Alexander's continued stream of obscenities in my thoughts. "He apologizes for his outburst. He simply asks for… time, to collect himself."

Father's anger simmered in his glare, but he seemed to keep it contained and gave a nod.

Though, I considered to myself, *while we're on the subject…*

"If my lord would permit," I said, habit taking control as I stood at attention with arms locked behind me. "I would like to make a request, on both our behalves."

"What request?" asked Father.

"Given the circumstances, I should think postponing the engagement would be appropriate? Not that we are ungrateful, but neither of us desire to make the women uncomfortable, with our condition. I would rather delay any weddings until Alexander and I were, well… normal."

Jaq snickered beside Lilli. She punched his shoulder, making him wince, and she sneered out the window in an indignant blush.

"Granted," father agreed, massaging his eyes. "Gods Almighty, what a mess…"

Shhhhk!

The compartment door slid open, and Octavius and Officer Ringëd shuffled inside.

Everyone quieted as the two slid the door closed behind them.

"Well?" I asked, his distant expression worrying. Ringëd held the same haunted look, a cigarette trailing with watery smoke between his lips as that feral ferret of his curled around his neck. I prodded, "Any word?"

Octavius held Shade in his arms and pressed the messenger against his chest for comfort. "Yeah," he hushed, sounding relieved yet puzzled. "It wasn't Mika. She's still at home."

"Thank *Oscha* for that," Officer Ringëd muttered, sucking on his cigarette and causing the singed tip to flare red. "She's never heard of any relatives up here either. I don't know where in Bloods this woman came from, but it's too freaky how much she looks like Mika."

I crossed my arms, humming. "We've considered Cilia may be one of your ancestors, Octavius. It's the only explanation that seems to fit."

Octavius's shoulders slumped, seeming frazzled. "I guess so… She looked *exactly* like my sister. Except for the lighter hair."

"And she's a fire-thrower, like that demon girl," Ringëd added, shaking his head. "It's just… *too* weird."

Octavius nodded emptily. "Same Hallows, same face… It's definitely creepy. And that Sentient looked like she recognized *me*, too."

Jaq scratched his scaled chin, not bothering to put on his peasant persona. "Do you resemble one of her siblings, you think?"

Octavius shrugged and sat down. "Maybe… I'm sorry, guys. I guess it's my fault this happened, sort of…"

My father stood slowly, exhaling through his nose. "Do not blame your-self for a demon's actions, young man. You've been chosen as a Reaper for a reason, the Mother Goddess would not have sent that messenger to you otherwise."

Mother intoned her agreement. "And I damn well wouldn't have consid-ered you as an apprentice, had you any willing affiliation with a demon. We do not have the luxury of choosing those whose blood we share… whether that blood has rotted black or not."

Octavius nodded stiffly, blushing slightly under Mistress's penetrating gaze. "O… okay…"

"In any case," Father said. "Now that we've received confirmation from this sister of yours, Alice and I will retire for the night. I heed you all regain your strength and prepare for New Aldamstria. We're to stay in Everland's castle. Please be on your best behavior."

"*Especially* you, Jaq," Mother snapped and shot the viper a warning glare. "I was lenient when you drowned Howllord Tykes with your drink last month—"

"He had it coming, Mistress," the viper justified, then retracted. "With all due respect."

"Oh, I Bloody well know he deserved it," Mother snorted. "The bastard was overdue for it, and I thank you for having kept me from tossing my own sherry at him… but we're in a different territory. One that, need I remind you, popularly hates our kind. We needn't give them more reason for it, nor do we want to risk a war between our nations. So, I must stress: best behav-ior. No throwing drinks at a single Roarlord, no matter how much they may deserve it. Am I clear?"

Her last words quivered with authority, causing both Jaq and I to spring at attention, speaking in unison. "Yes, Mistress! Your will is well heeded."

"For your sakes, I pray that it is," Mother muttered and left the com-partment with Father, her tail swishing behind her.

When the door slid closed, I allowed my shoulder to drip out of atten-tion, exhaling in relief.

Octavius ruffled his hair. "Speaking of drinks, I think I could use a stiff one."

I grimaced. "That's the best damned idea you've had all day."

"You're telling me, Howllord," Ringëd muttered. Then the officer paused, snapping his fingers. "Oh, Bloods! I almost forgot—Howllord, I need to talk with you."

I cocked an eyebrow at the officer. "About what?"

"The reason I came to find you," he said, snuffing his cigarette in the ash tray on one of the chair arms. "I didn't come here to find Octavius. I came to find you and Alex."

My brow knitted, bewildered. "Us? Both of us, specifically?"

"Yeah." The ferret on his shoulder scuttled onto a seat and curled into a ball, yawning before dozing off. "Exactly, both of you."

My laughter was nervous. "I, er, suppose you're unaware that my brother isn't here at the moment, then?"

"You can relax, Howllords." He waved a flippant hand at me, rummaging through a bag he'd set on the carpet. "I already know you're both in there, no point in making excuses."

I glared at Octavius, accusing in a mutter, "You told him, did you?"

Octavius shot up innocent hands. "I didn't say anything!"

"Calm down," Ringëd said, kneeling to search his bag more intently. "Tavius didn't tell me. I already knew, way before he met you two."

"How?" I demanded.

"I knew from the minute you woke up in Alex." Ringëd finally pulled out a velvet sack from the bag, untying the strings and revealing a fist-sized, crystal ball. "Or, I guess, sometime *after* the fact."

He lifted the ball to me, and as his fingers spewed azure lights, images of my own face spilled into the orb.

"I'm a Seer," Ringëd explained. "I See people's past mostly, where they've been, what they've done, little glimpses into their lives…"

I frowned at the crystal ball that began showing glimpses of Alexander and my past. "Are you saying," I began, "you think you can find my body for us…? Where it ended up?"

"No," Ringëd chuckled, tossing the crystal ball up and catching it in a grin. "I'm saying I've already found it."

In the crystal ball, a new image flitted. This one held a young face; the face of a teenaged boy with grey hair that was matted and tossed about his brow, a scar running down his right eye and cheek, with a cast encasing his broken leg.

It was *my* face.

With numb fingers, I touched the crystal ball, the air flying out of my lungs. "You've… you've *found* my body?" I stared at Ringëd: the Seer who showed me my body, as it had been those six years ago when my soul was torn from it. "A-Alive?"

"You bet, Howllord," Ringëd said smugly. "Alive and breathing."

"But... but I..." I didn't know how to reply, this was all happening so fast. "But you've only just met us? I-I thought a Seer needed to *touch* something that belongs to those they Saw visions of?"

"Yeah, that's the weird part," Ringëd said. "See, I *really* came here to finally meet you two in person." He laughed. "I've been Seeing both of your pasts for twenty Gods damned years. You're like nephews to me, in a weird way."

I scratched my bandaged cheek. "Then... that's how you knew of our co-existence?"

"I Saw the night you were thrown off, Howllord. And I Saw what your brother was doing while you were there. And I Saw a vision of your body, alive, hooked up to a machine in a Marincian clinic."

"A Marincian Clinic..." I hushed, shivering with a new spark of excitement. "You're certain it was Marincian?"

"The nurses there were speaking Marincian," he said flatly. "And I'm Marincian myself, so I hear them talking about how he's in a coma ward in that clinic, wherever it is."

My thrill deflated. "You don't know where it is?"

"Not specifically," he said apologetically. "And Marincia is a long trail of islands, it could be any of them. Sorry... that's the best I can do, right now."

"Then," I murmured, a new plan of action solidifying to mind. "We'll ask Bianca's Master which island he'd visited that day, when he claimed he'd seen Sirra-Lynn. Perhaps it will be one nearby that island?"

Jaq snorted from his seat, poking at the feral ferret next to him with a scaled finger. "*I* for one want to know why a Landish mammal speaks Marincian. Last I recall, most commoners don't care to learn more than their first language."

"Oh," Ringëd shrugged. "Marincian *is* my first language. Sure, my parents were Landish originally, I still have an uncle over in Brittleton even, but I was born and raised on a province to the west, called *Y'ahmelle Nayû.* My parents were big into other cultures and all, so that's just where they ended up."

"And what of your shift?" Lilli asked curiously from the back, the bat glancing at the feral rodent on the chair. "You seem to understand that one there, so I presume you're a ferret shifter. Yet, I don't recall seeing your ears?"

"Or so much as a claw," agreed Jaq in a huff.

From the door, Octavius laughed nervously. "Well, uh, Ringëd actually doesn't, uh... *have* a shift."

Jaq and I stared at Octavius now. "He doesn't what?" we questioned in unison.

Ringëd laughed and stretched his arms behind his head. "I have a rare birth defect. I can still understand Kurn over there, since I should have been a ferret shifter, but I don't have any parts to *shift* between."

I gapped at him. "Then… what *are* you?"

Ringëd rubbed his chin, thinking. "I guess you can call me…" He gave a toothy grin. "A Feral Human."

58

PREMONITIONS

WILLOW

I sat on soft grass, leaned against a tree in the familiar forest of the Weeping Woods. The terrain was cloaked in fog, the only light radiating from the lantern beside me. It was filled with a single speck of fallen light, and I took the lantern, rising to my feet and stepped into the thicket of willow trees. A gentle wind swept past, hushing the leaves like a sea of whispers.

A figure caught my eye.

Xavier vanished through a screen of veiling branches.

My heart leaping to life, I burst through the rustling leaves and caught a glimpse of his shadowed hair disappearing through other branches. I rushed after him, keeping the lantern before me while its light quivered with each step.

Flakes of ash swirled round me, and the faint tinkling of wind chimes echoed in the night. The notes sang a dreary tune, the Relic awaiting its Call.

I drew back the last screen of leaves, entering the hidden cave within, and stopped. Xavier was there, in the middle of the cavern with his back turned to me.

Before him was the towering Willow of Ashes.

Its white branches flaked in the wind while the Ashcrystal leaves chimed the Requiem's melody.

"Xavier?" I called, my voice trembling. How had he found this place? It was forbidden...

He turned to me, silent, the clattering, crystal leaves of the Willow of Ashes twinkling the solemn melody of the Requiem.

Xavier was slightly older, his jaw outlined in a clean beard. He was dressed in fine, black silks, and a silver crown with skulls was placed atop his shadow hair.

Pierced through his left ear was a diamond earring, and around his left, fourth finger was a matching wedding ring.

Beside him was his brother, Alexander. He practically mirrored Xavier, yet contrasted him greatly. Alexander's noble suit was dyed white, almost blending with the ashen tree behind them, and he was cleanly shaven. He stood by his brother expectantly, arms folded.

"Willow." Xavier stepped toward me and took my hand. He lifted my chin and softly stole my lips. "It's time, love. If I'm to protect you both, we can't wait any longer. Can you give the Call, and awake the Relic...?"

I gasped awake, jolting upright on the bed.

My pulse blistered, fear shivering my chilled skin as the dream burned into my memory. *Why ask to awake the Relic? Why would that be necessary?*

"You should rest more, Your Highness," a woman's voice advised across from me.

I realized belatedly that I was on a train's bed. The scenery outside was dark and zipping by smoothly, a quiet hum vibrating the carpeted floor.

I turned to the woman who'd spoken—and gawked.

She was absolutely *gorgeous*. She must have been in her early thirties, her pale face smooth and perfectly sculpted as if the God of beauty had blessed her personally. Her black eyes were sharp and angled like a fox, white lashes unbelievably long and white hair curling to her chin.

She wore a velvet, azure cloak with a wide cowl draped over her shoulders, hiding her thin frame, her collar opened round her slender neck. She sat poised before me, noble and elegant as though cut from the canvas of a beautiful painting, and had a bust that, enviously, made mine look mediocre.

She cocked her head, making me blush when realizing I was still staring.

"I..." My throat was dry. I felt sick, only now noticing that beads of sweat covered my skin, making me shiver. "Where am I?"

"Traveling to New Aldamstria with the High Howllord." Her voice was a soothing whisper, like listening to a flurry of crystals singing a lullaby. "I am Yulia. The Devouhs' personal Dreamcatcher. I was asked to watch your dreams as you slept, Princess. Forgive me if I've made you uncomfortable."

I attempted to stand, but the blood rushed to my skull and I swayed, wincing at the following migraine.

Yulia rose and gently steadied me. "Do take care, Your Highness. Your grandfather Dream would be most displeased with me if any harm came to you."

I shook my head and regained footing. My boots had been removed. I was barefoot, but still clothed in my tattered trousers and black cloak. Jewel fluttered to my shoulder, chirping in concern.

"I'll be fine." I swallowed the sprouting nausea. "Where is Xavier?"

Yulia hesitated. "He is… perhaps discussing plans in the other cars by now. Best you stayed and—"

I forced open the car door, stumbling into the next one, my white hair dragging over the floor. Those winged siblings were in here, starting at my sudden entrance, their skeptical gazes following me as I crossed the aisle and shoved my way to the next car.

Voices murmured within a private compartment here. I stormed over and slammed the door open, panting.

Everyone hushed at my entrance.

There!

Xavier stood at the center, blinking at me.

"W… Willow?" Xavier smiled, though it was turned up at one corner in cheered confusion. "How, er… how was your rest?"

I recalled my dream, where Xavier was older. Now, he looked young again, bandages wrapped round his face and hand, a splint at his ankle, and no beard to be seen.

I padded over and latched onto him, a winded gasp escaping his crushed lungs. "Thank the Gods you're still here…" My voice was weak, a painful croak rubbing my vocal chords. "I thought you'd leave again, or…"

He chuckled and stroked a bandaged hand through my hair. "Of course I didn't leave. How are you feel—will you GET OFF?!"

He shoved me away, and I stumbled on my tender leg, falling over Lilli in her seat. Biting down the pain, I inched my baffled gaze at him.

Xavier's blue eye had switched places. He was Alexander now. *That's right!* I thought, memory racing back. *I'd forgotten…*

Alex shot me a tempered scowl. "*You* are to keep ten feet away from us at all times. Do you hear me? This is *my* body he's using. I'll not have him partake in personal affection of any sort with *my* limbs or any other such appendages, thank you."

"I… hang on." My heart squeezed, Lilli helping me to my feet. "*Your* body? Wh… What of his? He's *not* alive…?"

Alex's eyes flicked up, then rolled before Xavier switched with him. Xavier took my hand assuredly. "I *am* alive. We've just confirmed it, Ringëd showed us. He's a Seer. He had a vision of my body. We only need to hurry and find it, and we'll be back to normal in no time."

"But until then!" Lilli huffed and snagged his wrist, jerking Xavier away from me. "You stay away from them, Willow! It's *my* fiancé they're sharing!"

Alex switched out and ripped his hand free of hers. "Must you bring that up? I never agreed to this arrangement in the first place."

"How can you say that?" Lilli cried, her wings dipping desperately. "You knew we were betrothed even back then!"

"I was ten! Do you expect me to know what 'betrothed' meant at that age? I… *argh*! Forget it!"

He stormed out and slammed the compartment door closed behind him, the frosted-glass pane rattling.

Jaq cackled from his seat, clutching his ribs—

Lilli kicked between the viper's legs, her boot *klunking* against the wooden seat's frame and shutting him right up.

She flopped into the seat in a furious growl. "Men!"

59

RELUCTANT ALLIES

XAVIER

I was stirred awake by a faint, jingling bell.

The swell had been so crystalline and pure, I hadn't known if it came from the darkened car of beds or my dissipating dream.

Groggy, I sat up, searching the car for the source of the sound. Our team slumbered softly, save for Jaq who snored like a Bonedragon that had lost its protective armor of bones, but that metallic quiver had faded into silence from my ears. Perhaps I *had* dreamt it. Or...

I remembered something and fished into my pocket. I pulled out the ribbon and bell I'd slipped in there after changing. I'd forgotten to return it to Willow.

I sighed and slipped out of the bolted bed, squinting against dim lights of everyone's scythe-spheres to find Willow's mattress on the other side of the aisle.

She wasn't there. The sheets had been ruffled and thrown asunder, left abandoned on the vacant bed.

Had she crossed cars? I shuffled through the aisle of my sleeping comrades and stepped through the connecting section between this car and the next.

Once in the empty hallway, I found light spilling from a single, private compartment. I walked over and turned the latch, sliding open the door.

Willow was startled by the sudden noise, but settled back in her seat after seeing it was only me. Jewel fluttered from her head, chirping in greeting at me.

I propped an arm against the doorframe, shifting weight to my uninjured ankle. "Darling?" I asked. "What are you up to in here?"

"I suppose…" She lifted her bare legs onto the seat as her gaze drifted to the window. "Hiding."

She wore a borrowed, silken nightgown, compliments of my mother. It didn't quite fit her, since Mistress was a tall woman and Willow… was not. But she didn't seem to mind. In fact, she didn't seem to mind anything around her, at the moment.

She lapsed into a silence, and I exhaled, sitting beside her. "Hiding from whom?" I asked.

A pause. "My… dreams," she said, hushed.

"Ah. And what dreams would those be?"

She glanced at me, as if debating whether to be defensive or relenting. It seemed the former had won. She returned her attention out the window in lieu of answering.

I sighed and offered her the bell and ribbon. "You dropped this, in Lindel. Thought you'd like it back."

Her eyes brightened at last, taking the items from me. "Thank you. I shouldn't have been so careless…"

"You were focused on keeping a psychotic Sentient at bay. I'd say that takes priority over a Bloody ribbon."

She chuckled. "I suppose it does…"

We watched the mountains pass in the distance, a crescent moon looming under a sea of tiny, stationary lights. I still couldn't wrap my head around these 'stars'. If they didn't come from the clouds, like ours in Grim, then where were they made? How far did this sky climb? Did it even have an end?

"Xavier?" Willow murmured, leaning into me.

I countered her weight, enjoying the warmth, and gave a tired hum. "Yes?"

"What happens now?" she asked. "Lucrine is dead. Cilia's disappeared. She'll rebuild her army, if she truly plans to kill the Relic Bloodlines. How do we prepare?"

"We'll have to wait and see how things unfold, I suppose." I rested my head against hers, the scent of spiced apples clinging to her hair as my lids fell heavy. "I'm afraid we can't control the future."

"No… but we can See it, if we watch close enough."

I nearly nodded off, but she slipped out from under me, taking the spiced fragrance with her, and she went to the doorway. By the time I rose to my sluggish feet, she'd paused and turned back to me, her expression muted with worry and fingers fiddling with the amulet around her neck.

"This war with the demons..." she said. "What if it goes farther than we think?"

I scratched my neck, yielding to a yawn. "Farther how?"

She took a separate breath, then seemed to decide against it. "Perhaps I need more rest... I fear my dreams may be getting the best of me."

She wished me good night, and left.

I went to follow after—but bumped into her. She'd stopped outside and was staring ahead in shock.

"Willow?" I walked around her. "What is..."

I flinched.

A lion-tailed man had appeared in the hall. It was that same, scarred warrior who'd been cropping up since we surfaced. That Healer woman was behind him also, clinging to his back and peeking round to see me.

"H... how did you get in here?" I demanded uncertainly. The other Death Knights had been ordered to keep passengers out of these last few cars. How could they slip past their notice? "Who are you?"

The warrior denied an answer, and instead gave a proposition. "We request to join your party."

I exchanged a skeptical glance with Willow. "Excuse me?" I asked.

His stern face refused to soften. "I need not ask again."

"We don't even know who you are. Why have you been following us?"

"It was not by our will that our paths have crossed so frequently. Neither was it our choice to overhear your dilemma."

I saw Willow tense beside me, and my hands balled. "How much have you heard?" I demanded.

"Enough." His gaze narrowed. "After killing the dragon, we watched you make the Bloodpact with the ghost. We heard your tale and learned of your co-existence within your twin. And now we wish to assist in your search. Do you accept or decline?"

"Why do you want to help us?"

He glanced back at the woman clinging to him. "It was not my decision. *She* feels we must aid you."

I craned to face the lioness. She blushed, ducking behind him. "Why?" I questioned.

The woman whispered something in the man's ear, and he relayed the message. "She believes you both are important."

I prodded, "Because?"

She whispered a reply, and he repeated it with a begrudged sigh. "An oracle told her you would bring back the rightful heir of Everland. She wishes to see that day come."

Willow took in a breath beside me. "You're part of the rebellion?"

Hesitant, he looked to the lioness for approval. She nodded. "We are," he affirmed.

I groaned, setting a fist at my side. "Bloods, more of you? We're already housing two rebels, both of whom are just as delusional about 'visions' regarding the Land Relicblood. I'd say that's more than enough for us."

"This oracle…" Willow glanced at the woman thoughtfully. "In the market the other day, I overheard you mentioning King Dream. My Grandfather. Is he the oracle who told you this?"

The lioness blushed again and shrank behind the man, but nodded.

"So, I'm not the only one he sent to find you two…" Willow muttered to me.

The warrior's lion tail twitched behind him, and he murmured. "If Dream was correct, we wish to join you. We know your secret and know the Death Princess travels with you as well. We're prepared to confront the Death King with this, should you deny our entry. Now, do you accept or decline?"

Death. My teeth gritted. *Was there even a choice in this?*

"Fine," I growled. They'd been helping us through this utter Void since we surfaced anyway, I doubted they had any ill intent. The worst risk, it seemed, would be to turn them away given what they knew. "We don't know anything about the 'lost heir', but… we accept to house you in exchange for your silence."

The man extended his thick hand to me. "A wise choice. I am Kurrick Everstien, of the Old Kingdom. And this is my companion, Anabelle. We thank you for your… *generous* hospitality."

I scowled, but took his hand, muttering, "No, no, the pleasure's all mine… I simply love attracting lunatics…"

Nira, please don't let this be a mistake.

EPILOGUE I

MACARIUS

"Look at this mess," I hissed to Cilia, furious. "I'd been sent as a copy not six hours ago, yet I return to find you've leveled the whole damned city?"

She was crouched in this disgusting alleyway, kneeling in the rubble. Her army had been cut down by squads of Reapers, precisely what I'd feared would happen if we revealed ourselves too soon.

I rubbed my intangible eyes under my spectacles, purely out of habit, as this was not a physical form of mine. "The citizens are either dead or have sought refuge in the other cities," I spat. "Our army is severely diminished, and one of our commanders was killed. And what do you do? You sit here simpering like a fool in the shadows!"

Had I physically been standing over her, I would have kicked the girl for her stupidity. But I was merely a copy, an observer, conjured by a Somniovoking Evocation while my original traveled to the capital to meet with Kael.

"Well?" I barked when she failed to reply. "What do you have to say for yourself, you blood-lusting simpleton?"

She was silent for a long, infuriating moment, then finally spoke.

"Caleb," she whispered, hollow.

The name made me stagger. "What?"

"Caleb," she said again, turning to look at me with white, glowing pupils. "I saw a boy, with the Reapers. A cat boy. And then I remembered… A name. *Caleb*. Then it all flooded back—I… I remembered a child, a small one. The Reaper was much older than he, but his eyes were just like…"

My anger flared, wishing desperately I was physically here to wring her tiny neck. *What boy in this day and age could have possibly reminded her of…*

I stopped. *Had she found one of HIS sons…?*

Cilia rose, like a doll with limp arms. "Who… is Caleb? And… why does that Reaper share his face…?"

"Do you really think you deserve another reward after you've ruined everything?"

Her cat ears curled back, snarling. "I've discovered the Death Princess is with the wolf boy. And there are plenty of new corpses here to rebuild my army. Lucrine was a fool anyway, I have two other commanders to take his place. And this ruined city will only help us further, the Everlanders are sure to think the Reapers brought this destruction. You tell me now—who is Caleb?"

I sighed, rubbing my eyes under my glasses. "Caleb," I drawled dully. "Was your son."

She was silent.

"As for this Reaper boy," I added in a grumble, my gaze sweeping the terrain. "Well, I suppose he may be something of a descendant of yours."

A shadow loomed over me suddenly. I lifted my gaze, spotting a white-cloaked Reaper with black wings watching me, hesitant, his face shielded by his cowl.

"And where have you been?" I demanded of the Reaper. "What part in this disaster did you have, Janson?"

The Reaper hopped down, removing his hood to reveal a hideous, scarred face and bald head. His right eye was sealed shut by old, melted skin, and his left pupil gleamed white.

"I'm sorry," he rasped. "Too much was happening for me to get close to them. I had to blend with the other Reapers to sneak anywhere."

I gave a hard breath. "At least you're still under their radar… We'll have to use you to get to the Shadowblood later."

I pivoted, arms folding. "You, my feathered friend, may be most useful… And quite soon, I should hope."

EPILOGUE II

ROCHELLE

"You didn't tell them anything, did you?" she asked from across my kitchen table, the ice in her tea having melted and diluted it.

I took a sip from my own glass, hunching forward. "I told them I didn't know anything… I directed them to Maveric instead, you know I'm a terrible liar."

She crossed her arms, one eyebrow cocking. "Rochelle, Maveric is even worse at keeping secrets. And since the boy's own brother is the one looking for him, you know he'll crumble. Damn it all, now we'll have to be ready for a meeting… maybe move him to a different site?"

I sighed and set down my glass with a small clink. "Are you sure we can't just tell them? They're risking so much to find him, I'm sure they would—"

"We can't take any chances," she interrupted. "You're a part of this just as much as I am. And you have more to lose. That boy we found was the first son of Lucas Devouh. The Death King's *Eyes*, Rochelle. If his second son found us, we would be shut down and you all would be executed. Do you like your head where it is, or would you rather it be mounted on some high lord's wall?"

I pursed my lips, tasting lipstick while my tongue brushed over them. "Well, no…" I mumbled. "But they're risking so much. And your son is so worried…"

Sirra-Lynn's pale green eyes wilted at the mention. "I know…" she lamented, sighing. "But if what you say is true, and he's one of them… what can I do? Octavius can't find out."

"Only because you decided so," I pointed out.

She glared at me sharply. "He doesn't need to be caught up in something this dangerous. It's not his fight."

"It's becoming his, Sirra." I let out a hard breath and rose, my chair legs scuffing the floorboards. "In any case… We should head out. We'll want to warn the others that they may be coming for the Devouh boy soon."

She rubbed her eyes and followed after me. "Just as well… My resurrection is almost over, anyway. I need to see my *Da'torr*. She's waiting for me in the square."

I gave a weary grin. "You picked one Void of a time to come visit me, Sirra. You should know better than to wander so far from the island with all these Fera. Your Necrovoker isn't suited for fighting."

"I did what I had to. My son came looking for me with the Devouh boy. With a distressing call like that, how could I not see you and plan for the worst?"

"You could have kept it strictly over com, for one thing. But, as always, you just had to come see to this problem personally…" I exhaled a dismal breath and went to grab my traveling cloak from the hanger. I wrapped on the garment and fiddled with the leather ties. "Let's hope your son doesn't find you. Does Octavius even know what happened to Claude?"

"Bloods, I hope not." Her voice was grave, orange cat ears folded down. "We both did what we could to keep everyone in the dark—especially Octavius. His infection Hallows would have caused more trouble. That boy may be shy, but if he knew who'd poisoned me, he'd likely hunt the man down."

She tried to hold it back, but I saw her lips crack into a sudden grin. "You know," she began in an afterthought, "I think he'll make a good Reaper. It was a shock, but… somehow, it suits him." The light in her eyes smoldered next, her tone dampening. "Gods, I hope he doesn't find his father. It's got me worried now."

"But not worried enough to tell him what actually happened?"

"He can't know what happened," she emphasized. "Not yet. And if we're going to save that Devouh boy, his brother can't know either."

I sighed again and opened the door to leave. "If you insist…"

PROLOGUE: SOUL SURVIVOR

JANSON

"*Die, Gods damn it!*" I ripped my scythe into the beast's sticky chest, *snapping* its rotted NecroSeam. Its corpse collapsed, blackened soul evaporating in a hiss—

Another Fera tore at my wing, feathers shredded, a yell scraping my throat. More leapt at me, one biting my arm, the others thrashing my side and legs. I tried to back away, but fell into a ditch and landed hard on my wings, screaming, the demons scuttling after—

"*Da'torr!*" my vassal, Rossette, screamed as she spread her green wings and flew between us. She thrust her hands at the Fera, vicious bolts of lightning shooting from her fingers and splashing over two beasts with a deafening *crash* of thunder, throwing the slithering things over the ditch.

The remaining beast shrieked and bolted for her.

"You eez watching self, Rossette!" My second, web-eared vassal called, sprinting to Rossette's side and swept a fogging hand at the demon. A pillar of ice crystalized from his fingers, encasing the creature in a solid, icy armor.

"Rossette…" I panted, groaning at my leaking side. "Nikolai… you should run. If you die again, I… might not… be here to resurrect you…"

"We cannot leave you to die, *Da'torr!*" Rossette stood her ground, her and Nikolai keeping back the demons that strayed into the ditch. "We swore to service you to the best of our ability when we made the Bloodpact. If you stay, we stay."

The villagers' screams bleated over the ditch, curdled voices muffled overhead, their sobs dampened under the incessant whine in my ears. *Have I lost some of my hearing?*

I peered over the edge.

Those skeletal nightmares swarmed the burning valley, their skin slithering with black muck. Nira, the things were deboning villagers like feral fish in the dry glow of the fire.

My stomach churned, wanting to vomit, but I swallowed and ducked behind the rocky ditch. My palms were caked with blood, straining to keep hold of my scythe. I tried unfolding my wings, but winced as they stiffened back in place. My feathers were shredded… Flying away wasn't an option. There was no way Rossette could lift me with her small muscles, her vessel was only a child, despite her soul's matured age… Even if she *could* have lifted me, I couldn't bring myself to leave Nikolai.

Fangs Lastings, I decided. *I have to call Fangs Lastings.*

I pulled out my communicator from my cloak's pocket, fingers shaking as I dialed the number I sought. The com's gears warbled to life, its cogs whirring as a screen of translucent light brightened, projecting from the vision-gem embedded in the center of the discus.

The screen's blue glow swirled in a slow, stirring motion, waiting for the other party to answer.

After a few panicked seconds, a wolf-eared man came into view in the framed light. Fangs Lastings drew back, alarmed at my grisly face.

"What in Land's name?" Fangs Lastings muttered. *"Who is this?"*

I raised a charred fist to my chest in salute. "Sir Janson Stane, requesting help, sir!"

"Help with… an attack? What is your squadron number?"

"13-A!" My voice fractured. "Trixer Sye's squad! Please, sir, I-I'm sorry for calling you directly, but I didn't know what else to do!" I ran a bloodied arm under my nose, blinking tears. "I-I… I need help, sir. Please…"

Lastings' brow furrowed as he shuffled through papers at his desk. *"13-A… you were sent to see to that distress call in the valley."* His finger traced down the documents, then he glanced at me. *"Two squads were already sent there from your sector. That wasn't enough?"*

"They're all dead, sir!" I choked back a sob, shivering. "I-I'm all that's left…!"

His wolf ears dropped to his neck. *"Even Trixers Sye and Flerran?"*

"All of them!" My voice quaked, remembering the screams of my friends—of my Brothers. "It's just me, now, sir! We… we weren't prepared for this, it was an ambush! They were waiting for us!"

Sir Lastings pushed his fists on his desk and hurriedly stood. *"Are you still in the valley?"*

"Y-yes, sir! And everything's burning, the Sentient girl is a Pyrovoker. She's not some lowly newborn either, sir, there's something not right about her!"

"Get out of there, Dueler. If everyone's dead, then there's no one left for you to help."

A cloud of smoke clung to my throat, and I coughed blood onto my tattered white sleeve. "I-I can't move my wings, sir… And I can't walk out there—there's too many of them. I-it's like she's gathered an army."

"How many?"

I glanced at the turmoil over the ditch, my head light as cotton. How much blood had I lost?

"Too… t-too many," I reported. "Hundreds, maybe thousands. They're everywhere." My eyes stung from the smog, tears only flushing so much debris. "I… I'm going to die here, aren't I, sir…?"

"Say that again, and I'll pull your Skull-pins from your cloak." He slammed an outraged hand on his desk, rattling the quill on his papers. *"Your squad leader's dead! That means you've been promoted to Trixer, soldier! And at your rank, you're not allowed to give up!"* His eyes flicked to my neck; to my white Death mark. *"What's your Hallows, Trixer?"*

I sniffed, hitting a fist to my chest. "It-it's death, sir!"

"Do you have any vassals who could help?"

I wiped the fallen ash from my eyes. "They're here now, but I… I don't know how much longer the two can hold them off. C… can you tell the others to cut my Seam when they get here, sir…?"

"Damn it, Trixer, if you say that again, I'll demote you back to a Singer! I'm sending reinforcements your way, but you have to hold strong. Now get the Void out of—"

Someone plucked the com out from my fingers.

An adolescent boy was suddenly standing over me. His skin was coated in bronze scales, brown hair grown to his chin with blond streaks.

"These devices grow stranger by the year," the young man hummed, firelight glinting off his half-moon eyeglasses. I watched him toss my com to the ground and absently scooted a severed head to the side with his boot.

He scrutinized me like a prize at an auction. "You're all that's left, are you?"

I shuffled back, fumbling for my scythe. "Stay back, Demon…!" *There are two Sentients?* But… but where was the Pyrovoker girl?

I stole a glance back at Rossette and Nikolai. They were focused on keeping the swarming beasts at bay, lightning and ice exploding in a chaotic frenzy. They hadn't noticed this newcomer.

The young man gave a disgusted sneer. "Do I look like those mongrels, you featherless twit?" His gaze lifted past me. "Did you hear that, Cilia? This ingrate thinks I'm one of your witless dogs."

A giggle bounced behind me. I spun so quick, my eyes were late to focus. *The Pyrovoker!*

The grey-haired girl crouched to meet my eyelevel and smiled. "Hello there, little bird. I seem to have missed you, haven't I?" Her green eyes flickered, white pupils bright and gleaming. She sighed dismally. "Oh, I'm terribly sorry. I hate to leave anyone out of a game."

She reached for me, and I cringed—

"Just a moment, Cilia." The young man knelt to me. "This one has a Death mark. And here I was beginning to think none from this lot were worth a damn… Tell me, Reaper: What is your Hallows?"

"Go Cleanse yourself in the Void, Demon," I spat.

He circled a finger over his temple. "This one lives to vex me… I doubt you're an Infeciovoker. Though I suppose another fire-thrower could be sufficient."

"Wrong," sang the girl, skipping playfully around me. "He's covered in burn scars. Fire cannot touch us Pyrovokers. I saw this one sowing his vassals to help, however." She nodded to Rossette and Nikolai. "He's a simple Necrovoker, to be sure."

The scaled man rose. "Interesting… Still, he'll be an imperative addition. Remember to keep his soul tied after you're finished, Cilia."

Her hand burst with fire. "Very well." She smiled. "It will be curious to have a corpse-raiser with us."

"St-stay away from me…!" I raised my scythe.

I was still losing blood, my head spinning like mad. *I can't fight like this. I-I have to get out of here.*

I scrambled up the ditch, forcing up my torn wings. I'd almost taken flight when the girl snagged my ankle and yanked me back to the dirt.

"I'm afraid you're too useful to let go, Reaper," she chided.

"I'll sooner be taken to the Void before I become one of you!" I turned my scythe round, pointing the tip at my own chest.

With a bracing inhale, I plunged the scythe into my ribs—screaming as the sharp metal slid through my breastplate and lodged into soft tissue.

Rossette and Nikolai screamed, dropping to their knees. They clutched at their chests, feeling my pain through our Pact.

"*Da'torr…!*" Rossette's voice was shrill as she spotted me.

Nikolai panted. "What eez… doing…?"

"I'm sorry…!" I gasped, the breath burning. I gripped my dripping scythe again. "I'm not… done yet…!"

I twisted the blade toward my Seam—

The Sentient ripped the blade out in a gush of blood.

Her enflamed hand raged with hot flames, and her fingers snatched my face, her claws sinking into my cheeks and scraping bone. I howled, the stink of melting skin simmering as her fire licked over my right eye and spread to my featherless head—

Something swooped down and slashed its talons across her face.

It was my messenger raven.

Nile!

The girl jerked away as the raven dove again, distracting her while I crouched over the dirt, bearing my melted skin.

I curled over the dirt, wheezing, my chest drenched in dark crimson, spots clouding my vision. I wanted to lie down and… and rest for a bit… just for a little while…

Your soul will rot, I remembered, sobering. *You'll be one of those damned demons!*

I found my scythe lying a few feet away. I heaved forward, crawling to it. *If I could just… cut my Seam…*

"Annoying little *rats!*" snarled the girl. She swatted Nile with a powerful *crack* and the bird hit the dirt in a puff of dust.

I screamed, my soul ripping in two.

"*NILE!*" Pain exploded, grief and panic slamming hard and sharp. I scrambled to my messenger and scooped up Nile, cupping the limp bird.

"N-Nile?" My voice cracked, tears flooding as the new pit in my soul shriveled. "Nile…! Please—No, no, no…!" I heaved gasps as I curled over the dead raven, the world shrinking away. "Nile…! Please… plea—*Hghck!*"

Something drove into my back.

Squrlch! Something wet squelched, an icy chill ripping from my ribs.

Everything went numb.

The girl sauntered around me, beaming like a proud child who couldn't wait for her promised reward. In her hands was a dark, drenched lump of muscle. It looked like a shifter's heart.

My gaze dropped, absently noting that the pulse in my ears was dimming.

Rossette and Nikolai's screams choked into silence. With my spotty vision, I saw their corpses were being scraped raw by the rotten beasts, their ghosts rising from their mangled bodies and huddling as the demons surrounded them.

"Keep his puppets from your beasts' teeth, would you?" the scaled man asked the girl, pushing up his eyeglasses. "I should think they'll make fair collateral."

"D…" Blood flooded up my throat, the taste of salty metal pouring over my tongue, vision blotting black. "Death save us…"

NIRUSSIAN TRAVEL GUIDE

CHARACTER REFERENCE LIST

Aiden Rogeteller	Vassal of Alice Devouh, robin shifter, former Stormchaser, Aerovoker
Alexander Devouh	Half Shadowblood, wolf shifter, Twin brother of Xavier. Possesses Necrovoking Hallows for vessel manipulation (Vassals: Vendy, Dalen), Reaper (Messenger: Mal)
Alice Devouh	Twins' mother/ Death King's General, wolf shifter, wife of Lucas, Necrovoker (Vassals: Aiden and more unmentioned), Reaper (Messenger: Ethil)
Anabelle	Lion shifter, Terravoker/Healer
Bianca Florenne	Childhood friend of the twins, Doctor, rabbit shifter, Healer
Cilia the Grim	Necrofera demon queen of Everland, Cat shifter, Pyrovoker
Dalen Tesler	Tessler sibling whose NecroSeam was cut early, hawk shifter, Herrin's older brother, Hallowless
Henry Cauldwell	Vendy's uncle, blacksmith, rabbit shifter, Terravoker
Herrin Tesler	Dalen's scholarly younger brother, hawk shifter, Hallowless
James (Jimmy) Grieves	Dreamcatcher, elk shifter, Somniovoker
Janson Stane	Reaper, crow shifter, Necrovoker
Jaqelle (Jaq) Mallory	Xavier and Alex's childhood friend, viper shifter, Hallowless, Reaper (Messenger: Bridge)

Kurn	Ringëd's pet ferret who thinks he's an exiled emperor from the planet *Hcah-Ah-Ah-Hcah*
Kurrick Everstien	Ana's bodyguard, Lion shifter, Hallowless
Lillianna (Lilli) Tessinger	Willow's Aide, Bat shifter, Necrovoker, Reaper
Linolius (Linus) Rennegaurd	Goat shifter, Seer: emphasis on visions of the present, rebel soldier against Everland's false king
Lucas Devouh	Twins' father/Death King's Eyes, wolf shifter, Necrovoker (Vassals: Nathaniel, Thateus, and more), Reaper (Messenger: Barrach)
Lucrine	Class 2 Sentient Necrofera, Cilia's underling, Horse shifter, Hallowless
Macarius Lysandre	Cobra shifter, exiled Dreamcatcher, Dual-Evocator: Decepiovoker/Somniovoker
Mikani Treble	Octavius's eldest sister and Ringëd's fiancée, cat shifter, Pyrovoker
Milann	Young girl from Lindel, sheep shifter, Hallowless, Reaper (messenger: killed)
Nathaniel Jorechoh	Vassal of Lucas Devouh, bear shifter, former pirate captain, Pyrovoker
Octavius Treble	Xavier and Alex's new friend and Brother-in-Arms, cat shifter, son of Claude and Sirra-Lynn, Infeciovoker, Reaper (Messenger: Shade)
Ringëd Fleetfûrt	Footrunner: Seeker department of investigations, Mika's husband, "feral human" (No shift), Seer: emphasis on visions of the past
Sirra-Lynn Treble	Octavius's deceased mother, cat shifter, Doctor, Healer

Vendy Cauldwell	Vassal of the twins, rabbit shifter, niece of Henry, Terravoker
Willow Ember	Relicblood of Death & Dream, Heiress to Grim's throne, Death's reincarnation, Reaper, fox-wolf hybrid shifter, 6 Hallows (Necro, Pyro, Infecio/Somnio, Decepio, Seer)
Xavier Devouh	Half Shadowblood, Body missing, but soul is attached to his twin brother, Alexander. Possesses Necrovoking for soul manipulation (Vassals: Vendy, Dalen), Reaper (No messenger)

NIRUSSIAN WORLD NOTES

Dragons of Nirus: For every element of magic Hallows (with the exception of Dream Hallows), there is a dragon that embodies that element. Land realm: Stonedragon/Barkdragon/Landragon, Sky realm: Skydragon/Shockdragon/Nimdragon, Ocean realm: Seadragon/Bindragon/ Frostdragon, Death realm: Bonedragon/Flamedragon/Poisondragon.

Evocators: A shifter born with magic Hallows is called an Evocator. Most Evocators only possess one element. In rare cases, some are born with two Hallows and are known as Dual-Evocators. Only the Relicbloods have ever possessed all three of their realm's Hallows.

Land:	Terravoker	Healer	Arborvoker
Sky:	Astravoker	Aerovoker	Imbrivoker
Ocean:	Aquavoker	Glaciavoker	Pregravoker
Dream:	Somniovoker	Decepiovoker	Seer
Death	Necrovoker	Pyrovoker	Infeciovoker

Hallows: These are the "Gods' Blessings", which are elemental magics to which certain shifters are born. A shifter's Hallows element is defined based on the realm they are from. There are fifteen Hallow elements in total. For each of the five realms in Nirus, there are three elements, as shown in the charts below.

LAND		SKY		OCEAN	
Rock	Terra	*Wind*	Aero	*Water*	Aqua
Plant	Arbor	*Rain*	Imbri	*Ice*	Glacia
Remedy	Healer	*Storm*	Astra	*Pressure*	Pregra

DREAM		DEATH	
Dream	Somnio	*Fire*	Pyro
Illusion	Decepio	*Death*	Necro
Prophecy	Seer	*Poison*	Infecio

NecroSeam: A ghostly thread which sews a soul to its vessel. When a shifter of Nirus dies, the soul is still bound to its body by their NecroSeam. If three days pass without a Reaper coming to cut the NecroSeam and free the soul from its deceased vessel, the trapped soul rots inside its corpse and merges into an undead creature called Necrofera that can only be killed by a weapon made of Spiritcrystal.

Nirussian Calendar: A month in Nirus is 60 days, or six weeks. One week is 10 days. There are 5 months in a year (300 days).

Realms of Nirus: There are 5 realms in this world. Land (surface realm split into two continents: Everland & Neverland), Sky (floating islands of Culatia in the sky inhabited primarily by flying shifters). Ocean (seaside isles of Marincia inhabited primarily by fish shifters), Dream (subconscious realm of Aspirre where shifters' souls visit in their dreams), Death (underground caverns of Grim where souls of the dead are protected in their afterlife).

Relicbloods: Shifters who are descendants of the Relic Children (those chosen by the Gods to be the ruler of a specific realm). The only Relic Child still alive today is Dream, who doesn't age at a regular pace due to his time-less residency in the subconscious plane of Aspirre.

The Relics: Magical artifacts of the Gods which are the sources of each realm's Hallows. (Land: Blossom of Gold, Sky: Phoenix of Scarlet, Ocean: Pearl of Emerald, Dream: Orbs of Azure, Death: Willow of Ashes)

Sentients: Necrofera who possess Hallows (Class 1), or a mongrel demon who has eaten ten thousand souls (Class 2). Sentients look like normal shifters, except their pupils are white.

Shifters: The world of Nirus is inhabited entirely by shifters, but they aren't quite the traditional shapeshifters who can transform from one human form to a full-on beast form. The shifters of Nirus are seen possessing traits of some kind (Ringëd Fleetfûrt is the only exception) but these traits usually only consist of wings, horns, claws, teeth, ears, tails, scales, fins, etc. Most shifters are born with a majority of their traits already showing (referred to as Primary Shifts), but some only appear when they are threatened or upset (teeth/talons/claws and even extra feathers/scales/fur). Mammals seem to be the main beings whose traits actually shift, with their ears, claws and teeth. Antlers and horns are always out and don't retract, nor do wings and scales. The fish shifters are the most unique due to their inherent ability to switch their Primary Shift to tails or legs when they are in or out of water, and this is the largest range of shifting that happens among the shifters.

The Void and Great unknown: A place that is considered purgatory for rotten and sinful souls in the Harmonist religion. It is believed that once the Goddess Nira has Cleansed these souls of their rot and sin, she takes them to the Great Unknown, which is thought to be the "waiting room" for souls to be reborn again.

NIRUSSIAN MINERALS/ TECHNOLOGY

Olium: a lightweight, extremely durable mineral that is found in the deeper caves of Grim, where the veins are closest to the planet's magma-filled mantle and are in a constant liquefied state until extracted and left to cool. Once cooled, the metal can be crafted, but forging the material is incredibly difficult and only skilled smiths are able to handle the task.

Spiritcrystal: a mineral found in the caverns of Grim. It is a unique crystal which physical skin cannot touch. Adversely, it is one of the few things ghosts can make contact with. The Reapers use this crystal to forge their specialized scythes which allows them to cut a shifter's NecroSeam without damaging the body.

Vision-gems: minerals found in the Land realm's mines which, when broken apart, can show what the other piece is reflecting. Modern technologies led by Culatia's top inventors in 2102 A.B. have learned to harness Vision-gems to bring devices such as Vision-screens, communicators, and other numerous devices.

Levi-stones: magnetized rocks that are repelled only by the planet's core, causing them to be pushed into the air and kept suspended so long as the oppositely-charged side is facing the core. Culatia's islands are made of these stones, which is speculated by many geologists as to the reason Culatia's islands float.

Storage-gems: a gummy, gel-like mineral found in Everland's mines. When an object is pushed inside it, that object's size and weight shrink to a fifth of its original mass until that object is removed.

Yinklît Gel: a sap from a long-leafed plant that is native to Culatia. It is similar to the Aloe vera plant, but instead of possessing soothing properties when applied to burns, Yinklît Gel dampens all Hallows effects when an Evocator's hands are coated in the substance. If the gel is ingested, it can cause serious damage to an Evocator's Hallows for several days, and in some cases, it can wipe their magic connection permanently.

Shotri: The latest ranged weapons created by Culatia's top weapon-smiths. They require ammunition made of meta-glass pellets with entrapped elemental magics which, when fired, cause damage or temporary paralysis on a target, depending on the element the pellet housed.

Meta-glass: an alloyed material which combines Flexi-glass as the outer layer and Yinklît Gel as the inner layer. With this, Culatia's top weapon-smiths have used these to make Shockspheres, Flamespheres, Splashspheres and the like, which are then used as ammunition for Shotri.

Flexi-glass: A gummy, gel-like glass found in Culatia's mountain peaks that can be stretched and manipulated with ease while still wet. Once it has been through a kiln, it solidifies and become as fragile as normal glass.

THE LAWS OF DEATH

I

One shall not end a shifter's life before their natural
time has expired. Exceptions shall be extended only
to those defending themselves or others.

II

Deceased souls shall never be left to rot in their expired vessels.
Their NecroSeam must be reaped once their vessel has died.

III

One shall not release a shifter's soul before
their vessel's time has ended.

IV

Permittance to wield weapons of pure and alloyed Spiritcrystal
shall be exclusively bestowed upon Reapers. Exceptions extend
toward a Reaper's vassals and their apprentices. Violators
may only be excused if the violation was broken for self-
preservation or the preservation of others in dire circumstances.

V

Should a shifter's NecroSeam be cut before their time
has expired, the breathing vessel must be put to rest.

VI

No harm shall be tolerated toward black birds of any kind.
Black birds shall not be kept captive. Exceptions of captivity are
extended toward black birds which must be nursed to heath.
though, once healed, the black birds must be released immediately.

DEAR READERS,

Thank you so much for reading Willow of Ashes, the first book in the NecroSeam Chronicles series. If you liked it, I would be extremely grateful if you tell others what you think by writing an honest review. It doesn't have to be long…a few words, or even just a rating would be much appreciated. Reviews are vital to an author's career and helps us not only sell books, but provides valuable feedback. Check out my review page at https://www.necroseam.com/reviews.

If you would you like to find out more about the NecroSeam Chronicles universe, including world notes, deleted scenes, character artwork, and even recorded songs from the books, check out my website at https://www.necroseam.com!

And while you are there, feel free to sign up for my newsletter to receive announcements on new releases, upcoming conventions I'll be attending, and special promotions!

You can also follow me on my social media accounts below:

Twitter: @AizelleRaine
www.Facebook.com/officialEllieRaine

Thank you again!
Ellie Raine

ABOUT THE AUTHOR

Ellie Raine is a voracious BookWyrm when it comes to epic adventures, detailed world-building, and thrilling battles. Growing up in a family of book lovers, comic readers, and video gamers, she always dreamed of making the next explosive game that would catch fire with her darker themes that put the spotlight on her favorite fable: the Grim Reaper. Her ongoing Hard Epic Fantasy pentalogy, *NecroSeam Chronicles*, was originally intended to be that video game series, but she's found that the book adaptation is far more fulfilling and exciting. Her other works include a paranormal-noir novella entitled *Nightingale*, published with Pro Se Productions.

Fueled by coffee-bean concoctions brewed by the finest caffeine alchemists in Georgia, Ellie only emerges from the depths of her daring tales when she is summoned by her loving king and their darling daughter: the Dragon Princess Felicity. She is a lover of ravens and a dreamer of dragons, but above all else, she is a scribe to the stories that guide her.

You can find out more about Ellie Raine and her
books at: https://www.EllieRaine.com